SOLDIER GIRLS

'Melleah will now give you a caning of twelve, mademoiselle. Bare-bottom caning, to us S'Ibayas, is a sacred ritual,' said Dr Crevasse. 'The squirming of a whipped bare croup is the swell of the desert dunes, or the ocean waves. The gasps of a female flogged naked are the winds of life to our sacred land.'

Lise eyed the male servant's penis, which was now fully erect again.

'My servants,' said the doctor, 'are under instruction to maintain themselves in a state of constant arousal. They will wank off as you are caned, and for your humiliation the male will spurt his sperm in your face. Now, inmate Gallard, stand with your buttocks raised and your belly on the chair back. You may not move in any way without my permission . . .'

SOLDIER GIRLS

Yolanda Celbridge

Nexus

This book is a work of fiction.
In real life, make sure you practise safe sex.

First published in 2001 by
Nexus
Thames Wharf Studios
Rainville Road
London W6 9HA

www.nexus-books.co.uk

Typeset by TW Typesetting, Plymouth, Devon

Printed and bound by
Cox & Wyman Ltd, Reading, Berks

ISBN 0 352 33586 6

Contents

1

Degraded

The jeep was parked awkwardly off the desert road, as though with an empty petrol tank; its cargo of medicaments packed tightly in styrofoam boxes. The nurse peered into the gloomy shed, escorted by a tall young male, in the traditional bafto robe, with a sword at his red and gold belt. Two other young males, their chiselled Nilotic faces smiling, stood inside.

'Which is your sick brother?' said the young nurse, brushing a blonde lock from her brow. 'I see no invalids here.'

Her escort stepped away, leaving her framed in the sunlight.

'We are all sick from priapism, sweet lady,' he said, sighing, in broken French, 'and need your help.'

The three young males swept back their baftos, revealing themselves naked underneath. Each had a dark, shining penis, monstrously erect. Sweating, the uniformed nurse looked back at her jeep. She travelled alone as the paved desert road was considered 'safe', just by virtue of being a paved road. Nevertheless, she was armed. Her automatic rifle hung cradled beneath the dashboard, and her handgun was still closed in the holster strapped to her belt.

'I have no drugs to cure priapism,' she stammered.

'Your body is our cure, mademoiselle,' said one of the males, stepping forward and raising his sword. 'Perhaps you will be more sympathetic after a caning of your bare French arse.'

'No!' cried the blonde girl, 'I'm not French, damn you, I'm English!'

'Your fesses will be prettier after a caning, whoever owns them,' said the sword-holder. 'A female, heated to lust by our African sun, must be thrashed on her naked croup, for the good of her soul.'

'No . . . please don't!' she whimpered.

The males conversed in amiable ritual, not in the Somali dialect of the Republic of Djibouti but in French. She recognised certain words: melons, peaches, ripe plums, the arse of a goddess . . .

'Such a beautiful derrière demands to be reddened by the rod, mademoiselle,' said one politely. 'And the exquisite hole within, to be filled by the fleshy rods of men.'

'Oh no, I beg you!' she sobbed, staring at the three dark, naked cocks.

Already, she was undoing the buttons of her blouse, trembling as she stripped, and begging them to be gentle. Her skirt fell with a thump from her holstered handgun. Her full, jutting breasts, the plums of her bare nipples stiffened in excitement, sprang free of her bra, to gasps of delight from the erect males. When she finally unzipped her boots and stepped from her shed skirt, she was nude but for stockings and suspender belt. Moaning, she crouched on the ground, with her bare bottom thrust upwards and the cheeks parted, to show her anus and dripping wet vulva. Her naked teats squashed the dirt; she raised her head and her mouth fastened on the immense dark glans of an erect penis. Taking the shaft right to the back of her throat, she began to fellate the male organ with squeezing lips and fast, bobbing movements of her head, while one of her hands rubbed her wet slit and the other pinched her nipples together.

Crack!

The sword-flat twanged as it lashed her bare buttocks. With vigorous fingers, the girl masturbated her clitoris; her huge quim-thatch was soaked in sweat and love juice, which flowed from her gash and glistened on her thighs as she sucked the penis to orgasm and swallowed the male's sperm. Its place in her mouth was taken by a second, which she

2

sucked with equal vigour, bringing the male off and swallowing his full emission. Constant caning reddened her bare, clenching bottom, the strokes of the springy sword-flat delivered at tantalising intervals of half a minute or more, and each cut making her shriek and masturbate faster.

'Ohh . . .' she sobbed, pausing in her fellation. 'No, please . . .'

She masturbated herself to her own squealing orgasm three times, as she tongued stiff cock-flesh, and her squirming, naked fesses were caned crimson. When she had taken a full twenty-one strokes on the bare, she groaned as a cock's helmet nuzzled her anus bud, then fully penetrated her hole with a hard thrust right to her root. She whimpered and sobbed as she was buggered by all three cocks in turn, those she had milked having rapidly firmed again. Horses whinnied and pawed the sand, outside the stone shed. They were the only sounds, apart from the gasping sobs of the buggered and masturbating girl, as the black cocks rammed her arse-root, and the grunts of the males, as each filled her anus with sperm.

There was a whirring noise, far away, which neared, and became a pulsing throb. The males, sated, replaced their baftos, and left the girl crouching in the dirt, rubbing her sore bottom and still masturbating.

'No . . .' she whimpered, 'please don't go! Fuck my cunt! Please!'

Horses thudded away. The girl wiped her tears and struggled into her uniform, a task only half completed, when a helicopter landed before the shed. The figure of a grizzled, middle-aged Legion policeman entered.

'I . . .' she began to stammer, but he put a finger to his lips.

'Save it for the tribunal, mademoiselle,' he said in a kindly voice. 'You poor young thing! These Djiboutians are the most sexually beautiful people on earth, I know. It's cruel of the Legion to provide females for us, but expect you nurses to remain virgins . . .'

'They forced me!' she cried. 'They whipped me! Look at my bottom!'

'Your cheeks must be smarting,' said the policeman, as he gently helped her into the helicopter, behind the pilot, and a third legionnaire took charge of her jeep. 'But then, I expect you've come to like it. Every month you deliver medical supplies to Fort Holhol, and every month you are unpredictably late. Unfortunately for you, Moussa, one of your paramours is our spy. I dread to think what his friends will do if they find out he has deprived them of your derrière! Those necklaces of theirs aren't made of chestnuts. Or, perhaps you could say, they are!'

The legionnaire slapped his thigh, laughing at his own crudity, then put a paternal arm around the shivering young nurse.

'Never mind, sweet. Whatever happens, just remember that the French Foreign Legion, like a good parent, always looks after its own. Moreover, you've never in all these months had your weapons or medicines stolen. Take that as a compliment! For those males to value your behind more than black market profit, you must have the arse of a goddess . . .'

'God, how I hate the fucking French,' Lise Gallard whispered to herself in a mantra of despair. 'God, how I hate the fucking French . . .'

She stood, sweat stinging her eyes, in full dress uniform of the nursing corps of the French Foreign Legion: white blouse, fastened to the neck, with an ultramarine brooch; tight red jacket, with brass buttons polished to brilliance; bottom-hugging ultramarine knee-length skirt, and matching heavy cotton stockings, with a fleur-de-lys pattern. Beneath, she was swaddled in a pinching ultramarine corset, with lacy bra, knickers and suspenders of the same hue. It was a long-standing joke amongst the girls of the Foreign Legion Nursing Corps that the French – the *fucking, blasted French* – were such sticklers for elegance that even a girl captured by virile Somali or Djiboutian nomads had to look chic when ravished. Her long blonde tresses were pinned tightly in the regulation bun under the white tricorn nurse's bonnet. All her garments were drenched with sweat, even the red, white and blue tricolour sash of the French Republic which cradled her full – *pure English!* – breasts and bottom. The zipped boots of dark blue rubber, like jackboots, with their casual French blend of practicality and elegance, only increased her discomfort.

God, how I hate the fucking French . . .

'Nurses . . . *attention!*'

The parade ground cracked as sixty pairs of female heels snapped together. At 9 a.m., it was already baking in 30-degree heat, and dust was blown by the hot wind from the Red Sea, just visible beyond the white sprawl of Djibouti city. Lise Gallard stood in the open before her comrades in the Foreign Legion Sisters of Mercy, soon to be her former comrades.

'After this ceremony of degradation,' pronounced the Sister-General, 'three of you will no longer be Sisters of Mercy, but common legionnaires. The tribunal has passed sentence and the malefactresses have accepted their degradation of rank and subsequent penalty: indefinite training in the Punishment Battalion at Fort Lafresne.'

Lise mentally translated the French into English, a habit she enforced on herself in order not to forget her proper tongue altogether. She found herself thinking in French most of the time, and hated herself for it. The Sister-General had not said 'punishment battalion' but '*Centre de Formation*', which could be equally applied to a harmless training school for teachers or dental hygienists, or the most savage prison, as Fort Lafresne was widely rumoured to be. The nominal similarity to the French prison of Fresnes was understood by all the girls, few of them French, as another odd, academic joke of which the Legion seemed so fond: like the colour ultramarine for their uniforms, meaning 'overseas'. The Legion's motto, however, was not a joke: *Legio Patria Nostra*: 'the Legion is our homeland'. Once a legionnaire donned the white hat, he or she was subject to a disciplinary code that had nothing to do with the laws of France, and in which any government, French or otherwise, tried to intervene at its peril. The Legion closed ranks, including those members it punished; the Legion was its own law.

Within the Hospital of Mercy at Djibouti that law was represented by Sister-General Louise Grenier, already, at thirty years of age, one of the highest-ranking female legionnaires. That a woman of such lush russet hair, pouting lips and full figure should choose the military life instead of marrying the millionaire of her choice, made her the subject of more than the usual vitriolic gossip: that she had murdered her husband and fled France; that she was the mistress of one of the Legion's male generals; inevitably that she was a lesbian and the mistress of one, or several, wives, high up in the French government; at the very least, that she conducted policy meetings with other senior female officers in the nude, in her whirlpool bath. Certainly, she was a strict disciplinarian, and took a personal interest in the humiliating punishments she imposed for minor infractions of discipline or the uniform code. An unpolished button might mean a girl's cleaning the latrines with her own panties and clad only in her skimpiest underthings under the watchful eye of the Sister-General.

Beside Lise, two other girls stood stiffly at attention. One was coltish, big of croup and full-breasted like Lise, and was a German aristocrat, Gabi von Titisee, known as 'Titzi' for short. She stood haughtily, as if the punishment to come was no more significant than a flea-bite to the proud beauty of her swelling Saxon croup. The other was compact, but ripe of body: a sultry, brown-skinned girl, her pendulous teats and full, taut buttocks tight under her clinging uniform, and her sensuous lips set off by an aquiline nose. Her enormously long Sri Lankan name was shortened to 'Sutra'. Lise figured that her own abbreviation of Elizabeth was to her advantage, and even preferable to the 'Liz' by which she had been known before the Legion. She knew both her sister-prisoners only slightly, the three girls being from different squads.

What was I like before the Legion? What was Sutra like, or Titzi?

Not 'before enlisting in the Legion', but 'before the Legion': that was how the girls called their previous lives, as though time before had no meaning, and would never have one again, outside the Legion. Lise knew, to her horror, that no matter what brutalities she must endure at

6

Fort Lafresne, found on no map, she would nevertheless defend the Legion to her last breath, *because she belonged to the Legion*. In this arid corner of northeast Africa, there was, in any case, no preferable alternative. The Republic of Djibouti, formerly the French Territory of Afars and Issas, consisted mostly of desert, with a nomadic Somalian population devoted to chewing narcotic *qat*. Djibouti was the African headquarters of the Legion, in a land as big as Belgium, with just 300 kilometres of paved roads and 100 kilometres of railways, the object of frequent terrorist attacks. Dependent on French money, the republic was claimed by the various bandit rulers of neighbouring Somalia; outside the capital, which contained three-quarters of its half million people, the law was the French Foreign Legion.

'The Legion has trained you in the manner of lady soldiers,' the Sister-General continued, 'and each of you has disgraced the name of soldier, the name of lady, and, far more important, the name of legionnaire. Thus shall your degradation be witnessed by your sisters as an example and an encouragement. You are still legionnaires, and the Legion looks after its own. However oppressive you may think your treatment, you must never forget your pride as legionnaires, nor your hope that one day you will be readmitted to the ranks of your sisters. Sergeant-major, commence!'

Brrrt! Brrrt! Brrrt! A snare drum, beaten by a nurse in dress uniform, began a tempo at once sinister and mocking. The sergeant-major, a petite Portuguese, stepped forward and unfastened the sashes of Titzi, Sutra and Lise. She handed the sashes separately to three orderly nurses, then removed the bonnets and throat brooches of all three girls. Each girl's insignia were fastened in a wooden box, stencilled with her serial number, since the sash of the French Republic, and the brooch and bonnet of a nurse legionnaire, must be kept as sacred. The sergeant-major signalled to three nurses armed with surgical knives.

'Commence!' barked the Portuguese in a deep contralto, surprising for a woman so feminine.

7

Brrrt! Brrrt! Brrrt! The drum seemed to beat more loudly. Each nurse stood in front of one degraded sister. Their lips and faces impassive as stone, the nurses began the ritual of degradation.

God, how I hate the fucking French, GodhowIhate thefuckingFrench . . .

Lise winced, as a clean stroke from the razor knife sheared open her uniform tunic, then her blouse, which flapped open, exposing her bright blue bra. Another two slices, and her skirt was slit, to fall to her ankles, revealing her pubic mound, swelling under the high-cut blue panties, and her jungle of blonde curls spilling out, to brush the lacy stocking-tops and garter belt. Beside her, and in exactly the same rhythm – their sister nurses had been *trained* to this task of humiliation! – Titzi and Sutra's garments were cut away. The three girls stood in their bras, panties, suspenders, boots and stockings. Their humiliants bent down as one and sliced open the rubber boots with three quick strokes to the uppers and one across the toes, so that the rubber fell completely away from the girls' feet; the knives never even brushed their stockings. The sergeant-major ordered the three prisoners, still at attention, to take two paces forward. All three obeyed, rigidly, like automata, and stood in their underwear with stockinged feet on the burning stone slabs.

The bras were the first intimate garments cut away: two clean strokes and the bras fell, exposing three pairs of bare breasts to tremble under the scorching sun. Swiftly, the panties were cut off, with clean slices at pubis and in the croup-cleft; then the suspender belts, and finally, each stocking was ripped apart with a long, slicing cut down the back seam, the razors never touching flesh – which seemed to add obscurely to their humiliation, as if their bodies were pieces of equipment, either too expensive to be damaged or too worthless to damage a knife. Again, two paces forward, and the girls obeyed, each stepping out of her shredded stockings.

The three girls stood nude and barefoot under the hot sun before their sisters, stiff at attention, until the Sister-

General ordered the ranks of nurses to stand at ease: the nude, humiliated prisoners no longer merited standing at attention. They were shackled with their wrists wedged behind their backs in the cleft of their bare buttocks, and ankles locked in iron hobble bars chained to their handcuffs. The final indignity was the removal of their hairclips, so that each girl's full, uncombed mane cascaded over her naked breasts and shoulders. Lise gasped, for she felt her nipples stiffening as her tresses stroked her bare breasts; at the pressure of her shackling her quim seeped moisture. She peeped and saw that both Sutra and Titzi had stiffened nipples and moist quims, and that Titzi's inner thighs glistened with juice dripping from her swollen gash lips. The German girl's erect clitty poked from its fleshy wet pouch, revealed by a severely cropped pubic bush. Sutra's pube-hair was dense and matted like Lise's, and trailed in wet fronds concealing her clit. Were the other girls as guilty and . . . *perverted* as Lise? Why had *they* joined the Legion?

'Prisoners!' cried Sister-General Grenier. 'Naked and without uniform, you are no longer sisters of the Legion, so you shall be transported naked to the place of your reformation. The Sisters of Mercy deny you!'

'Response!' barked the sergeant-major to the ranks of nurses.

With one voice, the Foreign Legion's Sisters of Mercy cried to their nude and shackled ex-comrades: 'We deny you!'

Titzi's lips twisted in a sneer, while Sutra's eyes were misted with tears as well as sweat. Three girls, barely twenty years of age, humiliated by shackling in the nude, and to be brutally imprisoned for offences against military discipline . . . Lise's lips tightened.

'God, how I hate the fucking French,' she murmured to herself.

After the second hour in the windowless prison van, Lise no longer bothered to count the minutes. The jolting ride over the unseen desert was hell. Each of the three girls was locked in a stifling cage, with two sets of three cages fitted on either side of the vehicle, but the side walls were corrugated iron, and the girls were positioned so that they could not see or speak to each other. Each girl remained nude and shackled for the entire journey, while the stifling, piss-stinking air grew hotter, and the only ventilation blew hot desert air, with accompanying dust that clung to Lise's sweat-soaked body. The seating in the cage was a throne of wire mesh with a hole in the van's chassis beneath. Her hands were still cuffed behind her, and her feet in the hobble bar, so she was helpless to wipe the sweat that stung her eyes. If she needed to piss or dung, she must do so through the coarse wire mesh which was her only seat, and which became uncomfortable after a mere half hour of travel; hideous thereafter, so that she was obliged to raise her bare bum from the wire for as long as her aching thighs could stand it. From the roof of the van dangled a rubber tube that constantly dripped drinking water. By an agonising stretch of her limbs and pressing her feet to the scalding hot metal floor, Lise could press her mouth to the tube and suck fluid, or let the water drip over her head and breasts. Beside the tube hung a metal brank, a head-frame with gag, and tongue-depressor. Its clanking against the wire cage was enough to quell any desire to speak. A burly legion policeman sat smoking, with a carbine on his knees, behind the driver, and the vehicle only stopped at intervals for them to change places.

Lise no longer bothered to chant her mantra to herself; she was a numbed, stricken animal, in a desert hell, than which nothing could be worse. Her only friend was the faithfully dripping water tube, from which she drank and bathed herself as often as her tortured limbs could stand it. At first, she had been embarrassed by the presence of male escorts, imagining their custodians would be female. Eventually she understood this was part of her humiliation, since the males did not glance lustfully at three voluptuous nude girls shackled before them, nor even bother to glance at all. Lise, Sutra and Titzi were just prisoners, so much meat in chains: denied by the Legion, they did not exist. Yet the Legion was taking care of them

10

with its own logic. The Legion would not allow its valuable investment to go to waste. Lise, like all other Legion nurses, had been speedily trained to do most of what a male legionnaire must do, except fight. The physical standards for nurses were as exacting as for males, but their training lacked the casual brutality of kicks and punches by which a male legionnaire was toughened. Nurses must swim, canoe, trek or parachute with a full kit of medical supplies, but received only rudimentary weapons training. Their pistols were for self-defence, or, in the last resort, to give the *coup de grâce* to a mortally wounded soldier, with the implicit instruction to save the last bullet for herself. Alone amongst the world's elite fighting forces, soldiers of the French Foreign Legion were not issued with poison capsules.

Completely disoriented, Lise had no idea how far they had travelled from Djibouti, nor in what direction. Yet a gush of gratitude washed over her: legionnaires were trained to survive hell. The water tube was Lise's friend, and it symbolised the care the Legion meant to take of her, and would always take. She could piss and stool as she wanted: once at Fort Lafresne, she would be released from the hell of her shackled nudity, would be fed, bathed, and the Legion, however brutally, would look after her. No imprisonment could be worse than this stinking bondage, and Lise realised that this too was part of the Legion's psychology of control: she *wanted* to get to Fort Lafresne, where she would be free, and expected to hate *the fucking French* even more ... The Legion wanted her to hate it! Prison would be liberation.

It was late afternoon when the three dazed girls emerged, blinking in the fierce sun, from the darkness of the prison van. They were drenched in sweat and piss, their long hair matted and damp from their water tubes, and each girl had fragments of dung clinging to her anus and smearing her lower buttocks. They stood in a vast sandy courtyard; like the town square in Djibouti, each side of the square was occupied by shady terraced arcades, like shops, except that most had barred windows. A gap at the far end of the

11

square led to another one, where a three-storeyed, turreted building of drab greyish-brown stone was visible, the original Fort Lafresne. A high wall with manned sentry posts enclosed the terrain, but the sentries' attention was directed outside, not inside, the fort. The van had entered the open gates as though entering a marketplace. It was parked in a row of similar wagons, trucks and jeeps, by the grandiose entry portals, topped with arabesque curlicues of wrought iron, and made of solid wood. Lise, Sutra and Titzi looked out – their last glance of freedom – and saw only desert. There was no need of barbed wire at Fort Lafresne, as any threat was from outside, not from escaping prisoners.

Camels sat in the shade of the colonnades, and beside them fine-boned Somalis, males and females, squatted in their bafto robes chewing *qat*, as they offered fruits, dates, dried meats or bric-a-brac spread on tarpaulins. They bargained, listlessly smiling, with prison staff or prisoners – Lise could not tell which at this distance. All were female, and most completely nude but for white prison caps, like sailors', stencilled with numbers, and rope sandals; or else wearing white corporals' kepis and badges of rank on otherwise nude bodies. The prisoners seemed at ease with their guards, though they carried canes on rubber waistbands. Lise grimaced, hopping, as the sand burnt her bare feet.

The square was drowsily alive with female bodies. One group of prisoners, entirely nude, with white rubber swimming caps buckled under the chin, drilled back and forth at the double, their unfettered breasts bouncing. A second group marched round and round in a circle, also nude, but shackled together at waist and ankles, and carrying large rocks in wire baskets clamped to their bare nipples, so that if a prisoner failed to support her burden, her teats would be stretched. A third group of nude prisoners dug a trench, shovelling sand from a deep hole in the middle of the square, and, as fast as they dug, the sand was shovelled back by another group. These groups were also shackled and carried smaller rocks, clamped to their nipples and labia, which swung, striking their skin, as they dug. They were bare-headed and shoeless, their bodies completely shaven, including the pubis, scalp and limbs. All these groups were supervised by cane-wielding corporals, themselves nude but for their hats and badges of rank. None paid any attention to the others, and the naked females who idled by the merchants did not glance at the sweating bodies under discipline, even when a cane cracked on a bare croup. All the naked prisoners gleamed white, and the air bore a curious perfume above the stink of sweat: the nude inmates were smeared with sun-blocking cream. *The Legion looks after its own ...*

The two legionnaires did not salute, as a naked, hatted prison corporal approached, bearing a clipboard and papers. Rather, the corporal saluted the two ordinary legionnaires. She was tall, with rippling thighs and breasts, and a firm, swelling croup. Under her sun screen of oil, her nude body glowed with an unbroken suntan. Her naked breasts bounced at her smart movement; her status was indicated by her hat, by two corporal's stripes as copper armbands on her bare right bicep, and by a double-stripe cloth name-badge of red and blue in a copper clasp, pinned through the pierced nipple of her right breast. A cane a metre in length dangled from her rubber thong waistband, and her pubis and scalp were shaved gleaming bare. It was impossible to tell the colour of her hair before the Legion, or before Fort Lafresne; the firm brown pears of her croup were etched with scars of past cane-stripes. Her shiny pubic hillock swelled like two breasts, with a deep dimple between, at the pubic bone. Beneath it, the pink slash of her large, gaping cunt glistened wetly, as though she had recently pissed, or was seeping come oil at the prospect of new prisoners to break. Her swollen, extruded clitoris, peeping from the cunt-folds, suggested the latter, and her cane quivered on her bare thigh. She wore white rubber nursing boots, instead of rope sandals, and clicked them to attention as she saluted.

'Inmate Corporal Lavoisier, detailed to escort prisoners!' she rapped, her stony face not concealing the contempt smouldering in her eyes for the shackled and bedunged newcomers.

13

Paperwork was signed and exchanged, and the males lit cigarettes, then ambled, without a backward glance, towards an elegant arcade, crisply labelled *Centre d'Acceuil* – 'Welcome Centre' – with tables, a bright crimson-striped awning, and coolers of food and drink. They paid no attention to the nude prisoners but sat at a table, where two waitresses at once brought them beer. They were lissom and sultry Somali girls of Lise's age, with sleek, black tresses clinging to the clefts of their buttocks, and were bare-breasted, their firm, conical teats topped by nipples like peeled chestnuts. They wore only sandals and white pleated mini-skirts, flaring loose, after tightly hugging their ample haunches and the delicate plums of their bottoms; gold necklaces hung piled in the valleys of their breasts. The legionnaires slapped each girl's bottom, on her thin cotton skirt, making her neck chains and breasts bob, and her flimsy garment flap, to show neither girl wore panties; their spanks were delicate, like a handshake. The girls giggled and sat down with the men, resting their bare teats coquettishly on the table, and accepting sips of beer.

Corporal Lavoisier unhooked her cane and whipped each prisoner once, on the bare. Her cuts were deliberate, not hasty, and hard. Lise gasped as the cane stung her bare bum, already sore from the mesh seat in the prison van; Titzi sneered silently; Sutra squealed as the cane cracked smartly on her full brown buttocks. The corporal slapped her hard across the mouth and followed her slap with a lash of her cane, squarely on both Sutra's naked nipples. The Sri Lankan girl's face contorted, her whipped bare breasts quivered and her eyes moistened, but she made no sound. Corporal Lavoisier nodded, leering.

'You come to Fort Lafresne as dirty little nursing sluts,' she barked, 'but you leave as soldier girls. Bare-body caning will see to that! Prisoners! At the double! Follow me to the reception centre!'

Trotting in her springy rubber boots, she led Lise, Titzi and Sutra, hopping in their ankle hobbles, past the squads of sweating, naked prisoners, in the opposite direction to the *Centre d'Acceuil*.

2

Bare Body

The girls showered twice: once before they were shaved and medically inspected, and once afterwards. First, they showered singly, with three minutes allotted. All stretched and sighed, as medical orderlies, nude but for white rubber bootees and fluffy socks, removed their hobbles, cuffs and shackles. The shower was sumptuous, with a shelf of plastic bottles containing lotions and scents, and the water blissfully cold, turning to hot at the flick of a switch. Each girl emerged, smiling radiantly, to be fed a cup of hot broth, then taken by orderlies into separate, spartan surgery rooms. Lise was ordered to lie on her back on an operating table.

Her body was still wet from the shower, and she had begun to sweat again in the dry heat. The buzz of an electric barber's shear startled her, then she closed her eyes and felt the teeth slicing off her long head-tresses until her scalp was only a stubble. The armpits were next, then, with a finer blade, her whole scalp, arms and legs were shaved smooth. She raised her legs and parted them, trembling, as the razor poked into the crevice of her thighs, beside her cunt lips, but not yet touching her pubic bush. She sat up, bending forward, for her back to be shaved, and finally was ordered to lie again with thighs spread wide and holding her arse-cheeks apart.

'Pity to lose such a splendid jungle,' said the orderly. 'I was quite proud of mine, when I was a nurse.'

The razor, on heavy blade, was muffled as it delved into Lise's pubic forest. The orderly nurse was elfin, yet

15

strongly muscled, with high cheekbones in a gamine face, and spoke French with a Scandinavian accent. Her right nipple was pierced with a copper pin, twisted at both ends, and holding her orderly's badge. Lise asked where she was from.

'Finland,' said the orderly. 'We're not supposed to talk. My, what a lovely bush.'

The girl had a trickle of come clearly visible from her pink cunt lips. As her pubis was shorn, Lise, too, gasped, as she felt the tell-tale wetness between her thighs. The Finnish girl slipped her free hand between her own cunt lips, and began to masturbate, by flicking her nubbin until it stood wet and red in her swollen pouch.

'Do you mind?' she whispered to Lise.

Lise shook her head.

'I'm Heidi.'

'Lise.'

'Lise, it's just that . . . you've such a lovely cunt-mound and arse, and such big titties, and I wish I had, too! Looking at you makes me feel all tingly. I'm not lesbian, you understand, but I like to wank a lot – all the girls do, here – and we don't get much chance to do it together. Usually, a girl only gets to wank herself at night, and always alone. Do you want to masturbate to keep me company?'

Without answering, Lise grasped her stiffened clitty and began to press it, while slipping the four fingers of her other hand into her already slimy cunt. Both girls masturbated in silence, come streaming on their thighs, while the orderly completed the shaving of Lise's pubis to a gleaming smoothness, and applied the razor to her perineum and anus bud.

'I wank off two or three times a day,' said the Finnish girl, with her own hand balled in a fist, and right inside her wet cunt, up to her wrist. 'O . . . *yes! Mmm . . .!* It's all right for the corporals, they can have cock from the drivers or helicopter pilots, sometimes even afford their own male slave. Or for a girl who is one of Dr Crevasse's lesbian pets. Yuk! I haven't tasted cock since I've been here, so I wank

16

off, just thinking of those gorgeous big Somali tools, so big and black and hard in my wet cunt, or ramming my bumhole . . . *Mmm!* Yes, I'm coming! *O! O! O!'*

Lise wanked harder as she saw the Finnish girl's belly convulse in her spasm, and soon gasped aloud as her own cunt gushed come, and the pulsing heat of orgasm filled her.

'The doctor will be here soon, for your examination,' said Heidi.

'Dr Crevasse?'

Heidi laughed.

'No, the medical doctor, Dr Frahl. Dr Crevasse will see you tomorrow morning. She is the fort psychiatrist, and she will evaluate you, give you the details of fort routine, and prescribe your own personal discipline regime. This doctor is a captain, but an inmate like the rest of us. Almost everyone except Dr Crevasse is a prisoner, apart from her *friend*, the nurse-general. Hm! The general is Crevasse's prisoner. But don't worry about Dr Crevasse. She won't molest or proposition you. She waits for *you* to beg *her.'*

'And you haven't, Heidi? You are lovely, you know.'

Heidi grimaced.

'I've masturbated for eight months . . . I can wank for as many years.'

Lise rubbed her eggshell-smooth scalp and pubis, and smiled.

'We're the same, now, Heidi,' she said. 'I feel better.'

'Just naked animals, with a number,' said Heidi. 'As you progress in rank, you get to wear uniform, but no matter how grand your costume, you must still bare your bottom or tits for caning. I get bum-caned, mostly, but you have such lovely big titties, you'd better beware of breast-whipping. It's unspeakable, but then, you've a beautiful bum, too. O, I'm sorry, I must be frightening you! You get used to it . . . look.'

Heidi turned, to show her bare, tightly muscled arse, suntanned evenly with the rest of her brown body. Numerous welts, some still fresh, criss-crossed her naked

17

buttocks, with older, fainter stripes on her bare teats. She said that it was forbidden for prisoners to talk to each other at all, and this obviously absurd rule was a blanket justification for any caning whatsoever. If Heidi were known to have spoken to Lise, let alone masturbated with her, she would lose her orderly badge and be caned a dozen on the bare, and obliged to wear a rock in her nipple piercing.

'Expect the cane most days,' she said. 'But I mustn't tell you too much, for if Dr Crevasse senses you've already been told, she'll know we've talked, and we'll both be punished. The corporals can give up to three strokes on bum or tits, or both, without reason, warning, or explanation. For a caning of six, there must be a witness, and you can choose to be stooled. Sometimes you get a dozen, or more, in a full-body caning. It's so shameful to be caned on the bare. And I can hardly bear to watch a full public whipping, though if you are caught closing your eyes, you get the same whipping yourself. The funny thing – the damned *Legion*! – is, that those promoted seem to be those most lashed.'

Heidi's fingers stroked Lise's bare bum, still ridged from the Somali's sword-caning, as well as the stripe from Corporal Lavoisier.

'You've been caned already . . .' she gasped.

'That was before I was sent here. That was *why* I was sent here. That, and moral turpitude. I like dark men's cocks too much, in my anus, and their canes on my bare behind. That's what I think of when I masturbate, Heidi. A man, caning my bare bum, then buggering me.'

'*I'm* here for moral turpitude!' said Heidi. 'It's hardly a crime, compared to thieving. I used to be a ward nurse, and I would pleasure soldiers in plaster, you know, wank or suck them off, or ride their cocks with my cunt – sometimes my anus. I went with Somalis, too, sometimes for anal sex. Isn't it gorgeous to be buggered by a huge black tool? O . . . I must wank again! I'm so glad you're not a thief.'

'Are there many thieves here?' asked Lise, as both girls recommended masturbating, fingers diving into sopping wet cunts.

'Well, none I know of. But . . . you *like* bare-arse caning, Lise? You wank off, dreaming of your naked bum being thrashed? O! *Mmm* . . . it's so lovely to wank with a friend! Wank faster, Lise, the doctor's coming. O! O! I'm . . . *Ohhh* . . .'

'*Mmm* . . .' gasped Lise, 'I'd like to be strapped and nude, for a big Somali male, thrashing my bare arse, right now, and his cock standing, ready to prong my bumhole. Caning my naked bottom, harder and harder, making me wriggle and squeal as my bum turns crimson. *Oh! Oh! Oh! Ohhh* . . .! I joined the Legion so that I would *stop* liking it . . .'

'That should be easy enough.'

Panting, Lise sighed.

'It isn't.'

Corporal Lavoisier entered the room, followed by the doctor, a tall, coltish woman with a crop of dark stubble on her scalp. She had a stethoscope around her neck, dangling between her heavy naked breasts; through one of her pierced nipples was pinned a silver coiled snake of Aesculapius, signifying her medical status. She wore white rubber knee-boots, with high pointed heels, and a white rubber skirt hanging just above the knee, which clung so tightly to her firm thighs and arse-globes, that she was obliged to hobble. She sniffed, and wrinkled her nose.

'I smell come,' she said. 'You have been masturbating, Orderly. There is juice at your cunt, your clitoris is stiff, and your thighs are moist. The new inmate's cunt is also wet, and you, as orderly, are responsible. You will touch your toes, for a caning of six, on the buttocks. Corporal Lavoisier, you will administer punishment when I command.'

The doctor swabbed Lise's own cunt and thighs dry with cotton wool, then inserted a pipette right to the neck of her womb, placing its open end in a metal dish that was wedged underneath Lise's buttocks. Heidi's face was stony as she bent over and touched her toes.

'Cane her as hard as possible, Corporal,' said the doctor. 'It is not the first time this inmate has been caught masturbating.'

19

'Ohhh . . .' moaned Heidi, as a stream of yellow pee hissed down her inside left thigh and wetted the pile of Lise's hair clippings on the floor.

'After your beating, Orderly, you will clean the floor of hair clippings with your mouth,' ordered Dr Frahl, 'then fill your vagina. Corporal Lavoisier, tape her for two hours, both cunt and anus.'

'Yes, Captain,' said the corporal, swishing her cane.

'If we were not so short of staff . . . hm! Commence punishment,' said the doctor. 'The new inmate will observe closely.'

Vip!

The first cut of the cane took Heidi on the tender top buttocks, which clenched as the girl's body trembled.

Vip!

The second lashed the same welt, and Heidi's buttocks began to squirm violently. Lise did not take her eyes from the naked caned bottom, and the dish where her buttocks nestled was slimy with her own come.

Vip! Vip!

The third landed on the fleshy mid-fesse, as did the fourth . . .

Vip! Vip!

. . . with the fifth and sixth cracking on the slender brown haunches. Her caning over, Heidi sobbed uncontrollably, and after only a brief prod from the corporal's cane, she crouched and began to collect Lise's piss-soaked hair with her mouth, spitting the clumps of golden hair onto the table. When this was done, she held open the lips of her cunt, while Corporal Lavoisier wadded every tuft of hair inside her. A roll of brown vinyl package tape was passed across her perineum and her gash several times, until Heidi's cunt and anus were thoroughly bandaged. The doctor removed the pipette and dish, brimming with come, from Lise's vulva, and decanted the contents into a titration tube. A smile played on her lips, as she gazed into Lise's eyes, then down to her wet cunt lips.

'Over twenty-three millimetres of titration,' she said. 'You are quite the heaviest comer I have examined, inmate.

20

Dr Crevasse will be interested to learn that your masturbatrix's caned bottom excited you.'

Lise blushed but remained silent, and the doctor conducted her examination in silence, which, like her pedantic 'masturbatrix', was coldly demeaning. After routine measurements and stethoscopy, speculums were inserted into both vulva and anus, and she was instructed to squeeze as tightly as she could. The doctor's rubber-gloved finger poked deeply into both Lise's holes, as well as measuring her clitoris, both before and after ordering Lise to rub herself to arousal. Lise gave a sample of her piss, but was unable to stool, so the doctor inserted a spoon into her anus, and scraped a smear of dung from her root.

At last, a sullen Heidi, her vulval tape squeaking, led her back to the shower area, where she rejoined Titzi and Sutra for their second cleansing. This time, they stood in a communal shower stall for hosing by the orderlies, without soap, and in brackish, tepid water. The naked girls had little time to inspect each other's newly shaven bodies, before Corporal Lavoisier issued each of them with a pair of rope sandals and ordered them, dripping wet, to follow her, running at the double, across the darkening square.

They entered the low, fetid hut of the refectory, joining a long line of girls, all still running on the spot and supervised by corporals, who dealt malingerers a canestroke on the buttocks, or even an occasional slash across the nipples. The canteen inmates were nude like the others, but wore chef's toque hats. When they reached the food dispensary, Lise, Sutra and Titzi were handed segmented trays, each of whose compartments received a slop of food, while the holder still ran in double time. Most of the food was spilt by the time the three reached their allotted places at the end of a bench, and slotted their trays into grooves that ran the entire length of the table. Each table was supervised by a corporal, standing at the end, and Lise felt Corporal Lavoisier's breath on her bare skin as she tried to eat. The inmates ate rapidly and without looking up, pausing to take draughts of cold water copiously provided in tin jugs. Exhausted, Lise picked at her food: some greasy

21

stew, stale bread, soggy leaves ... Suddenly, a whistle blew, and the corporals upended their tables: every food tray, emptied or not, slid down the grooves into a waste bin at the far end. Corporal Lavoisier leered: the three new inmates would go to bed hungry.

It was pitch dark outside, save for a sparkle of starlight, and they followed the snake of naked girls, still at the double, into the large dormitory, its thick stone walls pierced by slits that gave minimum illumination. They kept up their double time while queuing for the latrines, where the three new inmates were issued with toothbrush, dental floss and toothpaste. Lise pissed, but did not stool, but Titzi and Sutra dunged copiously into the communal sluice. There was no lights-out, for there were no lights. Lise, Titzi and Sutra were separated and each marched to straw mattresses on the bare earth floor, only an inch apart, with a water jug between bed and wall, and a toothbrush mug. There were no sheets or blankets. The girls lived, and slept, in the nude: packed together, their sweating naked bodies glistening like sardines. The girls' bodies were of every race, every hue, every nation, united by their naked humiliance, and by whatever impulse or yearning had drawn them to the Foreign Legion. A narrow aisle separated the facing rows of beds, just wide enough to allow a girl to pick her way to the latrines at each end of the dormitory, after begging permission from one of the patrolling corporals.

Lise lay on her back, not sleeping. There was no talking, none of the delicious whispering as at an English girls' boarding school. Nor, despite the closeness of the straw palliasses, was there any touching. The corporals patrolled with penlights directed at the empty inches between the mattresses. Girls constantly rose for permission to stool in the latrines. If this was granted, the corporal followed the girl and sometimes there were two or three canestrokes, after which the girl, having dunged insufficiently or not at all, returned in tears, rubbing her caned bottom. Girls wishing to pee simply squatted at the foot of their straw, and pissed into the bone-dry ground, which rapidly drank their piss.

Almost every girl masturbated. This was tolerated, or even tacitly encouraged, by the corporals, who ogled the spread wet cunts and flickering fingers of their prisoners, as they vigorously wanked themselves to come after come. The air gasped and moaned with orgasm, and was perfumed with the oily scent of cunt-juice. Forbidden to converse, the female prisoners expressed themselves by wanking off. Lise's fingers crept across her bare belly, stroking for moments the new nakedness of her pubic mound, before she too slipped fingers into her wet cunt and rubbed her clitty to stiffness. She parted her fesses, and poked her index finger, then forefinger also, into her anus bud, getting the two digits all the way into her elastic anal passage, and buggering herself as she wanked her erect clitty, while her fingers pinched the pulsing wet walls of her slit. She was not the only girl with fingers in anus as well as cunt. After her first orgasm, she rose to piss and emitted a thick golden stream, sparkling in Corporal Lavoisier's penlight, like drops of yellow rain. She held her cunt lips wide open so that the corporal could see, and, as Lise pissed, she continued to wank her clit; Corporal Lavoisier began to masturbate, too, her face slack with lust, as she wanked her stiff clitty.

Back on her palliasse, Lise opened her legs as wide as she could, and showily masturbated, fingering her clitty and gash, until her come was a lake, and the corporal's bare breasts and buttocks quivered, with come flowing from her own wanked cunt. Lise frotted herself more and more vigorously, threshing and sighing, but not allowing her body to stray from her own palliasse, sodden with her come. Corporal Lavoisier stood, legs apart, masturbating, as though transfixed; when the corporal shuddered in orgasm, Lise spasmed too, and as her belly heaved in climax, the corporal's cunt released a jet of steaming yellow piss. Lise Gallard's face wore a smile as she fell into a deep sleep on her first night in prison.

'Did you masturbate in the dormitory last night, inmate Gallard?' asked Dr Charlotte Crevasse. 'Corporal

Lavoisier reports that your palliasse was soaked in vaginal fluid.'

'Yes, Doctor,' said Lise. 'I ... I sensed that all the inmates masturbate regularly every night.'

'You sensed correctly,' said the doctor. 'It obviously does not distress you, since you admit to having joined them in masturbating.'

'With respect, Doctor, a prisoner's distress cannot count for much.'

'Are you a frequent masturbator? Your dossier suggests that you are, when male company is unavailable.'

'*My dossier* ...? Yes, I have always masturbated, Doctor, I admit. At least daily, before the Legion, and more often than that, as a celibate nurse legionnaire.'

'How many times did you orgasm last night?'

'Twice, Doctor. I am surprised *that* isn't in my dossier.'

The black woman smiled, and stroked her thigh near her pubic mound.

'After a few days, it will be,' she said. 'In my office, you are a subject of psychiatric evaluation, who happens to be a prisoner, and I recommend the regime of discipline best suited to reform you and secure your early release, or ... promotion. You may stand at ease, inmate. Your medical report indicates morbid nymphomania, and I will conduct a few tests, purely psychological, of my own. A prison psychiatrist's interview reflects the nature of the inmate's offence, so a compulsive pilferer, for example, would have opportunities to pocket valuables. Your offence is sexual in nature, and therefore the structure of your interview shall also be sexual. Your tribunal testimony indicates a strong addiction to bare-bottom chastisement and anal sex from males, yet you juiced heavily on watching your orderly's bottom caned by a *female*. Most inmates fear the cane, which is why it is unsparingly used to toughen and reform them. Yet you seem used to, and eager for, bare-bottom caning, so I may deem it necessary to cane you on the bare at some point in your interview. My task is to find out if your fesses will come to *crave* caning by females. Bluntly put, to see if your tendencies are lesbian as well as psycho-pathological.'

Dr Charlotte Crevasse rose and unbuttoned her white lab coat. Beneath it, she was nude, and she draped the garment over her chair back. She was taller than Lise, smoothly muscled, and her dark skin was like rich velvet chocolate, swathed in a film of gossamer. Her head was as shaven as any prisoner's, but the slender bare skull was the dome of a queen, not a slave. Her nose was proud and straight, her sloe eyes wide, her breasts and croup swollen to perfect, firmly muscled ripeness. Her sleek body, with its jutting teats, softly rippling thighs and buttocks, and massive bare cunt-mound, smelled powerfully, but of no perfume but her own. The teats wore gold nipple rings, not hanging, but one inch discs pierced, or sewn, into the skin surrounding the aureolae, so that the nipple buds were squeezed to a state of permanent erection, like chocolate berries. Her naked, shaven cunt was locked in a tiny golden padlock, its chain pierced through both labia; she wore a necklace with a golden key to fit the hole in her cunt-lock. From pendulous lobes hung earrings of black basalt, each in the form of an erect phallus and balls.

'I shall interview you nude,' said Dr Crevasse. 'I will allow you to tell me, in total discretion, of the origins of your nymphomania, and your cunt's secretions will inform me how you react to my own nudity. You may sit, keeping your thighs open, so that I may observe your vulva.'

Lise obeyed, her cunt already dripping come, as she gazed at the black Djiboutian's magnificent nudity. Dr Crevasse fixed her eyes on the girl's vulva, and smiled.

'You find Djiboutian people beautiful,' she murmured.

'Yes,' said Lise.

'Especially if they cane your bare fesses.'

'I . . . yes, Doctor.'

'Of course. You wish your buttocks to be scarred moons, as beautiful as our savage volcanic land, whipped, we say, by nature. For that shameful passion, you are here at Fort Lafresne.'

'Some say caned fesses are poetry, Doctor. This desert is poetry.'

'We are equal, Mademoiselle Lise. You see that I sit nude before you, with my own thighs spread and cunt bared for your inspection, just as I am inspecting you. We shall take coffee before you make me an account of yourself. Your dossier, which I have inspected, is the official perception of you, and it is my task to compare that with your self-perception, in order to prescribe your regime of discipline.'

Two servants entered, bearing trays of coffee and hot croissants, which Lise eyed hungrily.

'We feed you muck, on purpose, here in prison,' said Dr Crevasse. 'But in my office, you are not in prison. You may feast according to the custom of my S'Ibaya tribe, of which my shaven head denotes queenship.'

One servant was male and the other female, both of Lise's age, and both their basalt black bodies nude. The male's enormous penis was fully hard, with a high arc of erection. The female was a younger version of Dr Crevasse herself, the smooth globes of the fesses proudly jutting and the young belly flat over a hairless mound, although her breasts were more conic in shape than the doctor's huge teats, and were topped with oversized brown nipples that seemed to cling like clamshells to the smooth bare flesh. Both servants had sombre, grave faces, and while the male was completely shaven, like Dr Crevasse and Lise herself, the female had a mane of long straight hair, that flowed over her buttock tops. The wet flesh of her cunt, and the protruding clitty, glistened in the folds of her silken black pouch. The bare buttocks of both servants bore deeply etched cane marks, arranged in a crossed pattern, like a tattoo.

Lise accepted her coffee, and drank, her eyes closing momentarily, savouring the aroma. The girl put down a plate of croissants sliced open, and her fingertips began to rub the huge naked glans of the male. His eyes fixed on Dr Crevasse's wet cunt-folds. The girl frotted her clitty, wanking herself off as she masturbated the male, and her gash rapidly overflowed with copious come oil. Lise's own cunt juiced as she stared at the trembling of the male's helmet, the circumcised glans melding smoothly with the shaft of the giant cock, whose flesh was equally velvet, as though his cock was one long glans. The girl's rubbing of the shaft made his cock tremble as much as her rubbing of the helmet, and soon he groaned softly, an enormous jet of sperm spurting from his peehole, to splatter on the croissant bread; his spurt was sufficient to cream five of the croissants. When he had finished, the girl took each croissant and, still vigorously masturbating her clitoris, pressed it against her cunt, allowing her come oil to flow onto the bread until it was gleaming and sodden. Dr Crevasse accepted a croissant, and bit it in half as her tongue licked sperm and girl-come from her lips. Lise crammed a croissant into her mouth, wolfing it whole.

'The young men of my tribe may never touch my person unbidden,' said Dr Crevasse, 'but must express their submission and obedience mainly by masturbating, or being masturbated. You will note Afgoi's penis: our custom is the African circumcision of the male, whereby the whole skin of the penis is peeled and excised, not just the prepuce; it is, naturally, very painful, but leads to greater pleasure for the male when fully grown. Did the cocks that buggered you, mademoiselle, possess this hard, smooth sheen?'

'Yes,' blurted Lise, accepting another croissant dripping in come.

'Our females are not excised, as is the barbaric custom elsewere,' said Dr Crevasse. 'For eons, our tribe has had a queen, whose breasts carry the charms against the evil eye. My breast rings are those worn by S'Ibaa, the mother goddess of our tribe, in the time before the pharaohs of Egypt. Masturbation, to the male and female S'Ibaya, is a sacred ritual: one reason I am proud to serve the Legion in its female penitentiary, where girls addict themselves to self-pleasuring. Our women instruct both males and females in the masturbatory art from the moment of adulthood. Both are trained to experience multiple orgasm, the males without ejaculating, but reaching what the vulgar term the *coup de vinaigre*, or vinegar stroke, and maintaining themselves in an orgasmic state for many minutes, without loss of sperm; the females, to know the innermost secrets of their pouches, so that they can climax repeatedly, and produce copious cunt juice. Melleah, orgasm three times.'

The black girl parted her rippling thighs, and pushed two fingers into her cunt, delving right to the knuckles. She did not touch her clitoris.

'*Ahhh . . .*' she gasped, then, almost immediately, '*Ahh . . .*'

She withdrew her fingers and grasped her distended clitty, pinching its tip, kneading the nubbin, and pulling it hard, away from her body.

'*Ahhh!*' she gasped again, her belly contracting in her spasm, and a wide gush of come flowed down her trembling thighs.

'There are many techniques of female masturbation,' said Dr Crevasse, 'and time spent in Fort Lafresne eventually instructs a girl in the effective enjoyment of her own cunt: thus, to achieve the legion's ideal of self-sufficiency, enforced upon us nomads since the dawn of time. Too many girls wank off rapidly, and impatiently, with simple clit-frotting, and ignoring the slow and sensuous delight of the cunt lips, the cavern of the cunt itself, and of course stimulation of the nipples, anus and spinal nubbin. Masturbation becomes holy, when female or male wanks off during a bare-bottom caning with a rod cut from a baobab tree.'

Lise's cunt was flooded with come, and her fingers strayed near her throbbing stiff clitty, eyed lustfully by Dr Crevasse.

'Like the caning of twelve cuts which Melleah shall now give you, mademoiselle. Bare-bottom caning, to us S'Ibayas, is a sacred ritual,' said Dr Crevasse. 'The squirming of a whipped bare croup is the swell of the desert dunes, or the ocean waves. The gasps of a female flogged naked are the winds of life to our naked land.'

Lise eyed the male servant's penis, which was now fully erect again, and the girl's cunt, which continued to drip come.

'My servants,' said the doctor, 'are under instruction to maintain themselves in a state of constant arousal. They will wank off as they watch you caned, and for your humiliation the male will spurt his sperm in your face; you shall lick and swallow every drop that falls on your lips, but not touch the sperm that splashes your breasts. Now, inmate Gallard, stand with your buttocks raised and your belly on the chair back, with your hands grasping the arms of the chair. You may not move in any way without my permission.'

Trembling, Lise rose and bent over the back of her chair, with her bare bum raised and thighs wide, allowing the copious come to drip from the spread lips of her gash, as the black girl flexed a springy brown cane. Inches before her face, the young ebony male stroked his erect cock. Dr Crevasse remained seated, her thighs still open, but her fingers now wanking her swollen clitoris.

Vip!

'Ah!'

Lise jumped as the first cut from the girl's cane surprised her.

'No squealing, inmate,' said Dr Crevasse, wanking herself harder. 'I like to see a girl squirm silently, as the cane cuts make her gorge rise.'

Vip!

The second stroke made Lise gasp, and her bum clenched tight, but she did not squeal.

Vip!

'The rod of the baobab is one of the hardest instruments of discipline,' said Dr Crevasse, 'much harder than the fabled rattan, and much more adaptable. There are rods supple or hard to suit every caning purpose, and in my private clinic, I keep a stock of Caucasian silver birch sheaves, for my slaves' discipline.'

Vip!

Lise's buttocks were squirming frantically, as the cane seared her bare fesses; before her, the male stroked the silky knob of his cock. Her mouth gasped towards it as though to fellate him. Come trickled in a hot flow from her gaping vulva, down her thighs and calves, to her ankles. Dr Crevasse had one fist inside her cunt and was twisting her huge extruded clitoris with her other hand, the fingers twirling her nubbin as the sharp nails dug into the swollen clit-bud.

Vip! Vip! Vip!

Three strokes to the left haunch made Lise wriggle, and tears misted her eyes. She gasped ever more harshly.

Vip! Vip! Vip!

The right haunch took three.

'*Nnnhhh* . . .' Lise moaned, her striped bum squirming and clenching, and her arms trembling, with knuckles white as they clutched the chair.

Vip! Vip!

The final two slashes cut straight across Lise's middle fesses, with the black male's cock dancing, and the peehole seeming to smile at her pain. Suddenly, it disappeared and Lise gasped again, as the silken penis stroked her exposed anus bud. Dr Crevasse masturbated vigorously: little gasps, and twitches of her belly, with a blinking of her eyes, were all that indicated she had wanked herself to repeated orgasm. Her cunt was a lake of come, dripping onto her bare feet. She had her buttocks raised and two fingers inserted in her anal hole. The maidservant squatted at Lise's feet, wanking herself in tandem with her mistress, and her own puddle of come mingled with Dr Crevasse's even more copious flow, which shone on her black thighs like morning dew on basalt.

'*Ahh* . . .!'

Lise cried out as the cock of the male sank into her anus and his peehole touched her root. He began to bugger her, slamming his cock so hard into her bumhole that she almost toppled from her perch. His fingernails clawed the weals of her buttocks, trapping the writhing arse-flesh in his embrace. At the fifth stroke of his cock, Lise's belly heaved and her gasps became a moan, then she squealed.

'O, God, yes, fuck me! O, I'm coming! *Ohhh* . . .!'

As soon as he had brought Lise to orgasm, the male withdrew from her anus with a rapid, plopping sound, and resumed his position in front of her face, wanking off his ebony cock, now shiny with her arse-grease. Melleah rose and took his whole ball-sac in her mouth, as she inserted a finger into her own anus and another into the male's. Her own cunt was foot-fucked by Dr Crevasse's bare toes. The male gasped and a spray of spunk splashed on Lise's lips and nose, followed by further ejaculate which fell thickly on her titties and erect nips, until her whole bosom was slimed with his massive spurt of cream.

Dr Crevasse bounded from her chair like a panther and fastened her teeth on Lise's left teat, biting the nipple savagely, as her tongue flickered on the flesh, to lick all the male's sperm. She bit and chewed both of Lise's teats until they were licked dry, and clutched Lise's spread arse-moons; her fingers traced and scratched the weals raised by the baobab cane, then two digits found her buggered anal opening and penetrated the bum-shaft, driving to the very root of her anus. A golden ring shone, pierced into the top of the black woman's buttocks, just at the nubbin of her spine. Her other hand was wedged inside Lise's gushing cunt, fist-fucking hard. Her thumb pressed the clitty and, as she finger-fucked Lise's anus, two fingers inside the wet gash-pouch touched the skin to Lise's pubic bone.

'*Ahhh! Ahhhh . . .!*'

Lise screamed, and her body shuddered, as a second orgasm engulfed her. Almost at once, Dr Crevasse had resumed her seated position, watching Lise sit numbly down, while the two naked servants departed as silently as they had arrived. Lise perspired heavily, still quivering after her climax. Dr Crevasse's skin bore not a bead of sweat. She sniffed, then licked her fingers carefully, like a cat.

'Why did you enlist as a common nurse, Mademoiselle Gallard, and not as a superior?' she said, sneering slightly. 'It is Legion custom that lower ranks are foreign, and officers French. You are a French citizen, yet you chose to hide the fact and enlist as a slavey nurse.'

'I am English!' retorted Lise. 'And I am no slave . . .'

'Born of a French mother, in Trouville, Normandy,' said Dr Crevasse. 'That makes you a French citizen. Are you ashamed of the fact?'

'I . . . I don't know . . .'

'Now, Mademoiselle Lise Gallard,' said Dr Crevasse, 'you are going to tell me the truth: why you are an addict of masturbation, buggery and the cane, and why you serve, yet deny, your motherland.'

Her dark eyes pierced the prisoner girl's, and drank in the sight of Lise's nude body. Nipples and clit tingling, and cunt dripping come, Lise obeyed.

3

Flagellance Sinister

Reading Mods and Greats – classics – at St Hugh's
College, Oxford, had not been Lise's idea but her mother's.
Lise did not object out of swank – to show off that a rich
girl could afford such frivolity. There would be trips
to Mediterranean sunshine, beaches, Italian and Greek
boys . . .

But for Dr John Henric, the classics were anything but
frivolous. This suavely handsome classics don, lithely
muscular, and thirtyish, with distinguishing flecks of silver
in his cropped hair, enchanted Lise from the first. His
accent had the studied precision of someone whose first
language was not English, and Lise detected a French
nuance: his name, perhaps, anglicised. He was rumoured to
enjoy great wealth, and was disdainfully elitist, sneering
that the study of classics was not for cowherds and
mill-hands – his choice of insult placing him firmly at a
distance from the twenty-first century, which he despised,
as he did all centuries after the thirteenth. He never
referred to Mods and Greats by their customary abbrevi-
ations, but always as 'Moderation Honours' and 'Great
Honours'. St Hugh's was still largely a female college, but
there were a few males in Dr Henric's small group of
classicists. The other girls were, like Lise, smug and rich, a
far cry from the dowdy bluestockings of old.

Dr Henric was a born teacher, enthralling females and
males alike with a passion for any subject, even if he felt
little himself, as was the case with most of the syllabus,

with which he dealt quickly and expertly. When it was time for the Henrician view of the ancient world, he was more than enthralling. Dr Henric was a Platonic pagan: he believed in slavery, that the many should toil for the leisure of the cultivated few, thus freed to seek the True, the Beautiful, and the Good. Slavery was not only necessary, but virtuous, as the vile masses could only redeem themselves in the service of philosophers. It was, however, not enough to study and discuss the world of Apollo and Dionysus, Plato and Socrates: a philosopher must feel it. Students of the classical world must live the classical world. College cloisters were not the place to experience the liberating spirit of Ancient Greece: Birchwood, Dr Henric's sprawling, gladed estate, north of Kidlington, was more suitable. Weekend study groups could live nude, as casually as the ancient Athenians, and the male students were surprised, and smug, that supple young naked females did not, after a first few embarrassments, cause their cocks to rise.

Dr Henric customarily wore only a loose purple academic robe while his students were nude, but joined them to swim naked in his lake. Lise, like every other girl, noticed his unusually long and thick penis, shaven of pubic hair. It was not long before the female students and, soon, the male ones, practised pubic denudation. Dr Henric said that sleekness of body was sleekness of mind. The poems and philosophical texts they read were pagan and unchaste, teaching that freedom of the spirit lay in exposing and exploring the flesh, and thus rising above its pleasures. It was at Birchwood that Lise first submitted willingly to a bare-bottom caning.

'Whipping and caning the naked flesh has a sacred function,' Dr Henric explained. 'The threshing or reaping of the corn simulates the whip descending on the naked buttocks, symbols of the earth's fecundity. By whipping the human buttocks, or the whole back and croup, the Greeks urged Mother Earth to be fertile. In Sparta, naked young men were ritually flogged to unconsciousness by naked maidens of Demeter, with the additional function of urging on the soldiers of that militarist city. All of you come from proper schools, and thus are familiar with the noble tradition of bottom-caning, lamentably abandoned in this debased age.'

There was an awkward, but excited, silence, with stirrings of the males' cocks, until Dr Henric casually suggested that students of ancient Greece should emulate the ancient Greeks, who considered naked flogging a normal, even daily, ritual.

'I assume all of you have been caned during your schooling,' he said, 'but has any of you been caned, or birched, on the bare?'

Lise put up her hand, unable to prevent a dribble of come juice seeping from her shaven cunt.

'Lise!' said Dr Henric, as if she had excelled in some test. 'And you are still alive to tell the tale. Perhaps you would be kind enough to do so?'

'It's nothing, really,' said Lise, blushing, as she felt her nips stiffen and her cunt become wet. 'I was caught smoking and Miss Haughtrey, the headmistress, gave me six of the best, on the bare bum, with my skirt tucked up and my knickers at my ankles, bending over like a boy . . . I suppose.'

'Six of the best is scarcely nothing,' said Dr Henric. 'It must have hurt, as it was designed to.'

'It . . . it was awful,' said Lise, noticing that the two males present had stirring cocks, 'and I bore the weals for days. My bottom was all corrugated and leathery. But it was quite nice, in a way. Sort of glowing, and friendly.'

'Nevertheless, it deterred you from the offence of smoking.'

'Well, no, it didn't. I was caught, and caned quite frequently. My tariff went up to a dozen strokes, with my lower body completely naked, and all the prefects were there to observe my comportment. That was in the gymnasium, and I had to bend over a vaulting horse. Miss Haughtrey would make twelve strokes last ten minutes or more, which was awful. I mean, she knew I wanted to get it over with, so that I could have a good cry. But I never cried. Actually, knowing other girls were watching my bare bum caned, and wriggling, gave me a kind of thrill.'

The silence in the glade was electric. Tim and Peter, the two male students, had fully erect cocks, which they made no attempt to hide, and there were glistening smears of come at the vulvas of the two girls present as well as Lise, whose own cunt flowed copiously, as she confessed.

'Is it a thrill you would deny yourself the pleasure of repeating?' asked Dr Henric. 'Now, and willingly, amongst friends, in the Greek rite.'

'I . . . No, I would not deny myself that pleasure,' stammered Lise, her heart racing as her clit stiffened, and come wetted her thighs.

'You will submit to a bare-bottom caning, Lise?'

'Yes.'

'Before, when you were caned on the bare, at school, it was because you wished to be caned, was it not?'

'Y . . . yes.'

'At other times, you relieved yourself by beating your own naked buttocks with a stick, or hair-brush, or similar instrument. Am I correct?'

'Why . . . yes.'

'And you would masturbate straight away, after this cruel headmistress had caned you, or masturbate, as you beat your own buttocks.'

It was a statement, not a question. Lise nodded her head in ageement.

'I have always longed to be caned bare-bottom,' she murmured. 'I have never known why.'

'I now invite you to choose a cane for your croup, and determine the number of strokes your chastiser shall give you,' said Dr Henric.

Lise broke a branch from a young elm tree and gulped, as it looked much larger than she had thought. It was long, thin and springy, with a jagged green gash over creamy wood, where she had broken it.

'I think . . . a full dozen, sir.'

She had never called Dr Henric 'sir' before.

'Twelve strokes . . .? On your bare, Lise, don't forget.'

'I'll take twelve, sir. From *you*, please. And, yes, on the bare.'

'I shall not cane you softly, Lise. But if it is your wish . . .'

'It is as I wish, sir. But I request that you be nude, also.'

Dr Henric frowned, then nodded, and let his purple robe fall. His penis was stiff and huge. He took the sapling cane from Lise and swished the air, then invited Lise to place her hands on an overhanging branch, and cling to it for support, while spreading her legs wide. She did so, finding that she was obliged to stand on tiptoe. Her cunt dripped come onto the bright green sward, moistening the blades of grass.

'Pain is unavoidable in life,' said Dr Henric. 'The bare buttocks absorb our allotted pain, so that we may live joyously. On magnificent globes such as yours, made for the cane, weals are medals of beauty. O! the beauteous haunches, begging for stripes; the firm meat of fesses that long to quiver and redden under the cane; the lush shady furrow of the cleft, ripe with your sweet woman-stink! Do you wish me to flog you twelve on the croup alone, Lise, or divide the strokes between buttocks and back?'

'All on the bum – I mean, croup – sir,' Lise whispered.

'I make one condition,' said Dr Henric, as he positioned himself in flogging stance behind the girl's stretched bare body. 'I fully expect your buttocks to clench and squirm as they receive their strokes, and your whole body may shudder. Hold tightly to the branch above you. However, if you cry out even once, the flogging shall stop. Is that clear?'

'Yes, sir.'

Vip!

Without further warning, the sapling cane whipped Lise's bare bottom. She gasped, and her bum clenched, but she stifled any squeal.

Vip!

The second stroke, harder, took her on the underfesses.

Vip!

The third lashed her top buttocks, jolting her, and her whole body trembled and her knees gave way as she clung to the branch for support.

Vip! Vip!

The cane whipped each bare haunch, spinning her slightly like a top. Beneath her, the grass puddled with come, whose drip, from her cunt lips, became a steady trickle. Her bum-cleft clenched tightly.

Vip! Vip! Vip!

Remorselessly, and in silence, the doctor caned Lise her full twelve on the bare; the twelfth delivered, he complimented her crimson weals.

'O, God, sir!' cried Lise, at last, and no longer stifling her sobs. 'It smarts so! O God, it hurts! My bum! O! *Ouch!* O, how I need it . . .!'

'Yet your pain excites you, Lise, as it excites all of us,' said Dr Henric. 'Pleasure yourself, if you wish, as your pudendum is so wet.'

'Wank off, after caning, sir?' Lise said.

'Vulgarly put, but yes,' said Dr Henric. 'Caning normally excites girls to masturbate. When you witness the bare bottoms of Tim and Peter caned, as and when they offer themselves, you, Helen and Susan shall probably be unable to resist masturbating.'

Lise did not let go of the branch, but, holding on with one arm, rubbed her deep cane-welts with her free hand.

'Are they well crimson, sir?' she asked.

'Superbly,' said Dr Henric, 'and in minutes, should darken to purple.'

'I have been guilty of spoken vulgarity, sir,' said Lise, resuming her position, 'and beg for punishment of twelve strokes on the back.'

She took twelve stripes below her shoulders; the searing of her bare back was a new and awesome agony. When her punishment was complete, she squatted with thighs apart and gash open, and wanked off, in full view of the others, the males with straining cocks, and Helen and Susan's cunts brimming with shiny come. Tim and Peter were caned by Susan and Helen respectively, with both girls masturbating as they flogged the bare bums, and Lise wanking herself to a second orgasm as she watched. Dr Henric's cock stood stiff as a pillar, bulging under his robe, but he made no move to his own pleasure. Tim's cock spurted sperm at the tenth stroke of his flogging; Peter took the caning without climax, but when Helen touched his peehole lightly with her forefinger, he spurted at once. Dr Henric caned Susan, but Helen asked Peter to cane *her* bare bum, during which she masturbated, climaxing at the tenth stroke of her dozen.

All five of the students, caned on the bare that summer afternoon, were caned or whipped regularly in the weeks to come. On the fourth or fifth caning weekend, Dr Henric said that the Greek experience was not limited to flogging.

'The sodomic practice was also part of the philosopher's life, and Plato mistakenly glorified knowledge of another male's anus as the pathway to virtue. Although male homosexualists are not immoral as such, they commit the far more unspeakable crime of being boring. What knowledge can be gained from intimacy with your own image? Debased though the female animal may be, only intercourse with a female offers the philosopher the necessary touch of *otherness.*'

Lise's addiction to bare-bottom caning, she realised, had grown so strong that she did not react angrily to Dr Henric's insulting words. As though philosophers could only be male!

'Some of the female's baseness may be cleansed by regular whipping,' continued the doctor, 'or penile penetration of the orifices, vaginal or anal. Penetration of the anus was a sine qua non of the Greek philosophical rite, and so it is time, my friends, for you to acquaint yourselves with the sensations of buggery, both as giver and receiver.'

Tim and Peter paled, and Dr Henric assured them, with a smile, that since three such pleasant young females were available, they might, if they wished, open their anal orifices to a lady equipped with a suitable 'toy'. He produced a variety of sinister-looking phallic devices of rubber, which Lise soon came to know as 'strap-ons', or 'penetrators'.

'The females amongst us may enjoy adopting a male role, as Tim and Peter learn the sensation Plato felt indispensable to wisdom; the females may then learn the same, with the satisfaction of live flesh filling them.'

All five students were by now so much in Dr Henric's thrall, that they smiled at the prospect of buggering, and being buggered. Lise put a hand to her cunt and retrieved it, slimy with her come, which she licked. Since she had been the first subject of bare-bottom caning, she begged to be the first student buggered. The doctor's penis was stiff beneath his robe, and he looked at Lise as she voiced her request.

'If no one objects . . .?' he said. 'Choose your penetrator, Lise. Shall it be Tim or Peter?'

'It shall be you, sir,' Lise said.

Dr Henric accepted her command with a nod, as though she had answered correctly some question of Greek syntax. He instructed her to crouch, pressing her face to the grass, with her hands at her nape, and her knees parted wide, to reveal her anal aperture. Lise obeyed, trembling.

'You have not been buggered before, Lise?' he said.

He reached between her thighs, and began to masturbate her cunt, until his palm brimmed with her come. This he used to grease his erection and his fingers played at Lise's bumhole, smearing come in her crevice, so that her aperture shone with her own cunt's lubricant.

'Try to relax your sphincter,' he said. 'It will hurt, of course, and there will be a moment's resistance, but as my penis gains ground within your hole, you will find there is a delicious point of no return, at which your anal elastic, understanding your submission, will yield fully.'

He entered her, and it was so. As his glans pushed up her bumhole, Lise chewed the grass, but suddenly gasped in delight as her anal walls relaxed, allowing the huge stiff cock to penetrate her right to the root. Dr Henric arse-fucked her with extreme vigour, and said that now he had achieved satisfactory penetration, Lise might masturbate. One hand flew to her sopping wet cunt, grasping her clitty, and she came almost at once.

Suddenly she gasped in dismay as the male's cock plopped from her bumhole. Dr Henric said that Susan and

Helen, both wanking their clitties at the sight of Lise's buggery, must not be deprived of the same privilege. The procedure was the same: Lise remained squatting, masturbating hard, as the two other naked girls crouched beside her. Both Helen and Susan wanked off as vigorously as Lise, and their cunts dripped juice. Dr Henric penetrated each in the same manner, and buggered her with firm, bum-slapping thrusts, until she wanked off to come. He remarked that their bumholes were perfectly tight, although his ingress to Susan's was easier, and Susan, gasping as she wanked, admitted that she often masturbated with a vibrator in her anus.

Dr Henric returned to Lise's spread buttocks, and re-entered her, this time sliding into her anal canal with no resistance from her bumhole. It was in Lise's anus that he chose to spurt his own cream, a mighty jet of hot spunk so copious that it bubbled from Lise's stretched arse-ring, and trickled creamy and wet down her perineum to her engorged cunt lips, where her fingers wanked herself to another groaning climax.

Champagne refreshed them, and Dr Henric, with an impish smile, said that it was now the turn of the females to bugger Tim and Peter. He suggested a swift bare-bum caning first, six of the best, to warm their arses for anal penetration, and this was agreed by all three girls. The males touched their toes, and their bare arses jerked, as each girl, armed with a wand, caned two strokes at a time. Speedily, Lise, Helen and Susan strapped on 'penetrators', as Dr Henric termed the rubber prongs, and took turns at fucking the bumholes of the males, who groaned, sobbing and writhing, as they crouched in sodomite's pose. Yet, as their buggery proceeded, their cocks stood, and first Peter, then Tim, began to whimper in ecstasy, and demand to be fucked harder.

'It's so good . . .' Peter gasped, as Lise's hips slapped his arse, 'from a *girl* . . .! O God, yes! It hurts! Bugger me harder, split me . . . O! O!'

A huge jet of spunk spurted from his stiff cock, splattering the grass with creamy white globules. Tim, too, was not long in orgasming, his penis untouched and his sperm pooling on the grass with Peter's. Dr Henric stroked his chin, smiling, his penis risen under his robe. Lise did not cease to bugger the groaning male, and Dr Henric spanked her own bare bum with both his palms. Lise began to rub her clitty, masturbating fiercely at the hard bare spanking and arse-fucking the male, as if furious that his balls were spent and cock limp. Peter chewed the grass, squirming and crying, as his anus shuddered under Lise's relentless buggery, and she too whimpered as the teacher's palms cracked on her naked buttocks. Peter's cock trembled, stirred, and began to rise again.

Susan was buggering Tim, and Helen began to spank her buttocks; both the recipient and giver of the spanking wanked their clitties off with equal delight, and Susan's come trickled onto the writhing buttocks of the buggered young man. Suddenly, Susan groaned in embarrassment as a stream of steaming yellow piss squirted from her cunt, and bathed Tim's bum. At Dr Henric's suggestion, Helen squatted over Peter's head, twisting it to face her cunt, and with her shaven vulva inches from his mouth, she sprayed his face with a copious shower of piss. Buggered by Lise, Peter gulped and drank her friend's golden pee-stream.

Throughout that warm summer term, the weekends at Birchwood grew more debauched, with Dr Henric taking part in the rites, but always distant from the young flesh that whipped, buggered, pissed and drank under his approving gaze. Different rods played different roles in their rituals of pain: long canes of pickled wood, or else short, springy rods, for caning the breasts of women, or the balls of men, in imitation of the Ionian fertility mysteries; Dr Henric was especially fond of a rubber scourge or flail of thirteen thongs, which whipped the bare buttocks most painfully, but left especially vivid welts where the tips lashed the haunches. Dr Henric advised his charges to be proud of their marks as a joyful secret known only to initiates. The males were encouraged to drink copiously of the girls' piss, and to masturbate as they watched the girls bugger each other with the rubber penetrators, while awaiting the cunt-oiled dildos in their own bumholes. At each rite, Dr Henric awarded his own sperm as a precious gift to his favoured girl, though sometimes he refrained from sperming, preferring to observe the jets of spunk and floods of oily cunt juice of the young orgiasts.

There was another frequent visitor, seen, mysteriously, only from afar: a female of sumptuous figure, swathed from head to foot in white latex who, Dr Henric explained, was a visiting Professor of Psychology, interested in – or, he hinted, sexually obsessed with – the sacrificial ordeals of the ancients. He explained that, rather tiresomely, she fancied herself his slave, wishing to be humiliated and thrashed. An aperture in her latex suiting invited buggery, but – he shrugged – while he did what little he would to satisfy her, there really was no satisfying a submissive, nor wisdom to be gained from her humiliance. The pleasure of enslavement was the hatred of the slave. In kindness, Dr Henric would occasionally thrash her on the buttocks and breasts, or, with her rubber-suited body buried in mud, he might piss in her open mouth, a pink gash amid her rubber mask. Bound in wire over her rubber suiting, with only her hands free, she would, on his orders, masturbate her latex crotch, until her come and piss flowed through the anal aperture, to be collected in a cup of dried dung. This was raised to her lips, until she had drunk her own come and pee. She arrived and departed alone, and always, on her departure, sobbing bitterly; she always came back for further humiliance.

'She is a slave to her own *morbiditas erotica*,' Dr Henric said. 'She wishes to be sated and disgusted with anal lusts she thinks impure, so that she may remain virgin in cunt. Thus, I refuse buggery: her frustration is the only pleasure she affords me.'

Away from Birchwood, the friends avoided each other's company, afraid that dowdy academia would tarnish the gold of their ritual perversion. At Birchwood, nude, they became ancient Greeks. Life at Oxford lacked sense for Lise, away from the naked orgies at Birchwood, and she sensed that it was the same for the others. They were all

43

addicted to the cane, the whip, the shameful delight of buggery, and the approval of Dr Henric, when he deigned to show it, by filling a quivering young female anus with floods of hot spunk from that massive cock.

Other male students were anonymously introduced, naked but for goat masks. Fear of Dr Henric's sneer kept the girls from protesting, as Tim and Peter yielded to the newcomers, who whipped and buggered them *en série*, as Dr Henric put it, one after the other, with Lise, Susan and Helen's bums clenching under repeated canings of six strokes, and their anal chambers filled by the six or seven cocks in succession, until their vulval basins were lakes of spunk and cunt oil. The woman swathed in white rubber looked on, masturbating, while suspended from a sacred oak above water. At all times, the white rubber woman wanked off most fervidly during Dr Henric's buggery of the girls.

Lise had a French male friend, Thierry, who was studying theology at St Dunstan's. His family had grown rich from the coal mines of Bruay-en-Artois five generations ago, and had refashioned themselves as landed gentry with attitudes to fit. Thierry lived on the family estate near St-Omer, and said that a military career did not appeal to him, as gallant wars were no longer fought. As for the Foreign Legion ... he shrugged disdainfully. So, he was considering joining the Catholic priesthood. Celibacy, he said, was a particular pleasure, and he would remain virgin for ever, although Lise chided him on such a waste of his cherubic beauty. Thierry thought Oxford very *folklorique*, though the English lacked seriousness; Lise had a crush on him, his virginity and passion giving him the allure of the unobtainable.

Thierry had a special interest in the flagellants of the Middle Ages, and she began to drop hints about her salacious weekends at Birchwood to tease him, but when she found serious Thierry was unteasable, she confided in him more and more. Thierry agreed, for what Lise imagined a daring prank, to sleep naked with her, to prove his chastity. When he stripped, Lise gasped, seeing the welts covering his back, and Thierry admitted that he ritually scourged himself in penance for sins uncommitted. Nude, beside his huge snake of a penis that lay curled on his belly, Lise longed to arouse him, but his devotion to virginity was true and frightening. She was afraid to touch him, and unable even to masturbate though she longed to. They slept together often, Thierry observing her wealed bottom and raw, crimson anus with disinterest. Finally, she revealed the whole truth.

'The pagan way is not the true way,' he said. 'In degradation and mortification of the flesh, you should not find pleasure, only shame. Your lustful stripes are flagellance sinister: my own, flagellance pure.'

'My shame *is* my pleasure,' Lise said.

Thierry smiled with white lips.

'Your shame must be your shame,' he said.

At their next meeting, just before term's end, Lise's bottom was smarting from a particularly hard caning from Dr Henric; he had offered his own anus for buggery by her rubber tool, but something had made her demur, as if his proffered anus was mocking her, and to bugger the teacher would in some way be total surrender. Her twelve strokes on the bare from Dr Henric's raw sapling cane, and her subsequent buggery by Susan, Helen, Tim and Peter, all wearing goat masks, as well as four other males, had been her hardest ever. She had orgasmed twice, wanking as she was caned, and wanked herself to orgasm at every penetration of her anus, and every male spunking at her anal root. Thierry looked grave.

'I have obtained information about this Dr Henric. The family was French, and originally Henriques. The good doctor's ancestor, Armand Henriques, was an accomplice of the infamous sodomite and torturer Gilles de Rais, known as Bluebeard, and fled to England, to avoid burning. The family has properties in both England and France, and flits between one country and the other, but blood does not change. This term, in ever filthier debauches, Dr Henric has made you his toys. Like his ancestor, he will make you his slaves, and finally, his victims.'

Thierry permitted himself a shy smile.

'You English have a quaint phrase: "Let me take you away from all this". However you planned to spend the summer vacation, I offer instead my company and home in Artois for three months, during which you may study, reflect on your obsession with this sinister academic, and perhaps grow to share my pleasure in celibacy. Dr Henric is playing games with you, Lise, and life is not a game.'

Lise thought of Dr Henric's sudden petulant fury when she had refused to impale him with her rubber penetrator; of the others, all now in goat masks, and hooting like animals, as they gave her her desired – her *craved!* – caning. She shivered. Perhaps an attempt at celibacy would be advantageous; perhaps Thierry would even agree to satisfy her craving for bare-bum chastisement, despite her pleasure in her bum's smarting. Perhaps – she scarcely dared think of it – her pleasure would be ecstasy, if her stripes were as no game, but as earnest of punishment, like Thierry's autoflagellance. The Artois countryside, comfortingly near the white cliffs of Dover, was inviting. If she signed a paper identifying herself as Thierry's 'chattel' – a mere formality and one of the few remaining privileges of the nobility – she would be free of tiresome bureaucratic requirements, like registering her residence with the police. She agreed to join Thierry for the summer.

Dr Crevasse had taken notes throughout Lise's narration, pausing to masturbate with lazy flicks to her stiffened nubbin.

'Flagellance sinister, indeed,' she said. 'I feel there is more sinister to follow.'

'There is, Doctor,' said Lise.

Dr Crevasse put down her notepad, and began to masturbate her soaking slit and erect nubbin with both hands.

'Go on,' she ordered.

4

Flagellance Pure

'Take off your left boot,' said Thierry.

'*What?*'

He pinched Lise's cheek playfully.

'To please me,' he said.

Lise obeyed. One foot dangled bare but for sheer black lycra, the other remained tightly shod in a black leather knee-boot.

'One foot bare, or nearly bare!' she said. 'It feels sort of kinky, or naughty . . . I don't know why, nor why it should please you, Thierry.'

'It pleases me that you should obey,' he said.

The train hummed, deep under the English Channel. A few interested males stared briefly, or as long as was decent, at the succulent female foot revealed in black lycra, with the toes wriggling, then returned to their newspapers.

'May I take off my other boot?' she said.

'No, you may not,' said Thierry with a yawn. 'We are almost at Calais International station, where we disembark. You have time to visit the toilet. Please do so.'

'Thanks for reminding me,' said Lise, rising on imbalanced feet.

'You will piss standing up.'

'But I'm a girl! I have to squat! Thierry, what is going on? A game?'

'Not a game,' he said mildly. 'An amusing exercise. You will stand with your right booted foot on the toilet seat, comfortably parting your vulva, under your panties. You

47

will not remove your panties, but piss through the cloth, down your left stocking, so that your pee puddles the toilet floor. You will stand with your stockinged foot in your pee for three minutes, until the fabric is soaked. Then you will return to your seat, treating all vulgar stares with disdain.'

Three minutes later, a blushing Lise Gallard hobbled back to her seat, her piss-wet stocking squelching, and leaving wet footprints. Now, the other passengers did look. She sniffed, and raised her head haughtily.

'You stink,' said Thierry. 'Your first lesson in purity, Lise. An aristocrat may do whatever she likes, disregarding the vulgar.'

The Mercedes that awaited them outside the station had shaded glass. Leaving the engine running, the driver emerged from the far door, and walked stiffly to the passenger side to open the front door for Lise. When Lise had seated herself, the driver opened the rear door, and Thierry slipped in, seating himself directly behind Lise. The driver was a woman of perhaps twenty-five, wearing a wide peaked cap and a fetching military-style tunic of dark green, which pinched her waist to hour-glass thinness; a high mini-skirt revealed stockings seamed back and front, and the beginning of her garter straps on milky white thighs. Her boots were zipped to mid-calf, with stiletto heels. She leant over to pull Lise's seat belt out and clamp her in it, and Lise saw that beneath her uniform jacket, her teats were squeezed to melons by a tiny uplift bra, with a glimpse of wide pink nipples. Beneath, a corset fastened her. The skirt, equally tight, smoothly encased powerfully rippling bum and thighs, which, Lise suspected, were unknickered. Her eyes hid behind wraparound sunglasses, with her glossy chestnut hair pulled back in a stern bun. Her entire green uniform, the stockings, boots, and corset, too, was made of fresh-scented latex.

'May I beg the privilege of admiring Mademoiselle's perfume,' she said in a silken voice.

Before Lise could respond, she was jolted as the car roared into a u-turn and sped away. They quickly left the suburbs, then the main highway, and swerved through a series of small, twisting departmental roads, past somnolent farms. Thierry's hands took hold of Lise's and drew them beind her seat, where he held her wrists clamped.

'What . . .?'

With only one hand for steering the car, the driver plunged her right hand between Lise's parted thighs, found her quim, moulded by the wet panties, and began to rub her clitty. At first, Lise protested with a moan, that soon became a moan of satisfaction.

'Mmm . . . O, yes, wank me! I so love wanking! But Thierry, I thought you didn't want me to wank any more. Am I to be punished?'

Thierry did not reply. The driver continued to masturbate Lise's cunt, almost, but not quite, to orgasm, with firm, expert wanking strokes. Her eyes stared coldly ahead, until they reached the gates of Thierry's estate. A long driveway took them to a large mansion of white walls and grey tiled roof, steeply sloping in the northern French style.

'Thank you, Odette,' said Thierry to the driver.

'Will Monsieur require dinner?' said Odette. 'I have Mademoiselle's bath prepared, as you instructed.'

'Yes,' said Thierry. 'You may serve us together, after Mademoiselle has refreshed herself.'

With Lise still hobbling on her stockinged foot and single boot, their steps echoed through immaculately polished corridors and rooms with furniture under drapes, before ascending a wide oak staircase to the mezzanine. Thierry explained curtly that the house was empty for the season, apart from Odette, and a few 'peasants'.

'Aren't you supposed to call them citizens these days?' said Lise, eyes bright at the luxuries of her new home.

'Yes, they have the vote,' said Thierry. 'Unspeakable!'

He flung open a door, and Lise saw a four-poster bed, with gilt pillars and a coverlet of pink silk. Beneath the open window stretched a lush landscape of ponds, arbours and sculpted gardens. Thierry said that it was her bedroom and study.

'Thierry, it's beautiful!' she cried.

'It is the bridal suite,' he said.

'I am honoured,' she said, trying to sound ironic.

'Now, you may strip to your stockings, and remove your other boot. Do not remove your stockings, but do remove your panties. Your bath awaits, in the adjoining chamber.'

'What about my sussies?' said Lise.

'Clever girl! Leave them on.'

'Thierry,' she said shyly, 'I . . . I like this game. I mean, feeling such a slut. Are you trying to turn me on?'

'It is not a game!' he replied, and clawed a ladder in her left stocking with his thumbnail.

'Ow . . .!' gasped Lise, though his nail had not touched skin.

'Now, you are a slut!' he barked. 'Time for your bath, dirty slut!'

'Dirty sluts are spanked on the bare,' Lise blurted, 'or caned bare.'

Thierry slapped her face, hard, then grasped her cunt, removing fingers oily with come, seeped through her piss-damp panties.

'You disgust me!' he said. 'Finish stripping, slut!'

Lise stripped to her stockings and sussies, and padded after Thierry to the bathroom next door, where Odette awaited them, still in peaked cap, but otherwise clad only in stockings, sussies, boots, and the impossibly thin rubber corset. She had removed her bra, but the corset's rim was so hard that it pushed her bulging bare titties together. She stood beside an ornate gilt bathtub, filled to the brim, and in Odette's hand was a scourge of rubber thongs, like the whip favoured by Dr Henric for haunch-welts.

'Ohhh . . .' said Lise, blushing, as her cunt moistened.

'Get in,' Thierry ordered, 'with your head next to the taps.'

Lise placed a foot in the tepid liquid, then paused, wrinkling her nose: the bath was full of piss. She hesitated, and then squealed, as Odette lashed her bare bum with the rubber thongs.

'*Owww* . . .!' she cried, rubbing her haunch where the tips had wealed hard. 'I thought I was to give up flagellance, Thierry!'

He grasped her by the anal cleft and heaved her, so that she splashed into the bathtub, her head sinking under the pee for moments, before re-emerging with her hair plastered to her scalp. She screamed as Odette's quirt lashed her full across the bare titties. Thierry divided her hair into two ropes, which he knotted to each bath tap. Lise threshed, splashing her tormentors in piss, and received two lashes on her wet nipples. She began to sob.

'Why, Thierry . . . *why*?'

'To cleanse you of foulness, slut. To disgust you with debauchery, so that you will become pure when I take you as my bride. Odette has faithfully filled your bathtub with her golden rain, which she shall replenish every day, for it shall be your only bath.'

'Wait a minute . . . your *bride*?'

'I intend to marry you, in the flagellant thirteenth-century rite, when you are purified. Ours shall be a white marriage, free of carnality. We shall sleep together naked, in constant temptation, and constant vigilance, with flagellance pure, to punish the flesh for sins contemplated. Odette is a former Nurse-Major of the French Foreign Legion, and is skilled in the arts of discipline.'

Odette turned to show Lise the swelling bare plums of her fesses. Her naked croup was deeply etched with whip-welts. With a crack, she added a stinging lash of the quirt to her own bare.

'Am I your prisoner . . .?' Lise sobbed.

'You are the prisoner of your own filth,' said Thierry.

'You intend to whip me?'

'Odette shall flog you every day, until you have the serenity to whip yourself.'

Odette vaulted onto the bath rim and squatted, so that her vulva was inches from Lise's mouth. She pissed a long, steaming jet of yellow pee right into Lise's throat. Spluttering, the tethered girl swallowed the nurse's pee. Meanwhile, Thierry disrobed. He stood before the pissing nurse, with his huge penis fully erect.

'I am unclean,' he said.

'Then it is hypocrisy to hold me here against my will!' Lise cried.

'If you are a coward, you may depart. My bride must be no coward.'

Odette placed her hand in Lise's cunt, under the surface of her piss, prised the lips open, and began once more to wank her off, with hard flicks and squeezes to the clitoris.

'Ohhh ... Ohh ...' moaned Lise, splashing in her pee-bath. 'O, yes ...'

Thierry presented his buttocks for chastisement. As one hand masturbated the bathed girl, Odette's flogging arm began to whip her master's naked buttocks. Lise raised a hand, and found Odette's own cunt sopping wet.

'No, slut,' hissed Odette, yet her open, slimed cunt lips did not resist Lise's wank, and her hips writhed as Lise pinched her swollen clit.

As the nurse flogged Thierry's reddening fesses, the two girls mutually masturbated to orgasm. Thierry was at the fourteenth thrash of the scourge when, suddenly, his penis bucked and a copious jet of sperm spurted over Odette and Lise's breasts.

'Is Thierry truly virgin?' Lise asked.

'Yes. He voids his impurity only by the whip. I must masturbate alone, and scourge my own buttocks for my filthiness. I warn you, mademoiselle, that once you elect to stay, I shall administer full discipline, and your bare bottom shall be raw with welts, although whipping shall be the least of your correction. You tempt and disgust me, English slut.'

'I was born in France! So I am a French slut,' gasped Lise, 'and I do, still, crave naked whipping. There! I admit it! So I shan't go, just yet.'

Lise began every day with a bare-bottom caning. She slept nude in her four-poster bed in satin sheets, but with her ankles chained to the bedposts. If she needed to pee, she had to foul her own satin. Odette awoke her, unfastened her shackles, and replaced them with a forked dog's leash, clamped to her nipples. Lise was helpless to resist the pinching nip-clamps and followed Odette to the bathroom. After watching Odette piss into the tub of golden fluid, Lise was pinioned by the nurse and her head forced beneath the surface of the liquid. She remained immersed, Odette's hand twisting her hair, while her naked buttocks received six strokes of a willow cane, under the eyes of Thierry.

Her food was taken in the kitchen, where she crouched like a dog, ordered to hold her hands behind her back, with her buttocks parted, and an index finger inserted into her anus. She ate and drank from saucers of scraps, and Odette removed the dishes when she was only half-finished. Each morning, Odette wore a nurse's uniform, with regalia of the Legion.

The uniform mini-skirts and blouses varied from rubber, to leather, or pvc plastic, but always clung to her mound, titties and buttocks, and her legs were always graced with stockings. Her waist remained corseted to a pin. It was a hot summer, and Lise was happy to be nude, although she was allowed to bathe only in piss except when Odette took her for a walk, like a dog, on all fours, and leading her by her teat-leash. Then, she could plunge into one of the ornamental lakes, whose goldfish tickled her vulva and belly. She was forbidden to shave her body or comb her hair. If she felt cold in the evening, she could wear a single garment: a *discipline*, or hair shirt, many sizes too small that swathed her tightly from neck to ankle. Thierry informed her that Odette had woven the garment herself from her own pubic hairs. To wear it was torture, for it itched abominably, the itching made worse by the sprouting of new pubic growth on Lise's previously shorn cunt-mound.

After her miserable breakfast, she was given her morning task, designed to be as humiliating, arduous and useless as possible. She had to pick up each pebble from the driveway adjoining the front door, with her cunt, fill her slit with pebbles, hold them inside her, and run on the spot, until Odette decided the stones were sufficiently polished. Or she had to lick the toilet clean; polish the Louis XV furniture

53

with her cunt, after wanking herself to juice; shovel horse-dung, using only her breasts. Failure to comply meant strokes of the rubber quirt, either on buttocks or titties, or else a full formal whipping, which required Thierry's presence. She was whipped, tied to a flogging-post, with her wrists cuffed, and dangling from a peg that only just permitted her toes to brush the ground, as her back and buttocks received twelve stripes each, her arms wrenched in their sockets. She might also be flogged, shackled to a moving cart, or her torso strapped on the running Mercedes, her cunt pressed against the scorching grille and her titties against the hot bonnet.

When she merely grimaced one evening at the itching pain of her hair shirt, Thierry made her strip and had Odette wrap her in cling film, before the garment was replaced: now, the itching was as bad, but she poured with sweat, and was obliged to sit with her hands cuffed behind her back, while Thierry read to her from St Jerome, whose battle against fleshly lust he identified with his own. Thierry was for preference nude in Lise's company; if his penis rose, Odette whipped him on the bare, until, cursing, he spurted his spunk into Lise's face, and she had to let the copious sperm drip onto her nipples, down her breasts and belly, and into her growing cunt-bush. Odette always removed her skirt, and panties, if she had any on, for whipping Thierry, and wanked herself off to orgasm, as she flogged his wealed bare bum. She liked to smear Lise's titties with her own come, or put her fingers to the back of Lise's throat, and make her lick the spunk and come. Then, she ritually administered a dozen strokes to her own buttocks. This occurred every fourth or fifth day.

There was a tariff of rules, and punishments for breaking them, which Lise was not allowed to inspect. At the end of each day, Thierry computed her tariff, reading from a scroll: insolence, three strokes of the quirt on the breasts and three on the buttocks; laziness, a caning of six on the bare fesses; sluttish demeanour, a whipping of twelve strokes on the back and twelve on the buttocks. Adjustments would be made for mercy and Lise informed of her

54

evening whipping, which could amount to twenty-four strokes, in combinations of whip, quirt or willow cane, and on the breasts, back, or buttocks, or all those areas. She was suspended in a square flogging-frame in the drawing-room with a porcelain bowl beneath her cunt, to protect the astrakhan carpet from her come or pee. Her nude body was stretched in an X as Odette administered her flogging, with Thierry usually observing, although sometimes he was absent. On these occasions, Lise was sure that Odette masturbated as she whipped the girl's squirming bare fesses and back.

On her first evening of whipping, Lise cried out at the searing agony of the quirt on her buttocks, and pissed herself, the pee mingling with copious juice from her cunt that dripped loudly into the porcelain. Thereafter, she was gagged in a rusty iron brank, with a tongue depressor, and could only gurgle as she was flogged. But her come flowed as avidly as before, and often the cuts of the cane on her croup, after a savage back-scourging, would bring her to orgasm, after which she invariably pissed herself, the yellow stream hissing down her thighs and splashing into the bowl. The flogging over, her brank was removed, but she was only unbound after drinking the entire contents of the bowl, filled with her fluids.

Escorted to bed with nipples clamped to her leash, she was left shackled and alone, to sigh in pleasure at the luxury of her bridal bed. Lise would rub the weals on her ridged and puffy bottom, and wank her cunt to two or three orgasms as the tingling of her smarting bottom was assuaged, then sink into a blissful sleep. Every day, Thierry taunted her that she was free to leave, and every day she defied him. She sensed that Odette needed her, not least to show off her varied wardrobe of clinging rubber and leather costumes, and her peaked caps, with Foreign Legion insignia pinned to the cruellest and most intimidating dominatrix costume. Odette reminisced about the Legion and kept all her uniforms, tight skirts and under-things, which she deliberately soiled, pissing her panties before stuffing them in Lise's throat to gag her.

'Ah, the Legion,' she cried, masturbating to climax as Lise's flogged body danced like a puppet under the whipthongs, 'the Legion . . . the bondage of tight stockings and knickers, corsets and hobble-boots! You do not yet know hardship, slut. Nor does Thierry. His debauchery comes from books, mine from the slave markets of Djibouti. I deserted from the Legion, was sold by the S'Ibaya as a slave, and whipped every day, until I escaped back to the Legion. There, in Fort Lafresne, my whippings were worse, but they still did not cleanse me. I was mired in filth: girls wanked me and each other blatantly, and I served the black mistress as both slave and procuress. I escaped again, to Somalia, where I became the concubine of a warlord, who sold me back to the Legion. When my five-year term was finished, the Legion released me with my uniforms. Slowly, I am achieving purity, and my addiction to wanking and the lash is purged by having that sweet firm croup of yours to stripe.'

After these nostalgic longings, Odette, as in a dream, would brutally wank Lise off to come after come, still tethered in the flogging frame, tweaking and pinching Lise's swollen throbbing clit, and masturbating herself as she whipped the girl. Their come and piss brimmed the bowl, and both ladies sipped the acrid liquor, before Odette applied the thongs to her own bared buttocks, her rubber skirt rolled up to her titties, and her come a cascade, soaking her laddered stockings. Sometimes, Lise received her nightly whipping wrapped in rubber, or cling film, with Odette showing her expertise by whipping the cling film to shreds to fall from Lise's body like a sloughed skin. After her whipping, Lise received a treat, of 'choc-olate drops': Lise knelt with her face at Odette's anus, which emitted pellets of Belgian chocolate, which Lise swallowed avidly.

One day, Lise's head was shaved with a blunt razor, down to a ragged, ugly stubble. She was obliged to don a skimpy bra and soiled high-cut panties of Odette's, then blindfolded and taken to the Mercedes. They drove a short distance into the nearby village, and Lise had her arms cuffed around a tree branch, raising her on tiptoe. A dirty toilet seat was draped round her neck like a bridle. She was caned twelve times on the bare buttocks, left almost open by the skimpy thong, which stank of Odette's piss and come and pressed tightly into the anus. Then she received twelve lashes on the bare back, and hung, quivering and sopping with pee and cunt juice, as the Mercedes hummed away. She wore only the bra and panties; fired by her flogging, she rubbed her cunt against the rough tree-bark and brought herself to come. All night she hung there, shivering and masturbating, sobbing in her joy of humiliance, with her bladder open, so that a permanent trickle of piss dripped down her laddered stockings onto her feet.

In the morning, she heard the cruel laughter of early pedestrians. Then, gentle hands unbound her, and she stared at the kindly, grizzled features of a policeman, immaculate in his tan uniform of the Gendarmerie Nationale. He removed the toilet seat from her neck, chuckling that Monsieur Thierry had a way with his girl sinners. Before driving her back to the estate, he gave her hot chocolate and a blanket in his tiny police station, and Lise saw the bulge at his crotch, as she rubbed her welts, her bare arse exposed by the come-soaked modesty thong.

'Mlle Odette is a legionnaire through and through,' he said. 'Such ordeals as yours are common in the Legion. I was a legionnaire myself, and you never truly leave the Legion. As an ex-legionnaire and sergeant in the Gendarmerie Nationale, I am empowered to enrol volunteers in the Legion, in this very place! A volunteer must repeat the words, "I wish to join the Foreign Legion" three times. Sadly, I have as yet not had the privilege of enrolling any. And rarely do I enjoy the privilege of having such a beautiful female in custody.'

Lise's hand strayed to his massive erection.

'If you like . . .' she said.

'Sergeant Rastoff, of the Gendarmerie Nationale and ex-legionnaire, at your service, mademoiselle.'

Lise unzipped him. His erect penis sprang, and her lips fastened on the swollen glans, sucking it vigorously, while unconsciously inserting her index finger into her anus. Suddenly, she withdrew her mouth from his massive cock, and blurted that if *he* liked . . .

Lise draped herself over the gendarme's desk and spread the cheeks of her bottom. She fumbled with the buckle of his heavy service belt, and when he had removed both it and his trousers, she doubled the belt into a flogging tool. He whopped her bare bum very hard, two dozen times, leaving her fesses raw and squirming and her cunt gushing with come. He dipped his fingers into her slit, and masturbated her clitty, then greased his cock with her come. His stiff cock rammed her bumhole, penetrating the anus in a swift, practised thrust, and he began a forceful buggery. Lise masturbated as he buggered her and climaxed at his third stroke, her anal elastic milking the huge cock, until his cream washed her anal root. As his spunk spurted, her fingers wanked her clitty and she orgasmed again, bathed in his hot man-cream.

'God! I needed that! Do all legionnaires have such big cocks?' she said, half in jest.

'Yes,' he said. 'It is not a rule, but we tend to be large of cock. Nature designs some of us to be legionnaires, whether we know it or not. You, mademoiselle, have a deliciously elastic anus: you make me nostalgic for the girls of Djibouti, with their magnificent croups and tight holes.'

'Thank you! But I've been buggered before, quite a lot, actually – it's something a girl grows to need. Thierry wants me to be purified, as his bride. I don't know how seriously to take him.'

'Take him seriously, mademoiselle. His family own this village . . . The bridal ceremony shall either be your ultimate purity, or your ultimate humiliance. Either way, it shall be what you truly want, and what lady knows what she truly wants, until it happens to her? I am reminded of the lady bandaged in white rubber, who pestered Monsieur Thierry . . . most curious! Anyway, Mademoiselle Odette wants to be pure, but she, too, comes for my cock in her bumhole, and this desk is well moistened with her come. Afterwards, she scourges her naked arse, and . . .'

The gendarme exposed his bare nates, and Lise saw the scars of caning.

'I did time at Fort Lafresne's male penal battalion, where we were subject to the same corporal punishments as the females, though not so casually. How the female officers wanked themselves, watching us strapped naked to the whipping post while the drums rolled, to be flogged by women corporals for our extra shame! Legion women are celibate and untouchable to madden us males with martial energy. But the Legion knows that men and women together in the desert cannot remain chaste, just as they know a quarter of new recruits desert in the first three months. Desertion is punished, but not harshly. You are thought odd if you have not tried to desert at least once. The femmes, too, are kept on heat, by their constricting clothing. The nurses, wrapped in tight brown, blue or white skirts, rubber corsets, stockings, bras and panties too small . . . all to heat their juices in the fervent service of the Legion! Ah, they are subtle. I was flogged, for fucking – and caning bare-arse! – a frilly little nurse; Frachon, her name was, the property of a black lesbian slavemistress. She wore a padlock at her cunt, to remain virgin, as leader, or high priestess, of her tribe. She thought her virginity gave her the power to punish and enslave all those of us, begging your pardon, mam'selle, who are not. Those were rumours, but nothing is impossible in that desert hell, where obedience to the Legion is your only rock of safety.'

He sighed, and said he must drive her back to Therry's mansion.

'We all miss the Legion,' he said, as he deposited Lise at Thierry's front door, 'even Monsieur Thierry, who was rejected for service as an officer. I served in the ranks, since I am not French. I am Russian, and after five years' service I got my French passport. How I hate the French!'

He laughed.

'But it does not matter. Outside the Legion, life is only a game. The Legion is pure, for it is no game. And the Legion prison, or punishment battalion, in the scorching bare desert of Djibouti, is purest of all.'

Sgt Rastoff deposited the buggered Lise back at Thierry's mansion, and received Odette and Thierry's thanks. Lise's routine of humiliance continued: towards the end of her summer vacation, Lise was serially buggered by five of Thierry's peasants, while Thierry watched and Odette masturbated him, wearing rubber gloves. Lise had taken her evening's whipping of twenty-four lashes to the buttocks and been released, sobbing, from the flogging frame. She gasped, and her cunt flowed as the five stinking, hairy males entered, dropping their cotton working blues to reveal erect penises. She crouched, automatically, and bared her croup to reveal her bumhole. She oiled her anus with her own copious come before pressing her face in the carpet, sighing in humiliant pleasure, ready for the first cock.

They took her brutally and efficiently without a word, as though she were no more than a mare to be tupped. They spurted quickly, excited by her fervent wanking of her clit under their buggery. As she chewed the carpet, her pierced bum squirmed at their ruthless penetration. When she climaxed for the third time, Thierry spurted into Odette's rubber-gloved palm, and Odette brought Lise his spunk to drink as the last male orgasmed and bathed her anus in hot cream. Sperm bubbled and frothed at her stretched bum- hole, and trickled into her perineum and cunt, where it mingled with her own copious flow of wanked come. Swallowing Thierry's hot spunk, she masturbated herself to a final, convulsive orgasm. Her arsehole was aching and sore after five penetrations, and as Thierry cursed her for a slut, she began to sob.

'You are broken, slut,' he said. 'Our wedding will be tomorrow.'

'This is all in your dossier,' said Dr Crevasse. 'Odette's reports were remarkably detailed. But we are lacking the details of how you came to the Legion recruitment office in St-Omer.'

'Odette was a spy . . .?'

'An informant.'

'And my debaucheries at Oxford, from her also?'

'Yes. We are interested to know their provenance. Perhaps this exciting marriage ceremony of yours will provide a clue.'

'More than a clue,' said Lise bitterly. 'Damn the filthy lesbian slut, for tricking me!'

Dr Crevasse smiled.

'Go on,' she said, gently frotting her come-wet clitty. 'How did a filthy lesbian slut bring you to the Legion?'

5

Pink to Crimson

The day of her wedding, Lise received her normal six strokes on the bare with her head plunged in the bath of Odette's piss, but for longer than usual, so that when Odette finally released her, spluttering, she slapped her whipper hard, on the face. Thierry was not present; Odette smiled, her nostrils flaring.

'You slap hard, madame,' she said. 'I wonder if your palm would be so ready to spank a bare bum. Mine, I mean.'

'I, spank *you* . . .?'

'Don't you thirst for vengeance, for all your humiliance?'

'Thierry thinks I am broken, but . . . yes, just a little.'

'Well, then!'

Odette raised her white rubber skirt, so tight that she had to roll it up her thighs and knickerless buttocks, to bare them for chastisement. She bent over the bathtub, with her legs parted and buttocks spread, but without lowering her head into the piss. Her open quim dripped come.

'Why?' said Lise, lifting her arm.

'I want more than a bare spanking, Lise. The desire never leaves . . .'

'The whip?'

Crack!

Lise's palm slapped Odette across her bare buttocks, which clenched at the spank's impact.

'Mmm . . . yes . . .' moaned Odette.

Crack! Crack! Crack! Crack!

'O! O . . . !'

Odette's bum clenched and shuddered, pinking under four hard spanks.

Crack! Crack! Crack! Crack!

'*Ohhh!*'

Come flowed so copiously from her swollen cunt that its drips made a plopping sound as they puddled the floor beneath her gash.

Crack! Crack! Crack! Crack!

'O! O! Ohhh . . .! God, I'm dripping come! You spank so hard, Lise! I want a whipping, yes, till my bum's raw, and then you must tongue-fuck me in the bum while you wank me off, just like in the Legion.'

Crack! Crack! Crack! Crack!

'*Ahhh!*'

'You fucking lesbo,' Lise hissed, but her own cunt was pooling come on the floor beside Odette's puddle.

'Aren't *you*? Isn't every girl . . .? O! O!' moaned Odette, her pink bum reddening under the spanks.

Lise picked up the rubber scourge. Its whistle in the air was the only warning before its dry impact on Odette's bare bum.

Thwack!

'*Ah!* Ah! Ah! You *bitch!*' Odette squealed.

'You wanted to be whipped! And that other filthy stuff.'

Thwack! Thwack!

The rubber thongs wrapped themselves around Odette's naked haunches, with Lise pulling them away from their clinging embrace.

'O! O! *God,* that's hard!'

Thwack! Thwack! Thwack! Thwack!

'*Ahhh . . .!*'

The bare bum writhed and squirmed, with deep purple welts already etched on the tender haunches where the scourge's tips had bitten.

'What do you think *I've* endured, these past months?' hissed Lise, 'and why should I give in to your filthy pleasures?'

'You accepted your humiliance, just as at Birchwood . . . you *want* the lash on your bare fesses. O, don't stop whipping me!'

Thwack! Thwack! Thwack! Thwack!

Odette's legs shot rigid behind her at each set of welts from the scourge's thongs, and her bare was now darkening to crimson, framed by the purple, glowing haunch-welts, the skin already puffed and ridged.

'How do you know about Birchwood?'

Thwack!

'O! Harder, please! Do you really want to marry Thierry in the flagellant rite?'

Thwack! Thwack!

'O! Ahhh! That's better! God, I'm almost coming! Can't you see my cunt juicing? I've always wanted *you*, Lise . . . not just your bare arse.'

'It's not a real marriage! I am almost purified of the filthy lusts that drove me to Birchwood. The ceremony will be my cleansing, by flagellance pure.'

'Don't tell me you don't wank off every night, thinking of my cane and whip on your bum.'

Thwack! Thwack! Thwack!

'*Ah! Ah! Ahhh!* You *do* masturbate, thinking of my cane on your bum!'

'Yes, damn you, I wank! But how do you know about Birchwood?'

'The wedding won't be as you think! Tongue my anus and clit-suck me, Lise, and I'll take your place! I'll leave the Mercedes running and you can get away, as I am flogged and buggered. I'll wear the veil, and you, my Legion nurse's uniform, with peaked cap and dark glasses. *I* want to be Thierry's bride and take his accursed virginity from him.'

Lise began to wank her extruded hard clitty, as she rhythmically flogged Odette on the bare. The whipped nurse gasped and sobbed as her welted bum writhed, and her squirms grew more frantic.

'Say you'll do it, Lise! Wank and suck me, and I'll let you escape. You don't know what awaits! Dr Henric has never forgiven you for making a fool of him, refusing to bugger him.'

'Dr *Henric!*'

Lise lifted Odette by her slippery wet cunt, causing the woman to howl, and tipped her into the bath of piss. She plunged after her, still clutching the whip, and grabbed Odette's hair, to pull her head underneath the pee. Bubbles spurted in the golden fluid as Odette writhed helplessly. The two nude girls wrestled in piss, splashing and churning the yellow liquid. Lise got her knee between Odette's thighs and kneed her groin, making the spurt of bubbles more frantic. She pulled Odette up by the hair, baring her breasts, and slashed the quirt across the stiff wet nipples.

Thwack! Thwack! Thwack! Thwack!

'Ah! Ah! *Ahhh!*'

The breasts were wealed livid by stripes; still clutching Odette's twisted hair and kneeing her hard in the oily cunt, with Odette opening her thighs for her gash-pummelling, Lise bit her breasts several times, taking each distended nipple between her teeth and chewing, while flicking the stiff bud with her tongue. She plunged Odette back under the piss, with her head bent over beneath the surface, and the wet teats trembling just above. She continued to knee the groin, smashing her bone right on Odette's erect clit, while administering vigorous whipping to the wet bare breasts. The dry thwack of the thongs became a wet slapping as she flogged the stiff nipples, the aureolae widening to huge crimson gashes.

Splat! Splat! Splat! Splat!

'That's for your filthy pube-hair shirt, you bitch!' Lise cried in English.

The bare girl writhed like an eel in the lake of piss. At each three lashes to the breasts, Lise brought her up for air, then reimmersed her. During this tit-flogging, Lise vigorously masturbated her own clit, pushing her fingers inside her wet slit, to poke the neck of her womb and, watching the nipples quiver under the rubber thongs, she wanked herself to a shuddering come. After the thirtieth stroke, with Odette's teats now bruised purple, Lise plunged her own head beneath the surface, between Odette's parted thighs. Lise fastened her teeth on the erect clitty, chewed hard, and Odette's belly at once heaved in orgasm. Both girls emerged, panting and wiping their piss-wet manes. They shifted, with Odette's lips on Lise's quim, and Lise tonguing the opened anus of the lesbian. They sank beneath the piss, now warmed and frothed from their threshing, and gamahuched each other, with bums touching the surface, so that they could spank each other's wet buttocks, as their mouths sucked come from their flowing cunts.

Slap! Slap! Slap! Slap!

Bubbles gurgled to the surface of the pee, as the girls' bare bums quivered under vigorous spanking. Lise's tongue penetrated Odette's arsehole to its full depth, while her fingers jabbed to the neck's womb through the girl's gushing cunt-slime; Odette had her tongue in Lise's own cunt, with forefinger, then index finger as well, up her elastic anus tube and a thumb pronging Lise's throbbing clitty. Finger-fucking and tonguing cunt and anus, both girls threshed the bath of piss, as they orgasmed simultaneously for the second time.

'You did all this, with Dr Henric and the boys and girls at Oxford, didn't you?' Odette gasped, as they climbed out of the bath, fingers still wanking each other's cunts.

'I . . . I may have done,' Lise blurted. 'But it was impure, and . . . O! God! Don't stop wanking, you're bringing me off again!'

Her own fingers twitched at Odette's throbbing nubbin, greased with come, and both girls embraced, with wet nips pressed together, and masturbating their come-slimed cunts to a further orgasm.

'Now, who's the filthy lesbian?' said Odette, smirking, as she rubbed her bruised bare titties and the whip-welts on her bum.

Lise offered no resistance as Odette took her to her own bedroom, laced her to groaning in a steel-ribbed rubber corset, and dressed her in green rubber uniform, with rubber corset, panties and fishnet stockings, high stilettos and a whalebone cane. Lise then helped Odette with her wedding dress, a delicious confection of frothy pink chiffon, but preceded by the fastening of an even tighter corset, which made Odette's big bare teats bulge. She wore white silk stockings with lacy sussies, but no bra or knickers. Under the thin chiffon, the welts on her naked titties and arse-globes were clearly seen, and Odette said this would make their deception easier. She gave Lise the keys to the Mercedes, and veiled her face. Lise secreted the keys inside her cunt, then haltered her by the neck, and Odette crouched on all fours to be led to her flagellant wedding. They would whip her wedding dress to shreds until she was nude.

'Just one more wank . . .?' Odette pleaded.

Lise felt the power of her tight rubber uniform. Contemptuously, she inserted a boot between Odette's cunt-lips and began to poke her clitty, at the same time reaching below her belly into her tight green rubber knickers, to masturbate her own gash, still sopping from their previous wanks. Her boot was slippery with Odette's powerfully flowing come, and she inserted the toecap into the vulval slit, pressing the clit with her ankle. Odette squealed in come, and Lise followed soon, leaving smears of cunt-slime glistening all the way down her green rubber stockings.

Thierry awaited them in the great hall, by the wedding altar, a St Andrew's cross; he wore a white robe, like a friar's. Keeping the peak of her cap well down, Lise led Odette up the aisle by her halter, to deliver her to two male figures dressed in blue robes and wearing goat masks. A further three figures, in similar robes, sat before the altar in makeshift pews. Lise glanced back and saw the bonnet of the Mercedes, through the open doorway. Her two male guardians strapped Odette, in her wedding dress, to the St Andrew's cross, pinning her skirts up, and gagging her with the hem wiped in her wet cunt, to bare her buttocks. The cross was not upright, but tilted forward at an angle. Thierry reached forward and ripped a glaring ladder in each of the bride's white stockings.

'My bride-slut shall be whipped until her bare arse is raw, then flogged on the back and teats, until denuded of her wedding gown,' he said.

He stepped back and began to intone in Latin from a book in white leather binding, and each robed figure stood before the cross, opening his robe to reveal his naked body and erect penis. Lise saw the leader and gasped: it was Dr Henric. Thierry allowed his own robe to fall open; his cock was as stiff as all the rest. She kept her head down as he handed her a whip, and nodded that she was to deal the first stroke with the whip, although her whalebone cane hung at her waist. Lise did so, lashing Odette on her already wealed bare, and slamming her against the cross. Each robed figure took turns at flogging her naked arse, until she had taken six lashes, including Lise's. Then, one of the males mounted the tilted cross, straddling the girl's bare arse, and reached between her cunt lips to get lubricant for his cock. Penis shining with Odette's own come, he poked his swollen glans into her arse-pucker and pushed brutally inside, ramming his shaft all the way to his balls. He buggered her with strong slapping strokes, until he grunted in his spurt. Come dripped from Odette's cunt as she was buggered in her wedding dress.

The process was repeated: six strokes, then buggery by the next male. Lise felt her own cunt sopping as the bare buttocks writhed, purpled with welts, and began to rub her thighs together, pressing her clitty so that the flow of come dripped down her rubber stockings and pooled soggily inside her boots at the stockings' toes and heels. Dr Henric was last, and as he inserted his enormous erection into Odette's raw anus hole, Lise masturbated, gasping, to a shuddering orgasm. Dr Henric glanced at her, then began to bugger Odette with smooth strokes, her anal passage well distended from the other males' cocks, and greased by their spunk. Odette was squirming and squealing in real distress at the size of the doctor's buggering tool, and he arse-fucked her hard for five minutes, without any sign of approaching spurt. Lise looked again towards the Mercedes, figuring that, as all eyes awaited the doctor's climax, she could soon make a break for it. Suddenly, he withdrew his tool and darted to embrace Lise herself. She struggled, but he had her over his knee with her skirt rolled up and panties down, baring her bum. He began to spank Lise hard.

Whap! Whap! Whap!

The palm cracked hard on her wriggling bare bum.

'*Do the slut!*' hissed the bound Odette.

Whap! Whap! Whap! Whap!

'*Ah! Ah! Oooh! Let me go!*' Lise shrieked in English.

Thierry continued his Latin intonation but moved close to the St Andrew's cross, where the tip of his tool was within reach of Odette's bound hand. He placed a rubber glove on her fingers and she began a vigorous masturbation of his erect penis, as Lise was brutally spanked, with Dr Henric's massive erection poking her belly. She heard Odette giggle as she wanked off Thierry's stiff tool.

'Now I shall truly be your bride of flagellance, dear brother,' she cried.

Brother? Lise thought, sobbing under the merciless bare-bum spanking.

Thierry said that the false bride must have her robe whipped from her; Odette took his penis in her mouth and began to fellate him, as Lise was fastened on top of Odette's own spread body. Dr Henric pulled her panties up, then began to cane her on her stockings. Lise screamed at the pain, as the stockings were quickly shredded, then at the searing strokes on her rubber-clad buttocks, under which the thin latex soon shredded. The caning took a while longer to rip her jacket and corset, but after a good three dozen strokes, her bare skin was taking the wood. Dr Henric concentrated on her buttocks, wealing her haunches and top fesses with expert strokes, which had Lise's naked bum clenching and squirming as firm hands pinioned her on top of Odette. The caning suddenly stopped and Lise felt the tip of Dr Henric's massive cock enter her bum-bud to complete the ceremony by buggering her.

'Enjoying your cleansing, slut?' hissed Odette, pausing in her fellation of her brother.

Lise managed to stretch her hand, balled it in a fist, and punched Thierry in the groin. He screamed and doubled up, and the hands holding Lise loosened for a second. Dr Henric's cock was lodged in her anal shaft to a depth of his glans; she squeezed hard, trapping him, so that, as she sprang from her pose of submission, he was twisted, and toppled with his cock pinched in her anal hole. She hit his groin, and he too screamed as she expelled his cock from her anus; then Lise was running for the Mercedes, poking her fingers into her slimy cunt as she ran, until she found the car keys at the neck of her womb. The posse of debauchees pursued her at a leisurely pace, whips swishing and laughing as they removed their goat-heads: with Dr Henric were Peter and Tim, Helen and Susan, the girls wearing massive strap-on penetrators. Odette was no longer bound, but was being buggered by her brother, and her shrieks of agony and mocking laughter were louder than the hoots of the Birchwood debauchees.

Lise paused by the Mercedes for a moment to see that all the tyres were flat. Panting, she ran down the driveway as Dr Henric's crew began to inflate the tyres with a foot-pump. It was four kilometres to the village and Lise ran all the way. At the third kilometre, she heard the growl of the Mercedes, following her. She was nude, save for her boots, waist thong and tattered strips of green rubber, and air flowed through her massively grown, soggy cunt-bush, drying it of her come. She threw away the high-heeled boots and ran barefoot, grimacing as the roadway lacerated her bare soles. At the outskirts of the village, the Mercedes drew level, and a door opened, with Odette whirling a gladiator's net to ensnare her. She saw the French tricolour flying outside the Gendarmerie Nationale and burst inside, to see Sergeant Rastoff seated at the desk over which he had whipped and buggered her, weeks ago. The Mercedes screeched to a halt, and Thierry and Dr Henric followed almost at once.

'My bonded chattel has escaped, Sergeant!' said Thierry, regally aloof in his white monk's robe, while Dr Henric wore his normal dark suit and a college robe of St Hugh's.

'She is my student at Oxford, after her legal period of servitude,' rasped Dr Henric. 'She has suffered from a crisis of the nerves.'

'I want to stay here!' Lise cried, clinging to the burly Russian's tunic.

He smiled amiably at all three.

'I am afraid you cannot stay here, mademoiselle, unless you have committed any crimes,' he said.

'I have!' Lise blurted. 'I wish to confess!'

'Then I shall have to summon an examining magistrate,' said Sgt Rastoff, 'and in the meantime, release you to the custody of your legal guardians, however suspect. There was a mysterious woman in white rubber, I recall, who claimed, Monsieur Thierry, to have been disciplined by you beyond endurance, which explained her medicinal rubber swaddling – she wanted to escape and was not enchattelled, but had a French passport. Out of my own pocket, I was obliged to accommodate her with a one-way ticket to the Foreign Legion barracks in Lille, where she apparently thought she would be safe. It is not an expensive journey, though one must change trains at Hazebrouck.'

Dr Henric and Thierry each grasped Lise by a bare breast, and she squealed. The sergeant looked at her with raised eyebrows.

'It seems you have little choice, mademoiselle,' he said.

'Come on, slut!' Thierry snarled.

'But,' said the sergeant, standing to interpose himself between Lise and her tormentors, so that her bare breasts flopped free, 'little choice is not *no* choice, mademoiselle . . . if you recall our previous interview.'

Lise stared at him.

'I . . . *I wish to join the Foreign Legion*!' she cried.

'Aha! ' said Sgt Rastoff. 'You must repeat it twice more.'

'*I wish to join the Foreign Legion,   I wish to join the Foreign-Legion!*'

'In that case,' said Sgt Rastoff in an official growl, 'I must ask you gentlemen to desist from your harassment of a Legion volunteer!'

He smiled benignly at Lise, as he led her inside the station, her fingers already helping him undo the buckle of his heavy service belt.

'And you already have the uniform of a Legion Nurse, mademoiselle, or some of it,' he said. 'A nice springy cane, hanging at your delicious haunches! Your poor bottom is so temptingly bare.'

'Then, Sergeant,' said Lise, 'please punish my bare bottom for tempting you.'

The policeman grasped her springy whalebone cane, thrashed it once in the air, then thrashed her bare buttocks, poised over his desk.

'What an ordeal you've had,' he said. 'Don't you just *hate* the French?'

'And yet,' said Dr Crevasse, 'a primordial human instinct is to crave discipline, for discipline reassures us and makes us safe. That is why we join the Legion, our cruel but kind mother. A caned, or birched, bottom, is evidence of care, however harsh, and an emblem of belonging. A girl with striped fesses never feels lonely! I conclude from your dossier and your own testimony, inmate Gallard, that you have one of the deepest desires for bare-bottom discipline I have ever encountered, but there is another side to flagellance, as evidenced by your whipping of Odette. At Fort Lafresne we select those females who may learn versatility. You took vengeful pleasure in your whipping of Mlle Odette, and entered wholeheartedly into a lesbian encounter with her. Proper behaviour at Fort Lafresne can lead to a useful life as a female legionnaire, outside prison, and select *versatiles* are promoted, on my say-so, to the finishing school, or *école de finesse*, for further training in uninhibited duties. You will have already suspected that your sister inmates are all here for sexual outrage; there are no pickpockets. Fort Lafresne is not a prison for common criminals, but for sluts of the basest sexual desires.'

She paused. Lise hung her head, and a slow blush suffused her face.

'You are not insulted?' said Dr Crevasse softly.

'I am a prisoner of the Legion, Doctor. I have not privilege to be insulted.'

'Nor humiliated? A bare-bum caning, from a girl-slave, and a naked male slave bumming you, then spunking in your face?'

'I . . . I cannot be humiliated enough, Doctor,' Lise sobbed.

Dr Crevasse rose, and handed Lise the baobab cane.

'But I intend to humiliate you further,' she said. 'You will cane *my* bare croup, with six strokes, and wank yourself to come, as you beat me.'

She bent over her chair, with her velvet black arse-globes poised high, her long legs straight behind her, and the cheeks spread, showing her glistening cunt-meat, and the anus pucker nestling in its taut black bum-valley. As well as the ring pierced at her spinal nubbin, she wore a *guiche* ring pierced in her perineum, midway between the anus bud and the lower vee of her cunt flaps. Lise licked her lips, as come began to seep from her own slit.

'Frightened?' said Dr Crevasse.

'A little, Doctor. I might cane you too hard . . . I *want* to cane that gorgeous bum of yours . . . O! till she's raw and squirming and quivering like two luscious black plum jellies! You . . . you might hold a grudge.'

'Yes, I might,' agreed Dr Crevasse. 'I might think you not *versatile.*'

She twisted her head to watch her own bare-bum caning, with her fingers already masturbating and come dripping from her swollen pink cunt-folds. Lise raised her caning arm.

'I ordered you to masturbate, inmate Gallard,' said the black woman, 'and give me a bare-bottom caning of six strokes, on therapeutic grounds. Begin wanking off – strokes on the two seconds – now!'

Lise clutched her nubbin and she masturbated herself, as she caned Dr Crevasse's naked bottom.

Vip!

One, two . . .

Vip!

One, two . . .

Vip!

One, two . . .

Lise's cunt was slimy with flowing come as she wanked off, and at the fourth canestroke, she trembled as her orgasm shook her. Dr Crevasse smiled a leopard's smile, increasing the controlled pace of her own wank, and licked her pearl teeth as she watched Lise's belly and cunt convulse.

Vip!

One, two . . .

'Continue masturbating, inmate!' Dr Crevasse ordered. 'Raise your thigh and wank your clitty with your thumb, stretching your index finger, to get the fingernail inside your anus.'

Lise obeyed, her body shuddering with new pleasure as her anus was tickled and her clitty tingled under a thumb-pounding. The doctor wanked off with wide, sweeping strokes of her clitty and cunt that smeared cunt oil up and down her perineum, and right to the top of her arse-cleft; her guiche and kundalini rings glistened with her come.

Vip!

One, two . . .

Lise shuddered as she wanked her clit furiously, her fingernail lacerating the buggered ring of her arse-petal. She had striped the black woman's top buttocks, central and lower fesses, and haunches, yet the ebony satin bum-skin had scarcely trembled at the cane's slice.

Vip!

Dr Crevasse clenched her buttocks: too late, for Lise had delivered an upender, vertically, right in the cleft of the buttocks, and striking the anal bud and the lower vulval folds. Dr Crevasse groaned, and her come was a river gushing from her pulsing cunt as her bum and back stiffened, and she exhaled in a gasp of orgasm. Lise sobbed as a new climax swept her own body; not touching, yet touched by cane and woman-flow, the two naked females wanked themselves to orgasm together. Then Dr Crevasse rose, removed the key from her neck chain and, shivering, handed it to Lise. Then she sat down again, legs apart, and resumed masturbating. One hand caressed her come-slopped clitoris, while the other danced, slapping and pinching the buds of her nipples, extruded from their golden aureola rings.

'Inmate! Stand to attention!'

Lise's thighs and feet slammed shut as she obeyed.

'No other inmate has ever caned me so well . . . Is it safe to give you my treasure? The key to my vagina? A gamble, perhaps, Mademoiselle Gallard. Keep the key in your cunt or anus, the only safe places in this hellish prison. When you beg me, it shall unlock the key to my vulva, and my tutelage. There is a price to pay for your advancement: when my vulva is completely naked, you must pleasure me, at my orders. Until then, of the three punishment regimes of ascending harshness, I decide to assign you to regime number one, the most brutal. You will be ordered to report to Nurse-General Frachon to have your work detail officially signed. The sun will brown your bare body, inmate Gallard, but no matter how golden your skin, the weals of the cane will always stripe you, from pink to crimson. Soon, you will beg for the wetness and warmth of my cunt, which I now masturbate, at the thought of the lesbian and flagellant pleasures I shall enjoy with you in due course, when you have taken sufficient stripes for me to make you corporal. Your wanking friend, the orderly Heidi, is also a possible *versatile,* although she is as yet shy. If you could work on her affections – bring her bottom to me for stripes and her tongue for my clit – it might advance your own cause . . .'

'What of the commandant, Nurse-General Frachon, Doctor?'

'*Ahhh* . . .!' gasped Dr Charlotte Crevasse, smiling, as, with slender black fingers twitching her stiff nubbin, she wanked herself to a come-slimed, quivering orgasm. '*Ahhh* . . .! Nurse-General Frachon is my slave. You may now report to rock-breaking detail, under the hot sun, and the cane of Corporal Lavoisier, who is not.'

6

Arse-meat

The heavy Legion gasmask blinded Lise with sweat, as she pumped her legs, running on the square, to Corporal Lavoisier's barked orders. She squealed as the corporal's cane lashed her bare buttocks, but the squeal bubbled, deep in her throat. She was gagged, like Titzi and Sutra, by a mouthful of hot pebbles, scooped from the ground and wadded between her lips, before the humiliating gasmask was fitted. The three new inmates ran nude round and round the square, their feet hobbled by euphemistically named 'drill boots', which were in fact punishment boots. They were made of wood, like clogs, but perched on slabs of cast iron almost a foot high, like surgical boots. The naked miscreants were obliged to run at full speed in these restraints, with hands cuffed behind their backs. Lise was in the centre of the group, ordered to run in perfect pace together, and all she saw were the naked breasts of Sutra and Titzi, bouncing beside her own. Titzi's giant breasts, rock-hard, scarcely quivered, while Sutra's, equally large for her lithe frame, seemed to dance in a circular, sensuous rhythm, as though in mocking chorus to their owner's ordeal.

'Run, you filthy sluts! Do you want a public whipping?' screamed Corporal Lavoisier, her own nude body dancing effortlessly beside them, in rubber-soled track shoes.

Crack! Crack!

Her cane whipped Sutra and Titzi's pumping bare bums.

'You idle, dirty whores! Call yourself legionnaires? Run, filth, run! Let me see your arse-meat dance!'

Crack!

Lise winced and tears sprang to her eyes as the cane sliced her in the bum-cleft, dripping with sweat. She sobbed, her breath a roar under the gasmask, because it was so unfair . . . then chided herself for clinging to such a quaint, English concept, in the Legion. They had been caught talking, that was all! After the morning's drill and a bowl of broth for lunch, they had twenty minutes' repose before the afternoon's repetition. It was forbidden to enter the dormitory, so they sought the shade of the arcades, where the qat-chewing Somali merchants lounged beside their camels and wares. It seemed accepted as a neutral territory, where inmates could converse, albeit in murmurs, and even enjoy gruff pleasantries with the corporals who, a short while before, had been caning their bare bums on the square.

Sutra, Titzi and Lise found themselves together, pretending to scrutinise a listless display of trinkets on a rug, spread on the dirt. The merchants most visited were those who offered toiletries or even packaged snacks, for those girls who had received their weekly pay of five hundred Djiboutian francs, less than three euros. The three newcomers had no cash. Lise felt as hurt and bewildered as at her first day at boarding school. Only the slight discomfort of Dr Crevasse's cunt-key, lodged in her womb's neck, reminded her of the world beyond the punishment square. Across the square, on the terrace of the Welcome Centre, a few legionnaires drank beer, and flirted with the bare-breasted Somalian waitresses in their fluttering mini-skirts. They cast idle glances at the throng of nude, shaven prisoners, yet without lust in their eyes, as though they looked at a herd of cows. Sutra wiggled her bottom, without effect.

'You'd think the men would at least notice us,' she said.

'If they did,' sneered Titzi, 'wouldn't that spoil our wanks with fantasies we cannot enjoy? Better wank, dreaming of imaginary cocks, than live ones you'll never taste.'

'You are very philosophical, Titzi,' said Lise.

'We Germans are bred to be philosophical, inmate Lise,' said Titzi.

'Even in this hellhole,' said Sutra, 'obliged to live nude, like animals, and with wanking our only love?'

'Nudism is normal for us Germans,' said Titzi, 'and masturbation, for a woman, is both a necessary relief and a philosophical pleasure.'

'Did Dr Crevasse tell you that?' said Lise.

'I found Dr Crevasse distant, but correct,' said Titzi. 'Neither masturbation, or any sexual subject, was mentioned, except that she cautioned me against falling into my error of . . . of sexual voracity.'

'Me too! The cow's a bit full of herself,' said Sutra. 'Made me stand the whole time, with not even a glass of water. And you, Lise?'

'You're right, not even a glass of water,' Lise said.

'Dr Crevasse is right,' said Titzi, licking her lips, as she eyed the cane of a corporal standing nearby. 'Sexual voracity is a punishable crime, but I am here through a misunderstanding, and do not expect to remain long as a mere inmate.'

'What sort of misunderstanding, Titzi?' Lise said.

Titzi smiled thinly, and her hands strayed to her nipples, stroking them in a nervous mannerism.

'Discipline in my squad was not enforced thoroughly,' she said. 'I took it upon myself to enforce it. Lazy nurses received spankings, or the cane, on their bare arses, unbeknownst to our nurse-corporal.'

'Scarcely grounds for an indeterminate sentence at Fort Lafresne,' said Sutra. 'At least I know why I'm here – I fucked legionnaires. Any man with a big tool can have me, and all legionnaires seem to have big tools.'

Titzi's hand strayed to stroke her shaven pubic mound, as if in search of a stray, disorderly hair.

'I used to masturbate,' she murmured, 'while caning girls on the bare. One girl offered to lick my clitoris, if I would spare her a beating, and I agreed. She licked me to orgasm and swallowed my cunt-juice. We were observed . . . I am here for that moment of impardonable weakness. If only I had thrashed the girl, as she deserved!'

'My weakness,' said Lise, filling an expectant silence, 'was Djiboutian men. Their cocks submit to full circumcision, which makes them the smoothest, most velvety cocks on earth.'

'I had a Djiboutian once. God, I want to wank, just thinking of it!' Sutra cried, rubbing her thighs together and directing her noticeable seep of come down between her knees.

Her hand fastened on her glistening cunt lips, and she began to frot herself, in full view of a legionnaire in helicopter pilot's uniform, who was playing with the bare breasts of Damara, the ripely fessed Djiboutian hostess, wearing only a white skirt, on the terrace opposite. The sun blazed. Lise, too, began to wank her throbbing clitty, and even Titzi grunted, and stuck a finger in her bum-cleft, at her anus, while pinching the extruded nubbin of her clit. The Djiboutian girl smiled at them, and slid her hand under her pleated white skirt, showing them her bare pubis, and wanking too.

'Why your taste for caning girls on the bare, Titzi?' panted Lise, as she masturbated.

'*Inmate* von Titisee,' replied the German girl, herself wanking vigorously off. 'When I was a youth-hiking-girl, our troop leader, Fräulein Waltraut, used to take us to a sacred grove of oak stumps, overlooking the Rhine falls. These oak stumps, rounded by weather, resembled female arses, and she told us it was the custom of the folk to whip the stumps, and magically stimulate the flowing of the Rhine. We wore very skinny leather shorts, yellow socks and red boots, as well as yellow shirts and scarves. We asked to emulate the folk, and she agreed: with staves, we whipped the oaken stumps, as the mighty Rhine waters crashed below us. Waltraut was careful to let our desire grow of its own accord, merely hinting that in olden times, the buttocks of a living woman were whipped, bound to the tree stump, and it was not long before one of us – I, myself – suggested that we do likewise. At first, one of us hiking-girls would take a caning on her leather shorts, pulled tight. Then, we took turns caning each other, and finally, we were separated into those who caned, and those who were caned. I was the chief caner, though I had a rival for Waltraut's affections, a girl named Anna, an athletic, lithe young thing, whose big meaty bum I enjoyed thrashing, as much as she enjoyed being thrashed. She was a submissive, and . . . well. We wore no panties beneath the shorts, and were annoyed when one or two of us had her thin leather shorts ripped by caning, so we began to practise bare-bottom caning. It was not uncommon for a girl to masturbate as she was caned, or as she caned. I reinstalled the olden custom Waltraut described, that both caning and caned girl should be nude, and should masturbate to orgasm, to coincide exactly with the final stroke of the victim's beating: the come juice of the masturbating girls being a noble stimulus to the flowing of the Rhine. Waltraut was a photographer by profession, and photographed the bare-arse thrashings, buttocks wealed by caning, and the wet cunts of the masturbating girls. How I loved caning Anna's bare bum, watching her redden and writhe, with Waltraut herself masturbating, under her shorts, as we performed our ritual! At length, she wished to be caned herself, and bared her own arse, a most magnificent croup, suntanned all over. Each of us, caner and canee alike, had to cane her six strokes, and there were seventeen of us in the hiking-troop. I was in charge of photographing every nuance of Fräulein Waltraut's caning, every weal on her bare arse, every grimace and baring of her teeth. That was her last visit with us to the tree stumps, for Fräulein Waltraut announced her departure on a photo-safari to Djibouti, where there was a tribe of female cave-dwellers, descended from a goddess and devoted to the worship and flagellance of the bare female buttocks. She hoped her photographic portfolio would gain her admission, as evidence of her good faith and experience. One of us was to accompany her, and to my chagrin, it was Anna. I was guilty of jealousy, and of desiring revenge for Waltraut's betrayal of me, when I discovered that Anna was her own daughter! Our continued caning rituals were not the same without the clicking of her lens, to accompany our stripes. Soon afterwards, I joined the Legion, hoping for Djibouti, that I might find Fräulein Waltraut again, with Anna, and whip them for their duplicity, or else – I was so confused! – beg them both to thrash me, and accept my own submission. O! I'm coming, just thinking of Anna's sweet bare arse-meat, writhing under my cane . . .!'

'I'm coming, too!' gasped Sutra.

Lise shuddered, wordlessly, as orgasm flooded her belly and come poured over her wanking fingers. The lazy motions of the girls' masturbation seemed no more than the flick of camels' tails in the sun. It was then that Corporal Lavoisier pounced.

'*Talking*, you dirty little whores?' she hissed, ignoring the girls' wanks and the glistening rivulets of come on their naked thighs. '*Talking?* Whores' prattle means *special drill.*'

A cheer arose from the legionnaires on the terrace, as they raised their beer bottles in salute and squeezed the bare titties of their giggling girlfriends. So, Lise thought, as she double-stepped back onto the scorching square, men did watch nude female prisoners, after all . . .

The punishment continued, until all three girls dripped with sweat, their breasts rose and fell with harsh pants, and their running was scarcely more than a stagger. Beside them on the square, the other inmates drilled, all naked, but with various refinements of shackling: rocks clamped to teats or quim flaps, hands behind backs, or in hobble boots alone. One squad drilled entirely nude but for their rubber swimcaps, and barefoot, their faces grimacing in the pain of the scorching sand on their soles. Corporals lounged in the arcade, awaiting their turns in the sun, as drill mistresses, and the crop-haired Dr Frahl who had examined Lise, sat observing.

At last released, the three girls spat out their mouthfuls of pebbles and collapsed in the shelter of an arcade, beside a merchant and his camel. They lay, wracked with gasping sobs and oblivious to their surroundings. A knot of inmates and corporals giggled at them: their legs were splayed, and cunts open, as if they were part of the merchant's goods for sale. Three medical orderlies, one of them Heidi, came with buckets, and soused them with ice water, and Corporal Lavoisier ordered them to their feet: it was time to report to Nurse-General Frachon, to sign the documentation, accepting their decreed regime of punishment. Then, they would return to the square, and recommence normal drill. They ran at the double to the bulk of Fort Lafresne proper, with the corporal reminding them that their signatures, as with their contracts of enrolment in the Legion itself, were formalities. They were to sign, still running at the double, salute the Nurse-General, and return to the square.

They ran up the stone staircase, along a corridor, and waited, running on the spot, as Corporal Lavoisier rapped on the Nurse-General's door. The door was opened by a towering young Djiboutian male, nude but for the skimpy loinstring encasing his massive cock. Nurse-General Frachon sat in a swivel chair, looking out over the square. She turned to face the inmates, and, in silence, allowed them to continue running on the spot for two minutes, giving particular scrutiny to their bouncing bare teats. Then, she told Corporal Lavoisier to order the inmates at ease.

The corporal barked the order, and the girls slammed their feet apart, slapping their hands at the top of their bare buttocks, with their breasts coming to rest. The nurse general scrutinised the naked breasts as intently as when they jiggled.

'You may wait outside, Corporal,' she said, 'at attention, cane drawn.'

Corporal Lavoisier frowned for a fraction of a second, then saluted and about-turned.

'At your orders, Nurse-General!' she barked as she left.

The commandant was a trim woman, whose large, conical breasts were braless and held firmly by an olive green military blouse. Her rippling coltish thighs and full, taut buttocks swelled against a pleated skirt that did not cover her knees, sheathed in shiny lycra stockings, nor her dainty high-heeled fashion shoes of the same military colour. Her ash-blonde tresses cascaded fully over her shoulders, combed to a sheen, and as she spoke, the Djiboutian applied himself to combing her hair. There was no panty line visible beneath her skirt. She crossed her legs, showing a brief glimpse of suspender straps, and a hairy blonde cunt-mound.

'I am Nurse-General Jacqueline Frachon,' she said crisply. 'You will identify yourselves,' she said. 'Inmate Sutrapanaya!'

'Nurse-General!'

'Inmate von Titisee!'

'Nurse-General!

'Inmate Gallard!'

'Nurse-General!'

'Inmates, attention! About turn!'

The girls swivelled.

'At ease!'

After the Nurse-General had inspected their bare bottoms, she reversed the commands, and they once more faced her.

'Although I have observed you at special drill, for an infraction of discipline duly noted in your dossiers, none of you has received a punishment caning yet,' she said, 'although your bottom, I believe, inmate Gallard, is no stranger to the cane. Your *bare* bottom.'

A caning block stood prominently beside the commandant's desk, surmounted by a rack of canes. Lise remained silent. The Djiboutian youth handed each girl a paper and pen but the paper was folded over, leaving only the space for the signature visible. Each girl was instructed to sign, and did so. The black male removed the papers, the inmates' eyes following the swing of his penis under the thin loinstring.

'Caning on the bare bottom,' said the commandant, 'as my subordinate Dr Crevasse has undoubtedly explained to you, is an integral part of your formation as prisoners. You, von Titisee, and you, Sutrapanaya, have been assigned to regime three, which means that a formal caning

83

shall consist of six strokes. You, inmate Gallard, are on regime one, which means a formal caning for you shall be twelve strokes.'

Lise gasped.

'Unless you wish it to be more,' snapped the commandant. 'Dr Crevasse's report is quite damning, as to the disgrace of your sentencing to Fort Lafresne. You inmates have already observed the caning blocks, similar to the one beside me, placed at intervals throughout the compound. Caning is the least of punishments, as you shall find out. Formation shall consist of breaking you, with daily drill, daily labour and daily chastisement. You will receive no instruction other than the humiliance of your own naked bodies. Having learnt from humiliance, your stripes may promote you to corporals, but even NCOs must drill, at dusk, and are subject to caning from superior inmate officers. A perquisite of rank is permission to purchase a slave – technically, hire an indentured servant – male or female, like Muhammar, here. A slave costs about four hundred euros, and since your own pay of under three euros is paid to you with three-quarters withheld, to replace the uniforms formally shredded from your bodies at your ceremony of disgrace, it is unlikely, even if promoted, that you can contemplate the convenience of a slave for many years.'

She paused, to let her last two words sink in.

'That is right, inmates. You are aware that your sentences and regime of punishments are without limit, and without appeal, having just signed papers to that effect. In theory, you are eligible for parole, when you have reimbursed the Legion for the cost of your shredded uniforms, also four hundred euros. Few inmates are able to forgo the meagre enjoyments of their stipends, from the Somali merchants, to achieve replacement of their uniforms . . . or else find a slave more comforting than release. Any attempt to desert is unthinkable, no matter how much you may dream of reaching the lake of Abhe Bad and swimming to Ethiopia. You will hear – although all talking is forbidden – rumour of a tribe of troglodyte females, living as outlaws, underground in the so-called High Colon. Forget them. Between Fort Lafresne and Ethiopia, the desert swarms with lustful and immoral nomads, against which Fort Lafresne itself is the only civilised bastion. Deserters are invarably caught, if still alive, by one of the drivers or pilots you will observe at the Welcome Centre, or else make their own way back, begging to be readmitted as convicts. The penalty for desertion is short and sharp: a public whipping, followed by a period of solitary confinement in the Hole.'

The nurse-general stood, and positioned herself by the caning block. She lifted her uniform skirt above the waist, folded it, and tucked the skirt's hem into its waistband. She was indeed unknickered, with garter straps cutting sharply into her tanned thigh-skin, devoid of white strapmarks. Her pubis was trimmed into a neat triangle, but unthinned, so that the massive blonde thatch sprouted high on her sharply curving cunt-mound, in a forest of curls. The pube-hairs were carefully trimmed to show all of the naked cunt flaps, and the glistening clitoral nubbin strongly extruded from its pink envelope of cunt flesh. She turned, to reveal the firm caramel moons of her bare bum, framed by lacy yellow sussies, and smiled shyly.

'No legionnaire gives or orders punishment she herself cannot take,' she said, 'so you will each give my bare bottom four strokes of the cane.'

Only Titzi leered gleefully, as Muhammar gravely handed each girl a baobab cane. Sutra and Lise exchanged nervous glances. If they caned the commandant too hard, it would go in their dossiers, and if they caned too gently . . . it would go in their dossiers. More Legion mind games! Nurse-General Jacqueline Frachon stretched her lithe body over the caning-block, spreading the cheeks of her arse, so that the pink cunt flaps hung, seeping with moisture, and the wrinkled pucker of her anal nubbin was stretched like a mouth. Her anal cleft was taut as drumskin. The smooth expanse of the commandant's arse-meat was mottled by thin weals of a darker caramel than the surrounding skin. Even the anus bud was framed by two welts, like sycamore leaves, and the perineum was pinked with a large jagged weal. A golden ring pierced the skin at the base of her spine.

'You will take me in this order,' she said crisply. 'First, inmate von Titisee, second, inmate Sutrapanaya, and third, inmate Gallard. My bottom bears marks from regular canings, all taken on the bare, from ... from my own desire to attune myself to my inmates. I expect your strokes to be severe, and to stripe the entire fesse, and you will take care to mark me in existing welts. The strokes shall be delivered at five-second intervals, and I shall take the whole dozen without further break, so all canes must be ready. I warn you that squealing, gasping, or noise of any kind, will be punished. You shall cane me in silence, for one minute.'

Titzi raised her cane above the perfectly still bare fesses. The commandant's head was raised, with her spine curved, raising her buttocks to the full, and her head entirely shrouded by her mane of blonde tresses, spilling over her shoulders and breasts. She supported herself on splayed fingertips, in slots built into the block. Her buttocks remained spread and taut, as though moulded. Astonished, Lise glanced briefly at Sutra, whose eyes were wide too: the instruction not to squeal or gasp was normally given to the *victim* of a flogging.

'Begin, inmate von Titisee!'

Vip!

Titzi's cane lashed squarely across the mid-buttock, slicing both bare fesses, in a deep existing pink. The naked bum quivered slightly, not from the commandant's own nerve-ends, but from the jarring force of Titzi's cut. The slave stood with his arm behind his back, at ease, his eyes fixed on the woman's caned croup, and his groin swelling.

Vip!

Titzi took her on the underfesses, again in existing pink, and the muscled bum-flesh wobbled only slightly. Titzi licked her lips, eyes darting on the bare buttocks willingly presented, and she frowned. Her naked cunt was glazed with come that formed into a droplet beneath the lips, and

86

she reached down to catch the come-drop. She did not remove her palm oiled with her come, but pressed it to her clitoris and began to masturbate. Lise's cunt was juicing too, and Sutra's nubbin was fully erect; trembling, the two girls joined the German in masturbating.

Vip!

Titzi chose the left haunch for her third stroke, delivering a real stinger that darkened an already present welt. The commandant's buttocks were immobile, but Titzi's arse quivered as her wank increased in vigour.

Vip!

Titzi's fourth applied the same cut to the right haunch. Throughout the four, from the rippling muscles of Titzi's expert caning arm, the commandant's arse had remained stock-still and her hair was motionless; the only disturbance of her perfectly composed body was the quickening drip of come from her swollen gash lips. Her slave's penis was now perceptibly erect, and uncoiling like a giant snake that threatened to burst his fragile loinstring; as he gazed at the three vigorously masturbating girls, and the fresh pink that wealed his mistress's buttocks, the swollen glans of his cock burst from the skimpy cloth, snapping the threads that bound it to his waist and balls. The thong fell to the floor, and the male slave stood with his giant black penis shining hugely erect. He wore a cock-ring, in the shape of a butterfly, made of filigree silver, with wings atop below his giant shaft; as his cock trembled and stiffened, so too did the butterfly's wings expand and flutter. Titzi lowered her cane, but her eyes were fixed on the serpent's dark eye of the male's glans, and her wanking fingers became a blur, slamming her erect clitty. Come streamed down her rippling bare thighs.

Sutra, too, masturbated hard as she raised her cane to deliver the fifth stroke, precisely five seconds from the fourth. Her dark thighs trembled as she caned, slopped with the come that oozed from her glistening wet cunt. She delivered her first two strokes to Titzi's weals, then, instead of the haunches, targeted the tender top fesses, by the spinal nubbin. The ring pierced in the nurse-general's flesh shook at these two strokes, and the drip of come from her wet cunt was now a steady flow, puddling the floor between her spread thighs. The slave suddenly bent down, scooping a palmful of his mistress's come, and, with it, oiled the glans of his monstrously erect penis. His fingertips stroked back and forth along his peehole, and rubbed the base of the glans. The butterfly's wings were fully expanded, hugging the distended cockflesh. Lise's come was flowing so hard as she watched the male rub his stiff cock, that she had to force herself to count the required five seconds. She lifted her cane.

Vip! Vip!

She dealt a stinger to the left haunch, in Titzi's weal, and then matched it with a stroke to the right haunch. Her come now trickled over her bare feet, sliming the floor beneath her soles and squelching between her toes. She wanked furiously, almost coming as she gazed both at the wealed, still bumflesh of the prone commandant, and the black male lustfully rubbing and brandishing his insolent giant of a cock. She counted the seconds to five, then, suddenly, upended her cane.

Vip!

A strong cut right on the anal pucker jarred the woman's bare arse-meat, and the cane's tip just caught the bottom of her dripping cunt flaps.

Titzi and Sutra stared agog, both wanking hard and the slave now rubbed his cock-shaft vigorously, making the tight black balls dance in the rhythm of his slapping. His whole cock was shiny with the woman's come. Lise counted to five, then dealt the final stroke of the caning.

Vip!

She took the commandant right under the perineum, with the shaft of the cane landing hard in the gash, and the tip impacting the erect clitoris.

'O! O! O! God!' moaned the commandant, her blonde mane shaking from side to side.

One hand flew to her whipped cunt, and she began to masturbate furiously, her wanking hand splattering come in a spray on her calves and the soles of her feet. Her head sank, its blonde mane brushing the floor.

'Someone has squealed,' she moaned, 'and must be punished!'

Muhammar knelt and poised the tip of his cock at her arse bud, then with a smooth, fluid motion, slammed his penis right to the balls, until his butterfly cock-ring was embedded in her perineal skin. He arse-fucked her with hard, brutal strokes, his bare black buttocks writhing as though under cane, as the three inmates wanked themselves off to squirming, gasping comes, their cunt juices piddling the floor by the soles of their bare feet.

'O, punish the slut . . .' groaned the buggered woman, her caned bum rising to meet the ramming cock embedded in her bumhole. '*She* won't let me have a female slave . . . it's *her* fault! O! *God*! Bugger me harder, boy! Fuck my arse raw! Punish me for wanking! O! O!'

Her hand was a blur, masturbating her squelched cunt flaps and clitty.

'*Fuck me, slave*! Bugger my hole! Yes! O! I'm coming . . . *Ohhh* . . .!'

A heavy spurt of Muhammar's sperm bubbled from her anal lips, and the slave grunted in his own orgasm, his hips writhing like a snake as he poured his cream into the squirming arsehole of the woman. The spurt did not stop, but continued to spray the floor, where Nurse-General Frachon's come now puddled with the three wanking prisoners'. At last, her come ebbed to a series of mewling gasps, and Muhammar's buggering fury abated. His cock wilted a mere fraction, enough to let him plop from her bumhole; he speedily retrieved and refastened his loin-string, and took the canes from the three prisoners. He then left the room. The commandant's groans ceased and her blonde mane lifted. The three girls wiped the come from their cunts and thighs, and resumed their 'at ease' position, as the caned and buggered woman rose, smirking. She unfolded her wedged skirt and smoothed it down over her stockings, not regarding the fact that they were sopping in her own come. Her buggered anus, with the sycamore's wing of a cane welt on either side of the anal mouth, disappeared under the crisp military skirt – except that it

89

was neither a sycamore, nor a cane welt, but the indentation of a butterfly's wings. Then she sat down at her desk.

'There, inmates!' she said with a thin smile. 'That is how a proper soldier girl takes her caning! You shall have many, many opportunities to try and achieve the same serenity under the lash, since our code of discipline is based on necessary infraction. Inmates are forbidden to talk or masturbate, yet, like all girls, you will do nothing else, and your bare bottoms shall be caned, or whipped, for it. Muhammar! – O, where is the wretched boy? I really must ask for a *female* slave! – order Corporal Lavoisier to remove these inmates, and cane them for masturbating.'

The three girls paled, and their eyes widened.

'Not for the wanks you have had,' said the nurse-general, 'but for the wanks you are, inevitably, *going* to have.'

7

Nude on Ice

Every day, Lise Gallard, inmate of the Fort Lafresne
Centre of Formation, received at least one caning of twelve
strokes on her naked buttocks. The canings were awarded
for the slightest infraction, real or imaginary, of Legion
discipline. If Lise was found with another girl, then she
must be talking, and the other girl, too, was thrashed
bare-bum. For that reason, girls other than Sutra or Heidi
tended to avoid Lise, although Titzi condescended with an
occasional nod. If alone, she must be masturbating: the
sweat which dripped constantly from her naked body was
alleged to be her come oil. The canings were taken bent
over one of the numerous flogging-stools which peppered
the fort's corridors, and the same image was applied to
bare-bottom corporal punishment itself: a naked caning
was the pepper, or spice, in the simmering cauldron of Fort
Lafresne, and corporals would promise girls 'a good
arse-peppering'.

A corporal, more often than not Corporal Lavoisier,
would administer Lise's twelve strokes, with another
corporal, cone-breasted Hauser, or svelte Grimaldi, or
Kitchener, a raw-boned Scottish lass, of tattooed mound
and buttocks, as witness. That was in addition to breast-
lashings and fesse-cuts at random, from Lavoisier or one
of the other corporals during punishment drill, with her
nipples and cunt flaps clamped by heavy rocks, and her
face smothered in a gas mask. Every drill for Lise Gallard
on regime one was a punishment drill. Often, she saw the

dark face of Dr Crevasse, her body nude under a clinging bafto, with a scarlet and yellow belt, and barefoot, surveying her from the shade of an arcade, or from the terrace of the Welcome Centre, where she flirted with the young Legion helicopter pilots like Gilles, who brought Fort Lafresne its supplies. Dr Crevasse's eyes frequently smiled at Lise's, before straying, or returning, to her cane-striped bottom, or the pink gash of the cunt where, the doctor knew, the key to her own vulva lay hidden.

Sutra flirted with the male legionnaires, too, from a distance, even when sweating under punishment drill. Sutra confessed herself cock-crazy, and masturbated not just by clit-wanking, but with tubes, wooden staves, or any cucumbers or carrots she could filch from the waste barrels. Her own enrolment in the Legion was prompted by her nymphomania: in her home village near Trincomalee, she was known as a slut, who would take any well-endowed male for fucking. There were fights over her; once, she was caught in flagrante with a young male whose huge cock was destined for the virgin quim of the town beauty, of very rich family. No one expected the young man to be a virgin, but the custom was that he should slake his fleshly lusts with whores some distance from home. The village elders conferred, and sentenced Sutra to a public whipping, and a branding to follow: her naked breasts were to be marked with the Tamil symbol of impurity. She was strung naked from a tree, and took twenty strokes of the rattan cane on her bare buttocks, with twenty to her shoulders from her paramour, who, by whipping his slut, made amends to his bride.

The branding was set for the next day, and, by offering her anus to her jailer's cock, she managed to escape with enough stolen money to get her to Africa. Sutra found the whipping surprisingly tolerable, as, like most village girls, she was accustomed to bare-bottom discipline with a cane at home. However, she was terrified of being branded on her breasts, not for the agony of the hot iron, but because she felt her large firm titties were her most desirable attribute, in particular, the nipple domes on which men liked to chew, and which would be irredeemably scarred by the branding iron. The pilots evidently shared this view, and they eyed her creamy, coffee teats bouncing at drill, in pleasing harmony with her bare fesse-melons.

Occasionally, Dr Crevasse summoned Lise to the terrace, where she lounged over iced tea, with Gilles or another muscular young pilot, and the bare-titted Djiboutian hostesses like Damara, who seemed in charge. She allowed her bafto to fall half-open, so that Lise, running on the spot, could see her dark velvet hillock and the golden lock at her cunt lips. Dr Crevasse would idly place a hand under a girl's skirt and stroke the bare bottom beneath, as she asked if Lise was satisfied with her regime.

'Well satisfied, Doctor!' Lise barked.

'You like your bum peppered, inmate Gallard?' said the doctor.

'No, Doctor!' Lise rapped. 'Punishment hurts, as it is meant to!'

'You craved the canes of males, inmate Gallard.'

'Yes, Doctor!'

'But hate that of females?'

'Yes, Doctor!'

Dr Crevasse would nod to the corporal, who sent Lise back into the drill line with a sharp canestroke to her bare haunch. It was the same for her first week, for her second and third, and for her first and second months, under the burning sun that never changed. Every day she was caned, sobbing and squirming at the block, vowing to desert, as the cane wealed her naked flesh; every night she lay on her palliasse in the stinking, come-scented dorm, masturbating as she caressed her deepening arse-welts, and putting off her desertion until the next day. Every day at Fort Lafresne was the next day, since every day was the same day. She wanted Heidi to go with her.

'I can't,' Heidi said, 'I'm a legionnaire.'

The two girls were masturbating, pausing in their search for food scraps in the waste barrels behind the kitchen. Lise had her fingers inside Heidi's sopping slit, and thumbed her clitty, while Heidi wanked Lise's clit, with an index finger poking her bumhole. Both cunts dripped come, and their stiff nipples were caressed as they pressed breasts in long, slow strokes.

'Dr Crevasse hinted there was a way out,' said Lise carefully, and told Heidi about the finishing school, but without mentioning her own possession of the key to Dr Crevasse's cunt.

Heidi spat.

'I know,' she said. 'Every girl knows! Submit to Crevasse's perverted lusts and everything is easy.'

'Not every girl, Heidi,' said Lise. 'Me, perhaps, but you for certain.'

She diddled Heidi's clitty extra-hard, and Heidi moaned softly.

'I couldn't be a lesbo,' she said.

'But we all wank,' said Lise, getting her fingers at Heidi's wombneck, and squeezing the girl's index with her anal elastic, 'don't we . . .?'

'I mean, not the whole thing,' said Heidi. 'And even then . . . only with you, Lise. Not with that Dr Crevasse. Who knows what *she'd* want to do, with a naked girl, alone and powerless?'

'Much the same as me, Heidi,' said Lise, though uncertainly, 'and I'm no full lesbian. It's just like wanking, only a bit more cuddly.'

'You've done it before . . . gone the whole way?'

'Yes,' said Lise. 'Not often. It's not the same as being filled by cock, but it's nice, especially with a lovely caning on the bare.'

Heidi's fingers grew more insistent at Lise's clitty, and she poked a forefinger between Lise's opened anus lips.

'You're going to make me come,' Lise groaned, 'you awful *guine* . . .'

Teasing with the French for 'dyke', she began to pinch Heidi's clitty and got her own finger into the girl's anus. Heidi's cunt juiced with heavy come; the food scraps were forgotten in the intensity of their caresses.

'I'm coming,' Heidi hissed. 'What else can we do? I mean, spanking, or using toys . . .?'

'All that and more,' said Lise, 'but most important, we'd have time out on our own, not just for a wank, but to bathe, and, yes, spank and cane each other, and use toys for both our holes. There are strap-ons, called penetrators, and we could fuck and bugger each other.'

'O, God, *yes*, I'm coming,' gasped Heidi, 'O! O! *Ohhh* . . . But where could we get time on our own, sweet Lise?'

Her fingers pounded Lise's clitty, pushing deep in her bumhole and squelching wet slit, and Lise gasped in her own come.

'Mmm . . . *Ahhhh* . . .!' Lise moaned. 'We'd . . . we'd have to desert, Heidi. That, or become slaves of Dr Crevasse. O, wank me, O, *yes* . . .'

Every night, they and other girls wanked each other, as they rummaged, illegally, in the slops buckets of discarded food. The corporals made regular arrests, and both Heidi and Lise had received canings, but not for talking or wanking. Pilfering scraps of food was worse than public masturbation. Some girls, Sutra amongst them, dared to creep behind the Welcome Centre, and feast on soggy sandwiches or half-chewed sausage. The corporals could not be everywhere, and that was the Legion way, of necessary infraction. The quota of bare canings would be reached one way or another. Lise's buttocks, like those of her sister-inmates, were in a cruel and capricious lottery, but a lottery, it soon appeared, where some tickets were marked. Sutra often came to forage, wiping her lips with a sulky grimace, shortly before a corporal arrived to arrest the pilfering masturbators, but leaving Sutra alone. After one particularly brutal caning from Corporal Lavoisier, witnessed by Corporal Hauser, with a majority of strokes applied to her cleft and anus bud, Lise bitterly sneered at Sutra's apparent immunity.

'Do you think I haven't earnt it?' cried Sutra. 'Do you know what that bitch Lavoisier's piss and come taste like?'

'I'd rather desert,' whispered Lise, and Sutra sobbed.

After that, Sutra stopped coming to forage, and at drill her dark body seemed to glow with an inner heat. Her face wore a smirk, even when her bare arse took six strokes, or she drilled in a gasmask. In the shade of the arcade, Lise squatted beside her, in dunging position, and asked in a whisper what had happened to make her so contented. Sutra nodded to the terrace of the Welcome Centre, where a muscular legionnaire pilot was feeling inside the skirt of a Somali maid.

'Gilles,' she said. 'He's very understanding of a girl's needs . . .'

She patted her tummy, bum and pubis.

'Full bum, full gash, full belly,' she said, winking.

Sutra had been sentenced to one hour 'on the ice' by Corporal Lavoisier. For this, she had to be escorted through the rear door of the Welcome Centre to the ice room, where a huge block of ice stood, with a Djiboutian Somali maid chipping at it to make cubes for the guests' drinks. The sumptuous arse and bare breasts of the girl shivered at this task, and her dark teat-skin was pimpled with gooseflesh; her shivers turned to cruel laughter, as Sutra was hoisted astride the ice block, and her wrists and ankles bound, so that the whole weight of her body pressed her cunt and nipples to the ice. Corporal Lavoisier sat down for her hour's supervision of the girl on ice; leering at naked Sutra's grimaces of distress, she spread her thighs, touched her clitoris, and began a slow and leisurely wank. The Djiboutian girl watched, smiling at both Europeans, and put her hand under her dress, where she began her own rapid masturbation, her tongue flicking between her dazzling white teeth.

Corporal Lavoisier's own naked body began to pimple, and she beckoned to the Djiboutian girl for a blanket. The girl shrugged haughtily, and suddenly climbed onto the corporal, with her torso between the thighs, pressing the cunt, and began to rub her whole bare flesh up and down the corporal's teats, belly and pubis. Lavoisier lifted the girl's flimsy white skirt, and kneaded the cheeks of her arse, then began to spank her lightly on the bare buttocks. The girl's fesses were beautifully large, firm and pear-shaped, almost unnaturally so, as though subject to some hormone treatment, or age-old refinement of breeding.

'*Mmm! Oui! Oui!*' trilled the girl, excited by spanking, and rolling her arse-cheeks as though accustomed to bare-skin chastisement.

She leant back from the corporal's body, and began to rub and pinch her own nipples, while rubbing her cunt lips on the spanking woman's belly. Corporal Lavoisier inserted her free hand into the girl's cunt, and gripped her, pulling her down between her thighs, so that their quims touched. She continued to spank the wriggling bare bum, and each spank now jerked the girl's stiffened clit against her spanker's. The girl pinched her nipples to points, and began a mock-spanking of the Frenchwoman's nipples, which soon rose erect and stiff.

Suddenly, Lavoisier grasped the girl's pencil-thin waist, held her away, and flipped her upside down, so that her black hair was matted in the puddled floor. Lavoisier's muscled arms held the girl for instants, before plunging her face between her thighs, which locked the head against her cunt lips in a vice. The corporal's arms forced the girl's thighs almost straight apart, revealing a long, wet gash, seeping with shiny come, and an extruded stiff clitty, amid a jungle of come-soaked pube-hairs. Corporal Lavoisier fastened her teeth on the girl's clitty and began to chew, causing the Djiboutian to wriggle helplessly; her head bobbed back and forth, held prisoner by the corporal's thighs, and her tongue darted in and out of the Frenchwoman's wet cunt, with her nose tickling and poking the clitty. Holding the girl against her by the small of the back, the corporal raised her spanking arm, and spanked the girl's cunt, right on the gash flaps, and with the hardest spanks on the erect nubbin of the clitty.

The girl shrieked, and her spanked bum danced, as she pissed herself, the golden jet squirting right over Lavoisier's face, and into her nose and eyes. The corporal swallowed the girl's piss, then sniffed, licked and bit her arse-pucker, getting her tongue inside the anal hole, and darting in and out of the anus in a vigorous tongue-fucking. The girl giggled; the corporal recommenced chewing the clit and gash lips, and took whole hanks of the girl's pubic jungle between her teeth, ripping the hairs from her skin, and swallowing them. The girl squealed in alarm, until the Frenchwoman began spanking the wriggling bum with new severity, after oiling it with the girl's own copious come, and her wriggling spanked arse attested that her shrieks were now of pleasure. Lavoisier's own come flowed down her thighs, and soaked the girl's black mane, which became oily and sodden. When the corporal groaned and pissed herself, the Somali girl's dress was soaked, and her tresses absorbed the golden pee that poured from the corporal's pink writhing gash. Both females shrieked, as they gamahuched each other to shuddering, piss-soaked climaxes, their cunts gushing with oily juice, and each female swallowing the other's come. Gilles entered, to scold the Somali for tardiness, and roared with laughter at naked Sutra, her dark skin mauve with cold, and Corporal Lavoisier drinking the shrieking Djiboutian girl's gush of come juice.

'I'll give you something to shriek about, Damara, you slut,' she said. 'And it's not justice to leave that bitch up there to freeze. Release her, inmate corporal!'

He snatched Damara's quivering body from Corporal Lavoisier's embrace, and carefully unzipped her piss-soaked dress, which he folded and laid on the table. The girl murmured her thanks, and began wanking her swollen gash lips and clitty, as the male sat, removing his heavy Legion belt, pinioned her thighs on his own, and began to lash her bare buttocks with his belt. His erection was apparent beneath his thin cotton shorts; Damara paused in her wank to tug these away from his body, so that his huge stiff penis sprang up, and, by twisting her spine, presented her naked arse for the strap, while at the same time engorging the whole shaft of his cock between her sucking cunt lips.

Her bottom, already mauve from the corporal's spanking, now wealed and purpled as he reached the twentieth lash from his leather. Sutra saw her haunch muscles quiver, and her come soak the man's balls, as her bare bum jerked under the hard lashes of the belt. Corporal Lavoisier released Sutra from her own bondage, and forced the naked girl to her knees, to lick the corporal's still-erect clitty. She pushed Sutra's head hard into her cunt, so that her nose was squashed into the wet fleshy channel, and squirts of come oil invaded her nostrils and throat, choking her with the Frenchwoman's gush of cunt-juice. Bending over, the corporal began to spank Sutra's bare bum, very hard, until Sutra stopped licking her clitty. Snarling, the corporal pulled her by the ear, and demanded an explanation. Sutra sobbed that clit-sucking and come-drinking were *instead of* punishment, not *as well as*. The corporal chuckled, and agreed, saying that inmate Sutrapanaya must be mindful of their bargain in future, whenever the corporal felt 'juicy'. Sutra put herself to her work with feigned enthusiasm, sensing this was a new way of being liberated from the scorch of canemarks on her bare bum. The Djiboutian Somali girl giggled and shrieked with pleasure, wanking herself hard, as the legionnaire flogged her bare fesses, and looked at Sutra, uncomprehending that anyone could refuse a treat so delicious as a bare-bum thrashing.

Gilles grasped Damara by her piss-wet mat of hair, and made her squeal, and stand beside Sutra's head, bobbing at the corporal's cunt. The pilot continued to whip the girl's squirming bum, while sliding his giant cock into the cleft of Corporal Lavoisier's arse. No words were spoken; the corporal sighed with pleasure, and spread her arse-cheeks, bending over at an angle, and parting her legs, so that the legionnaire was easily able to penetrate her anus with his tool, lubricated with piss and come from Damara's hair. His swollen glans nuzzled her anal pucker for a moment, sliding the peehole in and out, until her bum-bud was gasping like a fish, and Gilles suddenly rammed his cock into her anus with full force, right up to his balls, which slammed hard against the corporal's arse-meat. Gilles continued to thrash the nude Djiboutian girl, who wriggled her superb buttocks to entice harder lashes, while she swooped low, to plunge her head between Sutra's own rapidly moistening gash flaps. As Sutra tongued and chewed the corporal's sopping cunt, her own cunt poured come, under the delicate tonguing of the impish Damara. Their bodies shook at the legionnaire's hard buggery of Corporal Lavoisier, until the corporal cried out in dismay as the tool plopped from her anus, and Gilles rasped that he must taste the inmate's arse, whose bare coffee globes he had long admired, pumping at drill on the square. Sutra found herself crouching over the prone body of Corporal Lavoisier, whose thighs were clamped around her face in a vice, while Gilles' massive cock pummelled Sutra's anus in a vigorous buggery, and Damara sat with her massive gash and bum on the corporal's face, wanking herself off and giggling, as she pissed into the Frenchwoman's mouth.

As her anus was firmly buggered, Sutra masturbated to come after come, until the legionnaire's jet of cream at her anal root made her buckle giddily in orgasm, and sag completely onto the corporal's come-soaked bare pubis. With her thighs trapping Sutra's nose in her soaked slit, the corporal began to buck up and down, as though being fucked, and Sutra's nostrils again spumed with the French-woman's come-gush. Gilles grunted as he spurted, Damara shrieked with little winces of ecstasy, and the corporal groaned, pissing into Sutra's face. Sutra herself felt her belly heave in a new spasm of come, as hot piss and cunt oil flowed down her neck and tits.

'A good tight arse,' said the legionnaire, slapping Sutra's buttocks, as he dressed, 'maybe even tighter than the German slut Titzi's, though not as tight as this S'Ibaya cave-girl's.'

Damara glowed with pleasure at the compliment.

'Certainly tighter than yours, Lavoisier! Your hole's slacker each visit! Time you went to Paris for a nip and tuck, or Crevasse will think you've had too many camels up you! Maybe it's your *cunt* I should fuck next time, though I don't normally go in for that sloppy nonsense – but yours might be tight as good bony S'Ibaya arse-elastic. We all know you Legion bitches are sworn to empty cunts!'

Damara wadded her cunt and anus with ice shavings, then carefully replaced and smoothed her white skirt, which she smoothed, with a haughty look at the corporal, over her shredded cunt-bush and the patches of bare brown skin between the remaining tufts.

'Ice for the customers,' she said, grinning, as she left with Gilles.

'Our bargain,' said Corporal Lavoisier, putting her finger to her lips, and Sutra nodded, lowering her head in shame, but with a wink at the departing legionnaire . . .

Titzi appeared one day, her nipple pierced with a corporal's badge, and caned Lise harder than any other corporal, even Lavoisier, for insolence: eighteen stingers, bent over in the middle of the square, with Lise's drill rocks still clamped to her aching titties and cunt lips. That was after her ordained drill; she took her caning at a crouch, and at each of Titzi's strokes, she winced, and sobbed, as her titties and cunt were dragged on the ground by the rocks. Afterwards, she was led shackled into the kitchen of the Welcome Centre, past another debonair young Legion pilot, who had eyed her on the first morning, and was chained to a coffin-sized slab of ice for an hour, her cunt and nipples face down, and blue with cold after her ordeal. Heidi took her at once to the infirmary, to bathe and dress her, and then it was time to endure the drilling of Corporal Lavoisier. Heidi and Lise could not decide who was the worse brute, Lavoisier or Titzi, but decided that an example must be made of one, to cow the other. For the trifling offence of idling, Lavoisier ordered Lise buried up to her neck in scorching sand, her only fluid nourishment the piss of each squad of drilled inmates, who pissed cloying golden pee into her gulping mouth. They decided it must be Lavoisier. Her comeuppance would shock Titzi from her new arrogance as corporal.

'Heidi,' whispered Lise, in the shade of the arcade, as they admired a young Somali's snakelike penis under his bafto, while pretending to consider the purchase of a half-used bar of Lux soap, 'I know Dr Crevasse fancies you. You and I wank, it's true. If we could go . . . all the way, as lesbians – pretend lesbians – we could be taken under her tutelage. If we're together, well, lesbianism would not be worse than this.'

'I'd rather desert, Lise,' said Heidi, 'though, if I wanted to go all the way, with gamahuching and toys and anal fist-fucking and everything, it would be with you. Let's humiliate Lavoisier first: from what Sutra says, she has too many secrets to make a fuss. Sutra is one of them, and I am sure she is getting buggered by Gilles, hoping to make corporal. We cannot entirely trust her. Whip the bitch Lavoisier, bugger her with a stave, and peg her out in the hour before dawn, on the square.'

'If we are caught, and she blabs, it'll mean a public whipping.'

'I can take it. Then we'll desert.'

'Being Crevasse's slaves might be better than deserting and getting caught.'

'If we get caught we'll be made her slaves anyway. Desertion is a sign of psychiatric disorder. Let's punish Lavoisier, then desert, anyway. In the desert, we can wank each other as much as we please, and who knows, Lise . . . maybe go all the way. Sweet Lise! If we could be *alone* . . .'

Lise thought for a moment. They heard Titzi's tread and the swish of her cane, approaching.

'OK,' she said, looking at Gilles, the young bronzed Legion pilot, swigging beer on the terrace, as he squeezed the bare breasts and ripely extruded fesses of the laughing Damara. 'But what if we could desert by helicopter . . .?'

It was Sutra who deserted first, on her own, and Heidi and Lise who took the blame for it. The Sri Lankan girl went missing after supper, and was last observed in Lise and Heidi's company, although they protested no conversation took place. Corporal Titzi escorted them, shuffling in ankle-hobbles, to the nurse-general's office, and reported them as 'conspirators'. The commandant seemed distracted, and, eyes bright with pleasure, ignored Lise and Heidi, as she knelt at the block and bared her bottom to Titzi, after handing her a stout baobab cane.

Nurse-General Frachon licked her lips, and said that the inmates must have another, *real* demonstration of how a soldier girl took punishment. Heidi and Lise watched Titzi give the commandant twelve hard strokes on the bare, which she took with the same impassive zeal as before, her flogged buttocks not even twitching. Her caning was followed, without instruction, by a sturdy buggering from the erect, masturbating Muhammar, which she took, writhing and squealing, until he spunked in her bumhole, and she cried out in orgasm; his sperm bubbled, frothing, from her anal lips, to drip into her come-puddle. After reskirting her caned arse, she seated herself primly, studiously ignoring the pool of come and spunk.

'I feel guilty, Nurse-General,' said Titzi, 'as the inmates Sutrapanaya and Gallard are of my own batch, and wish to offer my services in any search for the inmate Sutrapanaya. I shall gladly endure the desert.'

Damara knocked, with a message for the nurse-general, and was bade enter. She was bare, as always, apart from her white skirt, and waggled her breasts impishly at the solemn gathering, then raised her skirt, to show her bare bum, freshly caned with deep welts.

'Gilles is in love with me,' she said.

'Conspiracy! I don't think a mere caning is sufficient punishment for aiding and abetting desertion,' continued the nurse-general. 'The tribunal – myself and Dr Crevasse – will consider the case for public whipping.'

Damara smiled, and twirled her big plum nipples. The tribunal was speedily agreed, and Damara sent to Dr Crevasse's office to fetch her. Dr Crevasse arrived, wearing her bafto, with a burnished dagger swinging from her red and gold belt, barefoot, and accompanied by her slaves, Afgoi and Melleah, both attired only in loinstrings. Nurse-General Frachon blushed as Dr Crevasse stalked into the room, gazing with distaste at Muhammar's only half-somnolent penis, which stirred at the sight of Melleah's pert bare breasts and ripe arse-globes, almost entirely revealed by the skimpy loinstring. Dr Crevasse was given the case for the defence, both suspects being considered guilty unless shown innocent, and forbidden to speak at all. She inspected the two shackled girls with a smile, and said in their defence that they should not suffer loss of pay after their public flogging of twenty strokes on back, and caning of twenty on bare bottom, and a week's confinement in the Hole.

'However,' said Dr Crevasse, turning to face Nurse-General Frachon, 'I sense these two sluts are not the only guilty parties present. I observe your male slave is ill-trained, Nurse-General. His penis is scarcely quiet, and was not quiet as he arrived to summon me. My own slave Afgoi is quiescent, as he has been taught to faithfully drain his balls twice a day. You, Nurse-General, are, I fear, remiss. Unless there is another reason for his unseemliness.'

Nurse-General Frachon paled under her tan, and frowned.

'What other reason could there possibly be?' she quavered.

'The male Muhammar has recently taken pleasure,' said Dr Crevasse.

She suddenly grasped Muhammar's balls, under his loincloth, and squeezed, speaking rapidly to him in Somali. Wincing, the male gasped a few words. Dr Crevasse's face was stony as she stared down the commandant, but, suddenly, she smiled, licking her sharp white teeth.

'Buggery from such a tasty cock is only to be expected, Jacqui,' she said, 'and thank S'Ibaa I did not allow you a female slave, or I should be terribly jealous – but you know I must punish you for your shame, in front of the inmates.'

'Yes, Doctor,' mumbled the commandant.

'You may assume position, then, after giving me the cane your bottom likes least.'

The commandant rose and fetched a springy cane about a metre in length, but heavy, and handed it to Dr Crevasse with a curtsy. She knelt by the block, still warm from her caning by Titzi, and hoisted her skirt, to show her naked bottom still livid from her recent stripes, and the butterfly well idented into her anal crevice. Dr Crevasse gasped.

'Buggery is one thing, Jacqui, but someone else has caned your arse, which is mine alone to chastise,' she hissed. 'Who caned you, *slut*?'

Vip! Vip!

104

She accompanied her words with two sharp strokes to the raw welts on top fesse, and the commandant shrieked, with her bum squirming, quite unlike the ramrod-still arse that had taken Titzi's caning.

Vip! Vip!

Jacqueline Frachon sobbed and shuddered, as two more strokes took her on the tautly muscled, yet yielding underfesses.

'Please, Charlotte . . . no, please . . .'

Vip! Vip!

'*Dr Crevasse*, you whore!'

Vip! Vip!

'O! O! *Ahhh* . . .! O, Dr Crevasse, *please*, no . . .'

Vip! Vip! Vip Vip!

'*Ohhhh! Ahhhh!*'

The commandant's bare buttocks were reduced to quivering, helpless jellies, as she squirmed and clenched under a caning of twenty strokes.

'Now, Jacqui, confess. Did you permit your slave Muammar to cane you as well as bugger you? If so, you know the penalty: his bare arse shall be whipped publicly, until he is unconscious, with his balls and cock pincered by every corporal and sergeant in Fort Lafresne.'

Muhammar paled, and babbled in Somali.

'So,' said Dr Crevasse, gazing at the three trembling nude inmates, 'not the male. Who, then? If she does not confess, she shall take her public whipping with both anal and vaginal holes clamped, and stuffed with sandworms.'

Titzi swallowed, and seemed close to tears. The commandant sobbed, rubbing the bruised globes of her bottom.

'You, inmate Corporal von Titisee?' said Dr Crevasse, pleasantly.

Trembling, Titzi denied the charge, with a barely perceptible shake of her head, looking away from Lise and Heidi, and blushing deeply. Dr Crevasse parted the front of her bafto, extruded a silken black thigh, and pretended to scratch an itch. She allowed the cloth to fall from her thigh, until the shaven cunt-mountain gleamed, and the glistening wet gash lips began to writhe like snakes of their own accord, jiggling the golden lock that forbade ingress to her slit.

'Which of you two inmates, then?' she purred.

The top of her bafto fell away, revealing her jutting naked teats, the nipples massive and stiff, staring like eyes inside their golden rings.

'Be advised that I may recommend the culprit to my private psychiatric clinic for further treatment, after her ordained public whipping, and solitary confinement in the Hole,' she said.

She kicked Nurse-General Frachon hard, in her quim, with the sharp toenails of her left foot, then again, right in the anus bud.

'I do not think the nurse-general will raise any objections,' she said.

'Doctor, I –' Lise blurted.

'Doctor, I was –' Heidi gasped, at exactly the same moment.

Dr Crevasse smiled.

'So, we have two culprits, inmate Corporal von Titisee,' she said.

She pulled the sobbing Nurse-General Frachon by her hair, raising her to her feet, and drew her bejewelled dagger. With a swift slash, she severed the commandant's blonde mane close to her nape, and allowed the broad hank of hair to fall into the pool of come and sperm. She ordered the commandant to lie down on her back, with her shorn head in the come-puddle, and squatted over her face, as if to dung. She did not dung, but pissed copiously, a long, hard jet of steaming golden rain that was cut to spray by her cunt-locket, directed into the prone woman's mouth, and splattering her face and blouse.

'Drink, Jacqui,' she commanded, and the nurse-general swallowed.

Dr Crevasse ordered Muhammar and Afgoi to piss on her face, while Melleah, Lise, Titzi and Heidi were to take turns pissing on her uniform. Each male and each girl squirted a strong jet of piss, until the nurse-general's face, body and clothing were completely soaked in pee, and she lay, whimpering and spluttering, in a deep pool of liquid. She was ordered to raise her skirt and masturbate to orgasm, under the eyes of her pleasurers and inmates, and she did so, wanking her wet clit and cunt with more and more fervent strokes, until a strong flood of come flowed into the piss-puddle, and her buttocks and belly threshed in a groaning orgasm.

Dr Crevasse ripped the yellow sussies from the commandant's waist, dipped them in come and piss, then wadded the soaked garment in the woman's mouth.

'I expect the floor to be spotlessly clean when I return from witnessing the whipping of the two culprits,' she said. 'You are permitted to wipe the floor only with your mouth and titties, dear Jacqui. Your slave Muhammar's punishment for indecency shall be administered by my own slave Melleah, who shall wank him until his balls are completely drained of spunk, and continue wanking him even when there is no cream left. To maintain Muhammar's erection, my own slave Afgoi is permitted to bugger or cunt-fuck Melleah, as stimulus, while she attends to your slave's cock. *He* won't wish to fuck *any* holes for a long time . . .'

Dr Crevasse folded her bafto closed over her own naked cunt, which seeped with gleaming come, hiding the stiffened nubbins of her ringed bare nipple-pods. She smiled sweetly.

'Inmate Corporal von Titisee! Lead the culprits to the square. Their public whipping shall take place at once.'

8

Whipped Wet

O, God, this is my first public whipping.

Lise Gallard winced, as her wrists were cuffed to the headbar of the flogging-frame, which had been wheeled to the centre of the square. The little finger of Heidi's left hand touched that of Lise's right.

No, no, that's silly. I've been whipped publicly before.

The heavy ankle hobbles at the base of the flogging posts clanged into place, securing Heidi and Lise's nude bodies in splayed crosses for the double whipping. Every naked inmate of Fort Lafresne, as well as officers, medical staff and NCOs, whether in full uniforms, bare-breasted with skirts of rubber or cloth, or their haunches and teats pinched by bizarre Legion scanties, stood stiffly at attention around them.

I mean, I've been whipped in public before.

Corporals Lavoisier and Hauser lifted scourges of thirteen short studded thongs, and moved close to the girls' strung bodies. The first part of the flogging was twenty lashes to their bare backs. A tap was opened, and a shower of cold drinking water began to spray them. Public whippings were on wet skin, so that the strokes would smart more.

That is, people have watched me whipped and I didn't mind.

At the corporals' waists hung baobab canes, for the second part of their flogging, twenty strokes on their naked buttocks.

I love it when a man canes my bum, and other men watch, all stiff, and ready to bugger me. So a naked public flogging is nothing new . . .

Dr Charlotte Crevasse signalled the corporals to begin whipping the girls. The sultry air rustled, as they lifted their scourges.

O God! This is my first public whipping!

Thwap! Thwap!

O! God . . . O! My back! I can't take it . . .

Thwap! Thwap!

O! Please! NO . . .!

Beside Lise, Heidi's body was flung forward like a rag doll at each lash of the scourge, and ugly weals purpled her shoulders almost at once. The whipstrokes slammed Lise forwards, hurting her ankles and wrists, and forcing her body to the limit of her bonds, before bouncing back for her naked skin to meet the next stroke of the scourge. The stream of water danced on her deepening weals.

Thwap! Thwap!

O! O! God! Ohhh . . .!

Both girls' eyes streamed with tears, yet neither made any sound more than a muffled gasp of agony: they were gagged, their mouths completely filled by rubber bits, strapped to their napes. Their naked breasts bounced as their backs quivered under the whiplashes.

Thwap! Thwap! Thwap! Thwap!

O, no! No! How it smarts . . . O, pleasenopleaseno-PLEASENO . . . OHH!

Thwap! Thwap! Thwap! Thwap!

Dr Crevasse's eyes were glazed with pleasure as she watched the wet bare bodies shudder, their skins darkening with welts. Heidi was the first to piss herself, a golden steaming jet spurting between her writhing thighs; Dr Crevasse's nostrils flared as she smiled wide. Her hand, under her bafto, touched her cunt, and she began to masturbate.

Thwap! Thwap! Thwap! Thwap!

Dr Crevasse had ordered the flogging to be effected without pause, and no sooner had one stroke jarred their bodies, than they recoiled, to be lashed by the next. The faces of the inmates were either sullen and cowed, or gleefully smirking. Dr Crevasse's own dark features were serene. A trickle of come wetted her ankles and bare feet.

Thwap! Thwap! Thwap! Thwap!

Dr Crevasse masturbated faster, as the flogging progressed, and the girls' scarlet faces streamed with tears, with their teeth biting through their rubber gags. Lise pissed herself at the eighteenth stroke of the whipping of her back, the shuddering of her body, now darkly raw with welts, spraying her rain in a wide arc. At that moment, Dr Crevasse chose to bring herself off; she sighed, as she masturbated to an intense orgasm, and her cunt anointed her bare black feet with a river of come. When the girls had taken twenty on the bare back, they hung limply in their bonds, while the corporals swapped scourge for cane. There was otherwise no pause in the chastisement, and both girls arched their backs, shuddering again, as the first canestrokes lashed their naked buttocks.

Vap! Vap! Vap! Vap!

The heavy baobab wood, for long-reach caning, made a dry thudding as it slapped the naked arse-flesh, hissing as it sliced the fine spray that constantly watered the girls' bodies.

Ahh! O, God, it couldn't be worse! Rather the rattan . . . rather anything! I'll never ask a man to cane me again!

Vap! Vap! Vap! Vap!

O! O! Ohhh! God! O, God! Crevasse, you've won! I give in! Please let me submit, and stop this dreadful pain!

Vap! Vap! Vap! Vap!

O! O! O, Doctor, I'll wank and lick and drink you, open myself to you, let you do anything to me, just stop . . . this . . .

Vap! Vap! Vap! Vap!

AHHHH . . .!

By the end of the public whipping, both girls' bodies were livid with crimson and purple stripes, their shoulders and buttocks matching in a lurid symmetry of weals. They were quickly unbound and their ankles locked in hobble-bars, then placed belly down on stretchers and carried

110

underground to the cells. The inmates returned at once to their drill, and only a drying pool of girl-piss and girl-tears, and a smaller, oily pool of Dr Crevasse's come, indicated that a public whipping had ever taken place. The doctor followed the stretcher-bearers underground, doffing her bafto at the entrance to the cells; she went into the Hole nude but for her red and gold belt, which she knotted around her satin-black waist, and from which dangled her dagger and her cane.

Lise and Heidi were in separate cells, stinking, windowless holes, just long enough for a body to lie down, but not high enough for a body to stand. The doors were of solid rock, with a single slit, like a letter-box, and thudded shut on noiseless hinges. Dr Crevasse visited Heidi first, and Lise heard the doctor's voice, a soft and soothing murmur. Heidi laughed, hesitantly at first, then her laughter turned to giggles, which in turn became a fierce panting, a gasping, and a long, unmistakable cry of orgasm. Lise's door swung open, and the nude figure of Dr Crevasse padded to crouch beside her head, the glistening lake of come plainly visible between the black woman's spread and swollen cunt lips. Her extruded clitoris stood, jutting from its fleshy quim-pouch. The doctor carried two pots of ointment, applying the contents of the first to the weals on Lise's shoulders.

Lise's sobs turned to a groan, as the ointment stung, but she relaxed as a comforting glow suffused her welted skin. Dr Crevasse took the second pot, which smelt foully pungent, and rubbed the cream into Lise's buttock weals. This stung, and did not stop stinging, and Lise snuffled, wriggling her bottom. The doctor laughed softly.

'Only a little while,' she said, 'and your fesses will heal, after they have tasted the smart of enrichment. Heidi's buttocks, too, have begun the process, though hers require enrichment more than yours. She has agreed to join me in my private clinic, Lise. She said you persuaded her . . .'

'Not exactly,' Lise blurted, 'that is, I . . .'

'After your whipping, I think Heidi hates France almost as much as you, Lise,' said Dr Crevasse.

'I don't hate France,' Lise protested, 'just the French! I mean, Corporal Lavoisier and Sister-General Grenier, who sent me here, and that bitch Hauser . . . O! I didn't mean –'

'Corporal Hauser is a bitch, I agree,' said Dr Crevasse, continuing to massage Lise's buttocks, including her crevice, thighs and cunt mound, and with a generous penetration of her anus bud. 'Corporals are meant to be bitches. She is in fact Belgian, from the charming city of Liège.'

Dr Crevasse placed her hands under Lise's spread crotch, and found her clitoris. Placing her other hand between her own cunt flaps, she began to masturbate both nubbins. Soon, Lise sighed with pleasure, and her oiled buttocks squirmed as she pressed her stiffening clitty down on the doctor's fingers.

'You persuaded Heidi, Lise,' said the doctor, wanking expertly, 'and now I shall see if you have persuaded yourself, too.'

'I'd do anything to avoid another whipping,' Lise whimpered.

'Such a magnificent arse can scarcely expect to avoid thrashing, my beauty,' said the doctor, 'and certainly not when enriched to full ripeness. Your erotic craving for bare caning shall never abate, nor should it. I want, simply, to enhance it, to broaden your scope, as it were . . .'

Her fingers slid inside Lise's cunt, and she began to frig the slimy gash, with her thumb flicking the clitty. Lise moaned.

'Ohh . . . don't stop.'

Dr Crevasse tilted nearer Lise's face, so that come from her own dripping cunt trickled into Lise's mouth and eyes. Lise swallowed the black woman's come.

'What do you mean, *enriched*, Doctor . . .?' she moaned, her bum squirming hard on her masturbatrix's fingers.

Lise's come drenched the rough canvas of her stretcher.

'Your sacred number, that is, the measurement of your bottom, taken by Dr Frahl, who first examined you, is a hundred and two centimetres from clitoris to mid-fesse,' said Dr Crevasse, 'roughly a three-quarter *S'Ibaa*, the

112

goddess measurement. With the sacred volcanic *Gobaad* earth of Djibouti, you should reach a hundred and twenty, or more, and a corresponding, harmonious growth of the mound, haunches and thighs. Melleah and Damara's bums are about three-fifths a S'Ibaa; my own, seven-eighths. Titzi's arse is ripe and splendidly sculpted, but in fact, her sacred number is less than your own. Heidi shall benefit most spectacularly from our S'Ibaya wisdom. Sutra's sacred measurement is a hundred centimetres, most ripe for enrichment . . . if only the slut hadn't deserted! It was noble of you and Heidi to take the blame for Titzi's sin, and ignoble of the German slut to let you. I expect you want revenge.'

'*Sacred volcanic earth . . .?*' Lise gasped.

'Haven't you wondered why your Djiboutian paramours have such big cocks? Or why male legionnaires are so well-endowed?'

Her fingers pinched Lise's clitty very hard, and Lise squealed in pleasure, her cunt juicing copiously, and her hillock now squirming in a pool of come on the canvas. Dr Crevasse's fingers reached the neck of Lise's womb, and found the key to her own cunt secreted there. She did not remove the key, but used it as a masturbating tool, poking it further into Lise's cunt, and the hard pulsing meat of the wombneck.

'O! O! Mmm . . . *O, yes*! How did you know we lied?' Lise gasped.

'Muhammar told me. He, too, is S'Ibaya. You did not hear him speak Titzi's name, as he called her merely "the ripe-arsed slut".'

'But you still had us whipped?' Lise cried. 'O, don't stop wanking me!'

'That,' purred the doctor, licking her fingers of Lise's come, 'was for my own pleasure. I masturbated well, watching your arses wriggle. You have the arse of a queen, Mademoiselle Lise Gallard.'

'O! O!' Lise gasped. 'I'm going to come . . . Won't you wank to come with me, Doctor?'

'Only if you agree to join me in my private clinic,' said Dr Crevasse, rubbing Lise's clitty fast, and pummelling her

113

come-slimed slit. She was already, in fact, masturbating her own cunt just as hard.

'O! Anything!'

'As my slave, albeit a pampered one?'

'Anything! Wank me! *O, please, wank me off!*'

'With beautiful fesses for your masturbatrix to spank, and cane?'

'O! I'm coming! Wank me harder! O! O! *Yes . . .! Ahh . . .!*'

Dr Crevasse's own cunt gushed with come, as she brought herself off in time with her new slave's threshing climax, though only a slight whimper of contentment escaped the black woman's lips. She explained tersely that Heidi and Lise's automatic sentence of a week in the Hole was reduced to three days, after which they could credibly be released into her own psychiatric care.

'The purpose of confinement in the Hole is twofold,' she said casually. 'To meditate, and masturbate.'

'*What?* I don't quite . . .'

'You will have unlimited drinking water, as at all times in the Legion,' said Dr Crevasse. 'You will receive food, corresponding to the amount of come you wank from your cunt. Plastic pipettes are provided, and for every centimetre of titration you supply, you will receive a hundred grammes of food.'

'Dr Frahl said I produced twenty-three millimetres of juice, while I watched Heidi beaten,' said Lise faintly, 'and that was just one come, so to get enough to eat, I'll have to masturbate all day long, Doctor!'

'Exactly,' said Dr Crevasse. 'Both of you will receive a daily caning to whet your appetite, six strokes in Heidi's case, and twelve strokes in yours, Lise, as you are still on the regime-one discipline I prescribed for you. I suggest you find some particularly appealing fantasy that will enable you to wank sufficiently – for example, someone's bare bottom that you would like caned raw, in revenge for your own humiliation.'

'O . . . I'd thrill more if a male caned *me*,' sighed Lise. 'Or fucked me hard, in the cunt. I haven't been properly fucked for ages.'

'That shall not be on the menu for quite a while, Lise, although I may permit Afgoi's tool to penetrate your anus while he is beaten by Melleah. I tolerate only one male slave in my abode, and he must be well thrashed, to ensure proper and regular spermings. Remember that on your early release from the Hole – with four days' confinement merely *suspended* – I am your dominatrix, and masturbatrix. You and Lise shall be tools for my pleasure, which, if satisfactorily provided, may lead to your own. You shall address me as "Mistress", and obey me without question.'

'Damara, Doctor – I mean, Mistress – she is the girl in the Welcome Centre?'

'You know she is. You have admired her arse, and heard from Sutra of her sexual voracity with Gilles and the depraved Lavoisier.'

It was a statement, not a question.

'I have indeed admired her gorgeous arse, Mistress,' said Lise carefully. 'I should have guessed she was S'Ibaya.'

'We S'Ibaya are everywhere in Djibouti. You know the males by their massive, peeled cocks, and the females by their buttocks. Already, *you* have the arse of a queen, Lise, and if you obey and please me, you shall have the arse of a goddess! You must say, three times, as Heidi has already done, "I wish to be slave of S'Ibaa." '

Lise blurted: '*I wish to be slave of S'Ibaa, I wish to be slave of S'Ibaa, I wish to be slave of S'Ibaa.*'

Dr Crevasse smiled, and licked her lips.

'There is just one question, Mistress,' said Lise. 'It may sound silly, but – shall I be on inmate's pay, as your slave? I despair already of saving up for my new uniform, and if –'

'Uniforms,' said Dr Crevasse, 'will be provided.'

'I don't believe it,' said Lise, rubbing her red eyes.

Dr Crevasse slapped her face.

'Slaves address me as "Mistress",' she said.

'Yes, Mistress,' Lise blurted.

'You survived your three days in the Hole, with plenty to eat, slaves,' the doctor said to both Heidi and Lise, who still wore their hobble bars at their ankles, as Melleah escorted them into her compound. 'What were your fantasies, as you wanked off?'

'O . . .' said Lise, blushing. Dr Crevasse slapped her again, harder.

'I saw a bum caned raw, Mistress,' murmured Heidi.

'European or African?' asked the doctor.

'European, Mistress,' said Heidi coyly.

'And you, Lise?'

'Cock, Mistress. African, big and black and stiff, pulsing in my wet cunt,' said Lise. 'But I imagined a white girl's bum, too, squirming bare, and caned to crimson.'

'I wonder if it could be the same white girl,' said Dr Crevasse. 'There is some caning to be done while I dine. O, and some birching.'

Both girls trembled; Melleah grinned, and their mistress smiled.

'You do not wish to endure four more days of darkness, constant wanking off, and daily caning, in the Hole,' she said.

Both girls shook their heads, vigorously.

'You are no longer soldier girls, nor prisoners on numbered regimes, but slaves, and subject to my own discipline regime.'

'Yes, Mistress,' said Heidi and Lise together, at which Melleah obeyed her mistress's signal to free their feet from hobble.

Dr Crevasse had charge of six slaves, as well as Melleah, Afgoi, and now Heidi and Lise. She did not possess them outright: S'Ibaa possessed them. They slept in a shelter of mud and palm leaves, in the courtyard of Dr Crevasse's compound, dominated by the doctor's own mansion, of brick, slate and timber. The site was an oasis, with clusters of olive and jojoba, and flowering shrubs. Before the mansion was a lake with fish, and a fountain, surrounded by date palms. The slaves' shelter, shaded by palms, was like the inmates' dormitory, but airy, well-apertured and more luxurious, because less crowded. Afgoi did not share the female quarters. Each slave-girl had her own space, an armoire for clothing, a table and toilet things. There was a dunging-trench outside, and at the other end, a well for drinking water. Lise and Heidi had straw palliasses next to one another, and both gasped in delight to see that their armoires contained an array of clothing: real clothing, not Legion drab, or Legion punitive. They had frillies, skirts and blouses and underthings, many of silk, as well as leather and rubber, and there were wigs for head and pubis. Dr Crevasse said that Melleah would instruct them in their proper accoutrement, then escort them to the serving of luncheon, and the witnessing of punishment. Slaves were assigned not only to domestic service, but also to fieldwork within the oasis, and any girl slacking was, just as in the Legion proper, subject to rigorous discipline. The girls were left alone with Melleah; through the palm leaves, Fort Lafresne shimmered in the distance, which, in the heat haze, could have been a hundred metres or a thousand. Further away stood a similar structure, blurred in the heat, which Melleah said, casually, was the barracks for male prisoners. To the rear of the slave-girls' shelter stood a wooden shed, without shade, which was for slave-girls' 'hot punishment'.

'Our mistress intends one of you to be birched on the bare, today,' she said. 'You, I think, slave Lise. Tomorrow, or this evening, slave Heidi.'

'*Birched*? But . . . *why*?' Lise gasped, though she felt her quim moisten at the thrilling, comfortingly *English* phrase: *birched on the bare*.

'For being a slave of S'Ibaa,' shrugged Melleah, 'as Dr Crevasse says birch-oil helps the croup to ripen,' and rubbed her own voluptuous arse-melons with a sultry smirk. 'My bare arse has taken birch many times.'

'We did swear,' said Lise. 'After you swore, Heidi, I just had to.'

Heidi frowned.

'But I swore because Dr Crevasse told me *you* did,' she blurted, then sighed. 'I suppose I can take a birching – if you can, Lise.'

She smiled shyly, and her cunt lips seeped glistening juice.

117

'She tricked us both,' said Lise.

Melleah clapped her hands and slipped out of her loinstring.

'See, what a clever mistress we have!' she cried. 'We shall masturbate for joy, and I shall dress us three slaves for her proper service.'

They squatted cross-legged and wanked, with thighs spread and wet from dripping quims. Lise's slit was still seeping come after the triple wank, as she followed Heidi and Melleah into Dr Crevasse's mansion. She was dressed in frillies, as a French maid, complete with black lycra stockings, black silk sussies over a thin g-string and wobbling high heels. She had a long blonde wig. Her thin silk blouse, open to bare her nipples in an uplift bra, was already damp with sweat. The frilly tutu flounced up to show most of her bare bum, with the string snaking tight in her buttock crevice; Heidi and Melleah were identically attired, with wigs to suit.

They entered a large dining room, of panelled baobab wood, and decorated with paintings, photographs and a single statue. Dr Crevasse sat at the head of a long wooden dining table, beneath a larger-than-life photograph, in stark black and white, showing herself, in the nude, against a desert landscape studded with jagged black volcanic chimneys. She held a snake and a cane. In a crevice on the facing wall stood an ebony statue of a single nude female, holding a similar cane. Her breasts swelled as though to bursting, yet jutted like young volcanoes, and the sweep of her back flowed perfectly into the largest, ripest buttocks Lise had ever seen or could imagine. The hillock of the vulva swelled to match the croup, and was framed by thighs whose every ripple was caught by the sculptor. Along one wall hung black and white photographs of nude Nilotic girls, all magnificently fessed, and with painted bodies, and paintings of the same, with the colours starkly subdued, so that black body, rock brown and white sand were the only colours, save for a luminescent azure sky. Four items of furniture adorned the room. One was an aquarium of live crustaceans, the others wooden and festooned with restraints: an upright flogging-frame, a caning-stool and a birching-table, each with a rack of disciplinary instruments beside it.

'You admire my paintings,' said Dr Crévasse to Lise.

'Yes, Mistress,' Lise gasped. 'And your photos, and ... statue.'

Dr Crevasse laughed.

'The photographs are by another woman,' she said, 'and the statue of S'Ibaa is divine. Merely to suggest human provenance earns your naked fesses the birching I intend to give them, anyway.'

The other wall also showed paintings and photographs, but in bright colour, and the girls depicted were European, Asian or African. All wore superbly elegant and provocative Western dress, or just sexy underthings, in urban backgrounds identifiable as European, American or Oriental. They had silks, furs and jewels, or else sleek nylon skirts, stockings and figure-hugging bodices, as flight attendants or even police officers. Whatever their dress, the girls were all ripe of teat and buttock. Their eyes flirted with the camera, with tongues licking parted lips.

'Products of the *Ecole de Finesse*,' said Dr Crevasse.

'Permission to speak, Mistress?' Lise murmured.

'Granted, slave.'

'I know you'll think me silly, but I had the idea that *this* was the finishing school.'

'The finishing school is far from here,' said the black woman, 'yet not far. Djibouti is a small place, a volcanic crust on scarred earth, difficult to cross, except with wings, although, in ancient times, the S'Ibaya could walk across the valley that is now the Red Sea. A gazelle can easily run from here to the lake of Abhe Bad, and Ethiopia. You would have to desert, slave Lise Gallard, to find the finishing school, and your way back to the world. Don't tell me you and Heidi haven't plotted desertion.'

She gestured to the vast horizon beyond her window.

'The wastes of the *Grand Bara* are a prison without bars,' she said. 'Desert at your pleasure, if you can change into a gazelle, or a bird ...'

119

She sprang to her feet and plunged her bare hand into the aquarium, selecting a lobster, which she extracted, wriggling. She slew it with a swift needle stroke to the neck, then gave it to Melleah, for boiling.

'I abhor cruelty,' she said.

Afgoi led in three girls, shackled together, by wrists and ankles. Their naked bodies flowed with sweat from the hothouse. Heidi and Lise, instructed to kneel at their mistress's feet, gaped, astounded.

'Much occurred in the three days you were wanking off in the Hole,' mused Dr Crevasse. 'We have three unsuccessful deserters, sent to me for psychiatric evaluation, preceded, necessarily, by chastisement.'

Afgoi unchained the first prisoner, her face scarlet and sullen, and her buttocks two large moons, bulging smooth and uncaned. It was Titzi. No sooner had Afgoi unshackled her, than she was seized by the nape, and forced down to kneel over the high caning stool, with splayed legs that thrust her bum high. Her wrists and ankles were padlocked to the legs of the stool, spreading her big buttocks and revealing her pink, hairless cunt and anus bud. Afgoi's huge penis was limp within his loinstring, which emphasised his powerful musculature and the hardness in his eyes.

Luncheon was daintily served by Melleah, and Dr Crevasse handed Heidi her bafto, explaining that she customarily dined in the nude, to avoid staining its exquisite fabric. Butter dribbled down Dr Crevasse's breasts and belly as she chewed her lobster, and she indicated that Lise could lick up the hot droplets. Some of the melted butter splattered Dr Crevasse's pubis, and Lise licked those with particular care, daring to flick her mistress's prominent clitoris with her tongue-tip. Dr Crevasse made no sound, either of approval or disapproval, but her buttocks shifted and her thighs parted. Lise's lips kissed the little gold locket fastening her mistress's cunt, as though to remind Dr Crevasse that her own cunt held its key. Dr Crevasse smiled, and her fingers crept to her clitty, holding a lobster claw, with hot flesh peeping from the broiled shell. Touching her nubbin with the lobster-meat, the nude black woman masturbated. She instructed Melleah to use the hardest baobab rod from the rack; Melleah curtsied, and selected a gnarled, but long and whippy, cane.

Vip! Titzi's caning began.

Melleah caned her bare bum very hard; she slashed a vivid pink weal, right across the central fesses, then another, on top buttock, by the base of her spine, then one each to the haunches, which made a dry, slapping sound, and two more strokes to the soft underflesh of the thigh-tops. At the second stroke, the girl's cleft tightened. At the third, it tightened again, harder. The cleft tightened before the fourth, anticipating it, and after the fifth, she was clenching and unclenching, repeatedly, with her brow knotted in pain. There were intervals of six seconds between each stroke. Titzi made no noise, except for a soft choking in her throat at the sixth cut between her thighs, where a bright rivulet of come seeped from her jerking cunt lips. Lise shivered, as her tongue licked butter from her mistress's pubic mound, but could not help watching with mouth slack. Strokes to the thin skin of the haunches and top bum were the most painful and left the longest welts. Dr Crevasse dipped her lobster claw in her wet cunt, until it was slopped with her come, then popped the morsel of sauced meat in her mouth. Ripping another chunk of flesh from the lobster, she wanked her clit with it.

Melleah paused for exactly a minute. Then the second set of six began, caning exactly the same weals. Titzi did not cry, or even moan, but her whole body trembled. Tears streamed in silence down her face, matching the come that oiled her thigh-tops and soaked the swollen lips of her gash, with its clitty peeping hard and extruded from the cunt-folds. By the end of the second set, her welts were deep red. By the third, they were dark crimson bruises, deepening to welts. The other two slaves watched, cringing, as they awaited their beatings. Lise's cunt was juicing heavily, and she longed to masturbate, despite the ominous bulk of the birching table. Its surface was polished to a gleam, like the copper clamps for the victim's wrists and ankles at each corner, and it reflected the bottoms of the girls about to be flogged: four moons in a row.

At the twentieth stroke, Titzi's proud body went limp. She had fainted. At once, Afgoi doused her in cold water, and the caning continued. Now her raw buttocks were shiny wet, and a cane hurt twice as hard on bare skin. Afgoi grinned, showing white teeth, and his cock stirred beneath the loinstring. Titzi's cane welts were bruising purple, and her skin was mottled with puffy ridges. Titzi began to whimper, and her gasps grew louder, until she had taken five sets, a full thirty canestrokes, on her twitching, wealed bare bum. Afgoi's penis rose to full height and burst from his loinstring. At a nod from Dr Crevasse, he straddled Titzi, and pushed his swollen glans between her arse-cheeks. She howled, then sobbed violently, as he rammed the shaft of his massive black cock all the way into her anal elastic, grunting as his peehole struck her arse root. Afgoi began to bugger her hard, reaching down to wank her clitty, as his giant tool rammed her bumhole. Titzi jerked and squealed in tearful protest, but her come gushed in torrents from her swollen gash. After two minutes, she squealed in a powerful orgasm, and Afgoi at once withdrew from her anus, unspermed. She was released, and stood unsteadily, wiping the tears that streamed from her eyes. Her bottom globes were corrugated in dark welts, and her anus bud was raw and red.

The second girl was Sutra. She, too, was given thirty strokes of the cane on her bare buttocks, and took the punishment with placid resignation. Throughout the punishment, Dr Crevasse wanked her clit, which had swelled to full erection, using pieces of lobster meat, or else the shell itself, and always dipping the fragment into her gushing cunt juice before eating it, while Lise licked the come that glistened on her mistress's thighs. Dr Crevasse widened her thighs still further, and clasped Lise's head to her wet gash, so that she squinted, to see her friend flogged. Sutra screwed her eyes and clenched her buttocks tight, with her face a rictus of pain, until she had been caned to thirty. She took Afgoi's immediate buggery with every sign of enjoyment, and parted her thighs as wide as she could, for his masturbation of her clitty. It did not take long for her to cry out in an orgasm of joyous relief. She was released, smiling ruefully, and exhaled loudly, as though she had been holding her breath all the time. Her bare bottom was corrugated purple.

'Sutra deserts,' sighed Dr Crevasse, still wanking her clit. 'Corporal Lavoisier permits Titzi to go in search of her; when Titzi fails to return, Corporal Lavoisier goes to seek her; when the corporal does not return, *I* am put to the trouble of making a telephone call! Masturbate, if you wish, slaves, for I dare say your fantasies of revenge have come true.'

Lise's fingers delved beneath her loinstring and seized her clit, which she began to wank off vigorously. Heidi joined her, coyly pushing her fingers into her slit, but masturbating just as hard. The third girl was Corporal Lavoisier, who scowled at the black dominatrix, as she was strapped upright into the whipping frame. The frame was gallows-size, with clamps at each corner for ankles and wrists. In addition, a bar jutted at the centre of the frame, pushing on the victim's waist, and forcing her buttocks to protrude as a target for the cane, with her feet painfully balanced on the tips of her toes. Melleah first flogged her back with a whip of nine tongues, each a metre long. The corporal's nude body was rocked by each lash, but her clamps restrained her from falling forward. Nine vicious welts appeared on her back at each stroke of the thongs. After ten strokes, her back was raw and etched with deep weals. Her spine and ribcage stood out stark beneath the whipped, puffy skin.

Leaving the corporal dangling, sobbing, in the frame, Melleah began to cane her bare arse-globes. This time, there was no minute's pause between the sets of six strokes. Thirty strokes were delivered at intervals of six seconds, without a break. The woman's squirming became frantic. While she seemed to have taken her whipping quite calmly, the flogging of her buttocks maddened her, and she gasped and whimpered. Her tiptoes danced, the soles of her feet clenching and wrinkling at each stroke of the cane, just like the livid, whipped buttocks. At the twenty-seventh stroke, she pissed herself. A jet of golden liquid steamed from her spread cunt, flowing down her thighs and calves, and puddling the floor. Seeing this, Dr Crevasse masturbated faster and more gleefully.

'Give the bitch an extra ten strokes for foulness,' she murmured.

Corporal Lavoisier grimaced, and she gasped as Melleah continued the caning after the thirtieth stroke. At thirty-five, she screamed, full from her throat. Dr Crevasse's finger was a blur as she masturbated and come flowed from her swollen gash, almost too fast for Lise to lap and swallow her mistress's cunt-fluid, as she herself wanked off, sopping her frilly skirt and loinstring with her flowing hot come. Heidi's face was pink, her hand under the waistband of her tutu, and wanking hard. Suddenly, Lise's tongue pushed her mistress's finger out of the way, and found the erect clitoris, big as a walnut, in its fleshy den. Lise began to nibble her mistress's clitoris, and Dr Crevasse moaned, as the girl's mouth fastened to kiss her soaking cunt.

The final, fortieth stroke lashed the naked corporal; Dr Crevasse's belly contracted and heaved, as Lise tongued her to an orgasm which was utterly silent. Lise brought herself off, drenching her string knicker in come, and had to bite her lip to avoid crying out. Heidi wanked to orgasm at the same time, and whimpered softly, with streams of come glazing her fishnet black stockings. The corporal was buggered strongly for three minutes, then wanked to orgasm by Afgoi, and released, sobbing and clutching her wealed derrière, her welts darker than her raw cunt-gash. Afgoi approached his mistress, his penis raw and throbbing, greased from the bumholes of the three buggered girls. Melleah grasped his glans, and rubbed it softly, until, in moments, creamy spunk spurted in a powerful jet over Dr Crevasse's face and bare breasts. Lise licked the sperm, where it flowed down the black woman's quivering bare belly and over her cunt-mound, and her spunk-creamed tongue found her mistress's throbbing clitty. Lise swallowed the come that flowed uncontrollably from the quivering, slimed pouch, with her lips caressing the locket jangling over the swollen gash flaps. After three flicks of Lise's tongue to her clit, Dr Crevasse orgasmed again, this time crying, once, in a loud wail.

'I intend to birch you even harder, now, Lise,' panted Dr Crevasse.

'But why, Mistress?'

'Because you made me come so sweetly and lose control.'

'O! Yes, Mistress,' Lise gasped. 'Please – you had Sutra and Titzi chastised for desertion, which I understand. But why Corporal Lavoisier?'

'Didn't seeing her bare bum squirm make your cunt wet?'

'O, I did wank off in the Hole, thinking of her and Titzi's bums caned! But I still don't see why Lavoisier was caned *and* whipped.'

'Because she was cruel to you, Lise. *Only S'Ibaa is allowed to be cruel to you.* Now, smooth your dress and walk to the birching table.'

Lise rose, and obeyed.

9

Slave Games

Lise Gallard, slave of S'Ibaa, lay face down on the wood, scratching her breasts and cunt mound. Her frilly maid's uniform was pinned up to expose her bare buttocks for birching, and her sussie straps were unfastened, so that both her arse-globes shone pale and untrammelled. Afgoi and Melleah took her by arms and legs, splaying her in an X. Her wrists and ankles were tightly fastened in the copper clamps at each corner of the birching table, stretching her body so that she groaned. A padded cushion, pushed under her pubis, raised her buttocks for her birching and stretched her limbs still further. Dr Crevasse's hands stroked her bare bum-cheeks and cleft. A finger poked all the way into her pussy, and emerged wet. The oiled finger slid into Lise's exposed anus, to a depth of her fingernail. Lise shuddered and clenched her hole, then gasped, as a bucket of freezing water drenched her bare bum.

'You'll be birched on the wet, Lise, for maximum smarting. I intend to award extra punishment for making me come. Perhaps it won't be a punishment and you'll enjoy it, along with your birching of four dozen.'

'Four *dozen* . . .? O! Yes, Mistress . . .'

She squealed as Melleah rammed a massive dildo into her anus, lubricated with Lise's own come. The shaft of gnarled baobab wood sank right to her root, fully stretching her anal elastic. She grimaced at the slave-girl holding the dildo by a long handle.

'Melleah will bum-fuck you with one thrust of the knob for each stroke of the birch, Lise,' said Dr Crevasse. 'Get ready.'

She lifted the birch. It crackled and whispered in the air, like flower petals, although the instrument comprised thirty pickled rods. Dr Crevasse smiled at Lise's bare bottom, stretched helpless before her, and, as she lifted the flogging instrument, come glistened on her cunt lips and thighs. She positioned herself well back from the birching table, and her arm rose, the tips of the birch almost touching the ceiling. The birch whistled.

Crack!

'*Ahhh!*'

The twigs struck Lise's naked flesh and she screamed.

'Uhhh ... O! O!' she grunted at once, as Melleah plunged the tool against the root of her anus.

'Do I have to gag you with a brank?' asked Dr Crevasse sympathetically. 'I hope not. It would not be pleasant for you.'

'No ... no, thank you, Mistress,' Lise sobbed.

The dildo slithered from her anus, but its tip remained a finger's breadth inside her hole. The birch cracked again, on her naked rump. Lise's cleft twitched and clenched, but she made no sound, other than a choked sob. She gasped again at the dildo's second thrust in her anal shaft.

'Good girl,' said Dr Crevasse.

Crack!

The birch slashed her quivering bare bum again, followed by a savage push to her root.

'You'll be glad to hear,' Dr Crevasse said, panting a little, 'that we'll take a minute's pause after each set of twelve.'

'Thank you, Mistress,' Lise gasped, her voice hoarse.

The birch whipped her naked buttocks three more times; a delicate pattern of pink stripes now mottled the pure white skin. Dr Crevasse licked her lips, as both globes of Lise's birched croup squirmed with equal vigour. The set carried on to the twelfth stroke, which had Lise's skin now a delicate shade of crimson all over the nates. She shuddered, groaned and panted, clenching her buttocks. But each squirm only drove the walls of her anus harder against the invading dildo. Melleah wanked herself as she buggered the flogged girl, with the baobab shaft swallowed rhythmically by the arse-cleft between Lise's threshing fesses, to emerge shining and greased from the elastic anal tube.

Then, the second set. Lise was sobbing and her buttocks squirmed uncontrollably. As the twentieth swish of the birch striped her bare, now shuddering, buttocks, Dr Crevasse said that she should reach a plateau of tolerance soon, where the birch would seem less painful.

'I think I've reached it, Mistress,' Lise said. 'O, it smarts so! But I'm sure I can take it.'

Dr Crevasse laughed, her voice a tinkle of sweet bells.

'Why, you've no choice, Lise.'

A vertical birch stroke lashed Lise right on her anus and cunt lips, and made her jerk like a marionette. Melleah followed the stroke with a powerful thrust of the dildo, which she held in the girl's anus, twisting it like a screwdriver until Lise's hips writhed. The birching table gleamed with the pool of juice which seeped from the lips of her soaking, swollen cunt; Lise's clit rubbed stiff against the wet belly-pad.

'Uhh ... uhhh ...' she groaned. 'Again, please. Again ... *harder.*'

'Delirious,' said Melleah.

'No,' said Dr Crevasse, her own cunt dripping come, 'a willing slave.'

Her birching resumed, hard, and at each lash, the dildo corkscrewed her anus. Though Lise's naked buttocks squirmed as each stroke deepened her tracery of bum-welts, the flow of her cunt oil quickened. After the forty-seventh cut of the birch, and Melleah's ramming her anus with the tool, Dr Crevasse touched Lise's stiff clitty, just once. The girl screamed again, this time in an orgasm that shook her body in spasms as her cunt gushed oily come. As she was spasming, Dr Crevasse delivered the forty-eighth stroke, and Melleah rammed the dildo, still hot and greasy from Lise's anus, into Dr Crevasse's own cunt. This time, Dr Crevasse panted for a full minute as she orgasmed, her gasps chorused by Melleah, who thumbed her swollen clitoris and climaxed, with come streaming on her twitching thighs as though in obeisance to her mistress.

'Happily, that was only your *first* birching,' said Lise's new mistress.

'Inmates aren't birched at Fort Lafresne,' said Melleah, 'but you are no longer inmates. You are slaves of S'Ibaa's servant, Dr Crevasse. Neither do inmates receive enriching *gobaad* mud in their weals and crevices – bum mud, we call it. The weals of the birch sheaves, brought from so far, have long served to adorn and enrich the perfect croups of the S'Ibaya ... like the mud spewed from the boiling volcanic crevice, which S'Ibaa herself called the Earth Cunt. S'Ibayans believe a woman's come is the lava from the earth of her body, and whip-weals on bare buttocks are the smiles of mountains to the sky.'

Lise lay naked on her belly, in the slave-girls' quarters, while Melleah, bare-breasted over a pleated white skirt, applied pungent gluteal ointment to the wealed globes of Lise's arse. She masturbated as she massaged Lise's naked bottom; beside her, Heidi lay, wearing only her loinstring, with the thong drawn back to reveal wet cunt lips. Smiling shyly, she too masturbated, her eyelashes fluttering like the soft twitches of Lise's bare bum. On the palliasses opposite, the nude bodies of Sutra, Titzi and Corporal Lavoisier, glowing with weals, writhed in hobbles, tit-vices and cunt-clamps. Although the cunts of all three females glistened with come and their eyes feasted hungrily on Lise's bare arse, their restraints prevented them from masturbating. Heidi, promised a birching less severe than Lise's, smiled dreamily as she wanked off, and rubbed her bare bum as though the birch-welts were already on her. The slave-girl Melleah lazily flicked her engorged clitoris, pausing to smear her crevice and anus pucker with her own come, for her index finger to slide easily on her oiled perineum, for penetration of both cunt and bumhole.

'It hurts dreadfully, you know,' said Lise. 'Melleah! I know you wanked when you were buggering me – and *that* hurt, *too*! – and now you're wanking again? As for you, Heidi, how can you?'

'Mmm . . .' said Heidi. 'I had a lovely wank, watching your bum wriggle. I hope you'll pay me the same compliment when I am strapped down for birching. Then I'll have Melleah's hands on *my* arse! Look at her clit! So big, like the doctor's, an inch at least. I know female body-builders get big clits, but this is different. O, I want mine to be . . . like a Djibouti girl's! Don't you want to wank off with us, Lise?'

'Really! I . . . mmm, Melleah, don't stop.'

Melleah's fingers reached away from the birch-welts, stroking Lise's perineum, now shining with an increasing seep of come from her naked cunt lips. Melleah inserted a finger, wet from her own cunt, into Lise's slit, and probed her gash until only her knuckle was visible. Her thumb slid from her own swollen clitty, under Lise's belly, to her cunt-hillock. Lise shivered; her slit-flaps quivered, and gushed come.

'O, Melleah,' she whispered. 'Wank me. You know I want it . . .'

Her finger joined Melleah's in wanking her extruded stiff nubbin.

'Harder,' she moaned. 'Fist-fuck me, Melleah . . .'

Melleah balled her fist and, without ceasing to anoint Lise's weals, rammed it into Lise's clutching cunt-walls. Lise reached to grasp Melleah's own clitty, which she took between thumb and forefinger, rubbing the huge extruded button, as the ebony slave-girl punched Lise's cunt vigorously, making the girl writhe, part her thighs fully, and thrust up her birched arse. Still wanking her own clit, Heidi poked one come-oiled finger into Lise's anus, then another, and finally, she was finger-fucking Lise's squirming bum, with three fingers plunged right to the knuckle. Facing the masturbatrixes, Sutra managed to wriggle, so that her quim touched Titzi's, and began to rub her come-filled gash against the German girl's. Titzi moaned in faint

130

protest, but her hillock thrust to meet Sutra's, and soon the two girls were gamahuching, with their stiff clitties slapping each other, peeping like wet tongues from the fleshy cunt lips.

'Mistress will birch all the new slaves in due course,' said Melleah. 'Including the deserters, when their arses have recovered from my cane.'

'Lavoisier, Sutra and Titzi are new slaves?' Lise gasped.

'Of course,' said Melleah.

'Lise,' Heidi hissed, 'we mustn't be caught talking.'

'In slave-girls' quarters, talking is permitted,' Melleah said. 'Dr Crevasse likes us to intrigue, so that she can punish us for it.'

Her knuckles were slimed with Lise's come, as her fist slapped in and out of gash, with Heidi vigorously penetrating her anus. All three girls wanked their swollen nubbins, and Sutra and Titzi writhed in tribal dance, their shackles jangling as their bare clits smacked and slapped. Corporal Lavoisier glowered, her cunt gushing, and the nipples of her massive teats hugely erect, yet unable to pleasure herself.

'With you as her informant, no doubt,' said Lise. 'God, yes! O! It's fabulous! Do me harder! Both of you . . .'

'Of course I inform,' said Melleah. 'We all do. Damara, too.'

'And if we are caught masturbating?' Heidi gasped, the intensity of her cunt-wank, and fingering of Lise's anus, giving scant hint that she cared.

'O, God! Ah! Yes . . . I'm going to come!' Lise cried.

Sutra's buttocks squirmed as her clit rammed Titzi's, penetrating the upper folds of her vaginal skin. Their bare mounds slapped, slimy with sweat and come; both gamahuching girls had flowing cunts and bellies quivering in the approach of orgasm. Heidi took her fingers from her clit, and daubed bum-mud on her teats, nipples and on the nubbin itself. Melleah gulped and rubbed her erect clitoris hard out from her cunt, wedging the shiny nubbin between Lise's big and second toe, and jerking her ebony buttocks in the motions of fucking. The skin between Lise's toes was

131

encrusted with viscous cheesy scum, which soon clung to the erect clitty of the toe-fucking black girl.

Melleah began to gurgle in a strange ululation, and flecks of foam appeared at her lips. She bent suddenly, arching her back in an almost perfect U, and licked the cheese from Lise's feet, her clitty still rubbing between the toes, and her mouth a hair's breadth from her own clitoris. When she had licked Lise's toes clean, taking each digit wholly into her mouth, she pressed her mouth to her own cunt lips, sucking her clitoris, and swallowing her own come, mixed with Lise's toe-cheese. Rising, she tongued Lise's clit, lapping the come flowing from her cunt, and Lise cried that she could not hold back: steaming golden piss squirted from her gash, mingling with her cunt oil, and spraying Melleah's face in pee. The black slave-girl's tongue danced, slurping every droplet of Lise's fluid.

'O!' moaned Heidi, her own fingers bathed in come, and her fist-fucking hand slimy with Lise's anal grease. '*Ohhh . . .*'

She too pissed herself before moaning in orgasm. Sutra made Titzi come first before giving in to her own pleasure, and Lise came at the same time as Melleah's ululations rose to a thin shriek of ecstasy.

'Female self-pleasure,' gasped the black girl, 'is a rite sacred to the S'Ibaya. If you serve Mistress well, you may be privileged to learn it . . .'

Dr Crevasse now had eleven slaves, with the arrival of Lise, Heidi, Titzi, Sutra and the disgraced ex-Corporal Lavoisier. Three of the six existing slaves were Somali, S'Ibayan girls like Melleah, and the others were failed Legion deserters. The Somalis were Deydey, Guestir and Xiddigta, which, the dark-eyed S'Ibaya girl was fond of explaining, meant 'star'. She was tall and lithe, her firm plums of croup and teats hard and almost boyish, and with a large fleshy gash and extruded clit in sensuous counterpart. The black girls talked little, but smiled with dazzling pearl teeth; immodest, they stripped off without hesitation, before flinging their bare bodies on palliasses, usually with buttocks upward, to coyly show the marks of recent canings, etched deep in their silky chocolate bum-skin.

The deserters were less demonstrative – polite, rather than sullen – but still took a rueful pride in exhibiting their whipmarked skin. They were Toyo, an elfin but whip-muscled Japanese girl, her skin still translucent and white despite the desert sun; Loosje, an Afrikaner girl from Witwatersrand, and almost the image of Titzi; Kee, a Nigerian, whose magnificent jet-black croup was almost the equal of Dr Crevasse's. All were completely shaven, including scalp and pubis, and all had armoires crammed with sensuous garments and wigs, for every part of the body. It was the custom for all the slaves to remain nude in their quarters, ready to dress promptly in whatever costume their mistress's whim dictated. The message, summoning one or several girls to service, or arbitrary punishment, came via Afgoi, clad only in a loinstring, on which every girl's eye fastened: if his message was a summons to flogging, then his penis would be uncoiled and bulging in his thong.

Every slave-girl expected to receive, or administer, daily canings or whippings, as well as regular naked birchings. Although Melleah assumed a directing role in the more bizarre ceremonies, her bare bottom squirmed under as many, and just as severe, canings as the other girls'. On the square at Fort Lafresne, now a shimmering blur in the near distance, the girls were mere brutes, naked for the lash. Dr Crevasse transformed them as creatures of her fantasy, for punishments exquisitely more terrible, yet appealing in their whimsy. The slave-girls appeared before their mistress dressed as nurses, soldiers, schoolgirls, or else bound in rubber, leather, clamps and pins, even wearing gasmasks. The roles of punisher and victim changed at random: once, Lise toiled in humiliating bondage of rubber, mask and shackles, pitting dates under the sun, and obliged to wank off to moisten each date with her own come, while Sutra, her masturbating partner of the night before, whipped her bare bum raw. Then Lise dined nude beside Dr Crevasse, as Titzi, in black clinging leather and mask, whipped

Sutra's bare back and buttocks with a scourge, striping her naked flesh, until she had swallowed every one of the come-soaked dates. At the same time, Loosje bent over in schoolgirl's knickers and stockings, lowering her knickers to take a dozen on the bare from Toyo, in a rubber harness, with her nipples and cunt flaps tightly clamped, and Lavoisier, nude but for a gasmask and strapped arse-dildo, squirmed under Melleah's cane, while the black girl wanked herself into a silver come pot.

Dr Crevasse's chosen dinner companion had to wank vigorously throughout her meal, and drip her come into a come pot, from which all the slaves swallowed. If any caned girl had pissed herself under punishment, her pee, mixed with the come dripped from her own gash, would join the fluid in the pot. Lise frequently took her punishment bent over, with stockings ripped by the cane, and knickers shredded, dressed in proper Legion nurse's uniform. She pleased Dr Crevasse by pissing herself copiously, soaking her stockings, which were then torn off and wadded in her mouth, to gag her for an extra dozen on the bare.

Sometimes bare-breasted Damara, who acted as messenger between Dr Crevasse and the nurse-general, would join them, still in her fluttering white skirt, and making it flutter even more to reveal her bare bum and come-soaked pubis, as she caned unlucky slave-girls. Afgoi would bugger girls in gasmasks and handcuffs, the male slave standing with the girl perched on his tool, and his teeth chewing her bare nipples; or from behind, the crouching girl's hands free to wank, and her face immersed in a chamberpot full of pee and her own come; or even upside down, the girl's ankles held above Afgoi's buttocks, with his cock bent to take her anally, and one or two more slaves in nurse's or schoolgirl's uniform caning her cunt and breasts, while a third slave, nude, squatted on the victim's face and peed into her nose and mouth, while drinking the buggered girl's come flowing down her belly from her caned cunt. Afgoi would spurt on Dr Crevasse's command, usually in her own anus, which she presented stretched over the back of her dining-throne, and usually took buggery while caning either Lise's or Titzi's bare bum.

When Afgoi was slow in spurting his cream, Dr Crevasse stood him before the slave-girls, and caned him standing up. Arching his spine, Afgoi bent down and took the glans of his engorged cock into his own mouth, sucking himself off until he spurted cream down his balls. Lise, rubbing her bum after a particularly vicious fifteen strokes from Heidi, was ordered to lick Afgoi's spunk from his balls and swallow it. The shuddering of Afgoi's buttocks under cane made his spunk-drops spray over Lise's erect nipples, and splatter her teat-flesh, and when Afgoi's balls were licked clean of spunk, she lowered her head, delighted to find she could easily lick her own titties clean, and tit-wank herself by taking her engorged nips in her mouth, tonguing her erect buds to orgasm, with only a few frot-strokes of her clitty.

Once, a face slid under Lise's bum and got its tongue an inch into her anus, before beginning to drink from the channel of copious come, that flowed in the valley of Lise's perineum. The girl wanked herself vigorously, and gurgled in orgasm, as she swallowed every drop of Lise's cunt juice, even sucking back the come which her tongue had pushed into Lise's bumhole. The come pot beneath Lise's loins was empty, and that earnt her a caning of a dozen on bare from Afgoi, eager to avenge his own humiliation, and follow the caning with a penetration of Lise's as yet unbuggered anus; the intruder was Titzi.

'That was unfair,' Lise gasped, as she touched toes and squirmed at the first stinger from Afgoi's baobab rod, in the already raw welts of her caned bare bum. 'O! O! *Ouch*! God ... it *hurts*! I owe you a proper whipping for that, Titzi, one day ... just the two of us.'

Titzi leered, licking the last droplets of Lise's come from her lips, as the dozen strokes shook her bare arse, and smiled broadly, wanking herself copiously into her own come pot; Lise groaned, as Afgoi's newly erect cock slid between her clenched fesses, forcing open her bum-elastic. His glans slammed Lise's anal root; as her wealed bottom shook under Afgoi's buggery, all other slave-girls knelt at Dr Crevasse's feet, licking her come from her ankles as it flowed from her wanked cunt, and masturbating themselves, so that their pots brimmed with come.

Often, Damara and Melleah wheeled a hospital operating table into the chamber. Both girls glistened, Melleah's loinstring and Damara's white skirt both sodden with sweat. Tell-tale come gleamed on their thighs, and Dr Crevasse awarded them a dozen cuts of the baobab cane on the bare, for dawdling to wank on their mission from Fort Lafresne! Bare bums puce, the two caned girls joined slave-girls above the operating table, with canes raised. To the table was strapped a female figure entirely swathed in thin white latex bandages: the slave-girls caned the female in rubber, until every shred of latex had been whipped from her body, and only then would her decreed chastisement of a birching on the bare teats and buttocks take place, with swishes of the birch, until the instrument was denuded. The woman's head was encased in a metal diver's helmet with opaque glass, and as the girls flogged the trussed body, the latex covering gradually peeled until skin was revealed; the belly, bum and teats already wealed from their flogging under latex. Dr Crevasse applied a birching of, alternately, six swishes to the buttocks, then, with Guestir, Kee, Toyo and Titzi turning the naked female over, on her breasts. After this process was repeated six times, the birching was complete.

Dr Crevasse raised her leg to the birched female's cunt, with her toes catching the swollen clitoris. Damara rammed a long-handled baobab shaft up the anus, as Melleah held the buttocks apart, and, pirouetting like a ballerina, Dr Crevasse kicked the cunt until the lips were swollen and bruised and come flowed in a steady stream, soaking the canvas table. As Dr Crevasse bit the engorged clitty, the nude victim screamed, writhing in a powerful orgasm, and pissed herself, while the slaves masturbated, dripping come over her. This woman was Nurse-General Jacqueline Frachon . . .

The come pots were borne away either by Damara or Melleah, to the chamber where Dr Crevasse bathed daily in a tub of girl-come mixed with pee and *gobaad* mud. In slaves' quarters, Melleah's hands were always soothing with bum-mud, as those girls with beaten buttocks lay face down on their palliasses, to await anointment, and the slave-girls crooned in their slippery wanks, whispering of the next day's rituals of costume, slavery and the lash. There was no calendar; there was no time. The slave-girls lived for the cane, for the anointing of their weals, and for wanking off, with their pee and come collected in pots, taken away, or drunk by the girls still masturbating. If masturbation was tolerated at Fort Lafresne, Dr Crevasse frowned at its neglect. Even Lavoisier seemed to forget she had once been a corporal. Lise was detailed to cane her a dozen on the bare, the ex-corporal bewigged in blonde, tied in hempen ropes and gasmasked; after her bum was crimson from the beating, in pretty contrast to her tan flesh and the bright yellow ropes, now sodden with her sweat and come, Lise asked her why she had deserted.

'Foolishness,' gasped ex-Corporal Lavoisier.

Loosje was next in line for a beating from Lise's cane, with Lise herself nude but for a schoolgirl's pigtail wig, fluffy white socks, ox-yoke and rubber harness, and her clitoris clamped in a long-handled vice, which Dr Crevasse could squeeze to masturbate her as she caned.

Vip! Vip! Vip!

Lise's strokes were hard but unsteady as she thrashed the girl's bare arse, taking care to cut her right up the bum-cleft and make her squirm.

'Hurry and do me, Lise, you bitch!' hissed Heidi, already bent over with buttocks bared, and wanking as she watched Loosje's arse squirm.

Heidi too was dressed as a schoolgirl, her anus and cunt penetrated by the double prongs of a baobab dildo, glistening with come, as she wanked impatiently. Dr Crevasse masturbated on her throne, sitting on Afgoi's lap, with his tool trapped in her anus, while she kneaded her erect nipples and thumbed her clitty, with three fingers sunk in her vulva. The kneeling Nigerian and Japanese girls licked come from her feet, their naked rumps caned by Damara, who herself wanked off so hard, that her come stained the white dress and soaked the pleats to limpness.

'*Ach! O! O!*' Loosje squealed, her flaxen wig fluttering and her giant blonde pube-wig soaking in her cunt juice. 'Who could think of deserting? Isn't *this* what we really joined the Legion for?'

Vip! Vip! Vip! Vip!

Loosje's bare bum clenched, squirming as she jerked under Lise's cane. Come flowed from her cunt and her belly began to heave, as piss sprayed from her swollen cunt lips at the onset of her spasm. Lise's clit was pinched harder and faster by Dr Crevasse's vice, and, as she caned Loosje the last stinger on the blackened left haunch, she too pissed, her cunt spurting golden steam, drenching Loosje's bum and splattering Heidi's eager mouth.

Vip!

'*Yes . . .*' moaned Loosje, climaxing, as Lise's wet cunt soaked her in piss and come, and Heidi moaned too, wanking to a gasping orgasm.

Lise cried out, as Dr Crevasse squeezed her clit-vice, and she too came, before Heidi unsteadily took position for the caning she craved . . .

One night, Melleah was morose. Damara had delivered an envelope sealed in wax; Melleah, Toyo, Damara and the doctor had set off across the desert, the slave-girls alternately carrying Dr Crevasse in piggy-back, and Damara whipping them on: not towards Fort Lafresne, but to the male prison.

'Dr Crevasse is lesbian,' Melleah told Lise, as she showed the welts from Damara's cane on her bare bum. 'Despite, or because of, loving buggery, she resents males. Today, one of the male prisoners was whipped – Gilles, the pilot. He became intimate with a prisoner, and his punishment was caning, on the bare. Dr Crevasse is jealous. She has male slaves for anal sex, but her cunt is virgin.'

'So, she whipped Gilles in anger?'

Lise and Heidi masturbated, listening.

'Damara and I whipped Gilles,' said Melleah serenely. 'I cannot say I disliked seeing his bare arse redden, nor that

I failed to wank off as I beat him. He was whipped round the yard, riding the panther, which means that his erect tool was imprisoned in Dr Crevasse's anus. She pranced the square, forcing him to stumble behind her, as Damara and I caned him, until he spurted in her arse, and his cock softened and freed itself.'

'How many strokes?' said Titzi, licking her lips.

'One hundred and twenty-one,' said Melleah. 'Dr Crevasse made Damara suck his spunk before his flogging. Her games can be cruel, especially to her favourites. You see her treatment of Nurse-General Frachon, whose every whipping is more degrading. Frachon submits to her as a lesbian, and to a true lesbian like our mistress, there is no brute so contemptible as a submissive lesbian. I believe she wants you, especially, to submit, Lise.'

'And I believe I will.'

All the palliassed slave-girls were now wanking off.

'It means she wants to break you: force you to desert, by her cruelty,' said Melleah. 'You, Lise, have been birched four times, but the other newcomers only once. You receive correspondingly larger anointments of bum-mud, and your arse has been enhanced.'

Without ceasing to wank her distended clitty, Lise blushed, and rubbed her bare bottom, now swelling more ripely than ever. Her thighs were soaked in cunt oil and the come dripped so fast from her gash that it frothed slightly on its descent to her come pot.

'You are our heaviest comer, Lise,' Melleah continued, 'and your arse is riper by almost two centimetres. Mistress will whip you harder and harder, until you break and cannot endure it. The goddess S'Ibaa dictates submission to *ordeal*.'

She shivered.

'You, Lise, will be disciplined to the utmost, birched without cease, until you worship the female arse, and will truly be S'Ibaa's slave.'

'Just because my bum's the biggest?' snorted Lise. 'She said something about finishing school to me . . .'

'Me, too!' said Titzi.

Melleah laughed.

'Dr Crevasse likes to play games,' she said. 'The finishing school of the S'Ibaya is not the Legion's! I am S'Ibaya, like Damara and Afgoi, and may possess no desire other than S'Ibaa's. But you, soldier girls of the Legion? What are your desires? Don't forget I am Mistress's spy . . .'

She smiled, and her fingers caressed her nubbin, making her cunt brim with come. Ex-corporal Lavoisier wished to regain her rank, and recommence caning 'inmate scum'. Djiboutian Guestir shyly admitted that she wished to become admitted to the S'Ibaya tribe. Lise described in sadistic detail her planned revenge on Odette and Thierry, who had betrayed her, obliging her to enrol in the Legion, and to 'the fucking French' in general. Kee, Loosje and the others had similar ambitions, and wanked harder as Lise described how her Legion training could make her betrayers suffer exquisitely. Heidi, almost apologetically, said she was happy. Sutra said she wanted to desert again, but couldn't go it alone. Titzi, pressed, admitted that she, too, had been unable to achieve her goal: to find her mentor, Waltraut, who was in Djibouti, and that meant finding the cave of the S'Ibaya and the world's most glorious arses. Her eyes flashed.

'To have the ripest arse!' she cried, wanking vigorously, as she gazed at Lise's bare fesses. '*I* want to be supreme! I have appeared in magazines and films, in Germany, for connoisseurs of arse-worship. I want Waltraut to photograph me alone! My arse, the perfect arse.'

Sutra glowered.

'No wonder Lavoisier caught us so easily,' she said. 'Then stopped to drool over your bum, until all three of us were deserters!'

The slave-girls presented their bare buttocks to each other, masturbating eagerly, with fingers probing comegreased bumholes. Titzi stroked her own arse-globes, and was the first to come; Melleah followed, and then every slave-girl moaned in climax, finger-fucking both bum and streaming cunt. The tall shadow of another masturbatrix darkened the slaves' quarters, and there was a contemptuous hiss of pee, spraying the bare bums nearest to the nude body of Dr Crevasse, as she masturbated to her own orgasm. Beside her stood Dr Frahl, bearing a bundle of rubber strait-jackets, and with her hair grown longer; she wore extra decorations of rank in her pierced bare nipples, and wore snugly fitting rubber knickers in red and blue stripes. Gilles, behind her, was nude, his penis massively erect and encased in the two halves of a razor-clam shell, strapped to his organ by rings of tiny silver spikes. Damara led the gasmasked and strait-jacketed figure of Nurse-General Frachon crouching on a leash and twitching frantically. Her breasts and bottom were bare under the jacket which pinched her waist to a shard, and her nipples were domed in glass jars full of beetles. Her anus and cunt were taped shut. Buttocks and teats were pink with canemarks.

'A pretty sight,' Dr Crevasse said, 'which will be rewarded at dawn. Disloyal talk of desertion! As Melleah observed, S'Ibaa decrees ordeal. Scarring of females appeases the heavens, who have scarred our land.'

'*Ohh* . . .!'

Guestir, Deydey, Toyo, Loosje, Lavoisier, Kee, Heidi and Melleah – all the slave-girls except for Sutra, Lise, Titzi and Xiddigta – pissed themselves at once, their faces sunk in fear, as steaming jets of piss made their brimming come pots overflow.

'In reverence of S'Ibaa,' said Dr Crevasse, 'Nurse-General Frachon has her bumhole and cunt taped full of sandworms. Very itchy, though not so much as the baby scorpions they resemble, and which shall join them tomorrow. Willing compliance pleases the goddess: Jacqui's bare arse shall be privileged to denude nine birches, as will the four girls who failed to piss themselves on my entry, which I deem lacking in awe. First, Gilles shall attend to your anal chambers. As you see, his cock is enhanced by a Red Sea crust, which shall be most stimulating as he buggers each of you in turn. The anklets, please, Melleah.'

Trembling, Lise, Titzi, Xiddigta and Sutra stood, as Melleah fastened their ankles in hobble bars, through which she threaded a chain. The black girl's cunt juiced openly, and she smiled at the captives with wide lips and bright eyes, which clouded at Dr Crevasse's next words:

'The girls who did piss themselves I deem lacking in respect, so he shall bugger them also.'

'You have tricked us all . . . *Mistress*!' Lise spat.

'Yes, I enjoy tricks.'

Neither Drs Crevasse nor Frahl, Damara nor Gilles, made any move.

'My dining-room is at present unoccupied, and the open French windows lead directly onto the Grand Bara, in the direction of Lac Abhe Bad, as indicated by the constellation Orion,' said Dr Crevasse languidly. 'I take it most deserters would wish to swim the lake to Ethiopia. If, for example, you chose to flee, Lise, you would be pursued by helicopter. Except that Gilles will be unavailable for pilot duties for a while, as he must bugger slave-girls. If you choose to remain, you must face ordeal.'

Dr Crevasse began a slow and voluptuous masturbation of her gaping wet cunt and extruded clitty, waggling the massive nubbin like a small penis. Come flowed on her rippling black thighs, as she spread her fesses, and Gilles, on tiptoe, thrust his shelled cock slowly up her resisting arse cavern, to the root of her anus. Dr Crevasse sighed in joy.

'Isn't it time you deserted, Lise?' she whispered, as he buggered her.

Lise Gallard led three stumbling nude girls, chained by the ankles, through the French windows, past the statue of S'Ibaa, and out onto the cooled desert sand, through the jagged phallic volcanic chimneys in the direction of Lac Abhe Bad. The sky was starlit with a gibbous moon. Lise paused, letting Titzi lead, and took one look back at Dr Crevasse's clinic and the perfectly arsed statue of S'Ibaa, in shadow but now seen from the front. Under her swelling cunt-hillock protruded a clitoris of truly unnatural dimension, far larger, even, than Dr Crevasse's own. It coiled like a sleeping snake: *the arse-goddess S'Ibaa was androgyne*. Jolted by her shackle, Lise Gallard hobbled after the bouncing bare bums of Sutra, Xiddigta and Titzi. She shuddered: she had committed the ultimate crime. She had deserted from the Legion!

'O, *fuck* the fucking French!' she gasped to the moon-scape of Djibouti.

10

Colonel Said

Xiddigta led them by the stars, westwards, to Lac Abhe
Bad. The ground was hard under a layer of powdery silver
sand, which clung to their bare feet and muffled the
clanking of the chain which shackled them. There was no
loose rock, for a hammer to break their chain; only the
jagged black volcanic chimneys perched like sentinels on
the desert of the Grand Bara. Titzi said their chain was
titanium, and nearly impossible to break.

'Cheer up,' panted Sutra, 'Xiddigta must be leading us
in the right direction. Last time, I was going round in
circles. The lake is only forty or fifty kilometres away.'

'We can't swim the lake if we are chained together,' said
Lise.

'What do we do in Ethiopia?' said Titzi. 'Four nude
girls, with no passports, or money.'

At pink dawn, their approach made a pair of gazelles
thump away in fright. There was a cluster of date palms and a
small, glinting pool: an oasis. The water was only waist deep,
and they plunged in, sinking below the surface, and filling
their bellies with the cool drinking water. The palms offered
enough shade for the girls to shelter from the scorching rays
of the rising sun, and by shaking the trees, they secured
plentiful dates to eat. Lise and Sutra burst out laughing.

'A knight in shining armour is bound to show up,' Lise
said. 'If not, we can bundle dates in palm leaves to eat, and
we should be able to make water bottles if we knot the
leaves together.'

144

Sutra scanned the desert, crossed with tracks.

'A lot of traffic passes here,' she said.

'Antelopes, hyenas, jackals,' said Titzi.

'More than that,' said Xiddigta. 'Carts and camels.'

'And some tyre tracks,' said Lise. 'Land Rovers.'

'Or Legion jeeps,' said Sutra, yawning. 'Well, the doctor dared us to desert, and we did, and now . . . O, who cares?'

'I don't think the Legon will follow us,' Lise said. 'And some of the tracks are too wide for jeeps, or Land Rovers.'

'Sand yachts,' said Xiddigta. 'There is a resort on the northern end of Lac Abhe Bad, Club V . . . something. Volcano, I suppose. The tourists might venture this far.'

'One of us must keep watch for tourists, then, while the others sleep,' said Lise, and they laughed. 'I'll go first, if you like.'

The three pissed casually, their streams evaporating as soon as they struck the sand, and Xiddigta dunged, kicking her large hard pellets away under the sand. The others coyly did the same, making a large pile, and giggling at the similarity of their dungs; all except Lise curled on the sand.

'Fifty kilometres, say, at twenty a day,' Lise said. 'Let's hope there's another oasis. I suppose we'll get to know each other. I never thought I'd be on the run, in the desert, chained to a German arse-porno goddess!'

'What?' cried Titzi, wide awake and eyes blazing.

Xiddigta clasped Titzi by the breasts, restraining her. There was a buzzing overhead, very far above them: the silvery shape of a Legion helicopter passed far to the south, and the girls cowered.

'See? Not really looking for us,' Lise said. 'Maybe that was Gilles . . .'

'They don't look for deserters,' said Xiddigta. 'They wait for us to signal them when we can't take any more. This part of the desert is called the frying pan, it's so hot.'

'Take it back!' cried Titzi. 'Porno goddess, indeed!'

'What?' said Lise. 'Hell, Titzi, you said you posed for nude magazines and films. Don't tell me you're no movie queen.'

'Only for my boyfriend,' said Titzi, pretending to sulk. 'My then boyfriend. He made videos . . .'

'Spanking videos?' asked Sutra.

'And caning,' said Titzi, solemnly. 'Bare bum, naturally. But what he really liked was to film me being caned, then fucked by other men while I fellated him or wanked him off. I was caned really hard, and fucked by six or seven, one after the other, sometimes. But I got rid of that boyfriend, as Fraülein Waltraut was so much more interesting. Men can be such prudes! He would only let his friends cunt-fuck me, not give me what I really wanted. In the bumhole, I mean. True arse-worship . . .'

Xiddigta scanned the sky, where large birds circled lazily, far overhead.

'That's what it's called!' she trilled. 'The tourist resort. *Club Vautour.*'

'Meaning, Club Go-around?' said Sutra. 'For the adventurous?'

'*Vautour* means go-around,' Lise said, 'and it is French for vulture.'

The sun rose, beating the palms above the sleeping girls. Sutra snored loudest, her breasts shaking at each throaty gurgle. Xiddigta's snores made a humming sound, like a bird's, and Titzi gasped, mumbling to herself aloud, until her dream-talk flowed, punctuated with jerks of her body.

'*Ach, ja . . .*' she moaned, hand on her spread pubis, '*im Arsch . . .*'

Bare loins and buttocks writhing in the sand, Titzi began to masturbate, her babble of German punctuated by lustful gasps and squeals. Her fingers pinched her stiffened clitty, while her arse squirmed on the fingers of her other hand, whose index and forefinger wriggled inside her anus. Her fesses closed on her two fingers like a vice, leaving only the knuckles exposed, as she finger-fucked her own bumhole.

Sutra and Xiddigta groaned in their sleep, and their own hands cupped breasts, bellies and moistening gashes. The two girls began to masturbate, as though hypnotically led by Titzi's sleep-wank. Lise's own cunt seeped come as she watched the masturbating trio of nude girls wriggle on the sand beside her, and she let her eyes fall between her own stiff nips, to her pink wet cunt, whose lips she carefully parted, letting the bright hard nubbin spring out, naked and erect. She touched her clitoris and trembled, as the tingle of pleasure shot up her spine; squeezed the organ between finger and thumb, gasped, and began to rub hard, wanking herself faster and faster as the come dripped, then flowed, from her swollen cunt, to disappear into the sand.

Titzi rolled over; she removed her hand from her sopping wet cunt-cavern and poised it above her buttocks, then began to spank her bare bum. She rubbed her erect clitty in the sand, still gasping and mumbling in her native tongue. Xiddigta and Sutra both masturbated to the rhythm of Titzi's hard spanks to her own arse, and Lise's hand was soon pinching her clitty in the same tempo. A short distance away, the pile of girl-dung stirred, and a sandy tube of flesh emerged, to crawl towards the quartet of girls, all intent on their wanks. A tongue flickered from one end of the long tube creature. Titzi's spanking hand threshed the air between slaps, her fingers opening and closing, as though searching for something. She closed on the serpent's tail, and shrieked throatily for joy, as she rammed the phallus-thick meat of the snake into her cunt.

Her bum was crimson from her own spanking, and now she masturbated with fingers in arse, using the snake's tail as a live dildo. Lise wanked faster; Titzi was crouching, her teats squashed against the sand, and her bum raised for spanking, with thighs spread wide for her dual penetration. Lise moved closer, still masturbating, with two fingers stroking inside her soaking slit, and began to spank Titzi's bare fesses. Titzi shrieked in delight, ramming the snake's tail all the way into her gash. All four girls masturbated, and their shackling chain rattled.

'Ach, ja . . . ach, ja . . .'

Come streamed from the open gashes of Xiddigta and Sutra as they wanked, their liquid flowing so copiously that it puddled the sand without evaporating. Lise's own thighs were spread, her tits bouncing as she masturbated her clit and spanked Titzi's puffy bruised bum; suddenly she gasped, as the reptile's head found its way between the folds of her cunt-mouth, brushing her knuckles busy at

147

clitty-wank. Lise shuddered, and pulled the snake's head from her cunt. The serpent's eyes glittered and its tongue darted, the skull wet with her cunt juice. It was the size of a fist. Titzi moaned and wiggled her bum in protest at the pause in her spanking. The tail was still ramming Titzi's cunt, needing little pressure from the masturbatrix's own hand, and the fangs parted, to let the tongue flicker, an inch from Lise's throbbing clitty.

'No . . .' she moaned, yet relaxed her grip, so that the snake's tongue flickered directly on her clitoris.

'*God, yes* . . .' Lise panted, and resumed spanking Titzi's bare.

A stream of piss squirted from Titzi's cunt, wetting the body of the serpent, which writhed, and increased its flicking on Lise's nubbin. Come gushed from her swollen cunt; with a sigh, she jerked the snake's head from her quim, and parted her crevice to show her arse-pucker. Panting hard, and still with her hand delivering slaps to Titzi's quivering bare fesses, Lise allowed the snake's tongue to flicker at her anal bud. She relaxed her sphincter, and opened the pucker, letting the tongue intrude fully, and her bum wriggled, grasping it with her sphincter. Her fingers resumed her clit-wanking, and she howled, as the whole head of the serpent suddenly slid into her anal cavity and began to ram and tongue her arse-root. Her fesses and thighs locked on the creature, drawing it taut between her own bumhole and Titzi's gash; Sutra and Xiddigta both peed themselves, before whimpering in orgasm, and Lise flicked and pulled her clitty until she, too, exploded in her spasm, with the serpent's head slamming her arse-wall and licking her root. She spanked Titzi to orgasm, the German girl's come mingling with her last droplets of pee, to sizzle and disappear on the sand.

Suddenly, there was a loud crack, and the body of the serpent went limp, falling, severed, in two halves: one protruded from Titzi's cunt, and the other from Lise's anus. After only a moment, each half of the serpent jerked into furious life, and Lise's half left her anus with a soft plopping sound, tickling her anal elastic like a dung, while

148

Titzi's headless dildo wriggled from her gash, shiny with cunt-slime. Both halves of the serpent scuttled away, burying themselves into the sand. On the shackle, between Lise and Titzi, lay the tongue of a camel-whip.

'Curious creature, the Galafi dung-snake,' said a male voice. 'It has two nervous systems and, if severed midway, will grow again into two complete animals, one of each sex. The female, recognised by her drab, sandy colour, is one of the most poisonous reptiles on this planet.'

Sutra and Xiddigta awoke and sat up, rubbing their eyes, and joined Lise in gazing at the man who sat astride a camel. Titzi gaped up at him, forgetting to move from her exposed position. He looked with mild approval at her dripping gash and spanked bum.

'Naughty girls, eh?' he said. 'I see one of you has been spanked for her naughtiness, but spanking, as I am sure you will agree, is scarcely punishment enough for desertion.'

'You . . . you are from the Legion?' Lise blurted.

'Why, no, although I have the honour of being known by my Legion rank. I am Colonel Said, an auctioneer by trade. My peaceful intentions are signified by the white flag on my beast's tail.'

The camel did indeed sport a bright white pennant, drooping in the breezeless air. Its rider was swathed in white robes, and his head shaded by a vast wide-brimmed hat. His chiselled face was perfectly white, as were his teeth, between which flicked a tongue as bright and pink as his eyes. He flicked his whip, rolling the thong around the girls' shackle chain, and jerking them to their feet. With his free hand, he uncoiled a similar whip from his saddle, cracking it, to lash all four girls across the bottoms, and again, whipping their backs. The camel lurched, and the whip, knotted around their chain, pulled the quartet forward, into the sun.

'I regret your nudity and lack of headgear, ladies,' said Colonel Said, 'but I assure you that the walk to my warehouse shall be only an hour or so. I must remain covered, since, as you observe, I am an albino. As long as

149

you maintain a brisk pace, I shall not be obliged to whip you. However, your bottoms will all be well trained before I sell you at auction.'

There was a shrill, feminine giggle, and a head, adorned with lustrous black tresses, peeped from the front of Colonel Said's robe. This was followed by two bare conic breasts, bouncing in the rhythm of the camel's movement. The girl's bright eyes sparkled, and the writhing of her haunches was visible beneath the billowing white robe. Her fingers teased her nipples to hardness.

'Maintain position, please, Damara,' said the colonel, 'and treat the new stock with decorum, or I shall be obliged to whip your bottom, too.'

The camel flapped its tail, and the white pennant fluttered. It was Damara's skirt, from the Welcome Centre at Fort Lafresne.

'By the way, Nurse Gallard,' said Colonel Said, as the shackled girls hobbled in quickstep, 'how did you know that the snake feeding in your anus was not the deadly female of the species? The male's bright pink skin was obscured by sand, giving it the aspect of a poisonous female.'

'I didn't,' said Lise.

Colonel Said's 'warehouse' glimmered like a mirage through the heat haze. It was a huge, circular fort of smooth, white rock, without handholds, and very high. A slab of the rock swung outwards at their approach, and they passed through an arched portal, on the inside of which a sign read: *Club Vente Aux Enchères* – 'auction club'. The letters were formed in human hair, each hank in the shape of a 'V', as though a girl's entire cunt-fleece had been sheared in a single stroke. The rock slab slid smoothly shut after their passage, its electronic control operated from a booth by a young woman with lush blonde tresses that came almost to her knees. Her hair hid little of her ripe fesses and teats, and the strands clung to a huge pubic jungle; she was otherwise nude, save for a grotesquely large golden phallus, erect, and anchored to a prong embedded in her cunt.

The cortege was at the entrance to a complex of villas and bungalows, like a village, flowered with hibiscus and bougainvillea, shaded by jacaranda trees, and dominated in the midst by a large turquoise swimming pool. Smaller pools adjoined white villas, so that the entire complex shimmered turquoise. Beyond the villas, fountains and arbours, another wall bisected the domain, this one with a single steel door. Colonel Said spurred his camel, dealt a single whipstroke to the buttocks of each naked slave-girl, and they proceeded around the perimeter wall, on the track leading to the distant steel portal. Heads turned in curiosity as they passed, and the exhausted girls gazed, awestruck.

The pool was surrounded by sunbathers, all gleaming with oil or white cream. Most were female, and most in the nude, but some in clinging spandex or lycra one-piece swimsuits. Many wore rubber bathing caps. Males and females swam in the pool. There was an air of languid opulence, with drinks tables and the paraphernalia of a Caribbean or Pacific luxury resort, with none of the guests seeming over thirty years of age and all, male and female, of handsome physique. Surrounding the pool were life-guards, nude males and females alternating, and the males with cocks fully and permanently erect, the females with artificial phalli of dried hard sponge. At each end of the pool stood a frame, like a gallows. A nude girl, with the slabbed muscles of a body-builder, hung by her hair from the cross-beam. A nude male flogged her back with a scourge, while another fucked her in the cunt from the front, the jolts of the whip slamming her cunt onto his tool. Her hands were cuffed behind her back, and she screamed at each stroke of whip and cock. Colonel Said ordered his slave-girls to dive in and refresh themselves, chained as they were.

'Please,' he said. 'The water will only come up to your waists.'

The girls did not hesitate, and anyway had no choice but to follow Titzi, even after her head disappeared, with a horrified, bubbling scream, under the water. Lise followed, holding her breath, as the heavy chain dragged the four girls right to the bottom, at least twice out of their depth. They struggled to swim back up, but the chain pinned them. Their eyes wide with terror, each girl pissed and dunged in panic. Lise's lungs were bursting, when, suddenly, the floor moved; they stood on a net of fine mesh, which gathered and enfolded them, and they emerged, bagged and gasping, to the surface. The corners of the net were held by the circle of lifeguards, and the sunbathers around the pool applauded, laughing. Many of the nude females worked at body-building equipment, their muscles slabbed and rippling, and buttocks and breasts purpled with extruded veins; their clitties were enhanced, peeping like thumbs from their enlarged and firmed vaginal folds. Colonel Said freed the girls from the net, and they resumed marching position. He gave each girl two whipstrokes on the bare wet buttocks and one on the back. They were obliged to scoop up their dungs and carry them pressed to their cunt-mounds.

'That was a cruel joke!' he said.

Inside his robe, Damara chuckled gleefully, as her buttocks writhed.

'I am fond of cruel jokes,' said Colonel Said, 'for they teach a slave obedience and mistrust. A trustful slave is imperfect – only the delicious frisson of hatred in humiliance, can satisfy.'

He whipped their backs again, and they proceeded past the swimming pool. The sunbathers lay, belly or bum up, on mattresses made of the nude human bodies of both young males and young females, their skins of every hue, as in the Legion. All the males had erect cocks, some of them were in service. Two women chatted under a parasol, each squatting on a cock plunged into her cunt, and her loins writhing slowly. Two others, prone, and face down, conversed while two black males vigorously bum-fucked them; beside them, another pair of women spread their thighs and took cock in cunt, masturbating, yet still chattering, in little squeals and coos. A male lay on his belly with his head pillowed on the bare breasts of two

152

girls, one oriental, one European, while his cock was embedded, unmoving, in the open cunt of a black girl with thighs apart and masturbating. The male sipped clear oily liquid through a straw, as he read a book.

Beside him, his female companion was fucked in the cunt by a black youth, while she lay on her back with arms outstretched. Her head and back, too, were pillowed on naked female breasts, and each hand held a springy leather riding crop, with which she whopped the bare bums of a black male on her left and a Japanese girl on her right. The crop made a dry, tapping sound as the buttocks wriggled under the naked caning; the Japanese girl's white buttocks were already striped crimson, and the black male's deep purple. Both recipients of the riding crop squirmed and squealed, begging their mistress to stop. Lise frowned as she passed; blubbing was not the Legion way, and their distress seemed exaggerated, even though the lazy, but efficient, whopping had evidently lasted long.

The fucked lady smiled at their squeals and squirms; when her cunt-fucker spurted, he changed places with the caned slave, who began a vigorous bum-fucking, while the lady commenced caning the bum of the male who had spunked in her. When the newcomer had spurted in her anus, the Japanese girl was ordered to sit on the lady's face and wank off, so that the caning lady could drink her come, while she whopped both the raw male bottoms. Her husband, engrossed in his book, paused occasionally, to cane his wife's bare breasts, and at this kindness, she would wank herself to climax, after a tit-flogging of a dozen. Similar pleasures were enjoyed all around the pool, now clouded in heat haze, as Colonel Said's cortege headed for the portal, or 'barricade', as he put it.

'These are your training quarters, slaves,' he said, 'which include the auction arena itself. Slaves are hidden until auction.'

Now shaded by the wall, he opened his robe to reveal the naked Damara, wriggling on his lap, with his tool plunged in her anus. Lifting Damara by her nipples, then squeezing her whole teats in his pale hands, he used the

153

girl's nipples to bounce her on his huge white cockshaft, drawing her up until his glans was exposed, then slamming her down until her buttocks slapped his balls. This buggery resulted in a spurt so copious that it splattered from the lips of Damara's anus and mingled with the flow of come, which her vigorous wanking made flow from her swollen wet gash. Pressing a palmful of his spunk to her mouth as she wanked, Damara masturbated herself to orgasm, just as Colonel Said's ebbed.

'Good!' said Colonel Said. 'I leave you now, with Hawo.'

A Somali guard, with tresses to her buttocks and a golden phallus erect against her ebony, lush-curled mound, banged the door shut after them. Around her waist was a golden chain, from which dangled a whip and a cane. Her breasts and buttocks were volcanic in their ripeness, and rippled slightly as she leered at her new charges, then laughed, and, raising her whip, lashed all four across the nipples. She did not stop whipping their naked breasts, until tears glistened in all their eyes.

'Welcome to servitude,' she said.

The new slaves joined those already captive, in an unbending routine of obedience to strict rules, changed at whim. Any breaking of the day's rules resulted in a bare-bottom caning, or full body-whipping, in severe addition to those already prescribed by routine. Hawo was captain of slaves, as signified by her golden phallus, and had three sergeants, each with a silver phallus: a lissom, pear-breasted Italian, named Capri, a wiry, whipcord of a Japanese-Brazilian, named Nikko, and the other, a powerful, raw-boned body-builder from Leeds, named Sheila. Lise hoped that their common Englishness would form a bond, but no – Sheila, while kind enough, would not speak, or had forgotten, her English, and barked her orders in guttural legionnaire's French. Hawo did the explaining.

There were thirteen other slaves, including two one-legged European girls, and all talking was forbidden amongst them. However, at no time were the slaves unsupervised by Hawo, Capri, Nikko or Sheila, and a mode of conversation had evolved, using the guard as intermediary. All slave-girls lived nude, save when wearing punishment dress, either a rubber frogman's suit with diving helmet, or the hair shirt that Lise remembered from Thierry's, worn with a gasmask and surgical hobble boots. An apple was strapped inside the miscreant's vulva, and she was released from the rubber suit or hair shirt only when the fruit had completely rotted in her cunt juice and pee. Worse, her cunt, or anus, or both, might be filled with live sand-worms and taped shut. Some trained slaves were soon to be auctioned after a display of submission.

They slept in a coop, like the dormitory at Fort Lafresne. Still chained by the ankles, the four newcomers occupied adjacent palliasses. The walls and ceiling of the coop were lined with mirrors, so that girls could practise grooming, and watch themselves, and each other, masturbate. Wanking off was obligatory, and each slave had a tin come cup to fill before sleep. The duty sergeant measured the come, and emptied the cups into labelled flagons, with canings for those juicing insufficiently. The come refreshed the guests, in their poolside cocktails, and girls whose come was most in demand had to masturbate excessively, to top up their flagons. Their piss was also collected, in separate labelled flagons, and was requested as a drink mainly by the male guests. This was the only way prospective buyers could form a preference for a girl at auction time.

Outside the coop were the drill yard and the auction platform, known as the punishment zone. It was here that full-body whippings were administered. The slave yard was enclosed by the unclimbable outer wall, which contained a second entry gate, always shut. The other buildings were the guardhouse where the four officers lived, and the gymnasium, where slaves exercised at body-building. The slaves were free to accept the tutelage of Sheila as instructor; about half the slaves, including the two amputees, had thus opted, and their bodies had grown slabs of muscle, which did not hide their essential femininity. The chief attraction was the enhancement of the 'glutes', or buttock muscles, and the development of the clitoris which went with the increased muscle weight: customers prized the body beautiful. Adjoining them was the male slaves' yard, its prisoners nude and unreachable across the dividing wire fence.

Their function was to be broken for total obedience. Then, they would be auctioned as slaves to the guests, all with perverted tendencies impossible to indulge discreetly in other playgrounds of the rich. The slaves auctioned belonged to their new owners on nine-year leases; could be traded and punished freely, with only the hope that a sexually besotted owner might buy them freehold from Colonel Said, and take them home. Guests obliged to absent themselves sub-leased their slaves to others. Flagellance and sexual humiliation were the normal expressions of power, and slaves were trained to accept any degradation, however foul, with theatrical signs of extreme distress. The Legion, and Dr Charlotte Crevasse's so-called clinic, were mere playschools, and slaves at auction, all deserters, existed purely for the guests' sadistic pleasure. Some were hideously scarred by birthmarks, or were amputees, hopping on crutches, for fetishist clients. No Legion helicopters would rescue auction girls.

Slaves had to practise maquillage, and grow their hair untrimmed, sculpting it in various styles, to please prospective owners. Every month, the girls' pubic growth was checked, and selected girls shaven clean, the pubic hair first held in a hank, and sliced in a dagger stroke, then the remaining bristles dry-plucked, one by one. Only then was the girl's pubis razored clean. Rising at dawn, each slave touched toes by her bed, to receive a bare-bottom caning of ten strokes from the duty sergeant, and only then was she allowed to dung in the dung-bucket, and bathe in the fountain beside the punishment zone. Meals were simply piles of scraps, thrown at whim on the sand for the girls to fight over. There was always water to drink from the fountain, although the girls might spend a whole day with only a few morsels of slop to fight over. This, Hawo explained, was to break any Legion sentiments of personal loyalty or team spirit.

'It will be nine full years of hell,' she said, 'after which you will be nearly thirty years old, and useless. So the desert, or the Legion, may reclaim you. There is no remission, and your only hope, that your addiction to humiliance may entice a guest to buy you out, and exchange this slavery for another. A slave must *perform* . . .'

One performance demanded was the ritual caning of young males sent from across the wire; many of the perverted male guests were submissive and wanted female slaves as dominatrixes. Both sexes must learn to masturbate for their owners' pleasure, and the slave-girls would stand opposite the young males, each sex wanking themselves, on either side of the wire. Otherwise, no contact between the sexes was allowed. The males had female guards, forbidden to mingle with Hawo's crew. Colonel Said paid occasional visits to either side of the wire for his own special requirements; Damara fetched the dung buckets for him.

There was 'wrestle-box' for some extra morsel of food, closed in a tin box with sharp edges. There were no rules: all the girls, even amputees armed with crutches, had to fight with knees and claws and groin kicks for the prize, as its sharp sides lacerated their bare flesh, with the girl who could score a touch-down by the sergeant's feet being the winner, permitted to keep the contents of the box. All losers had to touch toes for ten strokes of the cane on the bare bum from the winner. Mornings were for drill and exercises, except for Sheila's body-builders, within the gymnasium, from which loud whipstrokes echoed.

Bare-bum canings of ten were given for imperfections, like a loose strand of hair or smudged make-up. Once a week, every girl automatically received a full bare-body whipping, suspended from one of the two flogging gallows. Girls were flogged in twos, with the second of the pair, just flogged or about to be, lying with mouth open beneath the whipped girl's open cunt. If the victim pissed herself, the prone girl had to drink every drop of her pee, on pain of double whipping. Both gallows had a metal hair clamp.

Girls for whipping first had their hands cuffed behind their backs, and ankles tied to each corner of the platform, spreading their legs. Each gallows clamped its victim's twisted head-hair, the clamp raised until she was suspended by her hair alone, with her bound feet dancing on tiptoe. Like this, she took twenty strokes of a four-thonged scourge on buttocks, breasts, shoulders and cunt lips, in thirty minutes. On average, a girl could count on at least two or three bare-bum canings a day, as well as the morning ritual. After every caning, girls were permitted to soak for thirty minutes in a hot bath of bubbling bum-mud. Nighttime had its own rituals, as Lise learnt on her first night.

The titanium anklets allowed just enough room for the four newcomers to manoeüvre their legs into a semblance of comfort. Lise had just stretched, exhausted, on her palliasse, when a bare scented body straddled hers. It was Hawo. Her huge golden phallus was warm, pressing against Lise's cunt, which Hawo began to masturbate, with rough fingers.

'What . . .? Mm!' Lise squealed, in sleepy protest, to be rewarded with a vicious slap on the bare breasts, with Hawo raking sharpened fingernails across her nipples.

Lise began to sob. Soon, her sobs turned to panting moans, as her come flowed under the crude but passionate wanking of the naked Somalian, who frotted her bare breasts and nipples against Lise's own. Hard fingers manipulated Lise's clit, until her cunt was sopping with come. She clasped the Somalian's hard bare bum, pressing the phallus into her wet slit.

'Yes . . .' Lise moaned, 'in my cunt, yes, yes, it's been so long . . .'

She gasped as the heavy golden tool rammed her soaking cunt, right to the wombneck, and began a vigorous fuck. Hawo directed Lise's fingers both to her clit and Lise's own, and, as the black girl cunt-fucked her, Lise wanked them both off to orgasm, twisting and squeezing both their throbbing naked clits, with the black girl's bigger and harder even than Lise's already powerful nubbin. Come gushed from her swollen slit lips, under the pounding of the black belly against her cunt-hillock. She saw the pumping arses of Nikko, Capri and Sheila, cunt-fucking Titzi, Xiddigta and Sutra, respectively. All the other slaves were kneeling, wanking with their spread arses and dripping cunts presented in position, and their fingers wanking anus and gash, as though beseeching their own fuck.

'Nine years of hell,' whispered Hawo. 'And no way out, Nurse Gallard . . . unless you co-operate.'

'Co-operate? How?' Lise whispered, still gasping as she wanked.

'I like *your* arse the best,' said Hawo. 'I long, just once, for that which is forbidden me. If you are body-whipped the first, with your hair not long enough, it must be suspension by nipples. It will be insupportable, and I can persuade Colonel Said, in mercy, to melt your chain from the others, with fire of earth-cunt. You may try and escape to . . .'

'To where, Captain Hawo?'

'Forget I spoke. Don't join Sergeant Sheila's body-builders.'

Hawo grasped her by the cunt and made her turn over, to present her arse in like manner. Lise continued to masturbate, but now into her come cup, as Hawo buggered her sphincter with the cunt-slimed phallus. Sheila was buggering Sutra likewise, as Capri and Nikko buggered the vigorously wanking Titzi and Xiddigta, before moving down the line of open arses, to fuck the cunts or anuses of the other slaves, mewling with desire. Those unfucked wanked into their come cups as they watched the other girls buggered and listened to their shrieks.

In the morning, Sutra, Titzi and Xiddigta opted for body-building, before their ritual caning of ten by Sheila, the duty sergeant. Sutra squealed, and her large tits shook with every slash of the rod to her bare bum; her eyes were screwed tight, seeping tears. Even Xiddigta's firm conic breasts quivered like her caned buttocks; she, Sutra and Titzi shrieked, like the other slaves, clenching their caned bums, and with arses squirming at each whistling smack of

159

the rod on skin. Many wanked off, filling their come cups to overflowing. Lise bit her lip, awaiting the scorch of the cane on her own bared nates, but she, too, wanked off, as she watched the squirming bare bums of the girls caned before her.

Vip! Vip! Vip! Vip! Vip!

Lise's gorge rose and she stifled a scream, as five fierce strokes cut her, all on the tender top bum.

Vip! Vip! Vip! Vip! Vip!

'*Nnnh* . . .!' she gasped, her only sound of distress throughout the vicious wealing, and Sheila said that her silence was impudence and earnt her another ten.

'Ohhh . . .' Lise sobbed, as the smarting of her welts now increased with a slower, even crueller, caning.

Vip! Vip!

'Ahhh!'

Vip! Vip!

Her fingers found her throbbing clitty, and she wanked hard as the cane whistled towards her squirming bare fesses. Come dripped with a plopping tinkle into her come cup and overflowed; her bum squirmed so violently that some drops of hot cunt juice splattered her bare feet.

Vip! Vip!

'*Ohh*! O! No!'

Vip! Vip!

'*Ahhh* . . .! Please, no!'

Her fingers were a blur, pounding the clitty that throbbed amid the wet, writhing folds of her swollen cunt. Come poured down her thighs and splashed the floor.

Vip! Vip!

'O! O! O! *Ahhh* . . .!' she screamed, as her belly spasmed in heavy orgasm and piss jetted from her slimed cunt lips.

'Good,' grunted Sheila, her caner.

On the first morning of nine years' bondage, Lise was learning to perform.

11

The Sacred Gash

The one-legged Latvian girl screamed as the clamp tightened and lifted her by the blonde hair, high on the whipping gallows. Her stump wriggled, like her buttocks, as her one leg sought balance in its ankle cuff, the toes a cruel hair's breadth from the platform. Her comrades in slavery giggled as they masturbated blatantly; so did the naked males, faces glued to the wire to observe, despite the female guards' canes that struck their bare buttocks if they showed signs of frottage. Each male's penis and scrotum were enclosed in a tight restrainer of wire mesh, which encouraged, rather than deterred, full, frustrating erection. Male slaves had different rules, but for females, flagellance, humiliance and constant self-pleasuring were the life of nine-year slaves and their only amusement. It was only at public whippings that girls could whisper to one another.

'Remember,' hissed Lise, 'we are still legionnaires!'

'We are deserters,' said Titzi, 'and the Legion has forgotten us.'

A helicopter whirred overhead, far in the distance.

'Perhaps we should forget the Legion,' added Sutra. 'If only we could be unchained and join Sergeant Sheila for body-building. Then, be bought by a rich owner, who would worship us . . .'

Sutra, Titzi and Xiddigta looked accusingly at Lise.

The one-legged girl received the first stroke of the heavy leather scourge on the bare buttocks, one of the thongs snaking to lash the extruded anal pucker, which resembled a wrinkled date, and this was followed almost at once by the crack of a second scourge across her naked breasts; there was a ripple of excitement, and cunts juiced heavily as the girls wanked. Some wiggled their scarred bottoms at the watching males, whose stiff cocks strained in their harnesses.

'I think we shall be unchained soon,' said Lise. 'Sheila will demand it.'

'But Colonel Said makes the rules,' said Sutra.

'It is just a hunch,' said Lise.

They shifted their eyes to the squirming arse of the unijambe, hanging from her hair, her naked body twisting madly as though to wrench it from its roots. The scourge, applied by the nude and sweating Capri, wealed her buttocks in a neat criss-cross of purpling welts. The one-legged girl's arse was pear-shaped to perfection, the smooth globes like plums. With bum wealed, the ridges of her puffed skin leered like gargoyles. The right breast hung considerably lower, and jutted more amply, than the left; it was her left leg which was amputated, and this gave her body a curious harmony. The dark puckered bud of her anus writhed like a wrinkled mouth as the thongs sliced it.

The second whipper was Nikko and, like Capri, her teeth flashed white in a smile, as each stroke made the girl's bare body shudder. Nikko's scourge was shorter than Capri's arse-whip for close work on the teats and especially the nipples. To vigorous masturbation of the watching girls, Nikko relished slicing the nipples, unnaturally large like beetroots. Nikko's own bare breasts bounced in brisk rhythm as she tit-whipped the screaming Latvian. At each thwack! of the whips on her bum and teats, the watching girls cheered, more and more exuberantly as their masturbation became more intense: rivulets of girl-come flowed down excited bare thighs, to plop and evaporate on the silvery sand.

Nikko and Capri paused and exchanged both whips and positions. Nikko, standing well back, applied the longer scourge to the Latvian's back and shoulders, so that the tips of the thongs snaked around her breasts, clinging momentarily after impact. Capri moved closer, stooping slightly, and began to whip the girl's naked cunt, full on the exposed pink of the vaginal gash.

Thwack! Thwack! Thwack! Thwack!

'*AHHHH! AHHHH!*'

The wriggling squirms, and the screams, of the whipped girl, were now so intense that her hair seemed likely to snap, as she gyrated under the cunt-strokes. Her fesses, no longer beaten, but deeply bruised, clenched in a staccato rhythm, and her back muscle rippled, shuddering, as Nikko's flail spread the thongs right from her nape to her mid-back. Capri lashed her cunt in alternate undercuts and forward slashes, the forward strokes targeting the upper vaginal folds and clitoris, while the undercuts stung the arse-cleft and taut perineum, with the thong-tips catching the anal bud, and the curved valley of her left stump. Every third or fourth stroke directly lashed the flesh of the stump, which squirmed like a third fesse, and these cuts drew the most piteous screams.

Thwack! Thwack! Thwack! Thwack!

'*Ohhhh! Ahhhh! For God's love, enough!*'

Thwack! Thwack! Thwack! Thwack!

'*Ooh! Nnnh . . . O, God! Please, no more!*'

Captain Hawo, watching with arms folded and clasping her cane, nodded her approval. One arm dropped, to the nape of her cunt-fold, where her clitoris stood throbbing, astride the shaft of her golden phallus, and her fingers began to masturbate her clit. Beneath the dangling cunt flaps, the steady seep of her come dripped.

Many of the male's cocks began to ejaculate jets of sperm through the fence, without any stimulation of their organs. Those who spurted were ordered to lie face down in the sand and receive an immediate caning of ten strokes on the buttocks. Some of the masturbating girl slaves knelt and lapped the spunk where it dripped on the fence wire, anointing the wire with their own squirting come. The Latvian girl's own cunt dripped come, faster and faster, as her stump and bum wriggled faster, and her bruised cunt swelled to reveal a clitoris engorged and stiff.

At last, she pissed herself; the partner in flogging, a black Somali girl with legs apart and mouth open who was herself wanking off, gurgled, swallowing the girl's stream of piss, and her belly convulsed in climax as she pounded her clitty vigorously throughout her pee-drink. Piss splattered her conic teats, and she rubbed the erect nipples and breast skin clean of pee, putting her piss-soaked fingers to her cunt, and squashing the golden pee into her flowing cunt-oil. She continued wanking off, right until her wrists were fastened behind her back, and she took the sobbing Latvian's place under the flogging-gallows. The Latvian girl bravely tossed her head, and smoothed her hair down over her flogged tits, as she hobbled unaided on her crutch.

As soon as she lay in her turn beneath the black girl's spread cunt, her sobs turned to sighs of pleasure, and she began to masturbate as the Somali's bum started squirming, even before the first lash stroked her. The black girl's teats were so large, smooth and firm, and the hillocks of her nipples so hugely conical, that she was selected for nipple suspension. She screamed and wriggled violently as the heavy clamps bit into her nips, and she was hoisted with a jerk towards the beam, her toes flailing in the air helplessly. The Latvian stroked her whipped stump, as well as the pink thumb of her clitty, and parted her fesses, to tickle and penetrate her swollen, bruised anus pucker; she cried in orgasm as the black girl pissed herself, right after the first stroke to her bare bum.

Thwack!

'Oooh!'

A golden stream burst from the wet flesh of her cunt, and sprayed the Latvian's face and teats, with most of the liquid falling into her gaping mouth. Her throat moved, and she caressed her stump as her fingers twitched her clitty; the Somali girl's scream at her second lash was drowned by the Latvian's squeals of orgasm. Her come drenched the baobab wood of the flogging-gallows. Captain Hawo's wank grew faster and her mouth hung open. Her nipples were rocks; suddenly, she nodded to the masturbating slaves on both sides of the gallows, and nodded in command. The slave-girls paired off, frequently with kicks exchanged to face, teat or cunt, to decide partnerships. Soon, every slave-girl was squatting, wanking, on another's face, with the full weight of her buttocks and thighs stifling the pressed girl. The girls in submission masturbated too, and their tongues and noses flicked on the clitties of their juicing oppressors, while they swallowed the heavy drips of come. Titzi's eyes gleamed; suddenly, Lise was flat on her back, tripped by a judo kick, and the full weight of Titzi's naked arse-meat pressed on her face.

She saw Sutra sitting on Xiddigta's face beside them, both girls masturbating with fingers, as Xiddigta tongued Sutra's swollen clit. Titzi's cunt juice flowed over Lise's squashed face, and the German girl spanked her bare nipples, to Lise's squeals of protest. Her mouth found Titzi's engorged clitty, and she bit hard, then chewed, making Titzi squeal. The force and speed of her spanks increased, and her claws scratched Lise's nipples. Titzi writhed, so that her anus bud trapped Lise's nose, then her tongue and lips, and Lise was smeared in Titzi's copious arse-grease, as well as the heavy spurts of come which she was obliged to swallow, in order to breathe. Her own cunt spouted come under her masturbating fingers, which Titzi's soon joined, having spanked and pinched Lise's nips to rawness. She began to torment her clitty in the same way, clawing and biting it, as she bent over Lise's writhing belly. Lise got a finger into Titzi's anus, then two, and began a finger-buggery of her slimy elastic bumhole, while the black girl's screams, and the crack of the whips on her bare cunt and back, now filled the arena. Few males were left to ogle, for almost all had spurted and lay on the sand, bare bums up to receive their canings. Captain Hawo glanced alternately at the naked croups of the caned young men, and the slave-girls gamahuching, and masturbated herself to an orgasm, followed speedily by a second, and third. Her eyes gazed, wide with longing, at Lise Gallard's wet arse and cunt.

As the last strokes thwacked on the black girl's quivering bare body, Titzi howled in an orgasm that almost choked Lise with the flood of come she was obliged to swallow; the pressure of Titzi's teeth on her clit, and three fingers shafting Lise's soaking slit, made her gurgle in her own spasm. Capri and Nikko put down their whips, and masturbated themselves very rapidly to orgasms which their come-drenched thighs indicated they had awaited with longing. Titzi sighed in satisfaction as she pissed directly to the back of Lise's throat, obliging the girl to swallow the whole squirt of hot acrid liquid. At last Lise rose, wiping her face, drenched in Titzi's come and pee.

'You fucking bitch,' she said. 'I said I owed you a whipping, and now, I really, really mean it!'

'Difficult, while we are chained,' sneered Titzi.

'That will not be for long,' said Captain Hawo. 'All of you are due for public whipping, and you will be un-chained one by one, in order of performance. The unchain-ing process is a sacred rite, and almost as painful as a flogging itself, especially as your hairs have now sprouted. Colonel Said himself will be in attendance. Which of you shall be first . . .?'

She looked directly at Lise.

'I beg for the honour, Captain,' Lise blurted.

'You have it,' said Captain Hawo, nodding. 'Follow me, at the double, to the sacred gash.'

Sheila emerged, to take charge of the gamahuching slaves, whipping them into sullen ranks of come-slimed naked bodies, and ordering a hundred push-ups and sit-ups before a punishment drill, running at the double with mouthfuls of sand. Lise and the others followed Hawo, Capri and Nikko. Behind the coop, a tunnel led steeply under the earth. The girls descended, Hawo carry-ing a flaming torch and shears, with Capri and Nikko at the rear, still carrying their scourges. It grew hotter and hotter, and the rocky floor of the tunnel burnt their soles.

'We come first to the temple of pleasure,' said Hawo, 'where you shall see that public whipping is not a slave's most exquisite delight.'

After fifteen minutes' descent, the girls were panting and their bodies shone, slippery with sweat, in the flicker of the torchlight. The tunnel emerged into a chamber, lit by a single candle, whose light flickered on metal devices of constraint and torture: a rack, an iron maiden, and various bondage frames, like grotesque insects, adorned with cuffs and pincers. The chamber echoed with a girl's throttled screams. A black girl was strapped to a frame of spiked metal, with her ankles and wrists cuffed behind her neck, exposing her entire nates and vulva. Two naked male slaves, one straddling her, and one beneath, fucked and buggered her in robotic and merciless rhythm, while a third fucked her in the throat. Three masturbating female slaves whipped her wealed breasts and belly, while spraying her with piss and their own come. Two females caned the naked buttocks of the male slaves as they fucked, and a docile, sullen line of males awaited their turn to fuck the bound female; they winced, as two more female slaves passed down the line, caning each naked croup to ensure the erection of their cocks. The bound girl's eyes were glazed with terror; suddenly, the male who mouth-fucked her groaned, and a stream of sperm bubbled at her lips, despite her attempts to swallow the come.

Almost at once, the slaves fucking her in arse and cunt came also, their spunk squirting from her holes. The trio withdrew, and the bound slave had a brief respite from penetration, during which the girl caners gave her twenty strokes on the taut bare buttocks, and ten straight on the gash flaps and erect clitoris. The black girl screamed, pissing herself, as the cane struck her naked nubbin, and received ten strokes on the anal pucker as reward. Her cunt flowed with come; one of her caners squatted full weight on her face, and pissed copiously in her mouth. The black girl spluttered as she swallowed the steaming fluid, while the squatter wanked off, adding a flood of cunt oil to her pee, before climaxing, and rubbing the girl's nose against her slimed cunt and anus.

'O . . . wank me off . . . please! *I beg you!*' the black girl moaned.

At once, her buggery, fellatio and cunt-fucking began anew. Lise and the others stared aghast, and one more sound rose above the girl's gurgling howls of protest; Hawo, alone among the spectators, had her eyes gleaming as she stared at the girl's flogged cunt and bum, and the pumping buttocks of the males fucking her.

'Mmm . . .' she moaned. 'O, yes . . .'

She was wanking hard, and rapidly masturbated herself to spasm, with rivulets of come spouting from her swollen cunt, to flow down her quivering black thighs.

'That slut was really naughty,' she said dreamily, as she led them from the chamber. 'She refused to squat on a male slave's face . . .'

They soon came to a cavern where no torch was needed, as the chamber was lit by the earth gash itself. The temperature was that of a furnace: in the centre of the vast cavern, a slit in the volcanic floor allowed a seething pool of red-hot magma, far below, to sear the air.

'The sacred gash,' said Captain Hawo. 'The earth cunt . . .'

The aperture was exactly in the shape of a female vulva. The cavern tilted at an angle; around the walls were openings, the size of drainage pipes, one side sucking the smoke away, and the other allowing an inflow of air. Hawo said they were natural formations, called wormholes. Millions of years previously, giant blind worms lived in these holes, nourished by the volcanic vapours of the earth cunt. The Djiboutian nomads spoke of 'penis worms', and when fossil remains were discovered in the 1920s, the reconstructed creatures had exactly the shape of the human penis, the glans being the tail. Their descendants lived on as Galafi sand-snakes.

'Colonel Said is in attendance,' she said, handing Capri the shears.

They focused on the nude, pearl-white body of the albino Colonel Said. He sat on a throne of marble, at the cavern's far end. The throne had two decks, of which he occupied the lower, and at the females' entrance, he raised his head; his penis rose from its bush of white curls, and stood hugely erect, almost to his navel, the exposed glans as pink as his albino's eyeballs. The seat of the throne's second deck contained an aperture, like a pillory, around the colonel's neck, and his own seat was open in the same way, exposing his bare nates and balls. His head fell back, to rest on a cushioned clamp, so that his face was upwards.

'One of the wormholes leads ... *outside*,' Hawo whispered to Lise. 'Your public whipping shall be more severe than usual; I shall interrupt it and remove you. When you have satisfied me, and done my bidding, I shall tell you which hole is your escape.'

Hawo ascended the second upper throne, and squatted, with her full weight on Colonel Said's face. Nikko positioned herself before the throne, with whip raised. Capri led the girls to the brink of the molten earth gash. Their faces grimaced as their bodies streamed with sweat, and their feet hopped on the hot rock. Capri positioned Sutra and Xiddigta at the rear, with Titzi beside the hole, and then whipped Lise smartly on the bare, with the command to jump to the far lip of the hole. Lise gaped down; a second, harder, lash struck her nipples, and she leapt across the flaming chasm, screaming, as a gust of hot gas seared her cunt. Then she stood on the far lip, the chain taut between her own ankle and Titzi's, over the lava. Titzi's face was a mask of agony, and her new pubic growth curled with a smell of singeing. Lise felt her own pubic sprouts smoking. The titanium chain softened, and became brighter, as it heated. Above them, there was a hissing sound, as Hawo pissed copiously on Colonel Said's face.

Thwack! Thwack! Thwack!

The Japanese girl skilfully whipped the male's exposed balls and fesses from beneath, while sucking the full length of his cock, deep in her throat, with her lips on his ball-sac.

Thwack! Thwack! Thwack!

Colonel Said groaned. His lips moved, eagerly licking every drop of the piss that flowed from Hawo's cunt, now mingled with copious come, as she wanked her clitty. Nikko too masturbated, come streaming freely from her pulsing pink gash, and evaporating as soon as it dripped onto the floor.

Thwack! Thwack! Thwack!

Colonel Said began to whimper, as the thongs stroked every part of his exposed buttocks and balls. Nikko's fellation became more intense, as Hawo above wanked ever more copious come into the male's avidly swallowing mouth. Hawo was pushing on her own golden phallus, half of whose length disappeared into her vulva, and evidently connected seamlessly to another prong, embedded in her cunt. Nikko flogged Colonel Said's bare bum faster as he moaned in the approach of climax. Suddenly, Hawo's cunt squirted forth a new jet of piss, quite as long and full as the first, and the male was unable to swallow all the flow of piss and cunt juice. The fluid trickled down to his pubis, where Nikko's mouth lapped Hawo's come and piss, as she tongued the giant pale cock. Capri raised her shears.

Thwack! Thwack! Thwack!

'*Ahhh . . . Yes!*'

Colonel Said's spunk bubbled at Nikko's fluttering lips, faster than she could suck and swallow it. At the same moment, Hawo groaned, as she masturbated herself to orgasm, her buttocks, thighs and cunt writhing, and slippery with pee and come, squashing the man's face. Nikko whipped his buttocks and ball-sac in a flurry of strokes.

Thwack! Thwack! Thwack! Thwack! Thwack!

'Ahhh . . . !' he screamed. 'God, yes . . .'

The bubble of his spunk continued as the force of his climax twitched Nikko's head from side to side, and she squealed, as her fingers wanked her own cunt to a massively flowing piss and orgasm, both her fluids hissing as they dried on the hot stone. Capri raised her shears, and suddenly snapped them on the titanium chain, which broke in two. Lise was free of her bound companions. Grimacing, she rubbed her scalded pubis, the new growth of cunt-hair singed away by the sacred gash. Hawo descended from her throne, and joined Capri, Nikko and the still-chained trio, after Nikko had delivered a final whipstroke to Colonel Said's nates. The colonel raised his head.

'Most satisfactory,' he said. 'I shall save the pleasure of further unchaining for later. The three body-builders-to-be may remain shackled.'

Glowering, the three still-chained slaves, whipped on by Nikko and Capri, wanking off as they thonged the girls' bare bums, followed Lise and Captain Hawo back through the temple of pleasure. The punished black slave was now the most enthusiastic caner of a russet-haired European girl, who had replaced her in bondage. They paused while Hawo masturbated herself to orgasm once again, spittle flecking her lips as the come flowed from her swollen cunt flaps. At a curve in the tunnel, Lise and Hawo were momentarily blocked from the view of the others.

'Please,' Lise hissed, 'what is it you want me to do, Captain Hawo? That which is forbidden? I don't understand . . .'

Hawo's eyes glittered. She touched her whip and the golden erect phallus whose twin prong was embedded in her slit.

'I want you to use these on me,' she whispered. 'Colonel Said shall never allow us officers to enjoy a slave's humiliance, but, just for once, *I* want to be serviced in bondage, in the temple of pleasure. *By you, Lise.*'

The auction of slaves traditionally began with a public whipping of one male and one female slave, to whet the buyers' appetites. Six slaves of each sex were up for auction, the first and last time the selected males were permitted to enter the female compound. The bidding took place during the whippings, and would end with the final stroke. Bidding took place in American dollars, and in cash. The female was whipped before the male, and Hawo explained to Lise, as she strapped her to the gallows, that European females spent more than males, especially for a black, well-penised male slave, even though the whipped slaves were saved as prizes for the following auction.

Auction whippings were especially cruel, as the subjects were strapped upside down, the spectacle of an inverted male being curiously exciting to females. While the female slave was whipped on the cunt, the male had also to suffer a birching directly on his exposed balls, with a light but stinging birch sheaf. This, too, excited the females to bid for a slave on which to practise the same. Bidding started at ten thousand dollars per slave, and was expected to reach several times that. The naked youth, his penis hugely erect, lay in position beneath Lise, ready to swallow her fluids, which must trickle from her cunt down her belly or back, and drip from her new growth of bristling blonde hair.

Lise's binding was by clamps on her cunt lips and nipples, with her arms and legs stretched in an X, but the ankles bound only loosely to the gallows bar with slack twine. The nipple and cunt chains twanged taut, and she groaned as her cunt flaps and teats stretched to pale white gussets. The cunt lips were parted wide, exposing her clitoris and the pink walls of her vulva, glistening with her already flowing come. Hawo planned to carry Lise away for medical attention, after Lise pretended to faint during her whipping. While the youth was whipped, Lise and Hawo would descend to the temple of pleasure, and Lise, excited and enraged by her own whipping, could wreak revenge on Hawo's body. With Lise gone through the designated wormhole, Hawo would remain in bondage, flogged and buggered with her own tool, and explain that the stronger girl had tricked and overpowered her. Lise whispered that she understood Hawo's desire to be whipped and anally tooled, for it was her own desire.

'It is every girl's desire,' Hawo sighed, as she tightened Lise's cunt and nipple clamps, making sure the girl's whole weight was on their chains.

'Ohhh . . .' Lise gasped, shivering, her eyes moistening, but with come already dripping over her exposed pubic mound.

Colonel Said mingled with the throng of sun-worshippers, seated before the whipping gallows and the auction space beneath, and ensuring that his guests were served drinks by females in French maids' costume, complete with stiletto heels and seamed fishnet stockings. The costumes were saved from incongruity by the low bodices and uplift bras which thrust the bare black breasts into prominence. Each nipple-plum was painted yellow, and pierced with a ring, from which dangled a coiled silver serpent. Damara, bare-breasted above her fluttering white skirt, danced in barefoot attendance on Colonel Said. A silver ring pierced her right nipple.

Sheila and Nikko were to administer flogging, while Hawo and Capri auctioned the nude female slaves. The young naked males were sold by their own guards, both heavy-breasted Somalis, with jewelled necklaces and iron plates hanging over their upper teats and thighs. Their heads and pubic mounds were entirely shaven, but painted, like their bare croups, with interwoven green and yellow snakes. They wore the same phallic earrings as Dr Crevasse, and looked on the Hawo and her crew with some haughtiness. They too wore the phallus at their cunts, but theirs were larger, to fit the male anus.

'S'Ibaya,' hissed Hawo, with venom in her voice, 'so make a good show for the bitches, Lise, and you can take it out on my arse later.'

She placed a finger in Lise's perineum, the nail penetrating her anus bud in a sign of good luck, and signalled that her whipping should begin.

Thwack! Thwack!

'*Ohhh!*' Lise screamed, in unfeigned agony, as the two scourges lashed her naked buttocks and breasts. 'Ahhh . . . O!'

Thwack! Thwack!

'*Ahhh . . .! Ahhh . . .!*'

Sheila, taking the buttocks, lashed harder, while Nikko's strokes on the bare teats were more refined, and she managed to strike the nipple-buds with the tip of one thong, while getting the leather to cover almost all of Lise's naked breast-flesh, instead of bunching the thongs for a single, though deeper, weal. Sheila's muscular cuts made no attempt at subtlety: she applied the thongs with full force to a particular zone of Lise's buttocks, such as mid- or underfesse, for three or four strokes, until Lise's wriggling and screaming made the flogging awkward, at which point Sheila switched to another zone, the top buttocks or one of the haunches, allowing Lise's pain to build in a new crescendo. Meanwhile, there was the constant agony of the nipple clamps and the teat-scourging, the more hideous because of its deadly, thoughtful accuracy. There were pauses of at least a minute between strokes, to allow time for auction, and to prolong the smarting of the whipped slave's flesh.

Thwack! Thwack!

'*O! God! No, please no!*'

Lise's bared buttocks quivered like crimson jellies and she squirmed helplessly, as a fountain of come spurted from her cunt, trickling down her whipped teats and towards her face. Beneath her, the black male's mouth opened eagerly, his tool a black pole. The come slopped over Lise's short scalp-hair, drenching her thoroughly, then began a steady drip into the male's mouth. He groaned, smiling, and swallowed the cunt juice, licking his lips; his stiff cock danced. The lashes to Lise's skin were echoed by daintier, but forceful strokes of Hawo's cane to the first female slave up for auction. She was a tall, wide-fessed girl, whose heavy dugs brushed the ground, as she touched toes for caning.

Vip! Vip! Vip!

'Oooh!'

She squealed energetically, while Capri played with her clitoris, with sighs from the customers, satisfied at her copious juicing. Capri delicately masturbated herself, as she wanked off the caned slave-girl, and squashed her nipples in the sand, rubbing them with her toes. The drips of her own come mingled with the slave's increasingly copious cunt juice. Damara strolled behind Colonel Said, through the throng of guests, with her skirt raised and tucked in her nipple-ring. Cunt bare, and lips well parted to show her wet slit, she masturbated herself slowly and voluptuously, dipping her fingers into the lake of come that wet her gash and thighs, and smearing her slimed fingers across a male or female guest's lips, sometimes allowing the guest to suck her fingers dry.

Vip! Vip! Vip!

'O! O! O! Please, no!'

A raised finger signified a ten thousand dollar bid; followed at once by a female, with twelve thousand.

Vip! Vip! Vip!

'*Ahhhh . . .!*'

The girl pissed herself, and Capri cupped her palms under the flowing cunt. When her hands were full of steaming liquid, she pressed them under the lips of the caned girl, who eagerly sucked and swallowed her own piss. The bidding went to fifteen, twenty, then thirty thousand, before the bids stopped, and the girl received her final, twenty-second stroke of the cane, with Capri sealing the sale by deftly masturbating the slave's clitoris, and her own, to simultaneous orgasm, with applause from the guests. The slave padded to the side of her new owner, a male, who promptly cuffed her in a spiked dog's collar, made her kneel and take his erect penis in her mouth.

Speaking loudly, and with the pride of ownership, he directed her to wank herself off as she fellated him, and continue masturbating until she had orgasmed three more times. At her third orgasm, she was to dung on her own feet, then bring her master to spunk, swallowing his whole emission, then recommence wanking herself, while treading her own dung into the ground with her bare toes. This done to her master's satisfaction, she was to wank off, and cane her own bare bum, until she had fellated him to new stiffness. Damara rewarded her purchaser with a palmful of her own come, which he lapped, and wiped his lips and nose with the index finger she had removed from her anus.

Next, a young European male was led forward, touched his toes, and received a vigorous caning on the bare bum from one of the S'Ibaya guards. Her breast-plates clanged as she delivered the strokes in quickfire rhythm, and the male's body trembled, with fesses clenching. Tears moistened his eyes, yet his cock stood stiff, which brought 'ahh's of appreciation from the crowd. The other guard grasped his glans and began to rub his peehole, increasing the force of her masturbation as the caning, and the bidding, went on, starting at fifteen thousand dollars, and proceeding to forty. All the bidders were female.

At forty thousand dollars, and after the boy's quivering fesses were crimson with welts, the guard straddled him and inserted her silver phallus a short way into the male's bumhole. He groaned, and with a merciless thrust, she sank the metal shaft to the anal root, ignoring his yelps of pain as she began a vigorous buggery. The crowd cheered, and Damara now inserted one finger after another into her own anus, as she continued to wank her clitty, brushing the guests' faces, male and female, with her arse-greased and cunt-slimed fingers. After several minutes' buggery, the guard grasped the sobbing male's whole cock-shaft, and deftly wanked him off to a huge spurt of cream. A final bid of fifty thousand dollars took him, and he, too, padded meekly to his new owner, who at once recommenced his caning, wanking his cock, until he was stiff again, and masturbating herself with the stem of her goblet; she spread her thighs, still sipping her drink of cloudy white fluid, and instructed her new slave to bugger her, as hard as his guard had buggered his own anus.

Thwack! Thwack!

'*O, God, no . . .!*'

Lise's breast- and bum-whippings continued, at cruelly slow intervals, and her come filled the black male's gulping mouth. Her screams were louder, and her squirming more frantic, than any auctioned slave. When two males, and two females were sold, Lise's whippers changed implements and positions. Sheila was to work on Lise's cunt, while Nikko flogged her back and shoulders.

Thwack!

'*Ahhh!*'

At Sheila's first vicious lash, right on the pink meat between her gaping wet cunt lips, Lise pissed herself, her pee mingling with her copious come and drenching her own breasts, face and lips, before flowing down her scalp and into the erect boy's eager throat. He moaned and writhed in his shackles, as a droplet of sperm appeared at the peehole of his throbbing cock.

Thwack! Thwack!

Nikko lashed the shoulders, right beneath the nape, then, almost at once, gave a full cut to the mid-back.

'O! O! *Ohhh!*'

Thwack!

Sheila's next stroke hit Lise squarely on her erect and throbbing clitoris, and her loins jerked; her come flowed in torrents. Below her, the boy's glans was wet with the beginning of his spunking. Lise moaned that she was going to come, and the boy's cock jerked as he gulped her gush of come and the last droplets of golden pee, while emitting a powerful jet of sperm from his quivering black glans. Damara leapt forward and squatted, to catch the sperm in her mouth.

She passed coquettishly amongst the female buyers, finally selecting one for a full kiss on the mouth, in which she transferred the black male's load of sperm to the eager European female, who masturbated vigorously as she swallowed the black male's spunk, and waved to raise the bidding. The auction continued, with high prices paid for male and female slaves agile enough to bend double, and autofellate themselves as they were caned. Lise's own flogging continued, until half the slaves were sold. She wept and screamed uncontrollably, her body whipped raw and threshing, as come poured from her cunt. At the last two, simultaneous strokes to her back and cunt, she howled in climax, pissing herself again, with the male below gulping her come, his cock once more an ebony spear.

Hawo supervised Lise's release and, in mock-outrage, protested that her flogging had been too severe. Hoisting Lise on her back, she marched towards the coop, doubling behind it, till they came to the deserted tunnel entrance, leading to the temple of pleasure. Lise watched Hawo's naked breasts bobbing as she was carried piggy-back, and her erect clitty rubbed against the shaft of Hawo's neck, through her lustrous tresses, silky on Lise's nubbin. She looked down at the swaying of the ripe black buttocks she was soon to cane, and at the new flow of come from her own rubbed gash; bucking on piggy-back, Lise rubbed her swollen clitty against the black woman's nape, and her cunt gushed again in new orgasm. Only Damara watched them depart, her eyes on Lise's whipped buttocks, and finally completed her wank. Damara's slit gushed in spasm and she blew a kiss, from cunt-slimed fingers, at Lise's wealed red arse. Still wanking her swollen clit, Damara squatted in the sand, dunging and pissing, and grinned at Lise in mischievous pleasure.

12

Mam'selle

'You won't hurt me too much?' whispered Hawo, trembling.

Lise laughed, softly, but not gently.

'Look,' she said, touching her scarred buttocks and breasts. 'You expect me not to hurt you, Hawo? You *wanted* me to bring you here.'

'I wanted to know what it is like to be a slave,' said Hawo, gazing at Lise's wealed bare skin. 'Why slaves seem to feel such joy in submission, while for us taskmistresses, it is such hard work. I've never been beaten seriously: Colonel Said has caned me on the bare, but only with three or four stripes, almost in jest. I masturbate of course, whipping girls, or watching girls whipped, but as I wank, I . . . I imagine my own bottom flogged. Now that I see how hard my girls have beaten you, I'm not so sure.'

They stood in the temple of pleasure, far from the din of the auction above. Lise slapped Hawo hard on the face.

'O! Why . . .?'

'You may abandon this plan, if you wish, Hawo. A willing slave myself, I have no time for an unwilling one. Go, Hawo.'

She slapped her other cheek, and this time Hawo took the blow in silence.

'I will not leave,' she said.

'Then you must do whatever I say,' said Lise, 'and accept whatever punishment I apply, without protest, and without crying.'

Hawo nodded. Around them, the frames of torture gleamed in the flickering light of Hawo's candle. Lise smiled grimly: Hawo's golden phallus already dripped moisture, seeping from her quim. Lise grasped the phallus, and pulled hard; the inner prong slid easily from Hawo's lubricated cunt. It was smaller than the outer phallus, and Lise told Hawo that such items were sold with the smaller prong usually intended for the partner's anus.

'However,' she added, strapping on the dildo, 'we don't want to interefere with your S'Ibaya tradition.'

She pushed the smaller prong as far as it would go, inside her own rapidly moistening slit.

'I am not S'Ibaya, but Issa,' Hawo spat. 'Unlike that bitch Damara . . .'

'Then your Issa arsehole should be well able to take buggery from your own phallus,' Lise said, putting her hands on her hips, with legs akimbo.

Hawo shuddered.

'In my own bumhole . . .' she whispered, eyes fluttering.

'Hold your candle high, Hawo, and tilt it slightly, so that the wax drips on your nipples, while I describe your punishment.'

Hawo obeyed, grimacing as the first drops of hot wax scalded her nipple plums, part of the wax congealing and forming an extra skin.

'This machine will be suitable,' Lise said, tapping a cast-iron caning frame, equipped with levers, struts and cogwheels, to move its strapped occupant through various positions of chastisement: spreading the cunt lips, or raising the buttocks, squeezing the breasts in a tit-vice, or the quim in a gash-clamp, or many such refinements at the same time.

Hawo trembled as the hot wax congealed on her nipples, the breasts now enlarged so that the droplets flowed down her belly and formed another hot skin around the erect bud of her clitoris. Both nips and clitty seemed to grow visibly with the accretion of wax, and Hawo's gasps ceased as the wax no longer dripped on bare skin.

'First, I think I'll give you a proper English caning,' said Lise, 'to warm your bum for harder discipline. Ten on the bare should do nicely, if you would be so kind as to assume the position, touching your toes, *Mademoiselle* Hawo.'

Lise took the candlestick from her, and the black girl bent over, spreading her thighs and buttocks wide, as directed. Lise selected a thin, springy cane, not long, but suitable for work at close quarters. Haro's perineum was stretched taut between the pears of her buttocks, with the gash and anus bud clear targets for the cane. Hot wax dripped.

'O!' Hawo squealed, clenching her arse-globes.

'I warned you, no noise,' snapped Lise. 'That earns you two extra strokes, a full dozen on your bare· bum, *mam'selle.*'

Lise had tilted the candle so that the wax dripped directly onto Hawo's anus pucker, wrinkled and extruded like a palm date. The wax continued to drip, until the anal lips were submerged in a waxen hillock, whose whorls replicated the wrinkles of the skin it covered.

'Th ... this is how English schoolgirls are caned?' quavered Hawo.

'Apart from the candle wax, yes,' said Lise. 'Although not always ... and an English schoolgirl remains partially clothed. She must bend over, and lower her knickers to her knees, then undo her garter straps, so that they tuck up into her suspender belt, and leave her whole bum bare for her stripes. The knickers are usually spread tight between her thighs, so that if she wets herself, or if her quim drips too much come, the knickers will be wet. That earns her an extra punishment of ten more on the bare, with her wet knickers stuffed in her mouth. There are stricter schools, where canings are given on the nude body, with fastenings for wrists and ankles, on a converted vaulting horse. Whippings, too, with a scourge of four or five thongs, and whippings by schoolgirls on other schoolgirls can be quite bestial. With the cane, and the victim dressed, a certain restraint, or decorum, is preserved. When the girl is to be flogged nude, and ignominiously strapped, decorum vanishes. That was my experience, at least ...'

Vip!

'O!'

'I have been whipped enough here, Hawo, for me to become quite bestial with you. I intend to place your body in severe restraint, on this flogging rack – tightening it at each stroke, either of cane or whip – and you shall be caned and whipped on the back, cunt and breasts, as well as further caning of your buttocks. At any undue noise, you shall be gagged. When I choose, I shall impale and bugger you one hundred times with your own phallus, making you drink your come after each buggery, but forbidding you to masturbate, no matter how wet your gash is.'

Vip!

'O!'

Vip!

'*Ohhh . . .!*'

'Not *too* much noise, mam'selle.'

'It stings, though, Miss Lise. O! I never realised how much a bare caning could smart! Colonel Said insists on pure sadism. We are forbidden to taste a slave's humiliation, lest we might sympathise and become lenient.'

Vip! Vip!

'Mm!'

'And your four on the bare?'

'A foretaste of what he *might* inflict, if slaves are insufficiently disciplined. Colonel Said teaches that guards must be cruel and slaves crushed. Only the Galafi snake, or a S'Ibaya, can be two things at once.'

Hawo's naked bottom was quivering, and her arse-globes clenching in a tight, automatic rhythm. The cane thrashed each buttock separately, not touching the whorled hillock of wax which adorned Hawo's arse-pucker.

Vip! Vip! Vip!

'O! Lise! O, you . . .'

'Hurt a lot?'

'Yes, but . . . something else, too. Warmth . . .'

Vip! Vip! Vip! Vip!

'O! *Oooh!*'

'That's your twelve, Hawo.'

Lise threw down the cane.

'Now, I have something else to warm you up. Something I didn't get.'

Hawo's nude body was chained to the frame by her waist, with her legs bent back, spine arched, and ankles cuffed in front of her throat, with her toes at her mouth. Her wrists were suspended behind and above her by a ceiling chain. Her thighs were splayed wide, revealing the wet cunt wide open, and the wax-crusted arse pucker and clit. The zones exposed for flogging were her back, cunt, breasts and thighs; the buttocks glowed purple from her dozen with the cane, and were within easy reach of a slicing whipstroke between the thigh-backs and spinal base.

Lise selected a whip of ten thongs, and explained that she would apply the instrument variously to breasts, cunt and back, until the candles were extinguished. Hawo's ankles would then be shifted to her waist-chain, one ankle bound to each hip; she would be placed on her belly, and her thighs fully parted, still with her arms suspended above her. This position would expose the buttocks for a vigorous buggery, after which her bum would receive a further ten canestrokes. When this was done, she would be laid on a revolving rack, which permitted the flogging of all her sensitive parts in sequence, as the rack moved at the pressure of Lise's foot on a treadle, like an old-fashioned sewing machine's.

'In olden times,' Lise said, 'this was called putting a victim to the question, and there are some questions I want answers to, mam'selle.'

'I don't understand . . . Candles . . .?' bleated Hawo, her ebony skin trembling and shiny with sweat, that mingled with the come now flowing copiously from her spread cunt lips.

Lise lit a second candle and sliced another in half, extracting the fresh wick, which she cut in four pieces. She let the candle drip hot wax, to add to Hawo's already voluminous nipple-mounds, while inserting two lengths of wick into the softened wax, so that the wick touched bare nipple skin. She did the same with her waxed anus-bud, and the stumpy walnut of her waxed clit, building it into a new candle like a misshapen toy castle. She lit all four candles; Hawo was burning at nipples, clitty and anus bud. The wax from her inverted arse-bud dripped down her perineum and into her wet cunt mouth, while the clit-wax seeped down her hillock, with globules of wax dripping from her nip-candles into her navel.

'I shall give you twenty strokes of the whip between your slit flaps, right in the cunt,' said Lise, 'taking care not to spoil the clitty-candle. The wax from your arse-candle will be uncomfortable as it drips into your open cunt. As the flame burns the wax and nears your nips, pucker and clitty, you may wish to answer some questions, and I may agree to blow out the candles before they gutter with the flame on your raw flesh.'

Vap!

'*Ahhh!*'

Lise's whip struck Hawo fully inside her vaginal slit, the tips flicking expertly to cover the entire pink cunt walls.

Vap!

'O! O!'

That stroke lashed her perineum; the next, the exposed lower fesses, above the arse-candle, and perilously close to the anus; the next, two rapid strokes in the cleft of her breasts, with care to weal the teats without disturbing the candles, whose flame glowed closer and closer to the nipples themselves.

'Ask,' sobbed Hawo. 'The wax is burning me so horribly ... O, rather my cunt flogged a hundred times ... than *this*!'

'Good!' said Lise.

Vap! Vap! Vap! Vap!

She lashed twice in Hawo's armpits, and twice on her bare back.

'*O! O!* Please, miss ...'

'A few answers, and we can blow out the flames before they singe your precious parts – as mine were singed by the sacred gash!'

'You are a slave,' groaned Hawo.

'And now you know what it feels like.'

'Ask, I beg you!' Hawo sobbed, her stretched arms jangling her chains.

'Very well,' said Lise.

Vap! Vap! She whipped a separate stroke to each cunt flap.

'*Mm! O!*' Hawo sobbed.

'With satisfactory answers, the flames will be blown out, and your nipples, clit and bum-bud flogged naked of wax, so that my phallus can penetrate and bugger your anus. *Then,* I might decide to accept your suggestion of a hundred – *cane*strokes, mind! – to the cunt and bare clit.'

Vap! Vap! Vap!

The ten-thonged whip covered Hawo's dripping cunt three times.

'*Ahhhh . . .!*'

Hawo sobbed answers, as her nude body writhed under Lise's whip. Yes, she was a slave, like Colonel Said, and Dr Crevasse, and everyone in the desert; even the lustful guests were slaves of their own desires. The Legion ruled everywhere, except . . .

Vap! Vap!

The whip lashed Hawo's waxed clitoris, and she screamed.

'*Ahhh . . . O*, God! It is forbidden to speak . . .'

Vap! Vap! Vap! Vap!

Four whipstrokes lashed her bare nates.

'Except?' Lise hissed.

Vap! Vap!

Hawo's bare black titties danced, and she squealed, sobbing.

'Except the cavern of the S'Ibaya. Some say that the S'Ibaya rule the Legion . . .! That Dr Crevasse is the reincarnation of S'Ibaa herself. The virgin goddess of this whipped earth of Djibouti, the fesses of the world. I can never be more than a mere taskmistress, my arse will never approach the sacred dimension! Unlike yours, Miss Lise! So big, so ripe . . . if only your fesses were sacred black!

184

The German woman was here, the photographer, with her daughter, looking for the perfect arse, the perfect female fesses, to photograph, and she left, recklessly seeking the S'Ibaya themselves. Only there is arse-perfection! They have the juice of the true earth cunt. Intruders to the sacred cavern cannot emerge unchanged!'

The candle flames were perilously close to her nips and clit, and the wax had entirely melted from her arse-bud, with a faint odour of singed downy hairs which adorned her perineum.

Vap! Vap! Vap!

'O! O! I'm pissing myself!'

A fierce spout of pee hissed from Hawo's pulsing cunt, splashing Lise's own pubis and the golden phallus, trickling down to her ankles. Lise jumped, as the hot pee washed her clitty, the nubbin standing firm and erect, and when Hawo looked round in embarrassment, her eyes widened: come was streaming down Lise's legs, spouting in a glistening gush from swollen gash lips, and mingling with Hawo's piss.

'*You* are sadist, too,' Hawo murmured.

'Bitch,' said Lise mildly, and landed three more strokes of the whip on either side of Hawo's clit-wax, bruising and swelling the engorged flaps of the girl's wet cunt.

'*Ahhh . . .!*'

Lise blew out the flames at her breasts and clit, then began a rapid whipping, until the nipples shone naked and erect, and the nubbin, extruded and shiny with come, was denuded of wax. She laid aside her whip as she straddled the massive black buttocks, now scarred with welts. She plunged a fist into Hawo's spread gash, and withdrew a palmful of oily come, which she used to lubricate the golden phallus. The tip of the huge carved glans forced Hawo's anus bud open.

'Don't resist,' said Lise.

She got the dildo into Hawo's anus, until the whole glans was swallowed. Hawo's buttocks squirmed, rubbing the tool, and she moaned.

'There!' Lise said. 'That's the hardest part. Now you must relax your sphincter . . .'

'O! O! It hurts! I can't!'

'Damn you, then!'

Whack! Whack! Whack!

Lise spanked the bruised bare fesses with both palms, then, with a powerful thrust of her hips and buttocks, plunged the phallus inside the black girl's resistant bumhole.

'Ahhh!' Hawo shrieked. 'No . . . no . . .'

Lise thrust again; the phallus stuck, briefly, and Hawo squealed louder, then her anus elastic suddenly burst open, and Lise sank the shaft right to the hilt, the glans slamming the hard nubbin of the anal root.

Whack! Whack! Whack! Whack!

Lise coninued to spank the black girl's naked haunches as she buggered her hole, and Hawo's arse squirmed vainly, as if to ease the pain of the spanks, and the relentless penetration of her anus. Come oil dripped faster and faster from her writhing cunt lips as she was buggered, and she swivelled her belly, trying to rub her clitty on the pile of solidified wax drippings beneath her cunt.

'There is more,' Lise panted.

'O! God! How it hurts!'

'It will hurt more unless you tell me everything.'

Hawo's come was a glistening torrent from her cunt, as she writhed under buggery, masturbating her clit against the wax, which softened and melted at her clit-wanking and the heat of her cunt juice.

'The Galafi snake . . .'

Spank! Spank! Spank! Spank!

Hawo's bruised haunches glowed purple.

'Ahh . . . God, you bitch!'

'A cunt-caning to come!' Lise cried, as she buggered. 'Seventy-eight, seventy-nine . . .'

'Ooh! Ooh! Don't stop! Bugger my arse, spank me, spank me harder, mam'selle, O! O . . . yes, O, I'm coming! *Ahhh . . . mam'selle!*'

Hawo's cunt flowed with come, the puddle of clear fluid joined almost at once by a hissing stream of gold, as she pissed into her come-pool. Lise continued her buggery of

186

the girl's bum to one hundred, now vigorously wanking her own clit, with her own come streaming down the crack of Hawo's ebony arse. She curled the thongs of her whip to make a cup, which she slopped full of the come and pee. Wanking her clit, she drank the oily mixture, then refilled the cup and pressed it to Hawo's lips. As the black girl thirstily drank her own fluids, Lise masturbated her clitty with the whip handle, while fist-fucking her own slimy gash, and gasped long and loud in orgasm.

Hawo's arms were released, and the rack lowered, to take the full length of her body, with wrists and ankles bound to each end. Lise's foot operated the treadle, and Hawo groaned as her body was stretched. Beneath her cunt-mound, a saddle forced her to maintain her thighs apart, and her buttocks raised and vulva exposed, in correct caning, or gamahuching, position. The small of her back dipped sharply, past her buttocks, so that the perineum, the buggered arse-bud and the gash were presented vertically, and the buttocks for caning from above. Lise plunged her tongue into the anal hole her dildo had buggered, pulled the phallus from her cunt, and began to masturbate Hawo's clit with its glans.

'Ohh ... don't stop,' Hawo mewled, 'snake my bum-hole.'

Lise inserted the phallus all the way up her own bumhole, squeezing it tightly, and slipped her whole tongue into Hawo's anus, slimy with arse-grease, for a tongue-buggery, while nipping the engorged clitty with finger and thumb. Her free hand masturbated herself, with two, then three, and finally four fingers straight inside her cunt, and feeling her wombneck, which her fingernails penetrated. Her thumb squashed her clitty in rhythmic movement, and when she was fully finger-fucking her own cunt, she removed her thumb from Hawo's clit and balled her fist, which slid after some resistance right to the hard wombneck of the black girl's tight, soaking cunt. Lise fist-fucked Hawo, her thighs squeezing the phallus inside her own bumhole, and her come was so copious that it flowed on her perineum, and made the golden dildo slippery. She took her tongue from Hawo's anus, and demanded the whole truth, then recommenced her anal tonguing, nuzzling her nose in the ripe cleft of Hawo's buggered and piss-soaked arse. She pressed the treadle, and the rack creaked. Her crevice and bumhole were so wet with her cunt-slime that the dildo slid from her anus and fell with a clang.

'Ahhh . . .!' Hawo screamed. 'O, don't stop! Tongue me, cane my cunt! Come back from the S'Ibaya enriched, Lise, and fuck me with your tool of flesh! So good to be a slave! Hurt me, make me come and come . . .'

She howled in another twitching orgasm, as the rack stretched her a notch, with her conic teats now flattened quivering jellies on her ribcage. Lise's wanking brought her to another, heaving come; she withdrew her tongue from Hawo's anus and her fist from the girl's streaming cunt. She pressed her mouth to Hawo's cunt, and began to drink her juices, picking up the small whippy cane, as she swallowed hot cunt oil.

'Piss again, Hawo, and I'll have something to cane your naughty gash for,' she whispered, mouth pressed against Hawo's cunt lips and her voice making them vibrate.

At once, Lise's mouth filled with hot steaming pee, and, greedily, she swallowed the whole stream, wanking her clit to new stiffness. Hawo groaned, and peed again, in little thin spurts, as her anus opened, and she dunged, the stools dropping on Lise's bare breasts, and one dung lodging at her cunt-lips, where her wanking squashed it into her throbbing clitty. Hawo's dunging brought Lise off, and she squealed in pleasure as she climaxed again. Straight away, she rose, trembling, still feeling her dung-slimed clitty, and began to cane Hawo on the slit, alternating strokes directly to the clitoris with full thrashing of the slimy cunt-walls.

'One hundred on the cunt, Hawo,' she said.

'Yes . . . *O! O! Yes!* Snake-whip my cunt! O . . . *Damara!*' Hawo drooled in a delirium of humiliant pleasure.

Vip! Vip! Vip! Vip!

The cane made a wet, slapping noise as it thrashed the girl's naked cunt. She began to babble.

'The supreme arse of S'Ibaa, the sacred measure ... snake can be cock or cunt, man or woman. The goddess who fucks herself ...'

Lise wanked herself and Hawo to another climax at the forty-first stroke to her gash, and again, at the eightieth. Hawo's cunt kept up a running dribble of piss, and she dunged copiously, in hard little pellets that spattered Lise's bare feet, as she babbled. Somewhere in the desert, the S'Ibaya inhabited a cavern, where ancient, and perhaps murderous, or cannibalistic rituals were enacted. Was this what the constantly buzzing Legion helicopters were trying to find, or why the pilot Gilles seemed so friendly with Damara and Dr Crevasse, S'Ibayas both? The ability of the S'Ibaya, both male and female, to autofellate, symbolised the eternal circle of the world snake, with its tail in its mouth: Afgoi could bend down to suck his own cock, and Melleah, to tongue her own cunt.

In S'Ibaya mythology, the Galafi snake tunnelled through rock, disguised as a male glans, or female croup, and enchanted its victims thus, before devouring them. Snakes could impersonate women wholly, for long periods, detectable by the grandeur of their arses. Snakes were feared and worshipped, and since they only assumed the form of a large-buttocked woman, it followed that the female arse was holy, and the female with the sacred proportion was worshipped as a goddess. The swelling of the arse resembled the stomach of the snake, with its victim inside; the gash of the female, the cavern of the snake's throat. Women were goddesses: it was sacred to be eaten alive by a woman's cunt, and become her arse. Her anus itself was the holiest temple.

Lise laid down the cane; quickly, she unbound Hawo, as there were noises above. Hawo led her to the furnace-like chamber of the sacred gash, and showed her the escape tunnel.

'I cannot escape,' Hawo said forlornly. 'The desert traps each of us in our circle of cruelty. Fort Lafresne is one circle, Dr Crevasse's clinic another, Colonel Said's auction house yet another. But even he is trapped – he can never be black, the colour of the true arse! All are trapped in their own circle, save the S'Ibaya, who move freely, from their own, innermost circle. That bitch Damara! How I want her to devour me!'

'What of the finishing school?' said Lise.

'The desert is the finishing school!' cried Hawo. 'The Legion *wants* us to desert ... to find our true circle of cruelty!'

'And the Legion is under S'Ibayan domination ...' mused Lise, as she squeezed into the scented tunnel, just fitting, like a cock in a cunt ...

Hawo said that the Galafi snakes of old were indeed of human size, and oiled the tunnels with venom, which smelled like female human come and was as slippery, but ebony in colour.

'The venom of the female Galafi snake is poisonous only to *male* humans,' she added, with a shy smile. 'Not to females.'

Lise was fully immersed in the tunnel. She shivered. There was only darkness in front of her. Behind her were the voices of Colonel Said, Sheila, Capri and Nikko.

'Why do you not escape, then?' she asked Hawo, as she began to scramble to her dark freedom.

'I would not be welcomed in the cavern of the S'Ibaya.'

Lise panted as she climbed the upward slope of the tunnel, which suddenly came to a knife-sharp turn that pinched her vulva, and she cried out. Her eyes blurred with sweat. She climbed on and suddenly began to slither downwards. The tunnel fell sharply, leaving Lise without a handhold, and helpless to stop her progress. The walls were getting slimier, and her naked body was greasy with the oil that smelled just like come, freshly exuded. The tunnel's gradient grew steeper, and Lise realised she was being carried below the level of the sacred gash, though far away from it.

'You've tricked me!' Lise screamed.

'Not entirely,' she heard Colonel Said's voice, a tinny echo, far away. 'Your session with Hawo was most helpful, Nurse Gallard, in revealing to us her true submissive nature, and your own, dare I extend the compliment, essentially dominant one. Damara enjoyed some delightful wanks as you cunt-caned and buggered Hawo, who shall be a worthy replacement slave for yourself. A few sessions of buggery from my own tool should have her well tamed in time for the next auction. Hawo did slightly mislead you, though. The tunnel oiled with snake-come, which is the same thing as snake venom – a melanin compound most interesting to scholars and albinos – is indeed harmless to human females, *but only if they are S'Ibayan.*'

Lise screamed, as the ever-thickening walls of slime slowed her progress in the darkened tunnel. She careered around corners, up and down slopes, like a human bobsled, the snake venom, or come, ever more viscous, and seeming to drown her in its fragrant slime. Her whole body was covered in thick, scented grease, which filled her mouth and nose, her cunt and anus, like sucking tentacles of come oil. She choked, as the dark come filled her throat, making her swallow. Her anus and cunt were full of the slime, and she felt it invade her womb and belly, creeping like tendrils, invading her, filling her. The come-venom palpitated within her quim and anus, as though the stiffening liquid was forming into twin cocks, fucking and buggering her, while her mouth sucked a third slime-cock. She tried to scream, but more of the slime filled her throat, and she swallowed, bloating her belly.

The slope of the tunnel slackened, and she saw a dim light ahead. Her descent became slower, and the tunnel seemed to narrow, grasping her body like a sphincter preparing to expel her; with a sudden, plopping sound, Lise spurted into a dim, ovoid chamber, with a mirrored ceiling and floor, of a glazed creamy substance. Sobbing, she stood, wiping the slime from her body. Her eyes were clouded, and she only dimly saw another figure in the chamber, apparently a long distance away, and unaware of Lise's presence. The dim light seemed to emanate from the floor and ceiling of the room, and the air was perfumed with girl-scent and girl-come.

Its other occupant was a black girl, of such stunning beauty, with arse, tits and belly of such perfect proportions over such superbly muscled coltish legs, that Lise turned away in embarrassment, trying to scoop the snake-come from her own body. The black girl had a shaven head and cunt. At last, Lise could no longer restrain her curiosity, and turned to find the girl facing her, unsmiling. The shock of her beauty was too much for Lise, and her cunt began to juice powerfully. Her hand flew to her vulva, pretending to scratch herself, but in fact masturbating hard on her erect and throbbing clitty. Come streamed from her cunt and trickled down her bare legs onto the glazed floor, into which it seemed to melt. Lise did not rub the sweat and slime from her eyes; the blurred image alone of the black goddess, her glorious proportions of arse and teat, was enough to bring her to a shuddering orgasm.

She wiped her eyes. The ovoid chamber widened, then narrowed, to a hanging door which was woven with hanks of girls' pube-hair. The black girl was staring there, too. Lise made another attempt to rub the black snake-come from her body. The black goddess did the same, which made Lise frown. She moved closer, determined to brazen it out with this insolent slut, who was so beautiful that she had caused Lise to forget her dignity, and publicly masturbate! The black girl approached Lise; the walls of the room were mirrors, glazed and creamy, like the floor and ceiling, so that the chamber now appeared to be quite small. Lise stared, mouth agape, and her reflection stared back. Lise felt her ebony skin, and found it bone dry.

She looked at the superb black girl in the mirror, the satin skin, the pink cunt-meat peeping under the dark bare mound and, as the heady, girl-scented air invaded her, her cunt began to seep come again. Slowly, deliberately, Lise Gallard masturbated again, rubbing her clit and playing with the folds of her vulva, giddy with delight at the contrast between her pink wet gash and the ebony magnificence of her body. There was not a drop of grease or sweat left on her silky skin. Lise swayed, twisting her back, then bent suddenly over, until her mouth was at her quim, and her erect clitty between her lips. She tongued her own clitty, and then slid her tongue all the way into her slit, and began to tongue-fuck herself. Come flowed from her cunt, and she swallowed every drop of her own love oil. After penetrating, sucking, and tonguing her own cunt for two minutes, she stood, breathless and on the brink of orgasm. Face slopped with her own come, she masturbated to a shameless, joyful climax, gazing at her own reflection in the looking-glass. Lise Gallard was a S'Ibaya.

13

Hanging Gallery

After pushing through the doorway of pubic tendrils, Lise heard a cane cracking twice on bare skin and a woman's scream. Two more strokes followed, and another scream, this voice more girlish and shrill.

'*O! O! Ach, ich kann nicht . . .*'

Vip! Vip!

'*Ahhh . . .!*' screamed the older female.

'*Du musst, Anna . . .*' she sobbed.

Vip! Vip!

'*Ahhh . . .!*'

Lise concealed herself in a darkened corner of a cavern, lit at the centre by a shimmering glow, which seemed to emanate from the walls themselves, made of the same glazed substance as the floor of the mirrored room. The low ceiling of the cavern was two large ovals, separated by a crevice, the whole roof resembling an enormous sculpted croup. From within this crevice hung life-size statues of three nude African females, made of gleaming white stone: marble or alabaster. The women were hanged by the neck, with sandstone snakes as nooses, and their wrists were bound behind their backs, tied to their ankles: the legs were bent up, pressing the soles against the small of the back, leaving the marble buttocks, cunts and bumholes completely exposed. All were etched to lifelike precision, with the conic teats jutting stiffly upwards, as though wrenched by invisible wire. The tails of the snakes led into a hole, like a human anus, the sculptures like bunches of grapes on a vine, rooted in this stone bumhole.

Further along the ceiling swellings lay a gash, like a human cunt. Three more females, ebony of skin, hung from ropes disappearing into a monstrous vagina; the sculptures were not hanged by the neck, but suspended from clamped cunts or nipples, with their wrists bound behind their backs, as lifelike as the hanged white sculptures. One was upside down, with feet crossed over her breasts and the toes crammed in her mouth, and held by strands from ankles to earlobes; her body hung from clamps on her clitoris and cunt lips, and an anal plug. All the mannequins dangled inches from the floor. The hanged white sculptures were Kee, Deydey and Guestir, and the ebony figures, Loosje, Toyo and Heidi, slaves of Dr Crevasse. The anally plugged girl was Heidi.

Beneath the sculptures, one wall was occupied by a row of young black females, the other by a row of males. All were nude and masturbating slowly, with their heads turned away from Lise towards two European females being caned, at the far end of the chamber. The fluids from the S'Ibayan girls' wanked cunts were so copious that come streamed in bright rivulets across the glazed flooring. Three S'Ibayan females armed with copper-tipped braided scourges supervised the masturbators, their bodies bare but for flaps of copper and iron which loosely covered their breasts, and skirts of the same metals for fesses and pubic mounds. Beneath their guards' armour, their nude bodies were painted, or tattooed, with garish snakes, whose tails curled around the nipples, and fangs gaped above the cunt lips. The armour plates clanked as the guards moved amongst six naked S'Ibayan girls, spreadeagled belly down on the come-soaked floor, and who seemed to be swimming. A frequent crack of a scourge on bare buttocks encouraged the swimmer in her task: the job of these slaves was to spread the come of the masturbating girls, and the two caned females, in an even glaze across the entire cavern floor, using their breasts and cunt-mounds as mops. The frequency of whipstrokes on their own bare buttocks, all well striped, meant that their own come added to the puddles trickling from the cunts of the masturbators.

The caned females were naked but for yellow scarves knotted around their necks, and perched side by side on two movable flogging-rails with wheels. The women's ankles were tied to the bases of the rails, also with yellow scarves. Their caned buttocks faced Lise, and the caners had their backs to her. The two females straddled their flogging rails with the crossbars pressed deep into their vaginas, and their whole body-weight thus taken by their cunts. The legs of the apparatus were splayed, so that the buttocks of the women were spread wide, showing gashes and anus buds, with the perineums taut, and the croups sitting right on the end of the rails, so that the whole bum-flesh was exposed to the cane.

One woman was perhaps forty years of age, the other half that; both had firm, athletic bodies and ripe buttock-pears, but the young woman's croup was larger than her elder's. Both women were tall, and both were knotted with muscle, with unbroken suntans, but the elder female's skin was more deeply browned. Her buttocks were harder, the cane seeming to land on the gluteal muscle itself, knotted under paper-thin hide. The younger girl had a hint of softness in her ripe, pear-shaped fesses, despite the muscles that squirmed visibly under the golden skin at each whop of the cane on her bare. The canes sliced the bum-buds, perineum and exposed cunt lips in alternate strokes. Their backs were erect and their arms stretched wide in traditional back-whipping position, but the wrists were unbound. Each female clung to ropes hanging from the cavern ceiling, their muscles of arms, back and shoulders knotted and rippling, as they tried to hoist their bodies up from the pressure of the crossbar.

The rail was a sculpted phallus, with the massive glans facing their bellies; the women's cunts sat not on the glans, but on a sharp, narrow tongue, like a snake's, which projected from the peehole of the phallus. Taut wires ran from each woman's pierced nipples to the snake's tail, pulling the titties down, so that by hoisting herself, to ease the pain in her cunt, she tightened her nipple-wires. Lise gasped; a seep of come wetted her thighs and her clitty

196

tingled; her fingers crept to rub her stiffening nipples, then her throbbing nubbin, already moist with come, as she watched the golden caned buttocks.

. . . dare I extend the compliment, essentially dominant . . .

Vip! Vip!

'*Ach! Gott!*'

Vip! Vip!

'O! O! O! *Ohhh . . .!*'

Both nude bodies wriggled on the snake's tongue, which bit deeper into their cunts at each canestroke, yet both cunts oozed come, which dripped from the tongue like the snake's saliva. Their heavy breasts jiggled and bounced at the caning of their bare croups, and two long blonde manes cascaded, writhing like snakes, on their jerking backs. Both the females had their hair braided, the younger one's knotted in ropes, and the elder's braided in two pigtails, each with a yellow ribbon. Lise watched their bodies quiver as their buttocks were caned, and saw them as two halves of one flogged being: mother and daughter. Even the rhythm of their agony was the same, their squirms and shudders in dreadful harmony. Lise counted thirty separate cane-weals on each bare croup, the strokes not crossed, but in a fine weft of crimson threads. Though their backs were to Lise, their shaking bare breasts were so large that their bums' squirming made them flap like balloons on either side of their torsos.

The caners were both black, male, and also nude, and the penis of each was massively erect. Two S'Ibayan girls, clad only in short, pleated white skirts, masturbated the cocks of the males, in time with their caning. Each girl had her hand under the other's skirt, as they rubbed the black satin of the fully circumcised cocks; the girls' breasts swayed softly, as they wanked each other off. Their skirts rode up, showing a portion of buttock, and the cotton was deeply stained with come from the sliver of swollen cunt meat just visible.

Vip! Vip! Vip! Vip!

'*Ahhh!*'

'*Ohhh!*' screamed the girl. '*Ach, Waltraut!*'

Lise shuddered. Titzi's words came back to her: the rival for Waltraut's affection, the big-bummed submissive girl: they *were* mother and daughter. Waltraut and Anna had found the S'Ibaya, or the S'Ibaya had found *them*. The long line of black girls swayed as they masturbated, watching the canings. Lise's own cunt was very wet, and she moved forward into the dim glow. All the wanking girls had their eyes fixed on the squirming bare croups of Waltraut and her daughter, with the yellow scarves, knotted at neck and ankles, fluttering as their lashed bodies quivered. The black girls' hips swayed in unison, as fingers delicately frotted stiff nubbins, and Lise joined the end of the line, wanking off in the same slow rhythm, with her land lowered to squeeze her swollen gash flaps, and turn her increasing seep of hot come into a spurt of fluid that squirted forward, before wetting her thighs and trickling down to her slippery bare toes. All the other girls played with themselves in the same manner, alternating clit-strokes with deep fingering of the cunt; Lise sighed as her fingertips found the hard wombneck and squeezed the key to Dr Crevasse's cunt, firmly lodged there, using it for deep masturbation.

Come flooded her wrists and the Somali girls began to croon, their bellies fluttering, as they approached orgasm. The rhythmic nature of the joint masturbation gave way to individual passion, as some girls raised their thighs to insert fingers into their bumholes; others bent down to tongue-fuck their own cunts; some played with their nipple plums, raising legs to their gashes and foot-fucking their pouches, or toe-frotting their extruded clitties.

Vip! Vip! Vip!

'*Ach . . . Ahhh!*'

'*O! O! O!*'

The cunts of Waltraut and her daughter also dripped with copious come, and their gulping cries were no longer of pain alone. Their bums now bore over forty stripes, and the strokes began to criss-cross, since every caning zone, from underfesse to top buttock, was now wealed, including both haunches, welted deep purple. The line of males

198

suddenly arched their backs, and, as one, took their penises into their mouths to autofellate themselves. Lise wanked harder and harder, now balancing on tiptoe with a foot deep in her cunt, and her toes wriggling against her wombneck, while three bunched fingers pummelled her anal root, sliding in and out of her arse pucker, shiny with bum-grease. Forefinger and thumb squeezed the dripping come from her lower cunt lips, while her whole free hand slapped her clitty, with pauses to pinch her hard expanded nips, and squeeze her titties.

Vip! Vip! Vip! Vip!

'*Ach . . . Gott, ich komme! Anna, Anna, kommst du?*'

Vip! Vip! Vip! Vip!

'*O ! O! Ja . . . ja . . .*'

Anna suddenly pissed herself, the steaming spray of pee flooding the backs of her legs, already shiny with her oozing come. Her mother groaned and pissed immediately after her daughter, and both females began to gasp at the onrush of orgasm. Their male caners were masturbated faster by the kneeling females, each of whom had her skirt between her teeth, baring cunt and bum entirely, and showing nimble fingers deep inside her sopping wet gash, while thumbing an enormously protruding stiff clitty.

Vip! Vip! Vip! Vip!

'*Ahhh . . . O!*'

'*Ahhh . . . Mm! Mm!*'

Both caned females convulsed in orgasm, and jets of sperm spurted from their caners' cocks, to splash hard on their squirming buttocks. The canes were lowered; still masturbating, the white-skirted girls rubbed the sperm into the weals of the German females, until each darkened bum was glazed with male spunk. One by one, the autofellating males rose and crossed the cavern to the line of wanking girls, who each knelt to receive his swollen organ into her throat and swallow his spunk. Lise held off her own come, until a massive dark glans thrust between her lips; eagerly, she gobbled the pulsing shaft until she almost choked, with the peehole against her uvula, then screamed in pleasure as her own come flooded her, and the male bathed her throat in spunk. She swallowed the spurts of hot cream, licking the shaft and glans of the huge black penis, until she had taken every sperm-drop. The penis softened only slightly as she continued to rub her tongue on his peehole.

The male knelt between her thighs, and began to tongue her clitty, licking and swallowing her own new flood of come; all the kneeling girls received the same homage from the males, each of whose cocks fully stiffened once more. The caners of Waltraut and Anna stood with hands on hips, as the white-skirted girls crouched beneath the caning rails and drank the come and piss of the two flogged women; their satin black cocks hardened again to new stiffness, and they resumed the bare-bum caning of Waltraut and Anna, while the two girls pressed their lips to the cunts of mother and daughter and began to tongue-fuck them. Soon, the two caned females were sobbing again in growing pleasure, as the African girls' white teeth shone, chewing on two raw pink nubbins, while allowing the copious flows of cunt juice to enter their throats.

The caning continued until the two females had orgasmed again, and the caners now handed their rods to the girls with come-slimed faces. They took position, each with his glans buried in the crevice of a caned arse, and waited until the first lashes of the cane struck their own bare fesses, before sliding their cocks into the German females' arse-puckers. Anna and her mother screamed, yet each parted her buttocks to allow the cock its anal ingress. Inch by inch, the black cock-meat penetrated the squirming pink arse-buds of the white women; at each onward penetration, Anna and Waltraut moaned more shrilly, but their moans turned to sobs of pleasure, as the cocks were plunged into their anal elastic, with only the ball-sacks still visible.

Vip! Vip!

The males made no sound, as the girls, still wanking off, caned their bare bums, and they began to bugger mother and daughter in the rhythm of their own canings. Their bellies slapped against the thrashed buttocks of the two buggered women, as they drove their cocks right to the hilt at each canestroke, then withdrew almost entirely, teasing the anal pucker with the slimy black glans, before another canestroke on their bare buttocks made them plunge into the bumholes of the white women, as though to seek sanctuary from their own caning. Lise's feet left the floor, and she found her face against the cavern wall, with the male holding her by the nipples, painfully wrenching her teats as he pressed them on the glazed surface. His hand plunged into her cunt and began to wank her clitty; withdrew, briefly, to oil his cock with her come, then returned, to begin a vigorous fist-fucking of her cunt, filling her slimy wet pouch to bursting.

Lise's hands supported herself against the cavern walls, which were hot and slippery as the glaze softened; the cavern itself was made of human come. She gasped, as the male's cock found her anal opening and slid inside her arsehole. She lifted her thighs as high and wide as she could to permit him entrance to her bum, but his tool was so large that his penetration was slow, and each thrust, wrenching her anal elastic, made Lise howl in pain and pleasure. Her cunt flowed come over the male's ball-sack and thighs, as he finally pressed his peehole to the root of her anus, then began a hard bum-fucking, drawing the massive tool out almost fully at each stroke, then plunging in hard, so that each stroke of his buggery was as painful as a new penetration. His fingers squeezed her wombneck as he fist-fucked her vulva, and Lise's haunches writhed, to wank her clitty against the viscous come-wall, where she squashed her tits, rubbing her nipples in a circular motion. Opposite, the caning of the males continued, as they buggered mother and daughter with harder and harder strokes. Anna and Waltraut were squealing at the penetration of their bumholes, and gasping in new approaching orgasm.

Lise wanked her clitty vigorously against the soft cavern wall, with the scent of male and female come, mingled with the sweat of fucking loins, now filling the cavern. She gasped as the giant cock relentlessly thudded her anal root, and Anna and Waltraut's cries of orgasm echoed through the cavern. The line of black girls beside Lise also enjoyed buggery by their males, a hard hand-spanking together with masturbation of their clits, or a fist-fucking. At the far end, she saw Melleah! Dr Crevasse's slave-girl writhed on Afgoi's fist, plunged in her cunt; she swung like a spinning top, his arm her only support, as she spanked her bare bum, while she wanked herself off, dripping her come on his feet. The floor was a lake of male cream and gleaming girl-come. The two white-skirted girls removed their skirts and solemnly wanked themselves to climax with the garments, then pissed long and deeply until their skirts were steaming wet rags, which they wadded into the mouths of Anna and Waltraut.

The two buggers, cocks still erect, unfastened the women's nipple chains and held them in their teeth. The Somali girls sprang onto the males' cocks, and lowered their bum-clefts onto the tools, until each girl was anally impaled. They wrapped their legs around the males' buttocks and took the nipple chains in their own teeth, allowing the males to lower their heads and bite the girls' breasts as they moved the wheeled caning-rails towards the hanged sculptures. Waltraut and Anna let go of their ropes and flopped onto the carved cocks, trying to grasp the slippery wires which drew them by their nipples, stretching their teats to long pale envelopes.

Melleah, wanked and buggered to climax, leapt from Afgoi's erect penis and took it into her mouth, sucking it vigorously until his spunk, mingled with her own bum-slime, bubbled from her lips. Then, climbing onto Heidi's teats, Melleah drew the nipple-wires and fixed Waltraut and her daughter to the anus in the ceiling, hoisting the two women until they dangled like the other sculptures, their entire weight taken by their stretched breasts. Dark fluid, with the aroma of *Gobaad* mud, began to drip from the giant anal aperture, slopping the two women until their skins were slimed and ebony. Waltraut and Anna sobbed and squealed, jerking on their restraints, until the two black males began a vigorous spanking of their bare bottoms, making the darkening arse-globes wriggle.

Lise watched this further torment, approaching her own climax as she frotted her clit, and squirming under the hard-slapping buggery, and without waiting for her bugger's spurt, she yelped in the flood of her own orgasm. The two spanking black males were masturbated to another climax by the now-naked caning girls, who wanked their cocks by hand, then knelt, with a final fellation, to swallow their new jets of spunk. Even as they climaxed, the males did not cease spanking the squirming bare bums of the German women. Lise stared. The human sculptures of hanged women had changed; their legs were now striped like zebras'. Eyes opened and come dripped from the cunts of the whitened Africans, and from the blackened Europeans, melting the skin dye, and restoring their legs and vulvas to true colour. The Africans were not suspended from the snake nooses, but merely embraced, which was why their breasts jutted up so sharply: they were hanging from their nipples alone. They were not sculptures: Heidi and the others were real.

Suddenly, Melleah's eyes met Lise's and she pointed at her with a burst of words in Somali. The black males ceased their spanking of Anna and Waltraut, and left them hanging with the other living sculptures. Lise's buggering male whirled, leaving her wriggling in mid-air, suspended by the prong of his tool. Several come-slimed hands grasped her, slippery on her body, pinching her clit and titties and the lips of her vulva, but in complete silence. The bodies of the living sculptures, apart from Anna and Waltraut, began to lift, the nipple-wires drawn from within the sculpted anus and cunt. One by one, silently, the girls disappeared into the monstrous holes. The last was Heidi.

'Heidi!' cried Lise, but received no reply.

A bundle of nipple-clamps fell on their wires back into the cavern. Melleah and Afgoi selected two pairs of clamps, still warm and oily with sweat, and soon Lise was sobbing helplessly beside Anna and Waltraut, as she dangled by her nipples and spread cunt flaps, the wire from her cunt-clamp pressed in her anal crevice and against her back, so that she was balanced vertically. The cunts of mother and daughter juiced as they watched Lise's restraint. Two pairs of hands held her ankles, two more twisted her arms up to her shoulders, binding her wrists to her neck, to fully expose both back and arse-globes. Lise was helpless and her cunt dripped come; she pissed herself copiously, her pee steaming on the glazed floor of come, but with no reaction. All was done in utter silence, broken only by the swish of wood, as Afgoi and Melleah prepared to cane Lise on the bare. She looked up through her tears. Heidi had gone into the cunt; Lise was suspended below the anus, beside the two naked Germans, whose wet skin now dripped with bum-mud and who gazed at the dry satin ebony of Lise's skin with jealous longing. Anna stared at Lise's croup as Melleah's fingers rubbed the bum-flesh, measuring it.

'Almost there, Lise,' she said pleasantly. 'The sacred measurement! Your bum has responded better than any other's, as though the desert has made it grow so big and firm. And now the true colour of beauty! Dr Crevasse will be pleased – or cruelly jealous.'

'How . . .?' Lise moaned.

Melleah's fingers marched up her spine, and her palms covered Lise's trapezoid muscles.

'Back-whipping is a different art from caning the bottom,' she said. 'I am better at bottoms, but I am learning to back-whip. Caning the bottom inflicts more pain, and more shame, but a girl's whipped back, with her arms above her, is somehow more . . . helpless. Let us try both, my black sister, while Afgoi buggers me again.'

Waltraut and Anna looked at Lise, teeth bared in delight, but Melleah returned their grins with one of scorn.

'All they are good for is cunt-poking,' she drawled. 'Two of my fellow-slaves can attend to them, while I flog you, Lise. Unless you'd rather I didn't.'

'N . . . no, Melleah,' Lise whispered. 'Beat me.'

'I must flog you to the bone, Lise,' said Melleah, 'for you are one of us S'Ibaya, and must be initiated by ordeal. Our queen greased your snake-tunnel with her own come to anoint you. To be worthy of her, and our goddess S'Ibaa, your bum and back must be flogged raw before you ascend into the hole of the goddess, to emerge perfect.'

Lise's clitty throbbed; her come flowed in torrents from her cunt. Around her, the throng of naked black girls rhythmically masturbated, their come flowing to the sound of the guards' whips lashing the bare bums of the mopping slaves. Waltraut and her daughter were now slick and sopping with bum-mud, and the drip from the high anus switched, to fall on Lise's nipples, titties, cunt flaps and poking clitoris, and on her croup; already ebony, they shone wetly with a new coating of dark liquid.

'Beat me,' she said.

Crack!

'*Ohh!*'

The long cane seared Lise's back, just beneath her shoulder-blades; expecting the cut on the croup, she had clenched her fesses, and gasped, in pain and shock.

Crack!

The wire of her cunt-clamp twanged, as the cane struck it, now directly on the shoulders, just below Lise's pinioned arms.

'The goddess has instructed her slave to flog you, until you give up the treasure,' Melleah said.

'Treasure? Wait . . .'

Crack!

'*Ohhh* . . . it hurts so! O, Melleah!'

The third stroke was lower, right at mid-back. The fourth and fifth took Lise in the same area of the upper back, the sixth and seventh in mid-back: this, then, was the area designated for her back-whipping. At each stroke, her body quivered, the clamps stretching her cunt and nipples as she writhed. Tears flowed down her breasts and moistened the stretched envelopes of her nips. After ten strokes the caning paused, and Lise looked round, her eyes and mouth grimacing; Afgoi, huge of penis, was mounting Melleah. With a slick thrust, his cock slammed between her parted arse-globes and penetrated her anus.

'Yes! Encule me!' Melleah hissed.

He began a vigorous buggery, while two other black males, equally massive of cock, slapped their bodies scornfully against the teats and bellies of the hanging Germans, and played their cock-tips for a moment at the wet lips of the vulvas, before thrusting inside the pouches. They cunt-fucked the German females hard, and the gashes of Waltraut and her daughter flowed with come, despite their squeals of protest.

Crack!

'*Ahhh!*'

Lise's caning recommenced, this time on the bare fesses, and she howled: the stroke took her on the tender skin at top buttock. The three black males fucked in rhythm, and a fourth joined them. Blocking Lise's view, he pressed his body to hers, and she moaned as a huge black penis penetrated her wet vulva. The male had to thrust hard to get his huge member inside her slit, wet though she was for him; when his glans reached her wombneck, her gash walls clutched and began to squeeze, milking the giant cock as Melleah's cane wealed her naked bum.

Crack!

Her arse squirmed frantically as the cock penetrated her cunt-slime.

'*Ahhh!* O, fuck me!' Lise moaned. 'Split my cunt, *fuck me* . . .!'

The male's belly slapped against hers as she met his thrusts, the whip of the cane on her fesses driving her pubis to slam against his own shaven hillock. His balls were slippery, rubbing her come-soaked thighs, and as the caning welted Lise's bare buttocks deeper and deeper, she began to sob. Orgasm welled in her cunt and belly, and her spine tingled, with the black male's pulsing cock-shaft hard against her clitty.

'O! O O!' she shrieked. 'O, yes . . . *Ohhh* . . .'

Come drooled from her quivering cunt flaps, splashing the glazed floor beneath her fesses. Beside her, the German mother and daughter also squealed in comes, as their cunts gushed under the fucking of hard black tools. Melleah's pants of exertion as she caned Lise mingled with high squeals, as Afgoi thrust into her anus; her canestrokes faltered, striking Lise on the upper thighs, underfesses or haunches, as she was buffeted by her bum-fucking. Her cunt, too, flowed with come, mingling with the pool of Lise, Waltraut and Anna's, and the anus aloft kept up its steady drip of bum-mud on Lise's sweating titties and arse.

Crack! Vap! Vap! Vap!

'*O! O! Ahhh!*'

'Your ordeal is quickly over, Lise, if you yield the treasure the goddess's servant gave you.'

'*What?*' Lise screamed, as a thonged whip joined Melleah's cane on her arse, and two more scourges whipped her bare back. '*Ah! O, God! No!*'

Vap! Vap! Vap! Crack!

Four flogging tools now shook her naked body, and she pissed herself into her pool of come. The male's cock exploded in come inside her pissing vulva, his sperm bubbling from her cunt lips. The cunts of Waltraut and Anna also dripped creamy white, as the fucking males spunked inside them.

'Melleah . . .' Lise begged turning to her caner, joined now by the metal-plated guards, all her chastisers masturbated their wet cunts as they flogged her nude, writhing body. '*Melleah . . .*'

'I'm sorry, Lise,' Melleah gasped, lashing her cane vertically up Lise's arse-crevice and slicing both cunt lips and anus pucker.

'*Ooh! God! That hurt!*'

'You are S'Ibaya, and must be offered *raw,* to the goddess, unless you give up the treasure you keep from her. Your feet must bathe in the come of your sisters.'

'Treasure? For God's pity . . .'

Vap! Vap! Vap!

'*O!* Please! Melleah! It's a mistake . . . *please, no!*'

Every girl in the chamber masturbated hard, on clit and in gash, flooding the floor with a tide of slimy girl-come.

Vap! Vap! Vap!

'*Ohhh!* How many strokes, Melleah? For God's sake, let me know.'

'To the bone, Lise . . . *or give up the treasure.*'

Vap! Vap! Vap! Crack!

Lise's body jerked like a marionette.

'No! *Ahh . . . please!*'

Suddenly, the whistle of the flogging instruments stilled. The only sound was of Lise's own convulsive sobbing. The tallest of the guards lifted the plates covering her massively jutting breasts, but her loins, arse and face remained covered. Her huge dark nipples were ringed in gold. Masturbators and whippers alike fell to their knees in the sea of come.

'Hoist her to high anus,' ordered Dr Crevasse.

'Yes, O Goddess S'Ibaa.'

Lise continued to sob, her weals now filled with the bum mud dripping from above. She moaned as the wires pulled her cunt and nip-clamps upwards towards the gaping high anus, and the source of the mud, which now bathed her whole body, filled her mouth and nose, and obliged her to swallow. Beneath her, Dr Crevasse's mouth opened wide, and she swallowed every drop of Lise's fast-flowing come, mingled with bum-mud. From the second vulval opening in the ceiling, the mound representing the clitoris uncurled into a twined rope of hissing pink Galafi snakes. Dr Crevasse waved, and at once the naked males began to ascend this ladder, to disappear into the folds of the vulva.

The doctor herself leapt onto Lise's shoulders; Lise's scream of pain at the sudden wrench to her cunt and nipples, was stifled by Dr Crevasse's own cunt and thighs wrapping themselves around her face, with her open flaps and stiff clitoris pressed to Lise's mouth. Lise could breathe only by swallowing the copious come which poured from the doctor's cunt as she wanked herself, rubbing her clitty on Lise's eyes. The clitty was monstrous and swollen, darting like a snake's head. Dr Crevasse's come overflowed Lise's lips and frothed down her black swollen nipples, the oily trickle of cunt juice drawn to the parted lips of Lise's own vulva.

'The German women shall be flogged, while fucked and buggered with their blasphemous apparatus,' she said stonily. 'My servant Crevasse permitted them to record her likeness, and she, too, must be punished, as must all S'Ibaya who have exposed the secrets of their croups.'

208

Lise's thoughts whirled: what schizoid mind games was Dr Crevasse playing? Or had she, too, succumbed to 'morbid nymphomania'? *The treasure: the key to Dr Crevasse's virgin cunt!* Now, Lise's only defence against whatever madness had engulfed the arse-worshipping tribe . . .

'My servant imperfectly entrusted you with my treasure,' she said to Lise. 'Since ordeal by whipping will not make you surrender it, we shall draw it by more painful means.'

Her face clamped by the cunt of Dr Crevasse, riding her, Lise entered the scented darkness of the high anus of S'Ibaa.

14

The High Colon

'We are graced in the high colon of the goddess S'Ibaa,' said Dr Charlotte Crevasse. 'Beyond,' she pointed to a narrow sphincter that led from the cramped chamber, 'lies the vulva of the goddess. Hawo, the Issa slut, showed you the sacred gash, merely the earth cunt.'

The anal aperture squashed greasily shut behind Lise; it writhed, hissing, formed of live snakes. The entire, foetid enclosure, like the buttocks forming the ceiling of the chamber of come, was snakeskin. The flaps of snakeskin were glued together with an aromatic glaze, smelling of female come, arse-grease, and *Gobaad* mud, like that which still coated Lise, dripping to the hide floor. Apart from her sopping wet and whip-wealed skin, Lise's ebony body was no different from the majority of nude female slaves crouching in the anal chamber. Kee, Deydey and Guestir, and the ebony figures, Loosje, Toyo and Heidi, squatted, their skin dye melting, along with Heidi, who was still anally plugged. The Latvian amputee was there, with some Somali single amputees, from knee or thigh, or shorn right to the hip, leaving the vulvas exposed like tree roots. All masturbated, the amputees rubbing their stumps with the come seeping from open cunts. Dr Crevasse lowered her breastplates, leaving her teats entirely bare, and the crouching slaves ululated in unison:

'S'Ibaa . . . S'Ibaa . . .'

Their come flowed, to soak the glutinous snakeskin floor, and the girl-slaves shamelessly pissed, the golden streams fast soaking into the leather. In one corner of the chamber sat a throne of scented cedarwood, in the shape of the female pudenda and nates, with the body of a white male bound and gagged at its base. It was Gilles, the Legion helicopter pilot. Dr Crevasse mounted the throne, which was open-seated, so that the bare buttocks of its occupant showed through, in perfect moulding with the throne's gluteal form. It was wreathed with the writhing bodies of live female Galafi snakes, which began a hissing penetration of Dr Crevasse's vulva and anus, though blocked by her locket chain from ingress to deep cunt. On the opposite wall was a large video screen. Dr Crevasse placed her feet on Gilles' buttocks and forced Lise to squat beside him, holding her by the wires attached to her cunt and nipples. Lise's wet cunt was next to Gilles' mouth; he licked his lips and grinned. Unconsciously, Lise began to wank off her clitty in time with the moaning, sweating girls.

Dr Crevasse touched controls on the arm of her throne, and the monitor flickered into life. Dr Crevasse sat with her thighs parted, and allowed her armour-flaps to fall to one side, exposing her cunt. She began to tug on her extruded, serpentine clitty, her masturbation increasing the fervour of the slaves' wanking and their ululations, as her come began to seep, trickle, then flow copiously from her pulsing swollen slit. She pissed, spraying fiercely, and her jet splattered the male's bare bum and the naked bodies of the black slaves, who rubbed her pee into their cunts and erect nipples.

'This male,' she hissed, 'aided the blasphemies you shall now witness and abhor. The foreign intruders wished to make photographic likenesses of the bare croups of S'Ibaa's slaves, which are her own sacred likeness, and sought the arse of S'Ibaa herself, her holiest temple, in which we now gather. For his part in transporting them, the goddess shall flog him. Every slave portrayed and recognised shall take fifty strokes of the cane on the bare buttocks, and the females, fifty on the open vulva, or half on the cunt, and half on stump; the males, fifty on the cock's helmet, at the peehole. The goddess will summon the slave known as Titzi, and her servant Dr Crevasse, for their own chastisement, for permitting pictorial display of their sacred fesses, in her house, next to the goddess. Dr Crevasse deserves, and shall receive, the severest chastisement, for aiding her male accomplice in his blasphemies.'

Gilles crouched foetally, wrists bound to ankles and buttocks bared for the first rod that chose to strike him. His expression was bland, even ironic, and his cock was massively erect. Dr Crevasse took his swollen glans between her toes, rubbed it, frowning, then desisted; Gilles grinned.

The screen showed film from his helicopter: shaky shots of desert, a lake, scorched earth dotted with black chimneys, and then, two mounds of black rock, eroded precisely into the shape of a perfect female arse.

'The bastion of the S'Ibaya,' intoned Dr Crevasse, 'where we now sit.'

Gilles could be seen at the controls of the helicopter, approaching the volcanic buttocks; Anna and Waltraut, both bare-breasted, with identical yellow scarves knotted round their necks and dangling from pierced nipples, and wearing pleated yellow skirts and fluffy yellow ankle socks. Anna, giggling, unfastening Gilles' zipper and taking his full erect penis to the back of her throat; Waltraut taking her place, sucking the glans and squeezing his balls, as the helicopter made an abrupt landing. Titzi, nude, emerging from the shade of a rock to greet them with hugs, and, after some delighted laughter, bending over Waltraut's crooked knee to take a hard hand-spanking on the bare, from Anna.

The film then showed Titzi, caned with a branch by Waltraut, while Anna masturbated to orgasm; Titzi, licking the come-wet cunts of both mother and daughter, her head bobbing under each yellow skirt, which was soon dampened with come, as she wanked herself off under a hard anal fucking from the nude Gilles. Titzi posing for arse-shots, quim-shots, titty-shots, holding her cunt flaps open and wanking off her soaking clit while Anna fingerfucked her bumhole. The whole operation was videoed from a tripod, and Waltraut's camera crept closer and closer to the anus bud and cunt lips, getting the lens right inside Titzi's vulva, then her daughter's. Anna with her mother, spanking her as Titzi and Waltraut masturbated together, and wanking herself off with the camera back, while shooting Waltraut's spread cunt. The three females in triple masturbation to orgasm, before Titzi summoned a tribe of nude S'Ibayan girls, who received beads and gold trinkets with delight, baring their intimate orifices for the same photography, and taking the same spankings, fifty or sixty slaps and bare-bum canings of ten or twelve. Some proudly bared their nipples for teat-canings, masturbating as their naked breasts bounced under the canes of the wanking German females, with Waltraut and Anna now bare-quimmed, their skirts cast aside.

A group of naked males emerged, all with cocks limp. Bare-bottom canings, ten strokes to each croup from Waltraut and Anna, stiffened them, while Titzi knelt and wanked herself off, licking their balls and anal clefts. The males caned and buggered Titzi, who touched her toes, her massive arse-globes wriggling like snakes, as they darkened with purple welts, while Anna and her mother masturbated. When each male had caned Titzi to ten, she held her arse-cheeks apart to expose her open anus, which they buggered until cream bubbled from her anus.

Gilles now buggered a succession of S'Ibayan girls, each masturbating herself to come as his cock rammed her anal hole, but without coming himself, until at last he forced Titzi to the ground, and whipped her bare arse with a baobab branch, while she wanked off, squealing, and then raised her sand-crusted bum for a forceful tooling of her anus. His cream bubbled over her arse lips; Anna and Waltraut, wanking each other, so that their come was swallowed by the sand, knelt to lick his spunk before the desert could claim it.

The S'Ibayan slaves, including two amputees to the hip, crouched, wanking for the camera, with their bums turned and their delicate fingers clawing their wet pink gashes and opened bumholes, masturbating and finger-fucking themselves, or each other. When Gilles had spunked and concluded his buggery, the S'Ibayan girls, still wanking with their arses spread to the camera, took rods and began to whip Titzi's bare bum as she lay squealing and squirming in the sand, soaked in her own come and wanking her own clit and titties as the African girls flogged her.

'The slave Titzi relishes chastisement on her bare buttocks,' pronounced Dr Crevasse with some scorn. 'I – I mean, my servant, Dr Crevasse, diagnosed her, as such – a manipulative submissive, passing for a dominant. At last, in roundabout way, the Legion has exposed her true nature. The Legion unearths the truth of all its *soldier girls* . . .'

The video showed an agitated and unproductive discussion with the S'Ibayan slaves. They would not permit access to the inner sanctum of S'Ibaa. The three German females apparently gave up, and the last shot showed Gilles piloting his helicopter away. The screen went blank.

'Titzi was recaptured and punished for deserting, of course,' said Dr Crevasse. 'The other sluts, not being of the Legion, could not be detained – until they sneaked back in darkness and gained access to the gallery.'

Canestrokes slapping bare flesh, and the screams of Anna and her mother, echoed faintly from below. Dr Crevasse smiled.

'Now it is time for the punishments to begin,' she said. 'Heidi, fetch the male miscreants.'

Heidi wriggled into the sphincter that led to the cunt of S'Ibaa, and returned, moments later, plopping bum first from the orifice. There followed a succession of the male S'Ibayans seen on Waltraut's film. All emerged nude, their bodies slimed from the sphincter, their cocks dangling. Dr Crevasse ordered two amputees to masturbate the males to stiffness with their stumps, and when their cocks were fully erect, she said that Lise Gallard's punishment must begin.

'You will await me,' she said, releasing Lise's nipple and cunt chains. Lise stood up amid the sea of wanking girls, rubbing her wealed buttocks, which they jostled to touch as they masturbated. Lise's clitty and cunt were invaded by gentle fingers, wanking her off. Her come streamed to the floor.

'Your punishment shall be terrible, Nurse Gallard,' said the doctor.

Dr Crevasse vanished, squirming up the sphincter. Lise trembled but could not help juicing, as numerous female fingers wanked her clitty, and those unable to approach her arched their backs to suck their own cunt juice. When the doctor returned after a few minutes, she was swathed from head to foot in white rubber, her face zipped in a white latex mask, with holes for eyes and mouth only; she carried a scourge.

'Your accomplice, Dr Crevasse, is the true criminal,' she said, her voice muffled by the white latex face-mask, 'so your punishment shall be both to observe, and inflict, *hers* – until you can no longer bear her agony and give up the treasure: the key to my goddess's cunt.'

Lise stared. The fingers at her cunt, poking deep inside, and within a hair's breadth of her wombneck where the key was secreted, made her quim wet with come, despite her confusion.

'I . . . yes, Doctor. I mean, yes . . .'

How did a nurse address a goddess?

'You mean, yes, *nurse*,' whimpered the rubber-swathed female, her voice suddenly coy and girlish. 'O, I have always wanted to be a nurse. O, please, mademoiselle Gallard, whip me until I am a nurse . . .'

She handed Lise the scourge.

'Whip me all over my body,' pleaded the rubber-swathed doctor. 'Whip my bum, my teats, my belly, whip false whitehood from me . . .'

Two S'Ibaa amputees clamped Dr Crevasse's rubber-booted feet between their cunts and thigh-stumps, while Heidi and Kee made a piggy-back in front of the latex figure, with Heidi holding Dr Crevasse's arms twisted in a lock behind her neck. Numbly, but with her cunt still eagerly wanked and gushing, Lise lifted the whip and slashed Dr Crevasse's buttocks. Dr Crevasse moaned and her bum quivered as the thin latex shredded slightly. Lise whipped her again, and again, the ululating wanks of the slave-girls reaching crescendo after crescendo of orgasmic delight, as the rubber turned to shreds under the four copper-tipped thongs of Lise's whip. Beneath the bum-rubber was a Legion blue nurse's skirt, in the red, white and blue of the French tricolour. Lise counted her whipstrokes until twenty, then ceased to count as she concentrated on the delicate task of whipping the woman to her nurse's uniform without further damage to her apparel.

Thwack! Thwack! Thwack! Thwack!

The heavy whip lashed the woman's shuddering body relentlessly, making easy work of the legs and back. Dr Crevasse had fleur-de-lys fishnet stockings, and when her captor amputees unzipped her fluffy white bootees, she wore black stilettos. Kee and Heidi shifted, so that Lise could whip the doctor's – goddess's? – nurse's? – breasts and belly. She flogged the breasts first, making Dr Crevasse squeal, and then lashed her hard on the cunt, using upenders to get all four thongs of the whip right into her slit and anal crevice. Dr Crevasse gasped; her skirt rode up, revealing white cotton panties soaked in come. The rubber shredded from her teats, revealing a white blouse and white scalloped bra, the blouse opened to the third button, and the bra showing the gold-ringed tops of her erect nipples. Lise whipped each nipple with four or five strokes, and Dr Crevasse rewarded her with squeals of anguish. Lise reached forward and unzipped her rubber face mask, and a uniformed Legion nurse stood before them, tears dripping from her eyes and her face contorted in pain.

'Naughty nurses like to be buggered by males with big tools, and must be whipped for liking it,' she mewled.

The amputee girls kept hold of her stiletto heels, which their feverish wanking soon made glisten with come. Kee and Heidi relinquished the nurse, and she bent over, hands on her bare black haunches beside the skimpy white knickers, and parted them for anal penetration. The knicker cloth stretched over her bum-cleft, and she stabbed a hole in the knickers, ripping until it was a slit, then plunged a clawed finger right to the knuckle inside her anus.

216

'O! It hurts!' she squealed. 'The naughty bitch has holed her Legion knickers! Fuck her bumhole, slaves, and shame her.'

The S'Ibayan males buggered her hard, each taking three or four minutes, and well over a hundred thrusts of cock in bumhole, before spurting his cream. As they buggered the squirming black arsehole, each male took a caning on his own bare buttocks, from Heidi, Kee and Loosje, alternately. Miscreant slave-girls identified from Waltraut's film lay down flat to receive bare-bum canings of fifty from their eager sisters, whose wanks made their victims' wriggling buttocks gleam with cunt juice. By the fifth buggery, Dr Crevasse's cunt was a lake of come, dripping into the amputee girls' swallowing throats, and her stocking tops were awash with mingled come and spunk. Her erect clitty seemed to grow, squirming as though whipped, from the folds of her cunt, its glistening pink shining hard yet prehensile.

'O! Yes! Right to the root! Burst her arse with your cocks! *Hurt the bitch*!' she squealed, as the cocks rammed her anal elastic.

When the fourteenth and last of the caned males had buggered her, she touched her toes. Her knickers were stained with spunk and her own arse-grease. Heidi handed Lise her cane, warm from the males' buttocks.

'The nurse doesn't deserve to wear Legion uniform,' sobbed Dr Crevasse. 'Her knickers are shredded . . . cane the bitch naked.'

The caned males were masturbated or sucked to full erection again for the second part of their punishment, fifty on the peehole. The females spread their thighs, and squeals filled the chamber, as they took their gash-canings, or, in the case of the amputees, caning half on gash and half on come-slimed stump.

Lise began a vigorous caning of the black arse-globes now presented to her, bare except for wisps of knicker, which soon fluttered away under her caning. The garter straps snapped, and the suspender belt shredded and slid down Dr Crevasse's come-sodden stockings. They, too, became ragged as Lise's cane lashed the quivering black thighs and calves. Dr Crevasse stood and bent backwards, so that her arms supported her in the crab position, and Lise began to cane the black breasts which bulged almost entirely bare from the skimpy white bra. Her cane sliced the bra in two, and the bare titties sprang out unfettered. Lise lashed the bare nipples raw, her cane clanging on the goddess's nipple-rings, then the nurse's blouse, which was quickly tatters. Dr Charlotte Crevasse was nude, her black satin flesh bruised in deep cane-welts, and sobbed, her eyes glazed and misty.

'If the bitch will not surrender the key,' she hissed, 'then Crevasse must be trussed and flogged full-body. Her cunt needs the rod.'

'I am the caner, nurse,' said Lise. 'The goddess has instructed me to attend to the male's punishment, while Crevasse is bound for her own.'

Lise's voice rang unprotested as she gave her orders. Gilles was released, while the nude body of Dr Crevasse was trussed: she was lying on her back, with her bum up and gash spread and with her legs fastened to her ankles at the back of her neck. Lise attached her own two nipple-clamps to Dr Crevasse's teats, and chained her to the feet of her throne.

'Well, Gilles,' she said, flexing her cane, 'the goddess has decreed a bare-bum caning for your misdeeds.'

Gilles glowered, looking uncertainly at the mass of naked females who blocked any exit.

'Nurse Lise,' he mumbled, sullenly, 'if it is really you, under that skin dye – this has gone too far.'

'Touch your toes, sir!' Lise rapped. 'If you won't accept divine punishment, I dare say you must accept a legionnaire's. Your commander in Djibouti would be displeased to hear of your use of Legion equipment as a vehicle for sightseeing.'

'Damara put me up to it . . .!' he blurted.

'The position, sir!' Lise cried, and, slowly, Gilles bent over, legs apart, and touched his toes. 'By the way, it is no skin dye. I am a black woman of the S'Ibaya. Does not our mother the Legion unearth what we really want and bring us to our true selves?'

Vip!

The cane slashed without warning across the man's bare bum, and he clenched his bum-crack.

'O! God! that was hard!'

'Only one, Gilles!'

'How many, then?'

'Forty, perhaps.'

'Forty on the bare! O, God . . .'

' "O Goddess" would be more appropriate. For that slip, we'll make it fifty, like the slaves, and if you behave, I shan't cane your penis. Does it always get rigid when you are thrashed, Gilles?'

Gilles' cock was indeed fully erect.

Vip! Vip! Vip! Vip!

'*Ahhh!*'

Lise delivered two strokes to his haunches, and two to top bum.

'Answer the question, please. Does my beating stiffen you, or is it the nude females wanking themselves off as they watch your stripes?'

'Yes . . . I mean no . . . both!'

Vip! Vip! Vip! Vip!

'Ahh! *Ahh! O!*'

The slave-girls masturbated eagerly as they watched the male's bare nates darken to crimson, then purple, streaked with the welts of a quite merciless caning, the cuts delivered to the whole expanse of the arse, from underfesses to top buttock, and well striping the haunches, which made them squeal. Despite the harder and harder squirming of his flogged buttocks, Gilles kept a military stiffness in his posture, even when Lise's cane accidentally flicked his straining ball-sac. A river of come flowed from Dr Crevasse's open cunt as she watched, helplessly, strapped egg-like for her own flogging. Snakes' tongues flickered on her thigh-tops, licking her come and darting on her distended clitty, as though kissing another, pink serpent.

Vip! Vip! Vip! Vip! Vip!

'*Ah! Ah!* O, Lise!'

'That makes fifty, Gilles.'

Vip!

'Ahhh!'

'And one more, for failing to address me properly as Nurse Lise. I see your cock is still stiff, and I suppose, like the dirty pup you are, you will seek relief in one of these juicing cunts . . .'

In a moment, a posse of slave-girls sat on Gilles, one girl's arse covering his face, and the others, his arms, legs and belly, but leaving the pole of his cock trembling and untouched. His captors wanked off, sliming his body with their cunt juices, and he was obliged to swallow the come from his face's captor, slurping her copious fluid in order to gulp air. He had to swallow her pee as well when she evacuated right between his gasping lips, and the girl-slaves took giggling turns at soaking his face with their generous flows of piss.

'Now,' said Lise, 'for the slut Crevasse's punishment. She begs for the rod on her cunt, indeed! Breaking the cunt chain would be damage to property, and I am loth to damage the property of a goddess . . . However, you may expect a caning everywhere except in the slit, Crevasse.'

Lise brushed aside the snakes and began to cane Dr Crevasse's naked clitoris. The black woman's cunt poured with come and her belly began to flutter; after six strokes to the coiling, serpentine clitty, Lise worked on the bare nipple domes, with a dozen strokes each, then commenced a caning of the thighs and lower buttocks. After two dozen strokes, she returned to the cunt, carefully caning the open, slimed walls without touching the barrier chain. Her cane approached the clitty, this time not thrashing it, but tickling it. Dr Crevasse moaned and pissed herself violently, as her belly shook in her orgasm. Lise continued the caning, past one hundred strokes, on belly, thighs and arms, as well as the vulval area and buttocks, which took the deepest welts.

The doctor's anus was raw from her repeated buggery by the male slaves and the anal pucker swollen; Lise's cane landed repeatedly in the wrinkled bud, making it open and close as the nates clenched, like a fish's mouth gasping for air. Crevasse orgasmed three times more, but still the vaginal chain remained unbroken, although the spread cunt-walls enclosing it were well bruised by the cane's tip. The snakeskin chamber, that was the high colon of the goddess S'Ibaa, echoed to the moans of the slave-girls masturbating to orgasm, and their slurps of Dr Crevasse's come and pee, as they jostled below her vulva, to swallow her fluids.

Vip! Vip! Vip! Vip!

'*Ahhhh . . .!*' cried Dr Crevasse, pissing herself again, as she spasmed in her fifth come, on a hard set of nipple-slices, forehand and backhand.

Vip!

A final stroke directly on her swollen clitty made her gasp, and Lise, her own cunt juicing profusely, lowered her cane. She motioned the squatting females away from Gilles, and grasped the tip of his swollen cock, using it to masturbate her own nubbin, as her hand plunged into her come-wet womb.

'Rod on cunt, lesbian slut,' she sneered, 'and rod on cunt you shall have. The Legion makes us what we really want, and what we really really are. Spread your bum, lesbian.'

The moaning black woman spread her naked arse cheeks and pucker, ready for further buggery. It was the fully erect Afgoi who took her anally, sliding deftly between the floor and her buttocks, raised by Lise's foot, so that he was sandwiched beneath his mistress, his tool impaling her anus. Lise grasped her own wombneck, and extracted the key to the locket on Dr Crevasse's cunt. She inserted Gilles' huge erect penis through Dr Crevasse's kundalini ring, her guiche and her cunt-ring. His organ fitted perfectly into all three rings.

'He is the one,' hissed Dr Crevasse. 'Let that cock fuck my cunt! I've waited so long . . .'

'The Legion unearths our truth, my lesbian mistress,' Lise said.

Without letting go of Gilles' cock, she unfastened the chain and opened Dr Crevasse's cunt. She pulled the penis towards the cunt flaps inside, then spanked Gilles on the buttocks, to make him thrust his cock to the balls inside the black woman's soaking cunt. Dr Crevasse howled as Gilles began a hard cunt-fucking, ramming his massive tool right to the hilt at each thrust, while beneath her, Afgoi penetrated her anal elastic. The woman writhed, sandwiched between her cunt-invader and the buggering slave. Lise lashed her across the nipples six times, then climbed onto her belly, springing onto Gilles' shoulders, and obliging him to tilt his head backwards. Her thighs clamped his head to her cunt, and her come poured over Dr Crevasse's belly, as Gilles began to tongue her.

'This is how S'Ibaa, or any woman, becomes a true goddess, Dr Crevasse,' Lise cried. 'Cock in cunt, fucking her to ecstasy.'

The snakeskin walls of the chamber seemed to blur, lowering themselves and swelling into the shape of female buttocks and cleft. There were live snakes secreted in the cunt-folds, and they began to twist, braiding themselves into a nubbin that emerged from the vagina delineated by further snake bodies. All were female. Lise's eyes blurred as she approached orgasm at the male's vigorous tongue-fucking. Melleah leapt onto Dr Crevasse's belly, squatted on her to piss, then sank in her steaming pool of come and pee, to rub her mistress's writhing clitty with her own stiff nubbin. The walls and ceiling of the chamber seemed to heave, all in the shapes of female buttocks and cunts, as though the goddess herself was summoned by the ulula-tions of the masturbating slave-girls. Lise approached her orgasm; head spinning, she saw a perfectly etched female bum, cunt and anus bud, and the giant serpentine clitty writhing atop the gaping slit. The snake-clit writhed down the cunt flaps, across the perineum and into the anus bud, its foremost part stiffening, to begin a buggery of the anal hole. As Lise squirmed and gasped in the delirium of her own orgasm, she heard the cries and squeals of Melleah, Afgoi, Gilles and the doctor, all coming at once; her face was drenched in snake-oil from the writhing bum-skin above her, as the goddess S'Ibaa buggered her own anus with her own clitty . . .

The pyramid of bodies dismembered itself, and Lise stood, gasping, above Dr Crevasse, released from bondage. The doctor rose and pressed her buttocks against Lise's, then reached backwards and began to stroke them with expert fingers. Her fingers found Lise's cunt and grasped her cunt lips, then the stiff nubbin; Lise responded, sliding her hands beneath the doctor's parted arse-cheeks, and sinking her fingers into the cunt still slimy with Gilles' copious spunk. She found Dr Crevasse's clitty, pulled the stiff nubbin and began to wank her, as the doctor wanked Lise's own clit. Both females masturbated rapidly to orgasm, each one pissing over the other's wanking fingers as she came. Dr Crevasse, gasping, ran her fingertips around Lise's arse, until she breathed:

'At last, the sacred measurement! You, Lise, are . . . *you are she!*'

The ululation of the masturbating slave-girls grew to thunderous climax:

'*S'Ibaa . . . S'Ibaa . . .*'

Heidi led the male slaves who had buggered Dr Crevasse towards the two women. Their tools were hard as the black rock chimneys in the desert outside. Dr Crevasse climbed onto the throne, opening her thighs and rubbing her clit, with her soaking pouch inviting penetration.

'You will forgive your servant's presumption, Nurse Gallard,' she said, 'but I see cocks intent on fucking, and my own cunt has suffered a long time of abstinence.'

She draped her thighs over the arms of the throne, and gasped as the first black tool penetrated her soaking slit, the slave's bum clenching as he slammed her cunt in a vigorous fucking. Come poured from Dr Crevasse's gash lips, down her thighs and perineum, wetting her bum pucker which she began, herself, to poke.

'The goddess,' she gasped. 'The great queen, Sheba . . . lover of King Solomon, who built the first Temple of Jerusalem, in honour of her divinity, the twin domes of the female arse! Here is her first temple, before the S'Ibaya crossed the land bridge to Arabia, twelve thousand years ago . . . O! Yes! Fuck me! Fuck harder! Yes . . .'

Spunk dribbled from her clutching cunt flaps as the first male spurted in her.

'Yes, good and hot, and now the next. Take your time, or I shall cane you! Long and hard, that is how I wish my tools and my submission. I am sorry you may not stay and watch, Nurse Gallard, but your slaves would surely tongue your clit to pieces if they knew it was the goddess's, reincarnate! I, though, can be cunt-fucked for ever. "Djibouti" means buttocks, clit, or arsehole, or cunt, or the whole vulval area, you see – scholars differ on this point, but this is not the time for etymology. Gilles has his helicopter waiting to take you back to Colonel Said and Damara at the finishing school.'

The second tool rammed her cunt.

'O! Yes! Fuck me! Ahh . . .'

'I don't understand . . .' Lise began.

'You are a true legionnaire, Lise, a true soldier girl. You have been broken, degraded, punished and humiliated, and now exalted as your true self! The all-punishing goddess! Yes, the Legion unearths us. O! O! Fuck me harder, boy!'

The black cocks spurted their cream, and bubbles of spunk joined the lake of come and spunk at Dr Crevasse's cunt and bum-cleft. A third male mounted her and began to fuck her gaping wet cunt. Gilles took Lise's hand, and led her through the throng of wanking nude girls to the slit in the hide wall, which writhed open for them. Beyond, shone the desert sun.

'You should pass the finishing school with ease, Nurse Gallard,' panted Dr Crevasse, now with three fingers wriggling in her own come-slimed anus as she was cunt-fucked. 'Colonel Said will explain, just as you may explain that, with Damara's permission of course, his white cock may now enter my black, unvirgin cunt, as he has begged for so long. Remember that, although you possess the sacred croup of the mother goddess of the S'Ibaya, you are still a nurse legionnaire, and the finishing school will prepare you for a vital task, in the interests of France. Even though I'm sure that like all legionnaires, you absolutely *hate* the French! O! O! Yes! I'm coming! Fuck

224

harder! Never trust lesbians, Lise, they have split person-
alities . . . Fuck me! Fill my cunt! *Ohhh . . .*'

Dr Charlotte Crevasse winked at Lise.

'Sometimes, Nurse Gallard,' she gasped, 'the Legion
works in mysterious ways.'

15

Brigade Sexuelle

'It is all quite simple,' said Colonel Said.

'Nothing in Djibouti seems very simple, sir,' said Lise, eyes wide at her sumptuous collection of tailor-made finery and underthings in the armoire of her luxury suite, overlooking the lake of Abhe Bad.

Colonel Said, dressed in a blue velvet tuxedo, made a vaguely conciliatory gesture.

'In such a small place, things tend to ... interlock,' he said, 'and the desert contains many mirages. I know about the legends of the S'Ibaya, the sacred buttocks and self-fucked arse of their goddess S'Ibaa, but what you make of it, Lise, is your affair. I expect you would like to get dressed. Your helicopter trip must have been draughty.'

'O ... yes.'

Lise stood nude, looking over the white sand beach of the Club des Vautours, with its sand yachts, windsurfers and sunbathers.

'I hadn't realised that the club was so close to your auction house, sir.'

'It is convenient. The curious name, 'The Vulture Club', appeals to the bourgeois, who imagine they are visiting somewhere exclusive and dangerously exciting,' said the colonel. 'Which, for our targets, it is. You have identified yours?'

Lise peered at a couple, apparently in their thirties, she in a white string bikini, scarcely containing her tan breast melons and sculpted buttocks; he, muscular, with an aggressive quiff, and, like his wife, a lot of gold.

'This is your required test, Lise,' said Colonel Said, 'and I have no doubt of your success. Damara could have done it, but the regulations stipulate you prove yourself on home ground before your real task in the field, as it were. Damara! What a clever trollop! Trust a S'Ibayan woman to know that only Gilles would fit my dear Dr Crevasse's triple rings, and persuade her to surrender her virginity, at last giving me a chance to . . . Anyway, Damara knew also that you would make it through your gruelling ordeal, Lise, like the soldier girl you are.'

'Monsieur and Madame Dejonckheere, from Paris,' Lise said, looking at the sunbathing couple, 'he an art dealer, she, with her own private beauty salon, catering to government and diplomatic wives and mistresses. My task is to seduce them both, separately?'

'It should not be difficult, as our dossiers on them indicate. Both serious tax evaders, of course, but, in this case, that is not the prime objective of blackmail. We want *her* hair-dryer gossip, and *his* information on his gangster friends, who launder money through the international art market.'

'Then I should introduce myself on the beach,' said Lise, reaching for a strapless swimsuit, in gossamer apricot latex, cut high at the hips and deep at the breast. 'But, sir, you said *our* dossiers. I didn't know the Legion was interested in money-laundering and political intrigue.'

'*We* are the section of the Legion affiliated to the DST, the Direction de la Surveillance du Territoire,' said Colonel Said, 'rather like your English MI6. The interests of the Legion, and France, are not always served with military hardware, and we of the *Brigade Sexuelle* are just as much soldiers as any legionnaire of the line. The Russians, today, as in communist times, have "honey traps", female agents schooled in the arts of seduction; the American CIA have such schools, though like hypocritical Anglo-Saxons they deny it; the English, however, have no need, since they are already admirably equipped with boarding schools for the female upper classes. You undoubtedly remember the famous Miss Haughtrey, once one of MI6's most successful field agents, in what they wittily call their "Bottoms Up" division.'

Lise wriggled into her apricot swimsuit, poking her bare black breasts into the tiny cups, and tugging the skimpy saddle over her dark bum-pears; Colonel Said smiled ruefully, not concealing the bulge at his groin.

'My own taste for caning girls on the bare, in particular Djiboutian girls, was the cause of *my* recruitment, many years ago, to avoid causing indelicacy to the Legion's reputation,' he mused. 'Actually, it was Waltraut who recruited me: so pleasing, she is ripening her daughter's bottom in her own image. Hm! Your own superb fesses, Lise . . .'

'O!' cried Lise, with a shy smile. 'If you'd like to cane me bare, sir?'

He shook his head.

'On duty,' he said crisply. 'Sexual blackmail has always been the most effective way of turning an enemy agent, even though, nowadays, the enemies are within: tax-evaders, polluters, one global mafia or another. Before, any sexual peccadillo was a convenient blackmail weapon, but in these libertarian times, mere sex is no shame: it must be deviant sex. That is why our friends at MI6 are so successful! Their wonderful tradition of *le vice anglais* makes sado-masochistic entrapment natural to them. But if the Americans tend to clumsiness, the English tend to over-specialisation, while the Legion prides itself on poly-perversity. Our soldier girls are trained to accept, and inflict, *every* degradation, punishment, or ecstasy.'

Lise picked up the folder on the Dejonckheere targets, which contained a 'Psychosexual Analysis' by Dr Charlotte Crevasse.

'So,' she said, 'he, outwardly aggressive, but a secret masochist and urinophile, having been caned by the school nurse for bedwetting; she, with unfulfilled lesbian tendencies, regretting her timid refusal of seduction by a lesbian while hitch-hiking as a teenager in Morocco.'

'As I said, quite simple,' said the colonel, 'and the beauty of it is, no one loses: the targets are in fact glad to be exposed, and happy to expose others in their turn, their reward being much more satisfying holidays at my auction club. The exposure and enjoyment of fetishism becomes an end in itself, with the added glory of serving France. The DST controls numerous means of communication, such as magazines and internet sites – your friend Titzi featured in *Arschgeist*, one of our German publications. What could be more delightful than identifiable photographs, with long, lascivious letters in the targets' forged handwriting, in a British mass market magazine like *Dreams Come True*, or our own French *En Cul*?'

It was agreed that Mme Dejonckheere should be seduced first, outdoors, with her husband distracted by a business opportunity; M. Dejonckheere would be dealt with later, in the privacy of Lise's bedroom. Colonel Said would ensure concealed cameras captured every scene. Lise selected a towel and beach things and opened the door. As the colonel was leaving, she said:

'Are you sure you don't want to cane me, sir?'

'A foolish question, Nurse Gallard! That beautiful black arse of yours!'

'That's just it, sir. I love being black. I feel like the real me! I'm frightened my ebony will go away, if I'm not jolted a little.'

'Don't worry. The melanin content of Galafi snake-oil is so high, it will ensure you stay as you wish, for as long as you wish. Drinking the come of a S'Ibayan girl will, of course, have the same effect . . .'

A little while later, a black girl turned heads on the beach as her arse-globes and titties bounced in an apricot rubber swimsuit, several sizes too small for them. She dropped her purse by M. and Mme Dejonckheere. The purse fell open to show a snapshot of her in full nurse's uniform, with fishnet stockings, a microskirt and stethoscope.

'Oops! I'm so sorry!' Lise exclaimed. 'O God! How embarrassing!'

She dropped her towel.

'Would you mind? I can't wait . . . I've got to pee!'

She turned towards the sea, then wailed, 'O! Darn it! too late!'

A steaming jet of pee burst from the thong of her rubber swimsuit, cascading down her legs and onto her bare feet, and heavily spraying the bodies of the sunbathing couple.

'I'm so awfully sorry!' Lise cried. 'I don't know what to say! And me a nurse! It's a . . . a micturomanic condition, something to do with my pouch being too tight . . .'

'Do please join us,' said M. and Mme Dejonckheere, in unison.

'This is so kind of you, Lise,' said Mme Dejonckheere, stretched out, sunbathing in her white string bikini, on the platform of the sand yacht. 'I'd never get the hang of this. We seem to be in the middle of nowhere!'

'I know the desert, madame,' said Lise, barefoot, and wearing a white blouse knotted above her navel, with a pleated white mini-skirt, fluttering above the Parisienne's head, to reveal she wore no knickers.

'Claudine, please.'

'Well, Claudine, since we are far from prying eyes, would you mind if I took off my blouse? We S'Ibaya are accustomed to going bare-breasted.'

'I would be delighted, Lise.'

Lise undid her blouse and draped it on the rudder of the sand yacht.

'What delicious breasts you have, Lise!' said Mme Dejonckheere. 'I myself prefer sunbathing in the nude.'

She sat up and wriggled out of her bikini, her pendulous titties swaying with only a slight bikini line.

'Why don't we both be nude?' she said playfully, 'and then I can admire all of you . . . I mean that lovely bum, too.'

'I don't know, Claudine . . .' said Lise.

Claudine reached suddenly and pulled away the elastic of Lise's waistband, then lowered the skirt to Lise's knees.

'O!' cried Lise, in mock-protest. 'Now I can't control the yacht unless I take it all the way off . . .'

In an instant, she was piloting the sand yacht stark naked, with the nude Claudine making no secret of her appreciation.

'How this reminds me of Morocco . . .' she said, stretching her breasts, then spreading her legs fully, for Lise to see her pink wet gash and clitty. 'But your bum is superb, Lise, much fuller than any other African girl's.'

'You've seen many, then?' Lise said impishly.

'Why, yes,' blurted Claudine. 'Touched them, too, intimately. Are you shocked, Lise?'

'No, Claudine, just curious, and . . . rather tingly.'

At that moment, Lise manoeuvred the yacht, so that the rear tyre burst and they skidded to a halt, beside an outcrop of black chimneys.

'O, no!' she cried. 'I'll have to change the wheel and we'll be late by at least a hour . . .'

'Does it matter?'

'As a staff nurse, I'm subject to the same strict discipline as everyone else,' said Lise, glumly. 'Displeasing a guest means punishment.'

She unfastened the spare wheel and rolled it in place. Claudine jumped down and put a hand on her bare bum, as though lending moral support.

'But you haven't displeased me!' she said. 'It was an accident!'

'Dr Said doesn't believe in accidents. I'll be caned bare-bum, for sure.'

'Caned! That's barbaric!' cried Claudine, her gash shiny with come.

Lise shrugged.

'Better than losing a day's pay,' she said. 'On the other hand . . .'

'Yes?' said Claudine, eagerly.

'If *you* caned me, Claudine, I mean, hard, so that I could show Dr Said that I'd been properly punished, then we could have more time together, and you could tell me about Morocco, and . . . you know.'

She put her palm on Claudine's bare arse.

'Anyway,' said Lise coyly, 'I feel that if you caned me, Claudine, it would . . . open things up between us.'

Lise finished the simple task of changing the huge bubble-tyre, then bent over it, with her legs and arse-cheeks splayed. Claudine held a sheaf of dried baobab branches over Lise's bare bottom, with her own cunt dripping come.

'Are you sure, Lise?' she said, fingers at her crotch.

'Twenty good welts, and Dr Said will be satisfied,' Lise replied.

'Twenty on your bare bottom! My goodness! Are you sure . . .?'

'Try me.'

Vip!

The rods lashed Lise's naked arse, and she clenched her cleft.

'Harder,' she groaned.

Vip!

'Mmm! Much harder . . .'

'Very well, Lise,' said Claudine, beginning to openly masturbate, as she raised the sheaf of rods to her full arm's height.

Vip!

'Ahhh . . . yes . . .'

Come dripped from Lise's cunt.

'You sound as if you enjoy being thrashed!' Claudine cried.

'When it gives pleasure to my chastiser, Claudine. Your wet cunt gives you away. You said you've touched black girls' bums – well, my bum has been caned before, and enjoyed it. Can't you see how I'm juicing?'

Vip! Vip!

'*Oooh!*'

'Yes,' murmured Claudine, rubbing her erect clitty, 'I can.'

Much later, Lise sat naked and wanking off, her bum impaled on Dr Said's cock, as they watched the videos of her sessions with both Mme and M. Dejonckheere. Colonel Said clapped as the filmed women gamahuched each other, with Lise sitting on Claudine's face, and allowing the older woman to lick her clitty, while swallowing her

232

copious come. They adopted the sixty-nine position, flooding the platform of the yacht with their cunt juices. Later, Claudine herself writhed under a bare-bum caning, wanking off, although she claimed it was her first masochistic experience, and unprotesting as Lise pissed into her open mouth. Claudine's buttocks were crimson from fifteen canestrokes and she swallowed Lise's pee with gasps of pleasure.

'Excellent,' said Colonel Said, stroking Lise's wealed flanks, as she shifted her buttocks on his penis. 'So much accomplished, so soon! And so effortlessly switching from submission to dominance! Don't squeeze too much, Nurse Gallard, as my next spurt is for Dr Crevasse's cunt. Let's see what your evening video has for us . . .'

A foolishly grinning M. Dejonckheere entered Lise's bedroom, and Lise, wearing a strapless, low-cut evening frock of black velvet, whose hem scarcely covered her knickerless pubis, exclaimed:

'I can't *believe* what you said, Max!'

'*Please*,' whined the male. 'Just don't tell Claudine.'

'Only to look, you promise?'

'I promise!'

'Pour us cognacs, then, and no peeking.'

Lise turned, and slipped out of her dress. Nude, she rummaged in her closet, extracting a full nurse's uniform. Max Dejonckheere peeked so much that he spilt brandy, but when Lise bade him turn round, she pretended not to notice. She wore full nursing regalia, with her blouse unbuttoned to below her scalloped pink bra, and her micro-skirt allowing him to see her pink g-string, with pink sussies over black fishnets. She held a stethoscope, and tapped his bulging crotch with the steel tip.

'I thought so!' she said. 'You dirty males are all the same! You want to do more than look . . .!'

'No!'

'Well, I do, you dirty little worm! I want to see your bum bared, for I'm going to punish your impudence! Unless you want me to tell Claudine, instead' – hitting his erection quite hard, with the stethoscope – 'about this absolute *disgrace*!'

Sweating, Max gulped his cognac.

'No! Anything but that!'

'Then get your panties down and lie down on my bed . . .'

He obeyed at once.

Whop! Whop! Whop! Whop!

Lise straddled the man's neck with her cunt, as she flogged his bare buttocks with the folded rubber tubes of her stethoscope.

'Over a hundred whops and you're still stiff, you dirty little boy! It is intriguingly big, though,' Lise panted, as she whipped the crimson fesses. 'Let's try a more direct approach. Turn over.'

Max did so, and found his face buried under Lise's cunt; she began to whop the bell-end of his cock with hard strokes from the rubber stethoscope. He squealed, but his cock did not wilt. Lise began a whipping with the steel earpieces, and he began to squirm, begging her to do it harder.

'Yes, Sister!' he cried. 'You are so right to despise me!'

Suddenly, a gush of piss spurted hot and yellow from Lise's cunt, all over his face, and his lips moved frantically to swallow her pee.

'Mmm! Mmm!' he groaned.

Whop!

She delivered a further stroke to his penis, looping it in the rubber stethoscope tubing. Max's face and neck were drenched in her piss, and he gurgled as his cock began to jerk, spurting spunk all over the stethoscope. Watching the scene, Lise writhed, squeezing Colonel Said's cock with her anal elastic.

'Now, Lise,' chided the colonel. 'That's enough. Excellent! You leave for Paris tomorrow. A very important mission, Dr Crevasse has been kind enough to confide in me. Mmm! Your lovely arse has got me full of spunk for her deflowered cunt . . .'

'It is an important mission, sir, and one that Dr Crevasse assures me is not to be hurried. She has a rather personal interest in it, and wanted me to prove myself before undertaking it. Time to win the confidence of the already debauched targets, and gain admission to their depravities, in the knowledge that I must undergo considerable physical distress.'

They mocked me, Lise, and left me unfulfilled. They shall not mock you, but try to exact hideous revenge on you. You have shown in Djibouti that you can submit to the most gruelling indignities, and with joy . . .

'Wait, sir, there's more film,' Lise added mischievously.

The video flickered, and the scene was once more Lise's bedroom. Now, Claudine was on her knees, sucking Lise's clit, as Afgoi buggered her, with Max Dejonckheere watching helplessly from the bed, to which his nude body was tied. Melleah squatted on his balls, pissing and dunging on him. As his wife climaxed under the black male's buggery, Melleah masturbated Max's own cock to spurt amid her dung-drops.

'No . . . No!' sobbed Claudine, frantically drinking Lise's come, as her buttocks writhed, milking the spunk from Afgoi's balls.

'O . . . yes!' sobbed her husband, as Melleah cupped her pee in her hands and poured it down his throat.

'Lise! Lise! O!' cried Colonel Said, as Lise milked his cock so tightly that he spurted his cream right at her anal root. 'O . . . you naughty girl!'

'I'm afraid I exceeded my authority, sir, in making the extra video, so I figured I might as well be hanged for a sheep as a lamb,' Lise said, plopping his cock from her anus, and, without bothering to wipe herself, bending over to present her come-slimed arse for a caning. 'You did say you wouldn't mind giving me a caning on the bare, and it would help me have some nice wanks in the toilet on that long flight to Paris tomorrow.'

Colonel Said raised his cane and began to lash her bare black arse-globes.

'You really *are* one extraordinary soldier girl,' he murmured.

The sight of a long-legged woman, perfect of croup and bosom, swathed from head to toe in white latex, striding across the platform of the Gare du Nord, and wheeling two huge suitcases, excited no more than passing interest from jaded Parisian eyes. Descending from her train in elegant St-Omer, she turned not a few provincial heads; her entrance to the village police station not far away caused Sgt Rastoff of the Gendarmerie Nationale merely to raise one eyebrow, then, as he inspected the magnificence of her swelling croup, the other.

'To what do I owe this unexpected pleasure, Madame?' he said.

'You remember me. I was here before, as a guest of Thierry and Odette.'

'Indeed I do. It is my job to keep dossiers and phone taps on all residents of distinction and their visitors. Although I have not the honour of knowing your name, madame, I sensed that you were somewhat disappointed in your last visit. Odette gives me to understand that names are not very important in their rituals, which, I regret to inform you, have now ceased. It seems M. Thierry is soon to be ordained to the priesthood, and that his family money has already ensured him the Archbishopric of Reims, and a seat in the College of Cardinals in Rome.'

'I am Legion Dr Charlotte Crevasse,' she said, showing an ID card.

At once, Sgt Rastoff leapt to his feet, and saluted.

'At your orders, madame!' he barked.

Lise Gallard smiled under her latex swaddle, as she saw his cock bulging.

'I did not realise the erotic power of an ID card,' she murmured.

'Madame is surely not unaware of her beauty,' said the sergeant. 'It is madame's privilege to mock, and my duty to obey.'

Lise slowly unpeeled the white rubber from her bum and crotch, revealing herself knickerless. She turned and spread her ebony arse-cheeks, the pink cunt-meat seeping slightly, before the sergeant, whose erection grew massive. Lise removed a folded slip of paper from her anal cleft, and handed it to Sgt Rastoff, who sniffed it and sighed.

'Those are your orders recalling you to the Legion Reserve, under my temporary command,' she said.

'Madame, your fesses are the only orders a humble sergeant requires,' gasped Sgt Rastoff, 'and their beauty places me under your eternal command.'

'Yes,' said Lise, 'they told me you were an admirer of the female bottom, Sergeant, and now, after you have helped me store one of my suitcases, is your chance to express your appreciation. A vigorous buggery before luncheon is the custom of our more sophisticated soldier girls, and I do not think this provincial backwater too benighted to oblige me.'

'I shall do everything in my power to satisfy you, madame,' panted Rastoff, as her fingers stroked her open anal pucker.

'Good. I shall, of course, require a little more than that.'

English discretion ensured that all glances were politely averted, as the lady swathed in white rubber reserved herself the best suite in Oxford's Randolph Hotel for a month, explaining that she would be coming and going at odd hours, as she had business in France and would be shuttling back and forth. A sound bare-bum spanking of the teenage bellboy, followed by a luxurious tit-wank with the promise of more to follow, brought Lise the latest gossip of town and gown. She was especially interested in St Hugh's College, and expressed her pleasure in learning that Dr John Henric was in line for Regius Professor, and was rumoured to have been appointed Deputy Director of MI6. At any rate, his summer weekends at Birchwood seemed to have ceased as abruptly as Thierry's debaucheries at St-Omer. The woman swathed in white rubber became a familiar figure in north Oxford and Kidlington, watching and waiting outside St Hugh's College or Dr Henric's property at Birchwood. She regularly stood outside Thierry's mansion in France, too, doing no more than stare. Eventually, Sgt Rastoff informed her that telephone calls were being made between St-Omer and Kidlington. Lise listened to the tapes.

'That blasted Crevasse woman . . .'

'Ruin everything, for both of us . . .'

'Damned lesbian . . .'

'Let's finish her . . .'

'Too risky . . .'

'Teach her a lesson, then, one she won't want to repeat . . .'

'Where?'

'Better here in France . . .'

'And Odette?'

'The slut is a deserter from the Legion! She won't talk . . .'

'It must be the soundest lesson imaginable . . .'

'For Odette, too, before I get rid of her . . .'

'One last time, then . . .'

'I can't wait . . .'

Not long after, the woman swathed in white rubber was kidnapped, efficiently, at dusk, and whisked in the boot of a Mercedes into the grounds of Thierry's mansion. The woman, extracted from her brief confinement, proved sullenly silent, and her rubber costume was not thin, sensuous latex but heavy rubber, impenetrably fastened like a diver's suit, with a series of zips, chains and padlocks. Only the zips at anus, mouth and cunt proved openable.

'A fetishist's dream,' snarled Dr John Henric, slapping the woman's face but drawing no response.

'We can do anything with her,' said Thierry, eyes agleam, and already with his erect cock in his hand. 'Can't we, Odette?'

'I'll whip the bitch, while you men fuck and bugger her,' said Odette.

All three stripped naked, the males with stiff cocks, and Odette with her cunt swimming in come as she wanked off.

'We'll have some fun before we send her away sobbing,' said Henric.

'We want to teach her a *lesson*,' snapped Thierry.

'Buggery is a fine lesson,' retorted Henric.

'Even through that rubber, she'll feel my cat-o'-nine-tails,' said Odette.

'I want to tool her bum, first,' said Dr Henric. 'The bitch was so ... *demanding*, before. I hate demanding sluts! Now, she seems properly submissive.'

'Waiting for us – to grant her salvation,' said Thierry. 'A plea, not a threat.'

Thwack! Thwack! Thwack!

Odette laced the rubber buttocks with her heavy cat, and the rubber-swathed female trembled at the impact. She followed this with slashes to the breasts and cunt, before Dr Henric elbowed her aside, grabbed the woman by the waist and anally impaled her. He buggered fiercely but did not come; rather, he handed her to Thierry, who vigorously cunt-fucked her, while Odette sucked Dr Henric's arse-greased cock. Awaiting her chance to renew the whipping, she masturbated until copious come streaked her bare legs. Equally plentiful was the come that dripped from the rubber woman over Thierry's pumping member, and suddenly he shrieked, as a fierce jet of piss streamed from her fucked cunt.

'The filthy whore!' he cried.

Grabbing the whip from Odette, he delivered a thorough scourging to the naked cunt flaps, which continued to pour with pee and come. Thierry inserted his cock into the anus, and began a strong buggery, until he withdrew with a further expression of disgust. Dung droppings smeared his glans, and plopped from the rubber woman's anus. Dr Henric, grinning, removed his cock from Odette's sucking lips, and plunged it once more into the rubber woman's anal passage, which he buggered with his balls sunk in her arse right to the hilt of his member. Again, he withdrew, and inserted his arse-greased cock into the unzipped lips of the female, driving his cock right to the back of her throat, mouth-fucking her brutally. Thierry furiously lashed Odette across her naked breasts, leaving a cluster of dark welts, and she screamed.

'You filthy whores are all the same!' he cried, applying the cat to her naked buttocks, and forcing her head onto his swollen cock. 'Lick me clean, slut, or I'll whip your arse raw.'

239

'Whip her raw anyway,' groaned Dr Henric. 'Why do you need the bitch? A Legion deserter – send her back, with her tits branded.'

'Yes!' Thierry cried. 'Let's brand both the sluts!'

Thwack! Thwack! Thwack!

Odette's naked arse-globes quivered and squirmed, as the cat's thongs streaked her bare bum with bruises. Her sucking of Thierry's cock grew more fervent, the darker her arse welted under his whipping.

'Mmm . . .' she groaned. 'Yes, Master! Brand my titties, for the filthy lesbian slut I am! But let me do her, first!'

She took over thirty strokes on her bare bum and breasts, wanking herself off to a squealing orgasm, before Thierry sent her to fetch hot coals and branding irons. When Odette returned, both males were fucking the rubber woman as though to burst her, one in cunt and the other in arse, both orifices spewing come, piss and dung stools over their pumping shafts. Neither had spunked; Thierry ordered Odette to brand the supplicant's left breast first, then the right, then both her buttocks, while the males fucked her. Odette applied the red-hot fork directly on the nipple-swelling, and there was a powerful plume of smoke and the smell of burnt rubber. Both Dr Henric and Thierry howled, spunking in her anus and cunt, the orifices bubbling over with their powerful jets of cream. Suddenly, there was a loud pop, as the rubber doll burst, and the naked trio were showered in the dung, come and piss, that had filled its innards.

Lise Gallard, in a tight-fitting khaki skirt and blouse, with white stockings, and military boots, entered the room, followed by Sgt Rastoff. The naked males stared, aghast.

'You!' hissed Dr Henric. 'The Gallard girl! But black! What . . .?'

'We have done nothing wrong!' wailed Thierry. 'Merely games with a sex toy!'

'Which you did not know was a sex toy,' said Sgt Rastoff. 'An interesting point of law, possibly neglected by the Napoleonic Code.'

Lise explained that, far from being in trouble, the two gentlemen had passed Colonel Said's test. She explained

240

the requirements of the *Brigade Sexuelle*, and said that Thierry and Dr Henric had shown themselves worthy of invitation to Colonel Said's auction club, in return for certain small favours, to the benefit of France: Thierry, as a prince of the Church; Dr Henric, as regius professor, and high-ranking MI6 officer. If they were foolish enough to refuse, their entire escapade with the rubber doll was captured on video, and would be disseminated, to their inevitable disgrace. Neither refused. Odette, as a Legion deserter, must regrettably serve a term of imprisonment at Fort Lafresne, whose regime was not kind.

'You mean, I'll be whipped?' said Odette.

'And caned bare-bum, every day,' said Lise, 'with your only solace unending masturbation and the hope of being sold into slavery.'

Smiling, Odette offered her wrists to Sgt Rastoff's handcuffs.

'You *are* submissive, then, Odette,' said Lise. 'Would you really have taken a branding on your bare breasts?'

'Yes, mam'selle,' said Odette.

'You should fare well in Djibouti,' said Lise.

All five of them travelled on a French military transport to Djibouti, with Odette uncomplainingly shackled, but proudly wearing her old Legion nurse's uniform, which, Lise explained, would be ceremonially cut and stripped from her until she was naked, like the other inmates.

'It will be a long time before you earn enough at prison to pay for your new uniform,' she sighed. 'Even I must do that.'

Dr Henric and Thierry were increasingly excited, as they scanned the lavish colour photographs of Colonel Said's auction club. From the plane they transferred to Gilles' helicopter which landed by the gate, with Colonel Said and Dr Crevasse there to welcome them. Odette remained in the helicopter, while Thierry and Dr Henric were given into the care of Hawo. They entered the slave complex, crammed with naked female slaves, and both males licked their lips until Hawo delivered them to her colleague in charge of the male slaves. Quickly, the female guards stripped, bound and gagged the two men, and strapped them up for an introductory flogging of thirty lashes on the bare back and thirty on the buttocks. The two naked men were flogged with hard rubber quirts of thirteen thongs, a suggestion for which Dr Crevasse and Colonel Said thanked Lise. They screamed and writhed under their floggings, and, when cut down, were forced to their knees at Dr Crevasse's feet. The two males sobbed as their cocks and ball-sacks were clamped into chastity harnesses.

'It seems, Lise, that you forgot to tell the gentlemen they would be visiting the auction club as slaves, rather than guests,' mused Dr Crevasse. 'I don't suppose anyone will buy these specimens though. Just imagine – nine years without a wank!'

'I can't,' said Lise.

16

Soldier Girls

Nurse-Sergeant Lise Gallard inspected her ebony nude body in the mirror adjoining the dining-table in her private compound outside Fort Lafresne. She stroked her waist-length raven locks, teasing them around her jutting breasts and dark chocolate nipple-domes, then on the sacred buttocks of the goddess S'Ibaa, whose statue occupied pride of place amidst the photographic studies of nude female bottoms, whipped and unwhipped, in her gallery of Waltraut's work. She rubbed her own buttocks, relishing their satin firmness and their size, the sacred number, then stroked the gold key on her neckchain which was her only clothing.

She smiled, looking at the androgyne goddess and the lithe, serpentine thickness of her own clitoris, enhanced, like her croup, by the sun, the earth of Djibouti, the come of the S'Ibayan maidens; in the months since her desertion, her memories had not dimmed, but rather, they had become sharper. She still masturbated at the memory of her privilege in witnessing Colonel Said's first cunt-fucking of Charlotte Crevasse, the huge cock pumping between the quivering dark thighs, the bodies bathed in the river of come from the writhing female's cunt, as Lise joyfully wanked. However, even Charlotte Crevasse smiled whenever the subject of the goddess, and the sacred number, the perfect arse, was mentioned. As sergeant, Lise caned Titzi's bare bottom every single day, whether Titzi – naughty, provocative Titzi! – had committed a formal offence or not. Their arse-rivalry had become their own private, half-serious affair, though, Lise suspected, a cause of some mild amusement to others, especially Damara, the bare-breasted welcome girl who seemed to be everywhere. Titzi insisted *she*, not Lise, had achieved the sacred arse . . . and Damara, fingering her own taut cleft, would flick her dancing titties as with twinkling eyes and flashing teeth, she teased them both: 'Mystical rites! Snakes, and sacred gashes, in the High Colon of S'Ibaa! Your head is turned by the desert sun, and all those lovely canings and wanks, Lise.'

The basalt of Lise's shaven mound swelled above her elongated cunt-slit, which began to seep come, but she kept her fingers from her tingling clitty: today was wanking day, when Damara would arrive with a posse of male and female S'Ibaya, for the weekly come ceremony. Lise possessed a refrigerated cellar full of corked bottles, each one neatly labelled with date of exudation, and she possessed enough S'Ibayan come juice for a year's drinking. However, the weekly wanking was such a delight for all, that she felt it an obligation to her people, the S'Ibaya, the daily drinking of whose come maintained the purity of her ebony skin, as one of them. To Colonel Said's amusement, Lise maintained a stock of male spunk which she drank also, insisting that it, too, contained the vital essence of the goddess. She drained the porcelain cup, from which she took her mid-morning refreshment, and wiped her lips of the creamy sperm.

She looked at her agenda and saw it a busy day indeed: in the afternoon, the come ceremony and a party of selected guests from the Club des Vautours, where Sutra, scarcely ever out of her white string bikini, was, to Colonel Said's satisfaction, a most vivacious Mistress of Ceremonies; before that, luncheon with Nurse-General Frachon, who would request her customary bare-bum fifty. First of all, a visit to her office, to confer with Dr Frahl, and a brief inspection of the square, although no official whippings were scheduled; at some point, a tour of inspection of the Hole, where the disobedient Titzi languished. Lise pinned her sergeant's ribbons through the plums of both pierced nipples, and hung the golden sergeant's stripes from her clit-ring.

'Nurse!' she cried, and, at once, the fully-uniformed figure of Legion Nurse Charlotte Crevasse appeared, curtsying, before declaring herself at her mistress's orders.

Nurse Crevasse wore a latex blue micro-skirt over fishnet blue stockings, cruelly teetering spiked heels and a white blouse, unbuttoned to the third button, which showed a generous portion of her braless teats. The back of the skirt was slit right to the top cleft of the bare, sumptuous buttocks, with velcro flaps on either side, for easy access, if Nurse Crevasse required bare-bum caning. Though knickerless, she wore a red suspender belt and garters, the sussies, blouse and stockings thus forming the Legion colours. Lise looked at the swaying black peach of her slave's buttocks, and told her, nonchalantly, to take position over the table for a caning. The nurse obeyed, stretching her arms across the very table where inmate Lise Gallard had taken her first naked birching. Buttocks were splayed, and her feet perched on the points of her shoes; between her legs stood a bone china come pot.

'Have I offended, Mistress?' she murmured.

Lise raked her claw fingernails across the slave's left thigh, leaving an ugly rip in her stocking.

'You are a slut, and have damaged Legion property,' she drawled, as she selected a thin, whippy cane from her rack. 'The cost of new stockings shall be deducted from your slave's stipend. Already, you must repay the nurse's uniform shredded by my whipping, in the high colon – I think you'll be my nurse for ever.'

'If it pleases you, Mistress. In the history of Fort Lafresne, no inmate has ever been known to reimburse the cost of her uniform.'

Lise raised her cane over the nurse's bare black fesses.

Vip!

'Ah! Thank you, Mistress.'

A tinkle in the receptacle beneath Nurse Crevasse's legs announced the first drip of come from her open cunt pouch.

Vip!

'O! Thank you, Mistress.'

The drip of come quickened.

Vip! Vip! Vip!

Three stingers took her on top buttocks and the black arse shuddered.

'Ahhh . . .! Th-thank you, Mistress.'

Her come was now a steady trickle, and her wealed bum-globes quivered like jellies.

Vip! Vip! Vip! Vip!

Lise thrashed the squirming slave on each of her haunches.

'Ahhh! Ahhh! Thank . . . you . . . Mistress!'

Lise continued to cane the bare buttocks until they were squirming hard and well wealed; at the fifteenth stroke, Nurse Crevasse cried:

'O! O! thank you, Mistress. Please, may I come?'

'You may wank off on twenty, and not before,' said Lise, 'and make sure you fill the pot.'

Five rapid strokes brought the black woman to a frenzy of squirming, and it took only a few touches to the engorged serpent of her clitty to make her come flow like a river and overflow the brimming pot, as she jerked and squealed in orgasm. Lise sipped the fresh come and nodded, then permitted Nurse Crevasse two swallows of her own fluid, before decanting the rest into a bottle, and applying a date and name label. She donned her sergeant's boots, with white socks, and ordered Nurse Crevasse to carry her, nude, on piggy-back, to her office at the fort. They were soon underway, the nurse carrying a parasol to shade her mistress's head, with its stem firmly clutched between her arse-cheeks.

'Is something on your mind, slave?' Lise asked, tapping the nurse's buttocks lightly with the English riding crop she used for such journeys.

'If you please, Mistress . . . it seems awfully long since I was fucked in the cunt,' said Nurse Crevasse.

Lise whopped her left buttock quite hard.

'You know the rules I imposed, slave,' she snapped. 'You may be fucked in cunt once for every ten buggeries, and so far this month, your bumhole has only had eight pokings.'

Nurse Crevasse sighed; they were nearly at the portal of Fort Lafresne, where a Legion helicopter was landing.

'There is no use sighing, slave,' said Lise. 'You used me as an instrument of your own revenge on that disgraceful trio, Odette, Thierry and Henric, expecting me to suffer. Your presumption is forgiven, but unforgotten. Just because you hated them for refusing your craved humiliance, that was no excuse for wishing it on my own person.'

'I hated them for refusing to degrade me, it's true! But at that time, with your confession of craving the cane, I felt you and I were one, Mistress!' cried Nurse Crevasse.

Whop! Whop!

'Ouch!'

'And I trust you always shall . . . Dr Crevasse.'

They entered the square of Fort Lafresne, little changed from the day Titzi, Sutra and Lise had disembarked from their prison van. Now a prisoner of importance was climbing from Flight-Sgt Rastoff's helicopter.

The sergeant touched his cap to Lise, who nodded as she climbed from Nurse Crevasse's shoulders, before staring, as she recognised the hobbled and shackled naked prisoner. It was Sister-General Louise Grenier, who had ordered the public stripping and humiliation of Lise, Sutra and Titzi back in Djibouti; her bare arse was striped with thick welts.

'This is outrageous!' she sobbed. 'I demand a telephone at once! I cannot be ousted and disgraced by a *male*, some debauched driver named Gilles, a mere colonel . . .!'

Lise struck her bare buttocks hard, three times, with her riding crop.

'Silence, inmate!' she commanded.

'You!' hissed inmate Grenier. 'I remember you and the other trollops.'

Lise lashed her six more on the bare and she sobbed.

'Troublesome one, Mam'selle Lise,' said Sgt Rastoff. 'I had to thrash her bum twice, with the machine on autopilot, to make her shut up, and even then she wouldn't, kept demanding I fuck her, as she wouldn't get cock for a while. Typical French bitch. How I hate the buggers!'

'And did you?' said Lise. 'Fuck her, I mean.'

'Buggered her, mam'selle. She's an inmate, after all, and a darn Frenchie, too. Seems she seduced one government wife too many, and the gent thought her bumhole far too slack as compensation . . .'

'I'll tell Dr Frahl to pay attention to her anus during her medical. Before you take her to the doctor, please give her to Corporal Heidi, and run her round the square, hobbled as she is, with that inmate in shackles and gasmask. Better slop her in sunscreen first.'

Heidi was running beside her gasmasked charge, and vigorously caning her bare buttocks as she hobbled. Heidi's sun-bronzed nude body bore the corporal's insignia pierced into her left nipple, and she saluted Lise.

'Punishment drill for the slut Lavoisier, Sergeant,' she said. 'Caught her masturbating in sleeping quarters.'

'Again?' cried Lise. 'Give the slut three days in the Hole and a daily birching of thirty. I'll send Nurse Crevasse over with a supply of rods.'

She proceeded to her office where her slaves Afgoi and Melleah awaited her, Afgoi, by permanent order in a state of erection, and Melleah already masturbating into her china pot as she tongued his glans. Lise ordered Afgoi to bugger Nurse Crevasse, then stretched, yawning.

'I think I need a bare-bum caning to wake me up,' she said to Melleah.

The slave-girl was ordered to cane Lise's own fesses, then lick her cunt to a come. Lise bent over beside the nurse and both groaned, as the nurse was buggered hard by the black slave, and Lise caned smartly on the bare by the female, to ten strokes, after which Melleah knelt and tongued Lise's extruded clit to orgasm, swallowing her copious come as she sucked the cunt lips, and chewed with her teeth on the big fleshy nubbin. Lise sighed in satisfaction, refreshing herself, during her caning and gamahuching, with sips from Melleah's pot of freshly wanked come.

Afgoi's sperm frothed at the lips of Crevasse's buggered anus as he groaned in his spurt. He withdrew his arse-slimed cock, only half wilted, and Lise directed Melleah to suck him to hardness again. As Melleah took the massive dripping cock to the back of her throat and tongued him, Afgoi quickly arose again, and Lise instructed him to repeat his buggery of Nurse Crevasse, who was herself wanking off, and flooding her stockings with slimy come.

'That way, you will have made your ten, and I shall unlock your cunt. You have permission to attend the welcome centre, naked, of course, and if Sgt Rastoff is in the mood, I would recommend his cock.'

Afgoi buggered the nurse for a good forty-five minutes, before he spurted again. While the nurse was writhing under the slams of his cock, Melleah knelt and licked her distended clitty, bringing Nurse Crevasse to frequent orgasms, while swallowing her cunt juices and the powerful jet of pee which her buggery made her unable to withold. During this time, Lise studied the medical reports on new inmates brought by Dr Frahl, who walked with a limp: Lise had guessed her penchant for bizarre costumes of rank, and obliged her whim. On this occasion, Dr Frahl's left leg was bare, and her right hobbled in a surgical boot. She wore a white rubber skirt, slit open at crotch and arse-crevice, and her right nipple was pinned with a selection of gaudy ribbons, signifying her numerous medical degrees, while the entire left breast was squashed flat to her ribs with packing tape. Her nose and lips were pierced with gold pins of the snake of Aesculapius, and a dainty guiche protruded between her arse-globes, pinned through her anal bud.

Lise unlocked the cunt of Nurse Crevasse and permitted her to visit the welcome centre, in search of cock. She marched briskly across the square, inspecting the squads of inmates, sweating at punishment drill, before ascending to Nurse-General Frachon's office. The Nurse-General, attended by her loinstringed male slave, was already strapped by the ankles to her caning frame, with her khaki skirt up and knickers pulled down over her knees. She wore seamed brown stockings, attached by side-garters to the sussie belt, thus leaving her buttocks bare. She blushed.

'I . . . I took the liberty . . .' she murmured.

Lise lifted her riding crop and ordered the slave to remove his loinstring and bend over. She caned his bare until he had achieved a full, massive erection, and Lise ordered him to take his own mistress in the anus, buggering her to a hundred pokes, but restraining his own come. The nurse-general squealed and writhed, with little squeals and cries of 'O, how it hurts!' and 'This is too much, Sergeant Gallard!' but with her come flowing copiously from her swollen gash, and staining her stockings dark brown. When she was dripping copiously, Lise began her caning, taking care to stripe every portion of her quivering bum-flans.

After fifty strokes, her bare arse was glowing crimson, and she was wanking hard with her left hand. The fiftieth stroke brought her to climax, and her face and bum glowed crimson with pleasure as she sat down to luncheon with Lise, whose chair was the thighs of the slave, with his erect cock impaling her own anus. As they ate, Lise was reminded of Jacqui Frachon's interviewing her on her return from Colonel Said's establishment, and the internment of Thierry and Henric. 'Jacqui', begging to be on first name terms, had said that in view of her excellence in the field, 'Lise' was offered permanence on Colonel Said's staff, or, should she prefer to remain at Fort Lafresne, the rank of her choice.

'Even including, it seems, my own. Dear me! You would be so . . . *dominant*, Lise.'

Lise had assured her the rank of sergeant was her pleasure and ambition, and – since some mysterious influence had accrued to her – she suggested that Sutra's bubbly personality, and Titzi's charms, might be better suited to the *Brigade Sexuelle*.

'Sutra – yes, Lise, of course – but Titzi – I don't know – acting very strangely, always in trouble . . . three public whippings, four confinements in the Hole, wanking off in exhibitionistic fashion, and the more she is flogged, the more she seems to relish it. A *submissive*! How the Legion, or its prison, can unearth a girl's truth! Like your own delicious ebony.'

Where, Lise had asked, had her glowing recommendation come from?

'Why, from Legion HQ at Djibouti, of course.'

'But from which general? Someone powerful enough to override both Colonel Said and Dr Crev – I mean you, Nurse-General.'

Jacqui was flustered.

'I don't know. Damara just brings me things, and tells me what's in them and where to sign. I can sign my name all right, you see. Otherwise, Lise, I'm – I'm functionally illiterate. There! Even Dr Crevasse doesn't know, only Damara. I don't know what I'd do without her. She is truly a goddess!'

'So *Damara* ordered my promotion?'

'Yes! I mean, in a way, she orders everything . . .'

Lise smiled, remembering how Titzi had reacted with both jealousy and delight to the news of her promotion. Now, over coffee and cake, she masturbated her wet slit, her bum squirming on the male's penis, and brought him to spurt as she devoured her last morsel of chocolate eclair. As the cake's cream slithered into her gullet, and the male's into her anal elastic, she wanked her clitty to a sweet, shuddering come. Next on her agenda were the come ceremony that afternoon and whatever surprises Damara might bring with her. *In a way, she orders everything . . .*

Just before Lise's appointment as sergeant became official, Heidi having become corporal weeks before, Damara had – not exactly ordered, but silently commanded, that Lise and Titzi clit-wrestle. This practice was an old S'Ibayan tradition, now encouraged, by Lise herself, as a display to enthuse recruits for Colonel Said's brigade of 'helpers'. Titzi mocked Lise's account of her experiences as a deserter, especially her 'delusions of arse-grandeur' – though she could not ignore, or hide her envy of, Lise's ebony S'Ibayan skin. Nude and wanking, the two girls oiled their bodies with their own cunt juices, then bent

251

over, with buttocks pressed. One arm was held behind the back; the other reached through the opponent's thighs, pressing the perineum, so that the fingers could squeeze, pull and pinch her erect clit. To Lise's disadvantage, her clit was already much larger and accessible than Titzi's, even though the German's was well extruded. The victrix was the girl who brought her opponent to orgasm first, if a caressing attack was chosen, or else obliged her to cry halt to the pain of clawing: or, ideally, both. The enhanced S'Ibayan clitoris made this an ideal, if cruel, form of mutual masturbation. Damara had quoted Colonel Said, or was it Dr Crevasse . . .?

We know that the female clitoris, in evolutionary terms, is a remnant or more compact version of the male glans. What if a tribe of females evolved . . . non-compactly, for their own pleasure? Worshipping their female archetype, the goddess S'Ibaa, whom we know from legend as the Queen Sheba, and expecting her return, reincarnate, with the perfect, sacred arse, the prehensile clitoris, the supreme vulval glory?

It was certainly Colonel Said who confessed his devotion to caned female buttocks, to worshipping the arse of the ebony female: to be facially squashed under the juicing cunt and writhing bum of a S'Ibayan girl was heaven.

'I, an albino, a white man even amongst white men, am privileged to know that if there is divinity, it is the earth-ripe blackness of an African maiden's arse-globes: "The Gateway of Apotheosis", as King Solomon called Sheba's arse, so mighty that he built a temple to replicate it.'

Lise had no hope of winning at clit-wrestling; Titzi's grip of her massively swollen clitty was too cruel, and too sweet, to stop Lise's cunt flowing with come and her belly fluttering towards orgasm at Titzi's first savage clit-attack – no matter how hard Lise raked her own claws on Titzi's naked clit. The girls' bare, slimy arses slapped and slithered, as they dug at each other's unprotected cunts, and it was not long before Lise's fluttering belly began to heave, her come gushing over Titzi's wanking fingers, and Lise cried out in a shuddering spasm of orgasm, with the

German girl pinching the tip of her nubbin between finger and thumb. Suddenly, in victory, Titzi was meekness itself.

'You promised me a whipping, Lise,' she whined.

'Yes, I remember.'

'When you are a sergeant you'll have no excuse not to.'

'Only if you admitted I had a goddess's arse, Titzi,' murmured Lise, rubbing her oily ebony bum-flans, and clitty, sore from Titzi's claws.

'I shall never admit that,' Titzi had smiled, rubbing her own.

After her luncheon with Nurse-General Frachon, Sgt Lise Gallard regained her compound, by the same vehicle as had carried her, but a vehicle now glowing with pleasure, having been vaginally fucked, and with cunt full of Sgt Rastoff's spunk. Lise was still in reminiscent mood, as she awaited Damara, Sutra and the troop of S'Ibayan slaves, who would attend the come ceremony along with her own. She kept Deydey, Guestir, Toyo, Loosje and Kee; the one-legged Latvian girl, acquired from the auction club, was a useful addition to her slaves' hut, but had expelled Lavoisier to the cruel mercies of Corporal Heidi, on square and in dormitory. Dr Crevasse slept on her nurse's palliasse under Lise's bed, beside her chamber pot. Lise awaited her guests seated at her dining, or, as she preferred to think, her birching table; she was nude, but for her fresh pair of socks, in fluffy white cotton, and her golden neckchain.

'Lise!' cried Sutra, breasts bobbing in her skimpy white string bikini, embracing her, and introducing four couples, including M. and Mme Dejonckheere, both nude and led on slender neckchains by cane-wielding Xiddigta, her white pleated skirt bobbing with her naked breasts.

On some occasions, the guests would be privileged to witness a public whipping, with the added frisson that one female, chosen at random, would be whipped too. Behind her came Damara, and a group of nude S'Ibayan slaves, male and female, who squatted by their come pots for the wanking ceremony. Damara's manner towards Lise on these occasions was different, as befitted a goddess . . .

unless it was part of the show. The slaves began to masturbate in unison, while Sutra explained to her guests the sacred significance of masturbation for the S'Ibaya, how their come both fertilised and sprang from the charred volcanic earth, beneath which seethed lava, like come in a woman's gash.

The female guests, clad only in short white skirts, and the males in loinstrings, began to masturbate joyfully, both their own clits, and the swelling cocks of their menfolk, as the S'Ibayan girls filled their come pots, and Lise herself wanked herself off in leisurely fashion, as befitted a goddess. She remembered Titzi, now sweating in the Hole. She had neglected to visit her, and must remember to do so, in the evening.

Two female S'Ibayan slaves were selected for a fierce display of clit-wrestling, which provoked such interest that Lise ordered Loosje and Kee to provide the same spectacle: the third, final bout was between the winners of the first two, and Loosje, victorious, was permitted to celebrate with a joyful wank into her mistress's come pot. Colonel Said was right: there were endlessly subtle ways of enticing 'helpers' for France and the Legion.

Damara was happy to crown the entertainment, before the drinking of come, by her own speciality: she hoisted herself by her own long hair over a beam, and knotted her hair to the beam, suspending her naked loins, with her white pleated skirt pinned up. She held her legs straight out in a ballerina's splits. Her buttocks and cunt lips swelled, and parted, admitting the cocks of four S'Ibayan slaves, who placed themselves, standing by her flanks: two fucked her in anus, and two in cunt, at the same time. Each cock plunged right to the ball-sack, into its chosen hole. Damara's come streamed down her quivering thighs and mingled with their spunkings, as she wanked off at clitty and nipples, sighing in orgasm after orgasm.

Cups of girl-come were passed, and drunk, as Lise took her place for her part in the rite. Bare-bum, she spread herself unbound across the birching table, and received six cane-strokes on the buttocks from each S'Ibayan maiden, followed by a full birching on the bare back and bum from her slave, Nurse Crevasse. Her come filled three pots, before she spread her arse-cheeks for her own ritual buggery by the S'Ibayan male slaves. She groaned, and smiled, as the first massive black cock penetrated her anus, and began to pummel her arse-root. Damara smiled at her, and into her memory swam a scene, the first time Damara had revealed herself, fleetingly, and perhaps merely as a teasing provocation, to Titzi and Lise. It had been in this very room, Damara inspecting the photo gallery of bare croups, and stroking the statue of S'Ibaa.

'A reincarnation of S'Ibaa herself, with her perfect arse? Hm!'

Damara's own superbly ripe croup began to swell, growing before their eyes, until it surpassed Titzi's, Dr Crevasse's, even Lise's. The ebony melons swelled monstrous and superb for a moment, revealing the come-brimmed gash and the open, writhing anal pucker, the clitoris swaying like a frond, or a serpent's head, at the portal of her vulva, then snaking across the skin of her perineum, to nibble at the anus bud. Damara was the image of the statue of the goddess S'Ibaa. Her clitoris coiled into her pouch, and her buttocks resumed their normal, compact fullness.

'How . . .?' gasped Lise.

'What you see as my normal arse, my tight little bum that Gilles so likes to bugger, is my *clenched* arse,' Damara said. 'Sometimes, I unclench. Bumfuck is a girl's glory; it is the way we enslave the male.'

'Then . . . *you* are the ruler here? *You* are the goddess S'Ibaa?' Lise blurted, and Damara laughed.

'Every female arse is the arse of a goddess,' she said sternly, then suddenly giggled. 'As for ruling this place – come on, Lise, who made you sergeant? All along, who exactly did you *think* was in charge?'

As she was buggered, Lise's mind drifted forward to the extra-hard caning she would give Titzi's insolent, gorgeous, bare arse in her cell in the Hole that evening, impassioned by her own buggery and birching. Her cunt flowed with come: Sutra's lips drank from her gash, then Xiddigta's, then Damara's herself. Finally, buggered raw, she spread her naked body for Nurse Crevasse's birching, and orgasmed as the very first stroke of the fresh sheaf struck her wealed bare bum.

'Oh, yes!' she cried, allowing her massive arse-globes to squirm violently and relishing the fervent masturbation, the homage of those who watched her naked ebony bum flogged. What else did Damara say to Lise? *A woman who chooses to be black, truly is black.*

Swish!

'Ohhh . . .!' Lise squealed, as the pickled wood wealed her bare arse, squirming and clenching, then unclenching, unclenching . . .

The watching guests masturbated, and the S'Ibayan slaves autofellated themselves in adoration, backs arched, to suck cocks or quims.

'O! *Ohhh!* O, God, it hurts, Dr Crevasse!'

'It is not I who flog you, Mistress,' said Lise's slave, Nurse Charlotte Crevasse, 'but the Legion and France our mother.'

Lise's naked body writhed, and she gripped the table corners as the birch descended on her writhing bare fesses, then on bare shoulders and back. Her cunt gushed come and she pissed herself, her mingled fluids lapped by her worshippers. She thought of her own wank, as she flogged Titzi's bare arse that evening, and the solemn words she would use which she had used every time, since Legion Nurse-Sgt Lise Gallard's first bare caning of that superb, proudly submissive German arse.

'I owe you a whipping, Titzi.'

'Yes, Sergeant Lise.'

The German girl spreading her naked bum-cheeks.

Thwack!

'Ahhh!'

The arse-melons shivering, as though blown in a desert wind.

Thwack!

'Ahhh! *Yesss* . . .!'

The come juices gushing from swollen cunt, on rippling bare thighs.

'Remember, it is not I who flogs you, inmate Titzi, but the Legion, and France, our mother.'

Thwack!

'Yes . . . yes . . . O, God, yes, whip me to come . . .!'

Thwack! Thwack! Thwack!

'*Ahhh* . . .'

The bare buttocks crimson and squirming, glistening come-flow, both girls masturbating throbbing pink clitties.

'It is France who whips you, Titzi . . .'

Thwack! Thwack! Thwack!

The girl's crimson bare buttocks clenching uncontrollably, her clit-wanking a blur, nearing spasm.

Thwack! Thwack! Thwack!

Titzi dunging, pissing, coming: her arse a fountain.

'Don't you just *hate* the bloody French, Titzi?'

'Ohhh! Yes! Yes! *Yesss* . . .!'

NEW BOOKS

Coming up from Nexus and Black Lace

Angel by Lindsay Gordon
8 February 2001   £5.99   0 352 33590 4
Angel is a Companion. He has sold his freedom for access to a world inhabited by the most ambitious, beautiful – and sometimes cruel – women imaginable: an executive who demands to be handled by a stranger in uniform; a celebrity who adores rope and wet under-things; a doctor who lives her secret life inside tight rubber skins. And it's not Angel's place to refuse.

Tie and Tease by Penny Birch
8 February 2001   £5.99   0 352 33591 2
Caught by a total stranger, Beth, while playing the fox in a bizarre hunting game, Penny finds herself compromised by Beth's failure to understand her submissive sexuality. Penny is determined to seduce the girl, but her efforts get her into more and more difficulty, involving ever more frequent punishments and humiliations until, turned on a roasting spit, she is unsure how much more even she can take.

Eroticon 2 Ed. J-P Spencer
8 February 2001   £5.99   0 352 33594 7
Like its companion volumes, a sample of excerpts from rare and once-forbidden works of erotic literature. Spanning three centuries, it ranges from Andrea de Nericat's eighteenth century *The Pleasures of Lolotte* to the Edwardian tale *Maudie*.

Whipping Boy by G. C. Scott
8 March 2001   £5.99   0 352 33595 5
Richard and his German girlfriend Helena have cocooned themselves in the English countryside, to live out their private – and elaborate – fantasies of submission and domination. But their rural idyll is threatened by the arrival of Helena's aunt Margaret – an imperious woman with very strict house rules and some very shady friends, who always gets what she wants. And what she wants is Richard . . .

Accidents Will Happen by Lucy Golden

8 March 2001   £5.99   0 352 33596 3

Julie Markham embarks on a game whose rules she does not know, and in just three short days her life is turned upside-down. On Friday she was happily engaged to be married. By Monday, she is crouching naked on a cold floor and suffering whatever any man or woman demands. The two days in between have been a very wet weekend – and the best of her life.

Eroticon 3 Ed. J-P Spencer

8 March 2001   £5.99   0 352 33597 1

Like its predecessors in the series, this volume contains a dozen extracts from once-forbidden erotic texts – from the harems of the Pashas (*A Night in a Moorish Harem*) to the not-so-chaste devotions of a French nunnery (*The Pleasures of Lolotte*).

BLACK
lace

Stella Does Hollywood by Stella Black
8 February 2001   £5.99   0 352 33588 2

Stella, fur-clad heroine of *Shameless*, returns to romp through the wilder reaches of California. On meeting an old acquaintance and finding he's now the chief of the largest adult entertainment empire in the USA, Stella plunges head-first into a career as a porn star, only to cause more trouble than even she bargained for. Settling down with cowgirl girlfriend Kitten to a life on the range seems like a good idea. But, for a girl like Stella, maybe in trouble's the place to be after all.

Up to No Good by Karen S. Smith
8 February 2001   £5.99   0 352 33589 0

Emma is resigned to attending her cousin's wedding, expecting the usual round of relatives and bad dancing. Instead she meets Kit: it's a passionate encounter, the kind that don't usually get repeated. But her current flame Geoff is not the jealous type, as she discovers when she bumps into Kit again unexpectedly. Over the course of one turbulent year, and two further weddings, she learns that they don't have to be such dull affairs after all.

Darker Than Love by Kristina Lloyd
8 February 2001   £5.99   0 352 33279 4

It's 1875 and the morals of Queen Victoria mean nothing to London's wayward elite. Young, beautiful Clarissa Longleigh is visiting London for the first time. Eager to meet Lord Marldon, the man to whom she is promised, she knows only that he is tall, dark and sophisticated. He is in fact depraved and louche, with a taste for sexual excess. Can Clarissa escape him, and the desires he wakes within her? A Black Lace special reprint.

sin.net by Helena Ravenscroft
8 March 2001   £5.99   0 352 33598 X

On the net, you can be who you like. In real life, Carrie Horton is as meek as a mouse. But her assertive, provocative on-line alter-ego, Dominique, is all the things that Carrie believes she is not and suddenly she finds herself controlling some sizzling situations. But is it submission or strength that she really desires? And can she blend the admirable attributes of Dominique into her real personality?

Two Weeks in Tangier by Annabel Lee
8 March 2001   £5.99   0 352 33599 8
When Melinda Carr inherits a property in Tangier from a wealthy, bohemian great aunt, she takes a holiday to visit the city. Instead of the harems, camels and sheikhs she's expecting to see, she finds instead a few family skeletons, and a cast of handsome men eager to show her just how her great aunt came into such wealth . . .

The Transformation by Natasha Rostova
8 March 2001   £5.99   0 352 33311 1
Three friends, three lives, one location: San Francisco, Lydia wants to transform an intellectual bookstore owner into the sophisticated lover of her dreams; vivacious socialite Molly meets her match in journalist Harker Trevane; and Cassie, a professor of literature, finally starts exploring her sapphic desires. Soon the friends discover things about themselves – and each other – they never knew existed. A Black Lace special reprint.

NEXUS BACKLIST

This information is correct at time of printing. For up-to-date information, please visit our website at www.nexus-books.co.uk

All books are priced £5.99 unless another price is given.

CONTEMPORARY EROTICA

THE BLACK MASQUE	Lisette Ashton
THE BLACK WIDOW	Lisette Ashton
THE BOND	Lindsay Gordon
BROUGHT TO HEEL	Arabella Knight
CANDY IN CAPTIVITY	Arabella Knight
DANCE OF SUBMISSION	Lisette Ashton
DARK DELIGHTS	Maria del Rey
DARK DESIRES	Maria del Rey
DISCIPLES OF SHAME	Stephanie Calvin
DISCIPLINE OF THE PRIVATE HOUSE	Esme Ombreux
DISCIPLINED SKIN	Wendy Swanscombe
DISPLAYS OF EXPERIENCE	Lucy Golden
AN EDUCATION IN THE PRIVATE HOUSE	Esme Ombreux
EMMA'S SECRET DOMINATION	Hilary James
GISELLE	Jean Aveline
GROOMING LUCY	Yvonne Marshall
HEART OF DESIRE	Maria del Rey
HIS MISTRESS'S VOICE	G.C. Scott
HOUSE RULES	G.C. Scott
IN FOR A PENNY	Penny Birch
ONE WEEK IN THE PRIVATE HOUSE	Esme Ombreux
THE ORDER	Nadine Somers
THE PALACE OF EROS	Delver Maddingley
PEEPING AT PAMELA	Yolanda Celbridge
PLAYTHING	Penny Birch

ANCIENT & FANTASY SETTINGS

EDWARDIAN, VICTORIAN & OLDER EROTICA

SAMPLERS & COLLECTIONS

NEXUS CLASSICS
A new imprint dedicated to putting the finest works of erotic fiction back in print